WHEN WINTER COMES

THE COLLECTED SERIAL

DANIEL WILLCOCKS

DEVIL·S ROCK PUBLISHING

OTHER TITLES BY DANIEL WILLCOCKS

The Rot Series (with Luke Kondor)

They Rot (Book 1)

They Remain (Book 2)

They Ruin (coming soon)

Keep My Bones

The Caitlin Chronicles (with Michael Anderle)

(1) Dawn of Chaos

(2) Into the Fire

(3) Hunting the Broken

(4) The City Revolts

(5) Chasing the Cure

Other Works

Twisted: A Collection of Dark Tales

Lazarus: Enter the Deadspace

The Mark of the Damned

Sins of Smoke

Keep up-to-date at

www.danielwillcocks.com

The faintest glimmer of frost signals the brightest dawn.

When I look at the Northern Lights... I see our ancestors dancing around a sacred fire, lighting the way for us when it's time for us to cross over from this physical world and join them.

— MOLLY LARKIN

PROLOGUE

And so the sky bled.

Or, so it appeared. The shimmering, waving pulses of magnetism that birthed the Aurora Borealis lost their green hue as a rift broke across the night sky and turned the phenomenon crimson.

It began slowly. Even as his final breaths escaped through cracked, frostbitten lips, it turned. The eerie alien glow that captivated the hearts of millions across the globe receding as the vein was pricked and the red spilled over. Oh, it still danced in the sky, giving the people the show they paid for, performing its ancient ritualistic routine while the sun lapped the world and clawed for its dominance against the sickle moon. Only, this haunting shade of red brought with it much more than the world would ever know, a message and a beacon for darker times to come. Times that Chikuk knew only too well were a simple part of the cogs and gears of nature whirring. Times that Aklaq had birthed himself. A waxing and waning of the tides of life. For every hour of light that comes, darkness must soon have its turn.

She lugged the ancient chieftain now, her delicate frame only just strong enough to lay him on the sled that Aklaq had crafted when he was a much younger man. Stronger and virile. A chieftain of great stature, Aklaq had once been an imposing figure, standing well over six-feet tall with the broad girth that would put the trunks of the great jack pines to shame. An Inuit leader who had conquered some of his tribe's greatest challenges, leading his Iñupiat subsect through the challenges of clinging on to their heritage, rituals, and values in an ever-modernizing world.

While many of the neighboring Inuit tribes had taken to integrating with the mainlanders, Aklaq had pacified the stubborn advances of this new breed of man and bargained to secure the Iñupiat peoples their own territories and borders along the Alaskan coast. His ancestors had fought for their traditions, and in that regard, the open wound of the sky was his fault, and his fault alone.

The last of a dying breed.

Chikuk snapped the reins, signaling for Kazu to begin his run. The pure white husky was almost invisible against the barren landscape around them, the edges of his fur blending into the snowy tundra. The only true sign of Kazu's acknowledgment of Chikuk's command were two dark eyes, ringed with amber as they cast their gaze back at her, and the sudden tension in the reins that jolted the sled into motion once those dark pinpricks faded.

Passage was slow. Chikuk knew that one dog would barely be enough for the journey, yet it wasn't worth waking the rest of the tribe. Their bearing toward their resting place was located down a slight gradient which bore their advantage, but still, she only wished they could have moved faster. Soon the others would come and claim what was theirs, and when they did, she knew that her only chance of survival was to be absent from their sight. She had dreaded this day for years, ever since her life-partner's body had shown its first sign of betrayal, evidence of the arthritic parasite that gnawed at his tendons and bones and chipped away at his youth. He fought valiantly, though, in the end, Time claims what it's owed. Time waits for no being.

As they glided through the silence of the night, Chikuk cradled her partner. She was no young jack herself and holding Aklaq steady sapped what little energy remained. She pulled his hood tighter about his face to shade him from the steady stream of chill air, but already a darkness was staining the flat of his broad nose and twisting lips that had once been pink and lithe to shades of frosty gray. As his organs ground to a halt, so too would the final remnants of warmth seep through his pores until all that was left was a frozen husk of a man. A cocoon sheltering only defunct meat and organs. The soul transitioned into the great beyond, living eternally in the dancing river of red in the sky.

Chikuk afforded herself a single tear, the droplet trailing down her cheek and landing upon Aklaq's lips. There it remained, a frozen gem of her love and devotion and, though she knew it was near impossible, she could have sworn his lips twitched into the ghost of a smile.

The Aurora continued its metamorphosis above them, staining the sky as it completed its kaleidoscopic transformation. Already the alien greens through which the phenomenon had gained its renown were almost gone, and Chikuk knew that if she was looking at it, so too were they.

A stretch of ancient pines came into view, cutting across the snow in front of them. A foreboding border which crossed in either direction as far as Chikuk could see, and it was here on the edge of the forest that she set up camp, easing Aklaq from her lap and covering him with thick, fur-lined blankets to fend off the coming cold. Her hands, gloved in the thick blubber of seals, dug expertly into the snow. She shoveled and compacted the fine powder into solid bricks which she arranged in their circle as the igloo began to take shape. For many, the igloo may take hours to build, but for the expert craftswoman, which Chikuk certainly had once been, she adjusted the final touches no more than an hour later.

Breathless, she turned her pink nose to the sky. Thick plumes of frozen air streamed from her mouth, masking her view of the Aurora. Around her, flakes of snow had started to descend, a gentle flurry for now, but soon things would elevate. Soon there would be little escape from its attack.

She shooed Kazu away from his bed beside his master. The husky had curled up in the crevices Aklaq's withering body had offered and, though she was sure his body heat would have helped to ease Aklaq's passing, she had no heart to spare for the creature while her own was dying inside.

With a gentle tug, she presented Aklaq's face to the night. She was unsurprised to find that he was dead, staring up into the sky with unblinking marble eyes. Eyes which had watched over these lands for decades, ruling with the iron fist that only an ancient legacy can pass down. Eyes which had seen death, had seen love, had seen unimaginable change across the beating heart of the land. Eyes which had fought for their little island of paradise and won.

But at what cost?

Aklaq's eyes reflected the undulating crimson lights, an illusion of a bloody fire raging inside the hollow of his skull, twinkling with anger and fear. For a moment Chikuk allowed herself to see him one last time, the imposing authoritative commander of the Iñupiat tribe.

With the tenderness that only love can spare, she leaned toward Aklaq and nuzzled her nose across his, ignoring the icy temperature of his skin on hers.

Kazu whined, padding his paws against the snow as his head crooked toward the forest, eyes grown wide as he sensed the others' arrival through the trees. She could sense them, too. Time was short and nothing would stop them. Their promise had been made, and now it must be kept. It was their time, now.

For a while, at least.

Delicately placing Aklaq into his final resting place in the snow, Chikuk worked as fast as her body would allow to unpack her meager provisions from the sled and bring them inside the igloo. She had brought enough food for the night, as well as resources to make a fire that would fend off the cold and allow her a barrier from the coming monsters. With trembling hands, she created the first spark and birthed a fire in the center of the igloo. The darkness retreated in a sudden burst of light at the exact moment that Kazu rent the night with a bone-chilling howl.

Chikuk crawled to the igloo's mouth and urgently ushered the dog inside. Anything left outside the confines of the iced hut would be gone by morning. Kazu reared on his haunches and yapped relentlessly, his stubby fangs bared at the pines. Chikuk afforded a glance in their direction, heart stopping at the sight of the first of their kind. A creature, as tall as it was thin, its bone-white mask leering at them with quiet impatience. In its long, slender fingers it held a stone knife which caught the light of the Aurora and flashed as if in warning.

Chikuk hissed at Kazu and the husky barreled toward her, its courage all but spent. She caught him around the neck and threw him roughly inside before glancing one more time at Aklaq, his body twisted and frozen where he lay. The sled empty of all except him. She only wished she could have dismantled the sled and brought it inside before they began. The journey home would be a difficult one come morning.

If she made it to then.

Chikuk scooped the snow to pack the entrance closed. The creature's cries summoned more of its kind and their marching feet beat a crunching rhythm through the snow. The wind picked up and whistled through the minute cracks in the igloo. Chikuk wrapped her blankets around herself, drawing Kazu closer. The dog's ears were flat to his head, his eyes wide. A low whine leaked from his throat like the hissing of air through a damaged pipe. She was certain that Kazu was exploring a map in his mind, using his bestial senses to track the invaders. She wondered how close they were already...

...if they had made it to his body.

Chikuk closed her eyes and listened, regretting it almost instantly. Outside the igloo hard objects clacked against each other. Their footsteps were indelicate and strange utterances came from their throats, spoken in a primal language that Chikuk's people had forgotten long ago. They whispered and growled. Arguments broke out—likely an angry debate as they protested the feasting order of their latest meal.

A dominating cry exploded. Chikuk flinched. She covered Kazu's mouth but couldn't stop his whine. The cry was like a gunshot, then silence followed.

Chikuk wasn't sure how long the silence lasted. Even the wind held its breath, slowing enough that the quiet fell thicker than the snow. A silvery pearl traced its way down her nose and touched her quivering lips, leaving a salty trail that she daren't touch with her tongue for fear of drawing their attention. They had made a promise, but promises were made to be broken. History had proven that.

The candy cane snap of bone broke the quiet. Chikuk's startled jump kicked Kazu into action, and he barked and howled and whined behind a hand that clamped his mouth. His teeth broke her skin, her blood mixing with his saliva but it was all she could do to muffle his din.

Not that the creatures outside paid any heed as they began their feast. Chikuk was all too familiar with the sound of crude tools slicing flesh. Her tribe were people of the frozen north, hunters of seal and wolf and bear. She had witnessed the grotesque smacking of lips as her tribesmen threw the bloodied carcasses of their latest catch to the dogs and the beasts tucked into their meal. Great slopping slaps of fat, blubber, tendon, and meat torn to pieces by dozens of fangs. The whites of the huskies' coats morphing from shades of black and white and gray to nightmarish crimson, their fur thick and clotted as they dined hungrily, eating in the way nature had intended.

The exact same way the creatures feasted now...

They showed no patience or manners in their attack. Chikuk screwed her eyes shut, fighting off the image of her husband torn to shreds as the savage creatures claimed what was rightfully theirs.

A heavy thud beat the side of the igloo, and Chikuk could only gasp, terrified that one of their kind might break through and come for her next. Who was she, anyway? A lone Inuit delivering the promised goods. If they came for her, she could not fight, and this they must know. They scrambled and tore and growled and rent the night with enthusiastic cackles while her life-partner ceased to be in soul and now body. She extinguished the fire and huddled closer to the wall, wrapping her sheets around her. She forced her eyes shut, blocked out the sound with thoughts of places far from here, focused her attention on something—anything—that would remove her from this nightmare.

At some point in the night Chikuk fell asleep, the adrenaline wearing through her body and sapping her of energy.

Her heavy eyes opened, the lids crusted with the remnants of sleep and tears. Something rough licked at her hands and she glanced down to find Kazu cleaning the wounds he had inflicted, an apologetic look in those great amber-ringed eyes.

She stroked his head absently and noticed for the first time that the ferocious feast of the creatures had reached its conclusion. The wind blew eagerly and resumed its whistling through the igloo's cracks, the storm no doubt continuing to build its bluster. Chikuk stared at the ashes of the fire, knowing that she needed to get heat going again if she was to fend off the coming cold. She had no idea how long she had slept for but knew that it didn't take long for the cold to creep inside your bones and chew you from the inside out.

But first, she wanted—no, *needed*—to see it for herself.

Confusion creased the deep trenches already set into her brow as she fought her way out of the igloo. There was considerably more snow blocking the entrance than she had expected. She whistled to Kazu and the husky worked the barricade with his paws, worming their way out into a world of spectral white.

The snow fell thick and fast, snowflakes the size of golf balls sweeping across the landscape in a dense flurry. She could hardly make out the sky and the bloodied lights beyond the blanket of gray clouds whipping the winds and snow around them in indelicate pirouettes. Chikuk's breath caught, her mouth hung open in awe of the power of the elements above her.

Kazu barked, the wind ripping the sound from his throat. Chikuk turned to the dog, his body once again almost lost in the blanket of white. She shielded her face with a thick sleeve and laboriously made her way through snow that came to a little above her knees, fresh powder which would soon compact and make travel all but impossible.

A single splinter of wood jutting from the snow like a rebellious sapling, its pointed tip laced with blood now turned pink. Chikuk swept a hand at the ground, revealing a shard of bone, snapped and filed to a point. A few stray strands of viscera clung desperately to what remained, but otherwise she knew that he was gone. They left little to spare, and what they had would now be claimed by the winter.

Chikuk rose to her full height and squared her shoulders, staring in the direction she knew the forest to be—not that she could see it any more through the storm. The snow whipped against the few square inches of skin left bare around her face and pricked her with icy needles. It was already increasing in fervor, the coming storm only just beginning to find its legs.

She shook a fist to the woods and expelled a grievous cry. Every ounce of pent-up emotion she had felt during the night came out in one long, primal note of rage that the wind sucked from her dry lips and carried in the direction of the woods, an obedient messenger serving the gods. She screamed until her lungs were empty. She screamed until her throat burned, and her legs would take no more. She folded to her knees, Kazu taking a stand beside her and joining her declaration with a long, singular howl.

Chikuk gasped for breath. She began her crawl toward the igloo. At least she had the forethought to create some kind of shelter before they came. At least she had packed some provisions. She would be able to survive inside, for a while, at least.

As she reached the shelter of her temporary abode, she spared one final glance at the world of white beyond.

Somewhere, far away in the distance, the creatures cackled.

EPISODE 1

THE FIRST FALL

1

CODY TREBECK

Monsters and memories swirled in the darkness.

Three hours past his usual bedtime and Cody Trebeck was still awake. His hands laced behind his head, he squinted at the strange patterns cast by the shadows clouding around the warped wooden beams in the gloom and pictured his previous life, the one where sunlight and above-freezing temperatures were a staple of the conditions of his existence and he could ride down the street on his BMX. A life in which he could see his friends until the late evening, not having to worry about the encroaching chill that came with the Alaskan sunset. He had never experienced anything like it. Sure, when the sun hit its zenith, the icy temperatures of the little town of Denridge Hills were just about bearable—as long as he wrapped up in several layers of thick, insulated clothing his uncle had purchased for him—but the moment the sun faded from sight it was as though the world had been dunked into an ice bath, and the cold sought succor in the marrow of his bones.

Cody hated it here, that much was clear in the visions that presented themselves to him. The darkness presented a kaleidoscopic showreel of his former England life. Days in which he once cursed the near-relentless drizzle that blanketed the permagray skies and slicked the paths and roads of London. A life in which summertime appeared for a six-week period and then you hauled your ass back to school. A world in which the weekends reigned supreme and every Monday to Friday was a never-ending waiting game just to have two more sweet days of freedom with your friends.

England had seemed awful at the time, but nothing quite prepared him for this. He had studied Alaska, researched the northern reaches of its coastline and seen the stunning vistas on the internet. A shimmering green glow in the sky, glittering sunsets across a world frosted in snow. When he had boarded the plane with his uncle, his heart trembled with excitement. His friends were jealous, wishing they could accompany their own families on a six-month research trip to one of the farthest inhabited reaches of the planet.

But it hadn't taken long to realize the reality of what he had done and where he was going.

Holly's face appeared before him, hovering inches from his bed. Her smile was playful and cute, if a little crooked. Freckles appeared drawn on her cheeks and her eyes shone with the same shimmering blue he had witnessed along the coastline of the Arctic Ocean. He could still smell her perfume if he tried hard enough, the scent of her which lingered on the collar of his school blazer after she embraced him with a warm hello.

Cody sighed, his breath rising in thin, misty clouds. Maybe that was part of what kept him awake. If Alex knew how to regulate the temperature in their temporary abode, perhaps he would be able to settle into sleep and let his dreams take wing. Despite the thick wool of his pajamas and the obscene density of the duvet that covered him, he couldn't remember the last time he had been warm. Two months into this trip and still he shivered daily, nightly, and ever so rightly.

Something knocked against his window, the sound as sudden a strike as if a bird had crashed and cracked its beak against the glass. Cody jumped. Holly's ghostly face dissipated into nothingness.

He lowered the duvet, regretting it almost instantly as he clambered to his knees and cautiously approached the window beside his bed. Outside, the dancing green light show of the Aurora Borealis performed its nightly routine, the top edges of the display taking on a slight pink hue. That was one thing the online photos had captured perfectly, at least. There was something magical in that light show. On his first night in Denridge, Cody had watched the Aurora for hours, unable to peel his eyes away from its entrancing display, his mind reeling back to his trip to Disney World with his parents and the amazing creations cast into the sky with projectors and the spray of water. In the shifting and pulsing lights of the Alaskan skyline, he saw the specters of animals and beasts dancing, projected images of the natural world that stretched from eons past to the present day. In its glow the world fell away and all that existed was a primal peace, an age-long gratitude, and a sincere under-standing of his minuscule part in the journey of life. A profound glimpse at the—

The crack came again, louder this time. The object caught Cody off guard and he fell back onto his ass. His eyes darted to his doorway where the thin slivers of the hallway lights leaked through the cracks, half expecting Alex to be standing there with a stern expression, about to ask him what the hell was going on.

Cody gripped the window ledge with fingers turned spectral green from the lights. He peered out into the street, eyes scanning over the snow-laden rooftops of his town neighbors. The night was still. In the distance he could make out the local chapel, its spire puncturing the skyline. Somewhere beyond that, a mile or so north, lay Denridge High School, the place where Cody had spent the last seven weeks acting as the trophy new kid.

And there, directly in the street below, a dark shape rearing back, about to hurl another projectile at his window. Cast under the light of the sodium arcs, his face was shadowed, but Cody knew who it was. His signature snow jacket—the bottom half a nondescript black, the upper half an offensive neon orange—reflected the light and called attention to the fifteen-year-old who had been assigned the lucky role of chaperoning the new kid during his first semester at school.

Cody eased the latch and opened the window. The cold rushed in to greet him. "Dude, what are you doing? You're going to wake my uncle."

Cody ducked inside as another stone cracked against the glass.

Hayden Locklear lowered his hood and grinned. He was a handsome kid, with boyish blond hair and the kind of facial symmetry that caused girls to swoon at the members of their favorite boybands. His eyes were an icy blue and he flashed snow-white teeth at Cody, a devilish look in his eye. "Get your ass out, pussy. We're playing ball."

Cody looked back at his clock. 00:33 am.

"Are you kidding me? Alex'll go nuts if he finds out I'm gone. Who's even playing, anyway? Everyone's asleep."

Hayden dug his hand in his pocket and tossed another stone at Cody's window. This time a small spider-web crack appeared in the upper corner.

"Just get your ass down, Trebeck. And bring your ball, this ain't going to happen without you."

Cody deliberated this. On the one hand, he hadn't been able to sleep, so maybe some exercise would help him wind down. On the other hand, if Alex caught him sneaking out in the middle of the night, he'd likely ground him for the rest of the trip, and then what? He'd be left shivering in this shit-heap cabin with nothing more than a pathetic excuse for a fire that could barely melt an ice cube.

Another stone.

Cody's cheeks flushed with warmth. "Dude!"

The grin remained on Hayden's face. "I'm not leaving until you get your ass down here. I told the others we'd collect them on the way." He fixed Cody with a fiery gaze. "You don't want to let Sophie down, do you?"

Cody's throat constricted. *Sophie Pearce... Denridge High School's equivalent of Holly Marsh.*

He tried to hide his sudden flutter of excitement, but Hayden saw right through it. He drew another stone from his pocket and tossed it casually up and down in his gloved palm. "I've got a pocket full of these bad boys. You want to test me?"

Cody sent a wary glance back at his door, still half terrified that his uncle could be watching him silently, also secretly half disappointed that he wasn't. At least if his uncle caught him, he'd have a valid excuse to remain indoors. On the other hand...

Sophie.

Cody wiped a hand across his brow and sighed. "Fine. Give me two minutes."

"Hurry your ass up. It's freezing out here."

Cody shivered as he pulled the window closed. *Yeah. You don't need to tell me.* He found his basketball and scooped it into his arms.

Navigating his way downstairs wasn't the trickiest part of his escape. Although the ancient cabin creaked and groaned with each step he took across the landing, he knew that his uncle was unlikely to immediately wake. The house spoke, had its own language. The Alaskan winds often battered the old shelter and caused the beams and supports to mutter and complain in the night. At first, even Alex had trouble sleeping through the ceaseless conversation, but after a week or two he had adjusted—much better than Cody ever had— and snored rhythmically over in the far room, tucked tightly in the confines of his own bed.

For Cody, the tricky part was donning his insulated clothes. While this particular style of outerwear did an okay job at keeping its wearer warm in sub-freezing temperatures, the synthetic material that covered the trousers and jackets created a racket when the material rubbed together. Cody found the farthest room from his uncle's bedroom in order to suit himself up for the snow, but even just walking to the front door sounded like someone was repeatedly tugging a zip up and down, up and down. Every step was another zipping tug, and as cautious as he knew he was being, every step closer to the door filled him with dread that his uncle would finally foil his plans.

Cody turned the key in the lock. The mechanism clicked, a single clap in the quiet. He flinched, screwed his eyes shut and teased the door open. The Aurora's light spilled inside as he eased himself out and closed it behind him.

With a final turn of his key, he was outside.

Cody breathed a sigh of relief, taking a moment to steady himself. "Took your time, didn't you?"

Cody jumped, glaring at Hayden, who stood just three feet away. "*Please*, keep your voice down. If my uncle catches me, he'll…"

"He'll what? Write about you in his books? Come on, dude. If anything, it'll give him more inspiration for his characters. They might actually be a lot more rounded. Experience and tragedy add depth." He snatched the ball from Cody's hands and smirked. "So I've heard."

"You've never read one of his books. How would you know?"

Hayden wasn't listening. Already he was making his way down the street, trying and failing to spin the ball on the end of one gloved finger. The ball fell from his grip and hit the ground with a soft thud and no bounce as the snow absorbed its motion.

Cody cast one more glance up at his uncle's bedroom window before pulling his hood tight about his head and following Hayden into the night.

Above them, the Aurora continued its metamorphosis, neither boy heeding the warning stretched clearly across the darkening sky…

2

TORI ASPLIN

The stale aroma of their sex hung in the air. A heady concoction of his scent and hers, entangled in the fabric of her bedroom as they lay side by side, content and sleepy under the glow of the crackling fire.

Tori Asplin's curtains were skewed, her typically neat bedroom evidence of her desperate lovemaking with the hulking man who now dozed beside her. A sliver of alien green pulsed in the night sky, undulating clouds creeping in from the horizon to steal the beauty of the dancing display. Around the room hung posters, postcards, and letters, gestures and well wishes mailed to her by fans across the world. They had sent her drawings, an array of homemade gifts, jewelry and trinkets, and these were neatly displayed along the wall and scattered across an ancient, carved oak desk.

A coy smile lingered on her pink lips, the glow of satisfaction that came after a session of furious physical activity keeping her warmer than the roaring embers which burned in the fireplace at the end of her bed.

Tori rolled over and curled her body up against Karl's. His skin was still slick with perspiration, and her hands found the contours and grooves of his body easily enough as she affectionately squeezed his titanic frame and kissed his back. She had never been attracted to such masculine men before, never understood the lure of a man who spent all day working outside under the thin haze of sun in the Alaskan tundra, never desired to be lifted and carried as easily as if she were nothing more than a paper bag, but something about Karl changed that within her. There was a chemistry there that she couldn't fight. Even now, as Karl's deep breaths showed the tell-tale signs that he was teetering into dreamland, she craved more. Wanted more. Needed more.

With a mischievous glint in her eye, she rolled to the edge of the bed and scooped up her phone. She chuckled as she opened her camera app and turned it to selfie mode. Angling the phone to get as much of the fleshy boulder in shot behind her, she propped her head in the lower corner of the screen and gave a cheeky thumbs up.

The shutter sounded. Tori flinched, forgetting to turn her phone to silent. A litter of notifications decorated the top bar of her phone. Ordinarily she would spend the next fifteen minutes swiping and tapping through mentions, likes, comments, and shares of her countless social media profiles, but this time she didn't get the chance as Karl shifted beneath the thick covers and faced her.

"What was that?" His voice was a low rumble.

Tori placed the phone back on the sideboard and propped herself up on her elbows. Her eyes lingered on Karl's chest, his dark skin matted with a thick layer of wiry hair. Somewhere beneath that hair was a mountainous region of abdominal muscles that even now made her salivate. She could still taste the salt tang of his skin on her tongue, still knew the map of his body, right down to the three deep grooves which cut along from his right nipple toward his belly-button where the forest of hair broke into clean sections, highlighting the puckered pink edges of a scar he had earned in years past.

"Nothing. Nothing for you to worry about, at least."

Her tone was jovial, playful. Although Tori was approaching her mid-twenties, there was still plenty of childlike youth in her. Maybe that was why she found Karl so alluring. He was approaching his forties and was measurably more mature than the other men that she had encountered that were her own age.

Not that she had many options to choose from in a place like Denridge Hills, where the population of the town barely exceeded 3,000 citizens across the thin stretch of frozen coastline that made the northern borders of Alaska.

Karl's expression did not mirror Tori's. His dark, hazel eyes glinted as he leaned across Tori and snatched her phone. His fingers were baguettes against the delicate screen and, though he couldn't unlock her phone, he stared at the endless display of notifications scattered across on her lock screen.

"You didn't share that, did you?"

Tori's playful expression wilted under the intense heat of Karl's gaze.

"No. Of course not. I was just... It was for me, more than anything else. I just wanted to capture this moment of peace. Before... well..."

For a second it appeared as though Karl was going to crush the phone in his hands. It would be easy. Simply apply pressure to the meaty vice of his grip and the phone would shatter to a million pieces. Tori felt a flutter of excitement in her chest at the idea of it, that she could hold the attention of someone who could easily take on anyone in a bar fight and emerge victorious.

She teased the phone from his fingers and returned it to its dock on her sideboard. Beside the dock was a notepad titled "To-do" with a series of quick scribbles detailing her top priorities to manage her online beauty blog and update her social media pages. Her online presence was the very heart of her business, bringing her in a steady stream of royalties from advertising and promotional opportunities that flooded her inbox every day and, though the destruction of her mobile phone would certainly put a large wrench in the works, there was a part of her that knew that Karl didn't have it in him.

Ever since their first sexual encounter, after finding each other alone and drunk in the thick heat of one of the town's three public houses, "The Wolf's Head," Karl had been the perfect gentleman. Under the blanket of darkness, they walked through the glittering snow together. He held the door open for her, and though their love-making was desperate and primal, only once had he physically brought her to the point of tears, letting his excitement get too much for her as he yanked at her ponytail and tore a small clump of hair from the back of her head.

Apologies flooded from his lips and he held her in an impossibly gentle embrace for someone of his size. His thick black beard tickled her forehead, brushed her lashes, and they remained that way for some time.

That moment was perfect. From chaos is born beauty.

If only Karl hadn't had to return home to his wife.

Karl rolled onto his back, tucking one hand behind his head. He stared at the ceiling, chest rising and falling. "I'm sorry," he said, lips barely moving. "I should probably head off soon."

Tori's phone screen flashed—another notification. She felt the instinctual need to answer her phone and view the latest nugget of micro-interaction but decided against it, rolling onto her side and propping her head up with her hand. She trailed a finger across Karl's stomach, twisting the thick coils of hair as she did so. "So soon? You know... I'm not going to wait around forever."

The only sign that Karl had heard was the minute movement of his nostrils flaring.

"I wanted to talk to you about something." Her breath came in nervous hitches as she worked the courage to say the things that had been plaguing her mind for some time. Even just the mention of his home, with his wife, and his child, was enough to make her chest burn. "We've been sneaking around for months now and... I can't keep holding in my feelings for you. We need to do something about this... situation."

"What do you suggest?"

Dismissive, unfeeling.

Tori shrugged. "I don't know. Something. Anything. We can't keep going on like this. Sneaking around in the middle of the night, pretending it's not happening, passing each other in the street and pretending we're strangers? It's impossible. All I want to do is run to you and tell you how much I love you. All I want to do is kiss these lips and never stop kissing you." She planted a kiss on his lips. His body responded, lips pressing back. The heat grew, his fingers tangling into her hair, her hands cupping his face. Her tongue danced with his, their breath stolen. When she finally came up for air, she smiled. "Can't you imagine it? This. All the time."

Karl closed his eyes. When he opened them again, they were murky with confusion. His brow furrowed as he sank into thought. "You love me?"

Tori frowned, taken slightly aback. "Of course. You love me, don't you?"

"I suppose."

It was weak, but Tori took it. She sat up and crossed her legs beneath her. "We're good together, me and you. Much better than you two ever were. You complain about her all the time. You groan about how she treats you, about how the spark is gone, about how you wish you didn't have to lie down like two corpses in the night. I can see it in your eyes, Karl. That dying light that comes every time we kiss goodbye, and you go out there into the cold."

She moved closer, her desperation growing. They had never fought before, but they had come close, on a few occasions. She felt her emotions surfacing and it scared her. She loved him, dammit. She loved him.

"Tell me you don't want this." She motioned to her naked body. "Tell me you don't want our late-night talks. Tell me you don't want to stare into my eyes and get lost in them like I do in yours. Tell me you'd rather live the lie you've been keeping and go back to her. That you want to live in misery when you could live in bliss."

Karl was silent.

Tori gave him a nudge with her hand, more forceful than she had planned. Still, she barely moved him. "Tell me."

Karl's dark eyes narrowed at the wooden beams on the ceiling— beams where Tori had spent countless nights staring into the dark, heart thumping, head full of Karl.

She waited for an answer. When one didn't come, she let out a frustrated growl, took her phone and opened the picture she had taken of the pair of them. It was the only picture she had managed to get of them both from the last five months, knowing how important it was to keep their affair a secret. She pointed to the corner of the image where a beaming Tori stared at the lens, her blonde hair tangled into a bird's nest on her head. "That's happiness. That's what we could have all the time. Every second. Every minute. Every day. All you have to do is tell her. Tell her you want to be here and tell her that you're mine. Who cares if it turns messy for a while? We'll figure it out together. I just... I want you."

To her dismay, Karl shook his head. "I can't. I..."

A sudden wave of anger burned through Tori. She pushed herself from the bed, standing as naked as the day she was born. "What, Karl? What is it? What possible reason could you have to stop us from starting our life together? You're worried what the townspeople will think? Fuck them. You're worried what your wife will think? Fuck her. You're worried about what your daughter..."

Tori knew she had gone too far.

Karl's head whipped toward Tori with such sudden speed that it frightened her. He pummeled a fist into the bed and sat up, the covers sliding down and revealing his upper torso in its entirety. "Don't you *dare* finish that sentence."

"Then what is it?" Tori's eyes blurred. Hot tears pooled in the corners. She crossed to the en suite door and shrugged her arms into her nightgown, fumbling to tie the belt around her waist. "We can't keep sneaking around. Sooner or later, they're going to find out. This is a small town. I'm surprised that people aren't already suspicious." A tear trailed down her face, tickling her nose and finding its resting place on her upper lip. "Please. Just tell me when. Tell me when we can start our goddamn life together and make it official. I need to know."

Karl clenched his teeth as he fought his internal battle. Tori presented her phone to Karl, the image lit brightly on the display. She hovered a finger over the DELETE button. "It's all in your hands. I want what's in this picture. Make a decision, because I can't keep falling further in love with you and watching my heart break every time you crawl back into bed with her."

Her lips trembled. She could barely see him through the tears streaming down her face, but she didn't want to give him the satisfaction of wiping them away.

An endless moment of time stretched before them. A thousand thoughts ran through Tori's head. A sudden regret flared inside of her, her mind catching up, understanding that she may have just ruined everything, terrified that he would choose the Get Out of Jail Free card that she had offered.

Yet, at the same time, she held on to the miniscule buzz of excitement that maybe this was what the giant lummox needed, a kick in the right direction. Tori wasn't going to wait around forever. She had more self-respect than to simply remain the other woman.

Karl growled and pushed himself off the bed. His steps were heavy as he slowly tramped his way around the room. Her eyes tracked his, her head craning upward to look into the eyes of the mountainous figure towering over her. In that moment she was very aware that he could snap her in half with ease—Lord knows he had picked her up and held her against these walls enough times for her to know the true magnitude of his strength. You didn't get to become one of Denridge Hill's most revered hunters without having the muscle and the dexterity to back it up. Tales still whispered among Karl's friends of his encounter with the polar bear that had caught him off guard while fishing along the coasts of the Arctic Ocean. Though the bear had taken a powerful swipe with his claws and caught Karl in the chest, he still managed to swing himself onto the bear's back, gripping the creature around the throat with the crook of his elbow. Holding his arm tight with his spare hand, he had constricted the bear's throat until his fellow hunters were able to respond with a volley of bullets which caught the bear's flank and stained the ice pink.

They stared at each other for a silent minute, Karl's exhalations coming out in warm gusts from his nostrils. Tori held his gaze, unblinking, knowing that she had made her bed and now she must lie in it, hoping that this would be the moment that she fought for—and won—what was rightfully hers.

Karl cradled Tori's cheek. His palm was calloused and rough, the cup of his hand enough to swallow her face. The ghost of a smile returned as she softened into his hand and let out a weak laugh.

Her smile died. Karl shook his head. He didn't even have the decency to use his words. He relieved Tori of her phone and pressed the glowing red button. The picture vanished into the digital ether, leaving behind the next picture in the gallery—an image of Tori's bare legs spilling out from bedsheets as she decorated the bed in boxes of "Ray Ray Self-tan." A bright orange streak of the tanning solution running from knee to ankle.

Tori opened her mouth, but the words stuck in her throat. A strange guttural sob escaped her throat as she glanced at her hands. When she finally managed to speak, the words were nothing more than a whisper. "Get out."

Karl remained where he stood, heat radiating from his bare flesh, his scent dizzying her senses as her body yearned for him but her mind screamed at him to leave.

Still, he did not move.

"What do you want from me?!" Tori roared the words at him now, her anger coming out like poison as she spat each syllable. "Just fucking go! Go back to her! Go back to that bitch and live your happy little fucking lives! Just go!" She shoved him, but she may as well have been trying to move a stone obelisk. "What are you waiting for? Just go! Get the fuck out of here. You don't want me, I don't want you! There. It's done. That's what you wanted, right?" The tears were hot in her eyes as she beat her fists against his chest. "Go! Just go!"

She broke down in tears, her body slumping and going slack as she nearly collapsed into the vanity table behind her. It was only after absorbing this moment of defeat that Karl silently turned and dressed, as though he had been waiting for her to rage...

...as though he was enjoying watching this side of her.

When, at last, he donned his final layer of thermal wear, he crossed to the door, pausing with his hand on the handle. He turned back to her, a pitying glimmer in his eye which only made her anger burn hotter. She wondered if, perhaps, he might change his mind, that maybe in the final moments of making his decision he had had a change of heart. Perhaps this was it, she needed to show the true depths of her feelings in order to wake him up and realize what he was throwing away. She was an online celebrity, for God's sake. Every day thousands of men showered her with adorations and sent messages wishing, just wishing they could spend an hour of time with her. Didn't he understand how lucky he was?

If any of that was on his mind, Karl didn't show it. "You won't tell anyone about this?"

Tori's face fell. Led by a blind, carnal hate, she grabbed the nearest object to her, which happened to be a large glass bottle of perfume her grandmother had handed to her before she passed away. She hurled the bottle at him, missing his shielding arm by inches as it smashed against the door and sent an explosion of its sweet scent into the room.

Karl's eyes flashed. He pulled at the door with such fervor that it threatened to rip clean from its moorings. He marched out of the room.

Tori chased after him, her gown flowing behind her as her bare feet padded on the wooden stairs. "I should have known all along that that's all you cared about. Your goddamn reputation! You think I'm not going to tell your wife about this? You think I'm not going to tell the whole fucking world?" She waved her phone in the air, not even sure of the words that were spilling from her lips anymore. In that moment, she didn't recognize herself and she didn't care, all she cared about was reciprocating the hurt he had inflicted upon her by denying her ultimatum.

Karl stopped at the front door, his face a contorted mess of fury. He pointed a thick finger toward her. "You tell a single soul about this, and you're going to regret it."

He opened the door. A flurry of cold swept into the room. Snow hammered from the skies, adding several inches of fresh powder to the hard, condensed layer that perpetually covered the ground. Tori wrapped her gown around her, her teeth already chattering. Even Karl squinted and shielded his eyes from the onslaught of the snowstorm, neither one of them noticing the slight hue of red which tinted the town.

The sudden blast of cold snapped Tori from her reverie. She made a step toward Karl. "Wait. Karl, please. Can we just talk about this? It's awful out there, you don't have to go."

With dark, unfeeling eyes, Karl spared a final glance back at her. He turned away. Stepped outside.

Then he was gone.

Snowflakes melted in the entryway, turning to gentle puddles on the wooden floor. Tori crossed to the nearest window and pulled the curtains aside. She hoped that maybe she might get a final glimpse of the man she had let herself fall for, but the storm had already taken Karl, the eddies and whirls of snow dancing furiously outside.

She allowed a few silent tears to fall as she closed the door and made her way back to her bedroom. Her hands shook so violently that her phone slipped and fell to the floor. She knelt to retrieve it and found the corner of the screen had cracked. She stared at the dark mirror of the unlit display and saw the reflection of a woman she didn't recognize. Swiping to unlock the device, her eyes fixed on the notifications. A whole dashboard of instant gratification awaited her. However, when she tried to dive into her security blanket of anonymous worshippers, she found that even this luxury had been stolen from her.

She banged the heel of her palm against the screen. "Come on, dammit." A red cross overlaid the symbol for her network carrier. She glanced at the window, staring daggers at the sliver of the storm she could view through her curtains. The weather reporters hadn't predicted adverse weather conditions for the town today—usually a storm this extreme would have carried a series of warnings that had been distributed by the town mayor. She'd have had enough of a warning to schedule content before her internet went down entirely and she was cast in a three-day blackout. But if any warning messages had been put out there, she had been oblivious to it.

Of course you were, you were too busy ogling your lover boy. You wouldn't have seen any kind of warning, even if it had been written in chocolate on the tip of his cock.

She tried to open her apps, but all that met her were the loading screens followed by an error message. Both her phone signal and her home internet—which was scrappy and rudimentary in this part of the world at best—showed no signs of cutting her a break. The notifications teased her, like letters from loved ones that she wasn't allowed to read. With a final dismissive grunt, she tossed the phone onto her bed and stared out at the storm, noting for the first time, the faint red glow that danced just beyond the blanket of roiling clouds.

3

CODY TREBECK

It was reassuring to see that Hayden spared no compassion when it came to waking the rest of their unlikely band of misfits.

His pockets had no end to their depths as he scouted each of their bedrooms and launched stones at windows with impressive precision.

Travis King was waiting by the door when they arrived. Apparently, Hayden had seen it fit to announce to *some* of their group that he'd be arriving like a specter in the night to lead the ballers' rebellion. After a brief curtain twitch, Travis appeared in the door with a grin as wide as his face.

"Alright, fuckwits?" He hopped over to Hayden and bumped his fist, pulling back following the initial impact and spreading his fingers as their mouths formed the trailing roll of an explosion, after which he turned to Cody and nodded. "New kid."

"Travis," Cody replied. "How long have you guys been planning this?"

"About a week." Travis dug his hands deep into his pockets and tucked his chin, hiding his mouth behind the high collar of his jacket. "Thought you were going to tell him, Hayden?"

Hayden chuckled. "Nah. More fun this way. Thought I was going to catch sight of the new kid in his bunny rabbit pjs, but no dice."

Cody shot him a look. While Hayden clearly had the run of the kids in tenth grade, Cody had been cautious of him since the day they had been paired up as chaperone and charge. He was a nice enough kid, sure, but sometimes Cody couldn't help but feel that there was a hollowness to his smile, an emptiness behind his eyes. What did anyone really know of Hayden, anyway?

Still, that didn't stop the girls from chatting animatedly behind their hands whenever he walked past them in the halls.

Hayden and Travis took the lead as they trudged on through town under the pulsing alien glow of the Aurora. The bleeding red continued its descent, but Cody was blind to it, keeping his head down and folding his arms tight around his chest. He had learned from an old Batman movie that it was best to keep the torso warm in the harsh cold. While a human could live with frostbitten hands, they would struggle to survive if the chill penetrated the organs.

Their next stop found them waiting outside a house that looked as though it would barely survive another winter. The roof was already bowed, the whole house standing at a slight angle. The front porch displayed beams that had all rotted or broken as the weight of the snow pressed down upon it. A number of the windows were cracked, with layers of blankets, cloths, and towels pressed up in sodden bunches against the corners to hold off the chill.

"Doesn't look like much, but the greatest treasure is always hidden in the most unlikely places," Hayden said before tossing a stone up at the window. A loud crack filled the street and Cody wished that Hayden would find another way to wake them up. Every crack of stone on glass was another chance for them to get discovered, dragged back to their houses, and reprimanded.

As if reading Cody's thoughts, Travis said, "Why don't you just call her? Amy's phone is always on."

"More romantic this way."

Travis scoffed. "Smashing her window and waking her parents is romantic? I'd hate to see your version of Romeo and Juliet."

A face appeared in the window, ghostly white with bright wide eyes. Amy Lawson grinned, and was soon teasing open a front door that seemed determined to scream like a banshee with every fragment of movement.

With only an inch left to close, Amy rolled her eyes and pulled the door roughly behind her. The sound was a thunderclap in a monastery. Cody examined the other houses for anyone who might have heard.

Amy skipped down the steps with unearned confidence. Her eyes met Cody's and she let out a small chuckle. "Oh, relax, new kid. Mom spent the evening doing shots and playing online Scrabble. She's out for the count." She closed in on Hayden and wrapped her arms around his neck, planting a passionate kiss on his lips. "Hey, baby."

"Hey, you."

Cody still couldn't believe that Hayden was dating a high school junior. A year older than the rest of them, it was unheard of. It was every high school boy's fantasy to get the chance to date an older woman, and here Hayden was, acting as though it was no big deal and that *she* was lucky to be dating him. Back in England, Cody had never seen anything like this. Women matured faster than men and, in most cases, the girls in his year group were already dating boys a year—sometimes two years–older than him.

"Who's next?" Travis asked once the pair finally unlocked lips.

Hayden shot a look toward Cody. "Sophie, of course." He grinned, though it was difficult to read under the shadows cast by his hood.

Cody looked away. Maybe it was just the idea of hanging out with Sophie Pearce in close quarters that put him on edge. He had only ever passed her in the hall, and even that had been enough to make his heart race. Even if he did have a thing for Holly Marsh, he was thousands of miles away. What happened in Alaska, stayed in Alaska, right? It wasn't like he was going to be here forever.

"Doesn't Brandon live near Sophie?" Cody asked, changing the subject.

Hayden and Travis were already walking down the street. Amy

turned over her shoulder, lip curled in disgust. "The fat kid? He's not joining us, is he?"

Cody half jogged, catching up with the rest of them. "You didn't invite him?"

"Fuck no," Hayden rebuked. "You think we're going to be dragging around that tub of lard if shit hits the fan?"

"What if the cops come?" Travis asked. "He'll blab everything. Ain't no way he's going to be outrunning them on those two stubby legs."

Cody overtook the group and turned to face them, walking backward to match their stride. Now that they were out in the cold air his sleepiness had gone and he felt a fresh wave of energy running through him. "He's a good guy. He's not going to dob us in if the cops come, okay. He's also got a spare ball, which'd be useful if something happens to the first one."

Plus, having him here would make me feel a whole lot easier about all of this.

Hayden considered this for a long moment as they passed under the glow of the streetlights and turned right onto Abbington Alley. Cody's gaze drifted above them to the Aurora, noting the strange red hue which had overtaken almost half of the green, and looked as though it was continuing to bleed across the lights.

"Fine," Hayden said. "You want your snuggle blanket, you can go get him. We're not slowing down for fatso just because you want him here."

Amy let go of Hayden's hand and threw down her fists. "Are you kidding me? You're letting *him* join?"

"Sure. Why not?" The grin was back on his face. "New kid makes a good point. If the cops come, we can use him as fodder to slow them down."

"Just like that joke about the bear." Travis touched his chin, his brow creasing. "How fast do you need to run to outrun a bear? It doesn't matter. Just run faster than the guy behind you."

"Or girl," Amy added.

Hayden nodded. "Exactly."

Travis took the basketball from Hayden and prodded the tough rubber. "The extra ball wouldn't go amiss, either. When was the last time this was pumped? 1982?"

Cody's brows knitted together but he remained silent. There was no use arguing with them, they had their opinions of Brandon, and he had his. If anything, he only felt thankful that he wasn't going to be left alone with Hayden and Amy. While Sophie's presence was definitely a helpful reason to be outside at this late hour, the farther he strayed from his house, the more he wished he had stayed indoors.

Why? So you can sit in your bed and shiver until your nipples are tough enough to cut glass?

Cody bit back a retort to Travis, his eyes lingering on the Aurora for a moment longer as the strange magnetic phenomenon continued its transformation.

THEY SPLIT up just five minutes later, Travis, Amy, and Hayden sparing little in the way of glances back. Cody pulled his arms tightly around his body and strode in the other direction, feeling the sudden weight of loneliness grow with every step.

Nighttime always made it worse. Back in London there was always someone nearby. During the day, the roads were choked with traffic and the pavements drummed the steady beat of pedestrian feet. Planes flew overhead, holiday-goers taking off from Stanstead to pursue adventures in Barcelona, Abu Dhabi, or Tokyo. Even at night, the steady hum from the roads outside cocooned Cody in a comforting drone, reminding him that he was not alone in this world.

But here...

Denridge Hills had been the last place he had expected to set up his temporary life. In the last few months, Cody's world had flipped on its head and there wasn't a part of it he now recognized. Six months ago, he had been a regular kid, living the life that any fifteen-year-old raised in London should be living. Never in a million years would he have believed that he could lose both of his parents in a single accident.

A flash of the scene came to him. He had never seen images of the aftermath (although there were many of them in the local newspapers the following day), but he and Alex had driven past the off-ramp on their way to the airport only a few weeks ago and he had imagined the ghost of it then. A jack-knifed semi-truck. A road, slick from a torrential downpour. Tailbacks of red brake lights as far as five miles along the M25.

Cody was told his parents hadn't suffered, that the impact had been immediate. There was no way that anyone would have survived a crash like that and, he supposed, for that he was thankful. Yet, that still didn't fight off the guilt that he felt in the very pit of his stomach that it had somehow been his fault. That, by arguing with his dad for that extra thirty seconds about inviting Erik over to play Call of Duty Warzone, he had somehow lined up the stars of fate in such perfect unity that he had personally guided his parents into the collision.

It was an insane notion, but the stillness of silence and the burden of isolation can do crazy things to a pubescent mind.

Cody spent nights researching the sleepy little town of Denridge Hills on Google Maps the instant his new guardian had informed him of his imminent research trip. At first it seemed exciting, getting the opportunity to travel miles away from the epicenter of his heartache and pain, to run away and escape the relentless misery that had withered his juvenile heart. He had viewed the unremarkable smattering of houses in the northernmost frozen coastlines of Alaska as a place to escape, the tiny town which was bordered by a horse-shoe of dense forests spreading out several miles in each direction.

Yet, it turned out that silence only magnified his wounds. In the witching hour it often felt as though they were still with him, whispering to fill the silent void that pressed in on him in all directions. No matter how far from home he ran, deep down he knew that his parents still lived inside of him and, somehow, he would have to manage his own pain.

Cody stopped outside of Brandon's house, recognizing it instantly by the way the thick paint peeled away from the wood like chipped, curling fingernails. In the upper right-hand window, the curtains were open an inch or so. Cody removed a glove, regretting it almost instantly, and dialed Brandon's number. Just because Hayden wanted to play Romeo, that didn't mean that Cody had to.

As the dial tone sounded, he glanced up and down the street. Snow started to fall around him, an emptiness stretching in either direction. The skin on the back of his neck prickled as a feeling of being watched settled on him.

A groggy voice spoke. "Cody? What is it? Is everything okay?"

"Hey, yeah. Everything's fine. Look, I know this is random as hell, and I'm sorry to wake you, but are you free to come out for a bit?"

A pause. Rustling. "Dude, it's just gone one in the morning." A second pause. "Are you okay? Having more of those dreams?"

"No, nothing like that... It's just..." Cody glanced in the direction he imagined the others to be. They were far from sight now, which was a concern. He hoped that all of this wasn't just an elaborate prank that would be regaled around the tight-knit community of Denridge High School come morning. He sighed and told Brandon what had happened.

"I thought I'd heard them talking about midnight basketball," Brandon said. "In fifth period, today. Didn't know they had you in mind. Just tell them you don't want to come out. It's got to be freezing out there." Brandon's round face appeared in the window, his bright eyes staring up at the Aurora. "Woah, dude. Have you seen the lights tonight?"

Cody turned skyward, unsettled by the dominating shade of crimson the lights had adopted. He had seen hues of pinks, and greens, and oranges, and blues in his short time here, but if he didn't know any better, he'd say that someone had cut open the sky and it was bleeding down upon them. "Freaky, right? Have you seen it like that before?"

Brandon pawed at his eye, naive to Cody's presence below. "Never. Must be some turn of the moon, or... I don't know. Something. I'll ask my dad in the morning. You should get some rest, tell Hayden to fuck off. He'll be pissed, sure, but do you really want to spend the night out there with him?"

"Look down."

Brandon turned his head and found Cody. "You have got to be kidding me."

Cody gave a weak grin. "C'mon, man. This might be my only chance to hang out with Sophie outside of school. Besides, it could be fun. You're always going on about adventure and excitement. This could be your chance to do something daring. Do you want to look back at this when you're fifty and regret not taking the opportunity?"

"I'd like to make it to fifty."

"Please?"

"It'll never happen with Sophie."

"It might. Hayden ended up with Amy. Who knows?" Cody held Brandon's stare. "Come on... I'll give you my '97 Legacy Michael Jordan card?"

"You'd do all this for Jordan?"

Cody chewed his lip, the cold making his teeth hurt. His hand had grown numb. "Okay, maybe not Jordan. But someone else... How about Charles Berkley?"

Brandon let out a heavy sigh. "Hold on..."

Cody hung up the phone and rushed to return the glove to his hand. It took a few minutes for his fingers to warm up, and by the time Brandon carefully closed the front door behind him, he could finally bend his fingers again.

"You know this is insane?" Brandon said through a mask of thick woolen scarves. He was easily twice as wide as Cody, and a few inches shorter. The layers of clothing didn't help him at all, adding extra puff to the parts of his body that were already squishy and wobbled when he walked. "Batshit insane. I'm only doing this for you because of your psychotic breakdown the other day."

Cody cringed, reliving the moment. It had come out of nowhere, a sudden, unshakeable sadness that paralyzed his body and had him burst into floods of tears in the middle of a cafeteria full of his peers. Aided by Brandon, Cody had fled the cafeteria—Hayden had been less than useless. They found succor in the health nurse's office, the kindly lady handing him a paper bag to inflate with each outbreath. As he stared at the grimy black and white tiled floor, all he could think was: is there anywhere that grief couldn't follow?

"Gee, thanks." Cody gave an appreciative smile. "Didn't the nurse tell you not to bring that up again?"

Brandon shrugged. "My dad always says the truth will set you free. You don't need the world lying to you right now, you need someone who's going to be upfront and honest. Someone who can smack reality into that head of yours and remind you that it takes time to heal."

"Wow. Poignant and brutal."

Brandon gave him a knowing look. Cody wondered what it would have been like for Brandon losing his own mother at such a young age. Maybe it would've spared the pain of understanding what loss truly is, his juvenile mind too young to process and comprehend.

"You've been through a lot. I'm not going to sugarcoat that shit, you know that don't you?"

"Does everything circle back to sugar with you?"

Brandon gave him a weak punch in the arm, the pair breaking into quiet laughter. "I'll let you have that one." He pointed a gloved hand up the road. "Sophie lives that way. Is that where the others are?"

Cody nodded.

Brandon sighed. "Fine. Let's get this over with. The things I do for signed NBA memorabilia."

"Oh, that reminds me. Can you grab your ball, too? We need a spare."

Brandon rolled his eyes before returning to his house.

4

ALEX GOINS

The wind hushed against the side of the house, a soothing lullaby to some, a nightmarish drone to others. No matter how insulated the houses were in Denridge Hills, the wind had its own intelligence. It could sneak into the cracks and find the tubes and chambers which created the most haunting of whistles. Soft enough that the resulting ghostly choir sounded like they were practicing their harmonies a thousand miles away.

He had been promised more than this, but still hadn't expected much. A seasoned traveler of the world, Alex Goins had ridden in the cramped fuselages of a hundred planes and aircrafts. He had developed sores against his thighs and feet from the discomfort of budget plastic and leather seating, his skin grown clammy as it rubbed together while he tucked into shrink-wrapped reconstituted meats and watched Cheers reruns for the tenth time in a row. He had stayed in humid rainforests surrounded by monolithic trees, sun-drenched hotels in which the air-conditioning was the only respite from a heat so intense that it drew the very moisture from your skin, cities in which buildings fought like plants for the title of the tallest tower, and mud-dried shanty towns where your closest sleeping companions were the rats and the Petri dish of diseases which ran rife through the poverty-stricken communities.

Alex had witnessed more of life than the average man could witness in three lifetimes, but still there was something about the Alaskan north that caught him off guard. He had stayed in the Alps on weekend skiing breaks, visited the frigid blue caverns of Iceland, climbed the heights of the Siberian mountains, and a big part of him thought that he would be used to the relentless colds that could sweep in with the frosty winds...

But nothing had prepared him for this.

There was a small landing strip on the western side of the town, nothing more than a flattened line of dirt that allowed the limited air traffic to land. On the day that he and his nephew, Cody, had glided over the miles of barren tundra, the pilot informed him that visits to Denridge Hills could be unpredictable at best, with many pilots refusing to bring their modest aircrafts that far north at all. The winds were often turbulent, and even on a sunny day the weather could take a turn and force the aircrafts to U-turn, haul ass, and high-tail it back to Deadhorse Airport in Prudhoe Bay, some two hundred miles away, where they would lie quiet until the storms died down. Only then would they attempt to head back to the safety of the southern mainland the first moment that chance allowed.

"So, you don't get a lot of visitors?" Alex squinted through his sunglasses at the burning shades of peaches and ripe fruit that bled from the sun and into the sky.

The pilot chewed gum which had to have turned flavorless by now, each grind of his teeth accompanied by a wet smack of his lips. "This ain't a tourist town. If you're born in Denridge, you die in Denridge. The rare few that escape never come back. It's a real primitive place. Family trees are tangled. A lot of third cousins fall into bed."

Cody scoffed, the roar of the plane's desperate engines not enough to cover up his disapproval.

Alex threw a glance at the kid over his shoulder. "They've still got Wi-Fi, though. Haven't they?"

Cody shifted behind him, his attention caught.

"Oh, sure, they've got Wi-Fi. Doesn't mean it's reliable. A couple cell towers which can easily be buffeted by the winds and snows. You'll be lucky to sustain a decent enough connection to jack off to those blue sites and reach your climax before the thing glitches out and you're left staring at a—"

"Alright, alright." Alex waved his hands, catching Cody's eye for just a moment before the kid returned his gaze to the sunset.

It was shortly after their pilot announced that they were closing in on the town that an involuntary shiver ran up Alex's spine. He peered through the windscreen, searching for the fabled town he'd seen in so many pictures online, hoping to catch his first real glimpse, but all he could see was the endless green ocean of pine trees below. Giant things that stretched out of the ground like witches' fingers, clustered so densely together that it was impossible to see the forest floor.

"What you're looking at is Drumtrie Forest, one of the last stretches of unexplored woods this side of the globe. That thing stretches for miles in either direction, wrapping its arms around the town. Once you're in Denridge, the only way back to reality is by plane, my friends. Unless you want to trek through that thing, or hit the Arctic by boat and paddle the dozen or so miles to the next thoroughfare out of there." He winked at Alex, chewed his gum. "Lucky you, eh?"

Alex had seen the forest on a pixelated digital map during his first dive into the few isolated locations left on Earth and had grown immediately curious by what he had seen. It was because of this unique living situation that he had chosen Denridge as the target of his latest research trip. When his most recent novel, "Burning Sands," had been released a little over a year ago, it had received a slew of literary acclaim. He had rejoiced in seeing his name in online features and magazines. His phone didn't stop ringing for weeks. When the paychecks came in a month later, and he saw the royalty statements, his cheeks ached from grinning. Finally, after years of toiling behind the clacking keys of his keyboard, he had made it as a writer.

"Burning Sands" hadn't been Alex's first novel. He had released many before, of course. Each one granting him a little extra glimpse of the success that he had been aiming for. His particular brand of fiction boasted an in-depth look into some of the world's most misunderstood cultures, bringing an authentic lens to foreign civilizations and cultures. "World Writers Magazine" commented that his writing: "Blew the competition out of the water. Goin's books, while not only microscopically researched to a standard that any tenured academic would envy, also delivered plot lines so thick with tension that the reader walked the high wire from beginning until end. One could get lost in the pages for hours, emerging at the end with a profound sense of confusion and disarray as they struggled to acclimatize once more with the world they had left behind."

Yet, after those first few weeks, Alex struggled with the dilemma that all successful professionals then faced. How to follow up on a global bestseller?

The money rolled in. Despite it all, Alex did his best to remain humble. He bought a house on the borders of London, and for a few months he allowed himself a number of reckless purchases of items he had desired greatly for a number of years (including his brand-new Honda HR-V), before placing the rest in a savings account.

Weeks passed where he sat at the keyboard, head in his hands, searching for his next great idea. He researched the Amazon rainforest; he considered an exploration of North Korea. After six months his agent started cranking up the heat, and it was in a desperate need to escape and clear his head that he found himself in an East-London pub with an old school friend.

"You're thinking too hard, that's the problem," Ian Vance said, his upper lip frothed with foam from his Carlsberg.

"I have to. This *has* to be good. A tale rich with enough story and background that the readers fall in love. It's not just the physical characters that the readers love, it's the world. The country, the ambience, the very setting is a character in itself."

Ian let out a small exhalation from his nose. "You sound like a right pretentious twat. Do you hear yourself?"

They laughed as the smattering of patrons mumbled around them. The stale scent of spilled beer and ale hung in the air, thick in the sticky residues left in the weaves of the carpets.

"Why don't you just strip back what you did before? Don't over-analyze it. Pare it all back and start from scratch. Think simple." Ian leaned forward suddenly, hand slapping the table as his eyes widened. "Why don't you do the *opposite* of what you've done before?"

Alex raised an eyebrow.

"No, think about it. Burning Sands was all about Egyptian culture and pyramids and all that shit that we've seen in a thousand documentaries, right? Mummies and traps and all that crap."

"I hope this isn't how you talk to other people about my books." Alex grinned, a slight shake in his head. "No wonder my sales are beginning to decline."

"Do the opposite. Go somewhere barren. Somewhere where there *is* no story. Somewhere that remains a mystery to most of the civilized world but could yield some interesting reading. Somewhere like... An island off the coast of New Zealand, or... the Atlantic..."

"That's an ocean."

"I'm just spitballing, here." Ian unlocked his phone screen and navigated to his Maps app. He flicked his finger across the globe until it settled on a mass of white at the northernmost reaches of Alaska. "There. That's where your next book is going to be set."

At the time, Alex had shrugged off Ian's enthusiasm, taking it as nothing more than the ramblings of a tipsy friend. Yet, as the days wore on, the notion wormed its way into his mind. It became a parasite, and soon it was all he could think about.

He lost himself in study, spending hours each day looking into the unremarkable community who chose to live hundreds of miles away from the embrace of modern civilization. Over time he unlocked the secrets of his next story, ideas percolating even as he booked his flight and prepared to jet off for his solo trip to Alaska. Mystery swam in the legends regaled around the Denridge campfires. Enigma shrouded them, coddled in the arms of the Drumtrie Forest.

Something was there, he was sure of it. Something he could shape into his next bestseller. Denridge Hills was his best chance at a future success...

But, oh that chill.

Alex hadn't been sure if it was the physical presence of isolation that seeped into his bone marrow from the moment they soared over the dense forest and Denridge came into view, or if it was perhaps the guilt of dragging a fifteen-year-old kid so far from home just months after his parents—Alex's sister and brother-in-law—had passed, but something was off. When they stepped off the plane, he accepted that chill as an unwelcome companion. There was no escape.

Even now, lying under the copious piles of sheets and blankets, his body refused to reach any kind of warmth in temperature. Lying in the dark and staring up at the beamed ceilings, his mind reeled. He could feel his tiredness weighing his lower lids. His lips were chapped and sore. His hair felt brittle and thick, more like straw than the soft texture he had been used to when able to live in warmer conditions.

Still, it'll all be worth it. Four more weeks and we'll be out of here.

His screen pulsed with a white glow from the corner of his room. He rarely turned his computer off, knowing that an idea could strike at any minute and, like catching a trout with your bare hands, if you didn't react fast, it could escape downriver and disappear beneath the mirk. A thick black block of text decorated the digital white page— the result of his latest writing sprint in which he chronicled his experiences of visiting the Iñupiat tribe who lived a couple of miles out toward the Arctic coastline. The Iñupiat were some of the last truly native Inuit to exist in the world. This far north, the tribe had struck a deal with the people of Denridge Hills that they would be allowed to hold on to their customs and the borders of their grounds in which they hunted, slept, bred, and survived, without fear of modern interference. Their ways were sacred, traditional, ancient, and primitive, and they were to be respected.

Alex had found a guide who was able to take him out into the barren tundra only a week ago. Together they barreled along the snow on a sled led by seven of the most beautiful and obedient dogs Alex had ever met. Their coats displayed shining blacks, whites, grays, and even oranges as they sprinted under the hazy glow of the low-hanging sun.

He had visited the Iñupiat people and stayed with them inside an igloo for a single night. With their conversation translated by Alex's guide, he asked the burning questions he could not find an answer to on any side of the internet. There he learned about their customs and their lore. He probed about their gods and their superstitions. While there were some questions that the Iñupiat people were lax to answer —particularly when it came to their tribal leader who had been taken with a sudden sickness—Alex gleaned enough from his visit to fill the entirety of a dozen pages of his notebook.

That visit had informed the first three chapters of his new novel, for which he had yet to adopt a title. He planned to go back there, if he could. One final visit to follow up on a number of questions which had sprung into his mind on the ride back to town. If only his guide would agree to take him back again.

Alex's mind buzzed with a hive of thoughts. He rolled over in his bed, eyes finding the line of amber light which spilled from beneath his door. Just two rooms away Cody would be fast asleep. At least in slumber the kid could escape the pains of the last few months. While Alex covered the pain of the loss of his sister by diving deeper into his book than he had with any other project, he wondered how the kid was truly coping. He couldn't imagine what it must be like to lose both of his parents so young. His recent breakdown at school showed that there were cracks there that were breaking, although when he was face-to-face with Cody, he hardly showed any emotion whatso-ever. After receiving the call from the school nurse, Alex tried to coax some information out of Cody, but all he was able to gather was a mild grunt followed by a soft shoulder shrug before Cody disap-peared into his room and shut the door behind him.

Alex rose from his bed and beelined for the desk like a lazy fly drawn to a UV light. There were small chips and scratches in the desk's surface, initials carved from the former residents of the rental house, an ink spill in the corner which could never be erased without a full tin of elbow grease. He read over the last paragraph he had written, foregoing sleep and deciding that he may as well make some kind of progress while he was up. Writing always made him feel better, no matter the situation.

His fingers worked away at the keys, dancing and clicking without conscious thought. His eyes rarely strayed to the keyboard anymore, his mind and body so familiar with its layout that there was little point. After an hour he had written another page, and to him that was good.

Alex reached for the glass beside him and found it empty. His fingertips cradled the lip which had developed a small ring of frosty condensation. His throat dry, he teased open his bedroom door and crossed to the bathroom.

Water rushed noisily from the tap. Alex flinched. When he shut the tap off, he waited in the ambience of the distant ghost choir and cocked his ear for any disturbance from Cody's room. When none came, he tiptoed back into the hall.

Halfway back to his room, he paused.

Cody's door was open. Not all the way open, but open enough to show a long line of darkness in the crack left by the latch resting against the doorjamb.

Alex pressed an ear to the door. When no sound returned, he gently eased the door open a couple of inches.

It took a moment to adjust to the darkness. There was a strange red glow around Cody's window, as though cast from a lava lamp of some kind. Alex had had one as a kid, the bubbles blue and the light green. When he stared up at the Aurora in the night sky he often thought back to that lamp, about a simpler time when the world made sense and his sister was still breathing.

But Cody had no lamp to speak of, and Alex doubted that Cody would have been able to purchase one from the modest Denridge shops. Those were mostly reserved for the necessities like groceries, butchers, fishing tackle, hardware, and clothing. Drawn in with a daunting curiosity, Alex opened the door further, now able to make out the shapes of Cody's furniture in the gloom. His eyes scanned the crooked doors of the wardrobe, glossed over the picture frames on the dresser, filled with familiar figures and long-lost smiles, and finally found the empty bed.

For a half second, Alex believed his mind was playing tricks on him. The strange red hue cast an almost dreamlike state over the room, and he was almost certain he would wake up at any minute. Another step into the room and he realized that that was not the case. Like a blind man exploring his surroundings with waving hands, he stumbled toward the bed and patted the sheets, as though Cody might be hiding somewhere underneath the mound of scrunched up material left gathered at the bottom of the bed.

"Cody?"

He dropped to his knees and checked beneath the bed, letting out a sudden cry as he fell backward onto his hands. Strange dark eyes glinted at him from beneath the bed, some wicked creature cloaked in darkness. Only, when Alex caught his breath, he realized there was no creature at all. Just the reflection of the large black buttons of one of Cody's London winter jackets.

Alex let out a weak laugh and pushed himself back to his feet. Something caught his attention from the corner of his eye, and he turned toward the break in the curtains.

"What the...?"

Alex floated toward the frosted glass in a dreamlike state, his attention now entirely belonging to the Aurora. It danced merrily in the sky, pulsing and waving for as far as he could see in either direction. Alex knew that the natives of Alaska and beyond once believed that the Aurora was the resting place of many of the world's fallen creatures. He had seen paintings and displays of deer and bear and fish and eagles created from the very fibers of the alien light, soaring across the sky in an enchanting array of color.

Yet, he had never seen anything like this.

The Aurora eddied and weaved in the hues of blood spilled from a fresh wound in a squealing hog. A flash of his visits to the slaughterhouses of eastern Ukraine arose, a number of barnyards in the ass end of nowhere, governed by a cluster of born and bred farmers who took sick delight in torturing the poor creatures until their final breaths.

A serpent of nausea coiled in Alex's stomach and slithered up his throat, teasing its tongue out of his mouth to taste the air. He swallowed hard and pushed the creature back down, wondering what possible natural phenomenon could make the sky look as though it had broken, and God was bleeding.

He turned his gaze down into the streets, wondering if anyone else had noticed this strange occurrence, expecting to see a neighbor or two standing outside of their houses to bear witness.

But no. The sleepy town slept on.

What Alex did notice, however, as the first flurries of a fresh storm of snow began to fall from the dark clouds gathering around the Aurora, were a series of fresh footprints in the snow, leading away from his house, and out into the town.

He turned back to the room, spying the empty space where Cody's basketball sat when it wasn't being bounced inside his room, and sighed. Ever since he had received news of Kathrin and Tom's accident, the burden of parenthood had been a constant nag in the back of his mind. Cody was fifteen, nearly sixteen, and for that he was somewhat thankful. Alex had avoided having children of his own, not because the opportunity hadn't presented itself, but because his work was his life, his love, his child. While he was thankful now that he didn't have to change Cody's nappies and feed him milk from a rubber nipple every few hours, the teenage years were always going to be some of the most trialing to any parent. Rebellion was baked into their blood and, to Alex, this might have just been the most reckless act that Cody could have taken. To wander off in the middle of the night in a strange town where nightly temperatures plummeted to well below freezing. In a part of the world where polar bears roaming the town weren't just fables from fiction, but a real threat, and wolves gathered in merciless packs searching for a fresh kill.

And then there was the case of the Aurora. Alex's mind struggled to comprehend any kind of possible science behind its bloody alien glow. Every eventuality he considered caused his gut to wither, his heart to beat faster.

Five minutes later, Alex strapped up his boots and pulled on his gloves. He raised his hood about his head and crunched out into the night. The only solace running through his mind that perhaps, somewhere further down the line, this whole experience would make a great story.

5

CODY TREBECK

T he wind and snow picked up. Great blustery hands buffeted the troop along, shoving them in all directions. They braced themselves, Cody clenching his teeth, trapping his gloved hands in the crevices of his armpits, squinting against the flakes of snow that flurried around them. For the tenth time in as many minutes he questioned his decision to blindly follow Hayden out into the night.

The four others walked ahead of Cody and Brandon. They barely batted an eyelid when the pair arrived at Sophie's house just as she was leaving through the back door and emerging through the side of the building. Amy, Hayden, and Travis sniggered and muttered something among themselves, sparing a single glance back at Cody and his companion before leading the way toward the school.

Only Sophie held Cody's gaze and offered a weak smile. It was enough to send a flush of warmth through his adrenal system and make his heart flutter.

But even that faded as Amy hooked her hand around Sophie's arm and led her onward, the group setting their sights on the fuzzy white distance, as they began their trek toward the school.

Denridge Hills High School lay at the farthest limits of the town.

Divided into a cluster of larger buildings, each unit looked to Cody more akin to the industrial warehouses dotted around London's spaghetti junction motorways than a place for education and learning. Their externals were painted corrugated metal with reinforced sloped roofs to take the strain of the town's heavy snowfalls. The windows were few and far between, and those that did break the endless walls of sheet metal and insulation were inches thick, designed to keep the elusive heat inside the building and resist the frigid temperatures.

Around the back of the buildings was a courtyard bordered with a high mesh fence. It was there that the school children were allowed their respite from the blinking fluorescent lights and endless droning of their teachers—but only on the days when the sun was high and the snow was forgiving. Out of the thirty school days Cody had been in attendance, the courtyard had been closed off for at least twenty-five of those days. There was a gymnasium inside the main compound that soon became crowded when all students gathered to find somewhere to break up the monotony of their day and chat with kids from the other classes.

And it was for that particular gymnasium that Hayden had set his sights.

Twenty minutes later, the school loomed from out of the growing snowfall like a freightliner through fog. Its emergency lights gave a dull spectral glow that appeared to Cody like the bright lights of some demonic hellbeast. Instinctively, he shuffled closer to Brandon, and Brandon shuffled closer to him. Hayden and the others appeared unfazed as they tossed the ball back and forth and sent laughter into the air.

"How are we supposed to get in?" Cody asked, scolding himself for not realizing the fault in their plan. "The school's locked up at night. The doors will be padlocked."

Brandon shrugged. Beneath the folds of his insulated clothing, only his eyes and the bridge of his nose poked out. When he spoke, Cody had to strain to hear the muffled tones. "How am I supposed to know? This was Hayden's great idea." His cheeks rose as he grinned.

"If there's no way in, we can just cut home. Sophie's not going to judge you for that, is she?"

Cody looked over at Sophie wrapped tightly in a snow-white puffy jacket that hid the alluring curves of her body. Curves which he found himself absently staring at whenever she walked ahead of him in the halls. There was something about Sophie that called out to him and made his knees weak, and he struggled to put a finger on it. Perhaps it was the fact that she was in the year above, and for high school kids we all know that those years mattered. If he could get into a relationship with an older woman, that would go a long way to accelerating his social status among the boys in his year who wouldn't let him forget his emotional breakdown.

Or maybe it was because she was just so...

Normal.

There was no other word for it. While Amy's ego was tied up in her appearance and the rat race of schoolyard popularity, Sophie didn't seem to care about any of that. She liked Amy as a friend (though Cody couldn't understand why), but she didn't act like the other girls in her year. When Cody had stepped out of the nurse's office after a large portion of the school had watched him drop his tray of food to the floor and scream into his hands, hot tears fuzzing the world around him, Sophie had been one of the first girls who had met his eye as he walked back to class. He expected her to turn away, giggle, maybe even shake her head in disgust. Instead, she had smiled.

"Tough being the new kid, huh?"

Cody's mouth flapped, the words refusing to materialize. A strange guttural sound escaped his throat.

Sophie let out a soft laugh. "We all go through it. It'll pass soon. Trust me, you'll be fine."

With that, she shouldered her bag and disappeared around the corner.

Cody was so lost in his thoughts for a moment that he almost walked into the back of Hayden. It was only thanks to a swift tug on the arm from Brandon that he looked up and realized they had stopped.

Hayden turned to Travis, his eyes flashing with excitement. "Did you bring them?"

"Do you even need to ask?" Travis unzipped his jacket, shielding himself from the brunt of the wind and masking himself in shadow. A moment later he revealed a pair of bolt cutters from the depths of his inner pockets. He stepped toward the mesh fence and opened their jaws.

Hayden rushed beside him and elbowed him out the way, snatching the cutters from his hands. "Let me. This is my rodeo."

Travis looked as though he was about to argue, then thought better of it.

Hayden worked greedily away at the fence until he had snipped a segment tall enough and wide enough to peel back the metal and slip through. He assisted Amy, offering a chivalrous hand, then waited impatiently for the others to follow.

Travis flinched as he pushed his way through the hole. A flash of orange launched at his face, bouncing with a rubbery smack. The force knocked his head backward and he stumbled several steps. He shook his head, hand massaging his forehead when he spotted the basketball rolling back toward Hayden and Amy.

Hayden grinned. "Ladies first, dickhead."

Amy let out a raucous heehaw of amusement. "Yeah. Where are your manners? Come on, Soph."

Sophie glanced guiltily at Travis, apology buried deep in her eyes as he stepped back and motioned for her to pass on through. When she was safe on the other side, Amy claimed Sophie's arm again and locked it in her own.

Travis tried once again to step through, when another projectile came flying at him. This time he was more prepared and ducked out the way before the hit could land. The basketball bounced off the fence and rolled off to the side. Cody and Brandon watched in stunned silence as, this time, Amy shouted, "We said *ladies* first."

Travis turned over his shoulder, letting out a derisive laugh at

Cody and Brandon waiting patiently for their turn. "You're kidding? Those two?"

Hayden fixed a steady gaze on Travis. "You heard her, let the ladies through."

Travis lowered his gaze to the floor and stepped back. Even he knew better than to argue with Hayden.

"After you," Travis mumbled.

Amy clapped her hands together. "We haven't got all night, girls. Get your asses in gear."

"You still think this is a good idea?" Brandon muttered before passing through the gate, his protruding belly scraping against the sharp claws of broken metal.

Cody wasted no time following after, desperately avoiding meeting Travis' gaze as he waited at the side. After Cody had passed through, Travis silently followed, momentarily catching the mirth in Hayden's eyes.

Without another word, Hayden turned away and made a beeline for the gymnasium. Still, Cody wondered how they were going to get inside the actual school, but after seeing Travis' preparedness, he didn't doubt that they eventually would. He was not disappointed when they reached the side entrance to the gym and Hayden examined the padlock on the door. Reaching into his pocket, he crouched down by the lock and produced two small lockpicks. He closed his eyes as he inserted the picks inside the mechanism and started slowly teasing and twisting them in either direction.

If he was trying to hear something inside the padlock, Cody had no idea how he would be able to. The wind howled around them, sending up dizzying eddies of fresh powder from the ground. Small white tornadoes kicked into the air, traveling only a few feet before colliding with another and breaking into pieces. The only solace he could draw from the coming storm was that the clouds which had crawled across the sky now covered the hellish red glow of the Aurora. Only a faint pinkish tinge was visible in the places where the clouds were the most thinly veiled, but at least it was out of sight.

Out of sight, out of mind, as his mother used to say.

A sharp pinch of longing struck his stomach, and he turned his thoughts away from his mother and father. Instead, he thought of his uncle, wondered whether he would still be fast asleep, tucked into the cozy warmth of his bed.

"Got it! Ha!" Hayden's tongue hung out his mouth as he made the final twist and freed the U-shaped bar from the lock. He tugged it free and discarded the lock to the side of the door.

There was little more warmth inside the empty school gymnasium, but at least they were free from the wind. Brandon was the last one in and when he pulled the door shut, the howling ceased at once, leaving them in a thick silence.

Their footsteps echoed, the laminated wood flooring and the sheet metal roofs creating an echo chamber of magnificent proportions. They lowered their hoods, taking a few explorative steps around the space.

"It's spooky at night." Amy huddled closer to Sophie, her eyes darting around the room. "It doesn't feel like the same place, does it?"

"No," Sophie agreed, her voice soft and musical. "It doesn't."

A resounding echo met the first bounce of the basketball on the floor. There was a hoop on either side of the gymnasium, fixed to the wall at just below the official ten-foot height, and it was Travis who barreled toward the hoop now, dribbling the ball with trained elegance as he set up his first layup. He launched the ball and watched it spin a revolution around the bright orange hoop before dropping with satisfaction through the center.

The net swished.

"Game's on, boys. Who's got what it takes to beat T-King?"

Hayden spun to the others, backward walking to the court. "Let's do me, Travis, and Amy versus Cody, Sophie, and fat boy?"

Brandon glared at Hayden. Amy laughed.

Hayden stuck out his tongue. "I mean Brandon, of course."

Sophie tsked, turning to Cody. "You any good?"

Cody grinned. "I can hold my own."

"And you?"

Brandon flushed. "I think you know the answer to that."

They set up on either side of the court, Hayden claiming the initial possession. He dribbled the ball between his legs, scooted it around his waist and advanced on the hoop. Cody bent his knees and spread his arms, preparing to block a shot or a pass around him.

Hayden rushed him, lowering his shoulder and knocking straight into Cody's sternum. Cody grimaced but held his ground, slowing down Hayden's advance as he growled. Hayden searched for Travis, found him on the outer rim of the key and bounce-passed the ball.

Travis waited for the ball to come to him, but that was his mistake. Sophie dashed out from behind him and claimed the ball, tearing down the center strip. Amy, who had lingered back at the halfway line, gave a surprised yelp as Sophie faked to the right and spun back to her left, swinging easily past her.

Travis rushed back, chasing her down and closing the distance. Before he could make it to the paint, Sophie paused a few feet from the net and bagged a graceful two-pointer.

Travis caught up with her, his chest heaving from the sudden exertion. "You can play?"

Sophie gave a playful shrug. "Shouldn't underestimate your opponents. You should know better than that."

Cody and Brandon watched from their own half, goofy grins creeping up their faces. Sophie jogged back and high-fived them both. "Come on, boys. Think I can hold the fort down by myself? Get involved." She laughed and took a defensive stance.

Cody and Brandon exchanged a glance.

Hayden scowled and demanded the ball back from Travis. The game resumed, a sudden intensity falling over Hayden's cocky face. He unzipped his coat and tossed it to the side, stretching his arms and limbering himself up. "Two-two."

"I don't think so," Cody retorted. "Two-zero."

"What about Travis' layup?"

"That doesn't count," Brandon said. "We hadn't picked teams."

"We started the minute we set foot in the gym." Hayden bounced the ball against the floor with extra vigor, catching it roughly in his hands. "Now, are you going to argue, or are you going to play ball?"

He took two steps forward, standing just outside the key, then took a jump shot. The ball arced through the air and whispered through the hoop, the rim untouched. "Five-two."

Cody's eyes narrowed. He shrugged off his own jacket and tossed it to the side of the court. The others followed suit, all except Amy and Brandon who had yet to exert themselves at all.

"Fine," Cody said. "Have it your way."

Without hesitation, he took a sprint up to the halfway line. More prepared this time, Travis stepped in his way to block his advance. Cody dribbled the ball between his legs, throwing a few fakes to confuse Travis and set him off course, keeping the ball moving.

"Not bad, rookie."

Cody's eyes fixed on Travis'. "That's not what they called me in London."

He threw another fake, then bounced the ball between Travis' legs. While Travis had made a name for himself as the MVP of his grade's basketball team, it had also made him overconfident. Cody hadn't had the chance to showcase any of his basketball skills to his new classmates, having missed the tryout deadlines a few weeks before he had joined the school, but now he finally had a chance to show Travis and Hayden what he was all about.

Pressing the advantage, Cody strode around Travis and advanced on the net. Somewhere behind him he could hear Brandon huffing, his jacket rustling loudly as he ran. To his left, a blur of movement called his attention to Sophie who had outsped Amy once again and was taking the lane down the wing.

Hayden waited for him at the key. Cody sneered, luring Hayden into a false sense of security as Cody closed the distance and drew him in. "See if you can block this," Cody yelled, stopping a foot away from Hayden. He jumped backward, looking as though he was about to shoot the fadeaway, but at the last minute he launched the ball to his left, straight into Sophie's hands. As he came down from his jump, Sophie completed the maneuver and sent the ball through the hoop.

Cody landed with a loud clap as his boots touched the ground.

He shared a smile with Sophie, throwing Cody fleetingly back to that moment in the hallway just a few weeks ago.

A red-hot pain exploded on Cody's face. His vision went black.

Cody was aware of falling through a dark void, pulsing stars wheeling a million miles away. He hit the floor, the back of his head landing with a heavy thud. Somewhere far away someone was shouting, "Go! Go!"

A moment later the unmistakable sound of a ball passing through net.

"What the hell are you doing!?" Sophie's voice, nearby.

Cody held his nose, a throbbing pain pulsing in the center of his face. Something warm slicked his hands. He peeled open eyes that were clouded with the tears he was holding back and in that instant he could see the Aurora before him, swallowing his vision. It was everywhere, and it was everything, stinging his eyes, swallowing his vision. He could feel its heat, could taste its metallic tang, the white-hot throb of hurt bleeding from the sky.

"Cody?"

He sat up and let the blood slip down his face and splatter on the floor.

"What the hell was that!?" Sophie's voice echoed around the gymnasium.

"Seven–four." There was a sick satisfaction in Hayden's voice. Cody found both Hayden and Sophie standing just a few feet from where he sat on the floor. "Not my fault your man can't take the pressure."

"You head-butted him, you freak." Sophie closed in on Hayden. A sharp clap resounded around the gym as she slapped his face. His amusement instantly melted into a sick shade of venom. "That was totally uncalled for."

"Leave him alone!" Amy called, running across the gymnasium. "He did no such thing. Cody just got in his way."

"Got in his way? Cody landed and Hayden went for him. Don't pretend you didn't see that."

She turned to Brandon who stood the farthest from the group, hands buried deep in his jacket pockets. There was a paralyzed expression on his face as he debated the pros and cons of siding with his friend or stepping up against the guy who had just attacked Cody.

Hayden sensed his hesitation and pressed it. "Yeah, you saw it. You really think I attacked Cody in cold blood? If I wanted to hurt him, he'd be knocked out cold by now."

Cody looked up at Brandon. He understood his plight and gave a gentle shake of the head.

"No," Brandon said at last, his voice hushed and devoid of emotion. "No, I didn't see anything."

"See!" Hayden sneered, wrapping an arm around Amy's neck and pulling her closer. "I told you we shouldn't have invited your gal pal, babe. One dodgy move from her teammate and she's already jumping off her leash and attacking me."

Sophie growled and raised a hand to strike him again. Amy stepped in the way and grabbed her wrist. "Will you calm your shit? Jesus. This is supposed to be fun. A bit of dangerous excitement. What's with all the hostility?"

Sophie shook her head in disbelief.

Cody dabbed a hand at his nose, pleased to find that the bleeding was slowing. He tentatively pushed himself to his feet and felt the low tide of a headache behind his eyes. Pinching with the material of his sleeve he wiped away the excess blood and gently shook his head. He staggered as he took a step.

Sophie rushed out and caught him, holding him steady by the arm. He could feel the heat from her skin, could smell the faint traces of yesterday's perfume. "Are you okay? Do you want to sit somewhere? Call it a day?"

Cody stared into Hayden's dark eyes, an unspoken threat communicated between them both. Cody had seen that look used on other kids in their grade, but he had hoped that his personal chaperone would never turn the tables on him.

"No, it's fine." Cody dabbed his nose and blinked away the remainder of his tears. "Seven–four to you guys. Let's play this to twenty-one."

Travis clapped loudly. "That's what I'm talking about."

Cody released himself from Sophie and picked up the ball. Brandon followed in step, whispering quietly enough so the others couldn't hear. "Are you sure about this? I don't feel good being here."

"It's just a game to twenty-one, what's the worst that could happen?"

"Apart from Hayden knocking you out?"

Cody took a deep breath. "Win or lose, the sooner we get this over with the sooner we can go home."

He dribbled the ball and tossed it to Brandon, taking his first steps back on court.

Outside the gymnasium, unknown to the six, the wind continued to rage, howling and roaring. Snowflakes grew to the size of golf balls, the land blanketed and white. Dense flurries of snow signaling only the beginning of the encroaching storm.

And through the snow they walked.

6

TORI ASPLIN

Tori sat at the foot of her bed, basking in the heat of the open fire. The flames cracked, occasional pops exploding as the fire found the knots in the wood and fought to overcome them. Tori had always marveled at the wonder of fire. In her world of ice and snow, fire was the yin to the yang. The only force powerful enough to allow people to live this far up north. Fire was the great equalizer, the destroyer of all things. Over time, fire could eat its way through anything. Ice, snow, paper, metal, body...

...and bone.

Raising a shaking hand to her lips, she tasted the ashen tang of smoke. She drew a deep drag of her cigarette and expelled a gray plume into the air. As the smoke worked its way through her body, she felt a nauseous calm fall over her. A steady beat of belonging mingled with the guilt that her fallout with Karl tonight had drawn her back to her old habits.

Yet another thing to hate him for.

It was easy to hate when you were in the confines of your own mind with no one to break you free or show you another perspective. To Tori, in a matter of moments, Karl had gone from the man of her dreams to the villainous monster of her fairy tale. The antagonist who broke her heart, only for her to fall in love later with her true prince.

Good riddance to bad news.

Though, did she truly believe that? Her eyes darted occasionally to the frosted window where the clouds had grown dark and the snow whipped across the town with increasing fury. As much as she wanted to hate the man, she hoped that he was okay out there. She hoped that he arrived home safely. She had been out in storms of this magnitude and the snow had been akin to metal pellets shot from a child's BB gun. A volley of projectiles striking the skin at once was enough to flush your face pink and cause a numbness that would later hold the possibility of bruising. In her lifetime at Denridge, she had seen some monster storms, had braved small journeys in hurricanes and blizzards, and even she wouldn't wish that kind of pain on her worst enemies.

"Let her have him." Her words barely audible, clamped out as the cigarette met her lips again.

She should have thrown away the pack. She wasn't sure why she hadn't, as though at some point she knew she'd need a safety blanket at a time in her life where her heart was in turmoil. She glanced down at her phone—a habit she had yet to realize she had developed—and tapped the screen. The signal was still dead. A hundred notifications teasing her with their serotonin hits. Each message, like, and follow a microscopic injection of ego designed to keep her afloat on a raft sailing across a lake of boredom and misery.

Now there was nothing more than Tori, alone, with a burning fire and her cigarettes.

She supposed that perhaps once the storm had blown over in the morning, she might feel different. The teams would go over to the towers and fix whatever had become blocked or broken and life would resume as normal. But, until then, she couldn't shake off this alien feeling that, even in the heat of the flames, caused her body to shiver. A pressing withdrawal that had a name that she couldn't quite put her finger on...

Loneliness?

With 46,000 followers across a number of social media platforms, Tori had always presumed that she was in good company. How could one ever feel alone, even at the farthest reaches of the inhabited globe, when 46,000 pairs of eyes were looking your way? Commenting and sending love hearts and celebrating the pictures and strange ramblings you posted. She knew that her situation in Denridge made her unique. Occasionally she would post pictures from around the town, granting the world a sample of life in the isolated clutches of Alaska, yet mostly she found that the pictures that performed the best were simply the ones of her in front of a mirror trying on new clothes. Cozy pictures by the fire of bare thighs and socks pulled over her knees. Pictures that her mother—were she still alive today—would have frowned upon and reprimanded her for.

Sex sells, Mom. That's all there is to it. Besides, for every like and comment she received, she increased her chances of ad revenue and income. It was a great way to make money in Denridge, when the only other alternatives were hunting, council, manufacturing, shop work, law, and medicine.

Tori rose from the bed and waved away a cloud of smoke she had just exhaled, flapping a hand until the particles dispersed into the room. She crossed over to the window and stared at the world outside. The strange redness of the Aurora had long since been hidden from view by the roiling clouds, and the snowfall was now so heavy that it was almost impossible to perceive the individual flakes. The world outside was white, the powder on the ground easily two feet deep. Right now, it would be possible to walk through the freshly fallen snow, but after a few hours of these temperatures the powder would crystalize and harden. Add to that the weight of the layers with each additional snowflake hurled from the clouds, and soon it would turn to a mulch that sapped the energy from the legs of anyone who attempted to walk through it. Even the smallest distances could take the most Herculean effort.

Tori glanced back at her phone, remembered that there was no signal, then turned back to the window. She caught a glimpse of her reflection, her usually bright eyes dark and heavy. Her lids were still puffy from the tears she had shed.

"He's not worth it," she reminded herself. "A man who can't choose the right woman over the wrong woman is no man at all."

Still, that did little to erase the emotional hurt he had inflicted upon her. She really thought that he would choose her. That they could finally embark on the relationship she knew they both deserved.

Tori pressed a hand against the glass and rested her head on its chill surface. She stared out into the storm and imagined that she could see Karl. Imagined that his bulky frame would arrive from out of the gloom, a silhouetted figure that acted as a beacon of hope. That maybe, just maybe, he would change his mind and return to her, knock on her door and tell her he made a mistake. He chose her. All would be well. He loved her and that was all there was to it. Come morning he would find a way to tell his wife that it was over, he didn't love her anymore, storm or no storm. It was her he chose. Her.

Tori.

It had always been Tori.

A weak smile appeared on Tori's lips, her heart falling still. She raised her head from the glass and cupped her hands to try and get a better look. It was impossible but... yes... someone was out there now. Someone with a hulking frame and a steady gait appearing before her, making their way toward her house.

"It can't be..."

But it was. She blinked, pawed at her eyes, strained to make sure that what she was seeing wasn't just a figment of her imagination. Yet, still the figure remained, growing larger with each staggered step. A man out in the snow...

Heart leaping with excitement, Tori tore downstairs, her fingers automatically going for the light switch. She was unsurprised to find that the electricity had gone down too, but that didn't bother her. In that moment, all she wanted to do was confirm that it was him. To know that Karl had returned. She could already smell his scent, imagine her fingers sliding through the hairs of his chest. Hear the growl in his words as he groggily rolled over to face her in bed. She yanked the living room curtains back and peered through the glass.

It was him. Karl had returned. She could make out the puffy girth of his thick beard, the sloping frame of his shoulders. It was him; he had come back.

Throat dry, mind wheeling, Tori twisted the locks on the door and yanked it open. The cold wasted no time in pressing against her, invading her house as the winds rushed inside, pleased to be granted entry. Snow skittered across the boards of her floor and numbed her feet, but she didn't care. All that she cared about was that he had come back. He was here, dear God. It was him.

"Karl!" Her words were half laughter, half tears. "Hurry up, it's freezing. You'll let all the heat out."

Karl staggered toward her, not showing any sign of increasing his speed. In the thick fall of the storm it was impossible to make out his features, but for the first time something struck her. The way that he was walking... was he... in pain?

"Karl?" The wind snatched her words. She wrapped her gown tightly about her, bare skin prickling into gooseflesh. "Karl, what is it?"

He was only twenty feet away now, each step an effort as he staggered side to side. She called out again and at the sound of her voice, he raised his head allowing her the first look at the fear in that face, in those eyes.

Eyes that weren't Karl Bowman's at all. Eyes which belonged to Stanley Miller, another of the town's hunters. Along with Karl, a half dozen of these broad-shouldered giants formed one of the many parties that provided the town with fresh meat for purchase at Meyok & Son's local butchers.

Aware that so much of her skin was on display, Tori pulled the door closer. Only her head poked out as she called out to the man. "Stanley? What are you doing out so late? It's awful out there."

Stanley's mouth flapped open, but no words came out. He lumbered forward another few steps, and it was then that Tori noticed the red trail of footsteps he left behind. His hands clutched his stomach and, although it looked like he was wearing bright crimson gloves, the daunting realization of the reality of what she was looking at struck her like an ice pick to a frozen heart.

"Oh, God. Stanley, what happened to you?"

Another mouth flap. A weak response, "Help."

Foregoing her better instincts, Tori rushed to his side, the icy snow sending a burning pain through the soles of her feet. She braced herself against the wind, its frosty fingers scratching at the bare flesh of her legs, arms, neck and face. Stanley closed some more of the distance but looked as though he was about to collapse. She caught him on the downfall, hooking his arm around her shoulder and raising him up. Together they staggered their way to the house, the short excursion leaving Tori breathless and exhausted as she closed the door and banished the cold outside.

She guided Stanley to the couch, her numb feet almost slipping on the slick trail of blood that snaked behind him. He lay down on the couch, holding his chest tightly while Tori lit a handful of candles. Once the gloomy light was flickering, she rushed over to her bathroom, looking for her first aid kit. She found it in the lower drawer of her bathroom unit, a bright green thing with a white cross. She opened it up, checked that it was stocked. Inside were reams of bandages and antiseptic. She waited a moment, clutching the edges of the bathroom sink as she stared at herself in her reflection, only able to make out the shadowy silhouette of her head and shoulders. Taking a long breath, she closed her eyes. All that met her was the glimpse she had seen of Stanley's.

"Fuck..." she whispered into the quiet.

A faraway groan from the living room was her reply.

Tori screwed her eyes shut and counted to five before returning to his side.

"It's okay. It's okay. Here, we'll make this better." Her words uncertain, devoid of the confidence she wished she could bestow. One proper look at his chest and all of her own hope drained.

Under the folds of blood-soaked clothing, Stanley's skin had been torn open. The gray bones of his ribs were on display through the gaping hole, cocooning organs which she could just make out pulsing inside their cage. The edges of the hole were shredded, as though an animal had been at his chest, some great polar bear with daggerlike teeth and claws that could puncture flesh as though it were the skin of a peach.

Tears clouded Tori's eyes. Stanley's breath came in ragged bursts. The metallic scent of his blood filled her nostrils. She could taste it in the air, ancient iron coating her tastebuds. Finding any excuse to keep active, swimming as if through a hazy nightmare, she unbundled the bandages and started working them around his body, trying her best to cover up the hole and plug the broken, bloody faucet. Stanley's eyelids flickered as his eyes rolled into the back of his head.

"No! Stay with me, Stanley. Talk to me, *please*. Tell me what did this to you."

But that wasn't the real question Tori wanted answers to. The real question Tori wanted to ask was: why had the universe played such a cruel trick on *her*? How had her night started so wonderfully, and ended up like this? What kind of cruel gods would put this upon her?

Stanley looked at Tori as if seeing her for the first time. He pawed at her hands, blood staining her pale flesh. "It's too late."

Tori frowned. "No. We can fix this. All we need to do is plug the hole and find a way to stitch it up. I'm sure there must be something in this pack for that... Something that..."

She fumbled through the first aid kit, but was immediately pulled back to Stanley as a rolling, aching roar crawled out from between his lips. He grabbed her wrist, his hold uncompromising, painful, as though every second that passed with his sticky, icy hands on her, someone was twisting the tourniquet tighter. Though her feet prickled with the sensation of her body fighting back the numbness, his hold cut off the circulation to her frosted fingertips.

"No!" He roared with such ferocity that Tori was momentarily paralyzed. His eyes were wide, pupils dilated, an urgency in every desperate breath. "They're coming... Dear God... They're coming."

"Who's coming?" Tori managed, her lips trembling. "Stanley, you're scaring me... What did this to you?"

A derisive exhalation leaked through his nose, his own lips wobbling as gummy strings of pink saliva stretched like taffy between the gap. He shook his head, losing himself in the pain and hurt of it all, eyes shimmering with tears as he gave a final half-shrug. "Run..."

Tori's blood ran cold, her head twisting toward the window as a sudden, belting cry rent over the town. A strange combination of an animal howl mixed with the banshee call of a creature in pain.

7

ALEX GOINS

Alex was halfway across the town when the red needle on the snow-o-meter closed in on "unbearable." Though he wrapped himself up in his warmest clothes, they did little to stave off the increasing chill that found its home beneath his skin. He longed for the tepid shelter of his rented shack, mind straying to his welcoming ghost choir. Wondering if the band had sought a new abode in the marrow of his bones, deciding to use his own hollow tubes to amplify the flutes and clarinets of their orchestra and follow him on his journey. If he listened close enough, could he hear their merry jig right now?

No. None of that would be possible in this roaring wind. No matter which way he turned he seemed to be pushing against the flurries, each step leeching him of his energy. A couple of times he paused around the corner of a sleepy house to catch his breath, though as the snow piled up around him, his urgency to find Cody grew. How reckless could that boy be? To head out in the middle of the night, straight into a blizzard?

Not a blizzard. Not yet, anyway. Maybe Cody didn't know any better...

But Alex knew. According to his research, the official parameters for a blizzard hadn't yet been met, although they were well on their way. For the snowfall to class as a true blizzard, the winds had to rage at over 35 miles per hour.

An animated gust shoved Alex sideways, causing him to fight to regain balance.

Check.

The visibility had to be reduced to less than a quarter of a mile.

Alex squinted ahead, barely able to see five houses ahead before all was masked in snow.

Check.

The storm had to have lasted at least three hours.

Alex glanced at his watch, just able to make out the face between the sleeves of his puffer jacket and the cuff of his gloves. It had been almost an hour since he had noticed the first snowfall from the embracing comfort of his bed.

He gritted his teeth and inhaled sharply. Snow streamed into the open gap between his lips and stung his teeth, spreading its chill to his gums. He ducked down and curled into himself so he could breathe without interruption, basking for a moment in a maternal warmth of a mother hen coddling its eggs, then continued his pursuit.

With every step he trod he thought of Cody. Hoped the kid was okay. He couldn't imagine that Cody would have embarked into the darkness on his own, and there was some solace in that. If Cody was with another kid, at least they'd be able to work together to navigate their way home. For all Alex knew, Cody was already back at the cabin, settled into his bed and trying to stay as quiet as possible so as to not wake Alex as he warmed his frozen bones.

Still, something deep inside told Alex that wasn't the case. The basketball was gone, the tracks leading into town pointed in this direction. He had lost the footprints a mile or two ago, but there was only one place in town where a game of basketball could be played, unless one wanted to attempt to bounce a ball in slush. He imagined Cody trying to battle through the snow to play on the outdoor court of the school. Maybe his larger friend... Brendan, was it? Maybe Brendan was with him, too. Cody running circles around the kid as he practiced his layups and expelled his pent-up frustration at the cruelty of the world.

"Don't worry, Kathrin. I'll find him for you."

He mumbled the words to no one, and yet the wind ruthlessly tore them away. A bubble of guilt popped in his stomach as he felt the weight of the responsibility of his charge. Tom and Kathrin had left Cody to him. He was the boy's guardian, by choice. And already, he had let them down.

Alex turned right at the end of the street, passing Ludlow's Hardware Store. In the belly of the storm the window ledges were piled with powder, the door almost blocked by a three-foot drift of snow. In his mind's eye he could see the jolly old store manager shoveling away at the snow and fighting to keep the shop open come morning. Storms like this were Tomlin's bread and butter, the items inside the shop the perfect tools to repair any damages that had occurred due to native elemental damage. His shovels sold like hot cakes, insulation flew off the shelves, and timber and nails were in fresh demand once a storm had beaten its chest and disappeared over the horizon.

Alex braced himself as a fresh gust charged him. He turned away from the store and looked up the street, wishing he knew how much farther he had to walk. He was only vaguely aware of the direction of the high school, having trusted Cody to make his way there every day for class. Alex didn't mind Cody's insistence that he wanted to walk alone, knowing that the original intent of Alex's trip was to research the life and stories of Denridge Hills. Its families, its histories, its fauna, its ecosystem. The more information he could gather on the sleepy town before his scheduled return to modern civilization, the better. He hadn't expected to have to accommodate a hormonal teen when he originally planned his trip, and Cody showed himself to be older than his years in many ways—at least to Alex.

"Just make sure you watch out for them polars," Tomlin had grinned one morning while handing Alex his change during their third week of residency in the town. "You might think they respect our borders, but nighttimes are the worst. That's when they come.

Harmless enough if you're inside, but remember they're built to hunt meat—any meat. Protein is protein, at the end of the day."

As if triggered by the sudden memory, an animalistic cry broke out over the storm.

Alex stopped in his tracks, trying to glean the direction of the sound. He turned to his right and ducked in the small alley that separated the two nearest houses. Shrouded in darkness and only slightly protected from the storm, he strained his ears and listened. The cry was long, a howling that rang with the keen edge of human triumph, mixed with the raging growls of some predatory creature. In the quiet moments that followed after, Alex wiped his brow, aware that as fleeting as the sound had been, his skin was tacky with sweat.

A minute passed. Might have been two.

With stiff legs he trudged toward the corner of the house. He could see nothing in either direction of the street, only empty space buffeted by snow.

"That was no polar," he whispered when another cry rent the quiet. A moment later another joined, then another.

Alex's heart leaped into his mouth, the edges of his vision blurring as adrenaline focused his sight to what lay ahead of him. He couldn't understand what creatures could make such a noise. He'd heard wolves howl, eagles cry, and walruses grunt, but no creature had he ever witnessed emitting a sound of that caliber.

And then came a sound that he did recognize. The unmistakable sound of a human screaming in pain. Its abrupt pulses of noise coming from all directions as the dizzying winds turned the mono howl of torture into a surround sound experience. Alex's throat constricted as the scream grew in desperation, accompanied by the furious hunger of whatever creature was jeering and toying with its food.

Alex ducked behind the house and pressed his back against the wall. He clamped his eyes shut and counted to ten, wondering whether now would be the time to showcase bravery. A lonely British writer, given the opportunity to play the part of protagonist and help a fellow human in need. Now, there's a story. Although he had no

weapon to speak of, he pictured himself barreling toward the predators, voice hoarse from roaring, waving his arms in the air and
displaying his dominance. That was how you scared off a bear. He
had seen that once on National Geographic. Humans who exerted
their power over creatures and sent them fleeing in panic.

But who was Alex kidding? He wasn't the hero. That's why he
wrote about them. We write about the things we wish to be.

The shrieks of pain vanished into the night. It was abrupt. It was
brief. And then he was alone. Just the howling wind's frigid embrace
for company.

Fuck.

Alex shivered, though now it was from more than just the cold.
Fear met adrenaline as he plotted his next move, knowing that he
had to make a decision, and soon. Another brief minute passed
before he teased his head around the corner, finding the coast
clear.

He turned in the other direction, wondering whether it was best
to carry onward and try to find Cody, or to head on back home. By
pursuing Cody, he was committing to a long journey in elements that
no non-native to this part of the world should face. Elements he was
neither physically nor mentally prepared for.

Yet, if he headed home without Cody and discovered that something had happened in the night, how could he live with himself? He
had been entrusted with the life of a boy—his *nephew*. Cody was
blood. The same blood which ran through Alex's and Kathrin's
veins—

A long whistle blasted, followed by a sudden hollow *thunk*. Alex's
blood finally turned to ice as his eyes fixed on the dart which had
found its way into the wooden support beams of the house beside
him. At least three inches long, with a display of black feathers
fanning from the back, painted with crude symbols which looked
vaguely familiar.

Unsure why he was doing so, he wrestled the dart from the wood
and examined the tip. A thick bitumen-like paste covered the needled
edge. The dart looked to be hand-crafted. Almost tribal. As Alex

turned from the dart into the direction from which it had been sent, he let out a soft gasp.

A figure stood just thirty feet from him, any definition of its features lost in the fuzzy boundaries of the snowfall. The only things he knew for sure were that the figure had two long arms, two long legs, and that the figure meant to do him harm.

Alex's impulse was to run. The ghost choir concurred as they started their own storm of intense, staccato beats. Still, Alex found himself rooted to the spot, his throat sandpaper dry. His heart beat so violently against his chest that he was surprised he couldn't see it through his jacket. There was something strange about that figure something...

Inhuman.

The figure raised a slender arm, the small tubelike instrument moving back to its mouth. At this distance, it could easily have been mistaken for a carved, wooden flute.

Alex knew better, his muscles finally finding utility.

As the dart sailed through the air, Alex ran.

8

TORI ASPLIN

S he sat with the dying man in the dark, invisible insects crawling along her spine.

After the creature's howl fell to silence, Tori remembered that she had the ability to move and forced her leaden legs upstairs. She quelled the heat from the open fire with great difficulty, smothering the flames with the flour-like powder she had bought from the store, then tamping out the embers with a damp blanket. She worked quickly, fingers trembling and fumbling with the items until her bedroom window no longer leaked the light into the street and gave away her position. She envisioned her house from the outside, window appearing like a giant's eye winking in the storm. A beacon to draw the creatures—whatever they may be—toward her.

As Stanley groaned and complained downstairs, Tori turned her attention to her need for warmth. In the sudden lack of heat expelled from the fire, she donned a thick pair of woolen trousers and shrugged on two knitted jumpers that she hadn't worn in some time.

She whirled around the room, head in a tizzy, desperately clawing for anything else that she could do. Stanley's words echoed on loop, the urgency in each syllable enough to flood her bloodstream with adrenaline.

They're coming.

Tori stood in the center of her room, ears alert to the outside world. Her chest rose and fell in rapid beats. She searched around the room, feeling as though she needed to do something else, but unsure what that thing was. If something was coming for Stanley, something that could rip out a section of his chest and expose his insides, then she needed—

—*a weapon.*

She found the ancient rifle in a wooden box at the back of her wardrobe. A .338 Winchester Magnum her father handed down to her before he passed, knowing that his baby girl was going to be living alone. She had never been much of a gun enthusiast, but her father showed her the basic mechanics of cleaning and maintaining a weapon, as well as how to load, aim, and fire.

"Point and shoot. Simple as that?"

"Attagirl."

He also gifted Tori's sister one of his treasure trove of firearms on the day that she first moved out of their family home. A 7mm Remington Magnum that was soon adopted by Tori's brother-in-law. At the time they had both joked about how they would hardly need to use something that kicked out such violence but, then again, not once did Tori ever envision that a man would be bleeding out on her couch, a strange creature howling in the womb of the storm.

The darkness cloaked her. She clutched the Winchester in shaking hands. Stanley was still breathing, but only just, and Tori knew there was little more she could do for him here. She had managed to bandage the wounds, enough only to cover the horrific sight of his organs, but without proper medical help, he would be a lost cause. The storm was too violent. The lines were dead. She could hardly drag him outside to the doctor now, could she?

"Stay with me, Stanley. We'll find a way to get help. I promise." She was surprised by the hollowness of her words. She knew the promise was empty. How was she going to get help, when there was something out there that was capable of doing this to a human?

When the storm was causing the house to sway and the idea of carrying him to the town's physician was nothing short of ludicrous.

I have to do something.

There had been no more animal calls for a few minutes and Tori began to wonder if what she had been hearing was only an illusion fueled by Stanley's ravings echoing around the chamber of her mind. If perhaps adrenaline and a sudden bodily reaction to her situation had caused her to imagine the things she had heard.

Come on. Even you're not that stupid. If that was the case, then come up with one alternative scenario as to how Stanley could have ended up with a fucking shredded chasm in his stomach. Nothing? Didn't think so.

Feeling fundamentally useless, all thoughts of Karl Bowman knocked from her mind, Tori rose to her feet and stalked across the darkened room. If she could only see what was out there, if she could only get a picture of what stood in her way, maybe it would be enough to push her onward, to find a way to help Stanley. If only...

Stanley groaned, each breath a rasping struggle coming in hauntingly slow bursts. Tori glanced back, her eyes stinging with tears. She wanted to help him. She couldn't just let him die like this—

The windows rattled violently. Something crashed against the glass. Stood only two feet away, Tori let out a piercing scream.

A man stared at her through the window—if you could call it that. A snow-white face, staring intently in her direction with eyes that had lost the ability to blink. Eyes in which the lids were almost non-existent. Lightning cracks of blood trailed across the thin orbs of sclera toward pupils so dilated that there was almost no other color but black in those circles. A thin line stretched across the face where lips should be, nothing more than a dark scar in their place. He wore no clothes that she could see from his position in the window, just the vague decorations of dark paint splattered across a body as white as the snow falling from the sky.

His head cocked to the side, a bird studying the worm. He met Tori's gaze, the stare intense. For a heart-stopping moment, the corners of his thin mouth flickered with a smile.

Crash. He smashed his hand against the glass, the jolting bang enough to cause Tori to take a step backward.

Crash. This time with the ring of his fist. Glass rattled dangerously in the frame.

She raised the rifle, her eye lining up with the rifle's sight. "Stay back! I'm warning you, this thing's loaded."

No fear was found in those eyes, only a strange morbid curiosity. Intelligence wasn't a language it spoke, that much was clear by the several repeated bangs that followed as he hit the flat of his palm against the glass, once, twice, a third time, repeating the steady drumbeat until the first spider-leg cracks appeared in the corner.

"I won't say it again!" Tori didn't recognize her voice. Her words scratched her throat as fear created tiny hooks which betrayed her own body, as if they were doing everything to stay deep down inside, where it was safe.

That face. There's something wrong with that face.

A tear rolled down Tori's cheek as Stanley mumbled incoherently, his fear mixing with the final beatings of his dying heart.

"Please... Stop! I'll shoot!"

Her words did little to assuage the man. If anything, they spurred him on. His face, devoid of any emotion, continued that infinite stare. A disturbing addition to a haunting human.

Human?

"No, no, no, no..."

Crash.

A second fist against a second window. A woman this time, hair twisted and tangled, thick with lumps of something she could only assume was dried blood. Eyes wide and a hungry look on her face, lips dark and stained with sticky residue.

Were these the creatures who had attacked Stanley? These strange tribal beasts who seemed unbothered by the blizzard, brave enough to stalk outside naked as temperatures plummeted to below what any normal human could survive without aid? She threw a glance back at Stanley, even as the drumbeats grew louder and more desperate. He had stopped moving, stopped breathing. Whatever hope there had been—and she doubted there had ever been any in the first place—was gone. A dead man lay in her house. Attackers struck from the outside.

A soft fairylike tinkle as something gave way. Glass glittered to the ground as the hammering palm of the man finally yielded its result. A thin gust crept into her house, followed swiftly by the man's hand as he reached inside and attempted to continue his dissection of the window. His skin scraped across the jagged edges, the glass dragging its way along his pale flesh, though the man showed no sign of pain. As he reached toward her, she noticed with sudden clarity that his fingertips were blackened and pointed, the whites of his palms crossing the spectrum of gray as the frostbite took his extremities.

For that's what it was. She had seen enough incidences of frostbite, had been passed enough cautionary tales in her school days to know what the cold could do to the human body if left to its own devices. Yet, across all of her lessons of how extreme frostbite deadened nerve endings and destroyed the regenerative capabilities of soft tissue, it appeared to have done little to impair this man's basic motor skills. His fingers worked as if unafflicted, tugging and tearing away sections of the glass until the gap in the window was large enough for him to climb through.

Which was exactly where he was when Tori's attention snapped urgently back to the present, one foot balancing on the windowsill, arms stretched wide with the ghoulish length of some deranged manbat steadying itself to take flight. It poised, what little muscles remaining in its malnourished body tensed and ready to strike. A hollow choking sound leaked from between his lips as the woman at the other window howled in triumph, her own hand reaching through the glass.

Another howl joined her own. Then a second, third, fourth…

And so on, until Tori knew nothing but howling. A disharmonious chorus of syncopated howls bursting like machine-gun fire.

How many of them were there? How many encircled her house and closed in on their prey, their hungry mouths wet with saliva at the prospect of the kill.

For that was the intent that called to her from the man's eyes. A language of only death and hurt and pain and—

Hunger.

A still moment of clarity passed between Tori and the creature, a moment in which the world stopped turning and the silent conversation was all there was. Tori's throat was desert-dry, her bones brittle and ready to snap. She fixed her gaze on the dark pits of his eyes, her lips forming the hollow word, "No."

And then he was in the air, leaping toward her with such suddenness that her body could only react by instinct. Her fingers tensed, pulling the trigger as the rifle recoiled in her hands, the butt jarring her shoulder. The bullet found the creature's chest, creating an almost identical wound to the man lying dead on her couch. His triumphant arc was disturbed, his trajectory interrupted, and he fell just a short distance from her feet, writhing and jerking in pain as a bone-chilling shriek erupted from the split of his lips.

Tori heard something behind her and whipped her head around. Stanley stared at her, eyes laced with terror, a single word repeating from his mouth. "Run."

For a fleeting moment, Tori could only stare in confusion at the man she had presumed dead. Then the crash of glass indicated the woman's full entry into the house. Another cry and the clawing grip of a third came as the vacated window was quickly inhabited by more of the ghoulish creatures.

Tori wasted no more time in obeying Stanley's final commands. Feeling awful at leaving him behind, but knowing she must get out, *had* to get out, she fled through the living room door and into the kitchen. She slammed the door behind her so hard that it bounced against its frame, then made her way to the back of the house. With hands that didn't feel like her own, trapped in the visage of some strange nightmare, she indelicately shoved the key in the lock and opened the back door. She had time enough to grab a pair of shoes, but had no time to put them on her feet. On the other side of the house the din of shattered glass and the beating hands of the invaders mixed with the howling winds. She imagined the horror on Stanley's face as those things... whatever they were, closed in on him, ready to finish the job they had started.

She only hoped that he was already dead when their fingers found his flesh.

Tori ran, ran into the white, ran into the maelstrom of the growing blizzard. The world beyond her cone of vision was masked in a fuzzy blur of snow and gloom. She had lived in this town all of her life, but now she was running across an alien plane, no clue which way she was heading. Her compass only held one direction and that was far away from whatever the fuck those creatures were.

Her feet grew numb, her socks wet. The thick carpet of snow sapped her energy as she narrowed in on a set of houses she did not recognize and found succor from the wind in the alleys in-between. With her back to the wall, she kept her ears to the wind and slipped on her shoes, knowing that she'd never get her feet warm while they were wet, but doing whatever she could to add an extra barrier between herself and the freezing ground.

Another cry. Distant this time.

That was something, at least. Tori closed her eyes and gathered her breath, her body threatening to spill its tears and throw her into a spiral of frenzied emotion. She wanted to throw up. She wanted to cry. She wanted to laugh. She fought against all those things, tightening her grip on the rifle, her only protection. Her fingers were already numb and, for a moment, as her blurry eyes stared down at her hands, she saw the man's own fingers, their frostbitten tips blackened and cracked, filed to points.

"What the fuck is going on?" she asked the wind, considering what her next move should be. She studied the gold lettering on the side of the rifle and thought back to her sister, the only family she had remaining in Denridge Hills.

If these... things were attacking the center of the town, who's to say that anyone was safe? Could there be more out there? Could they be closing in on her sister, breaking through the glass and coming for her nephew?

Tori tried not to imagine it to be true, but knew she had to warn her. Had to find comfort in the arms of someone familiar.

What about Karl? Aren't you concerned about him?

She was concerned. That much was true. But given Karl's physical stature and the fact that he hunted for a living, she imagined that he would likely be the most prepared for a situation like this. On more than one occasion he had bragged about his armory, and the multitude of weapons he had stored aside for his hunting trips. He would be fine, tucked in his nice cozy marital bed with his wife. He would be just fine.

Just fine.

Isn't that all the more reason to go to him? He lives closer than Naomi does. Make a detour to his house, get some protection.

Tori shook her head, snow gathering on the tips of her lashes and weighing them down. There was no time to debate this, no time to argue. She had to make a choice, before the frosty teeth of the blizzard bit into her and made the decision for her.

She started forward, working her way into the small pathways between houses, her arms wrapped tightly around her body. Her teeth chattered, her eyes mere slits to brace against the wind and the snow. Another cry came from somewhere in the town.

Tori let out an involuntary yelp as something dark moved in front of her. She was sure of it. Something lean and nimble. She tucked herself into a nearby crevice, soaking in the momentary shelter from the snow, wondering when she would be lucky enough to catch a goddamn break. Where was the rest of the town? Why hadn't they woken up? Was she truly just in the throes of a terrible dream, cast alone in a world of white while monsters ate up the very fabric of her known reality?

She peeked around the corner and was relieved to find the way ahead deserted. She crept out further, her whole body exposed once more, then caught the faint crunch of feet on snow.

Tori had enough time to stare into those dark eyes before a hand clamped her mouth and muted her scream.

9

CODY TREBECK

I t all came down to this... the final shot.

Two games had swiftly blurred into a third. Although Cody's nose throbbed relentlessly and he was pretty sure that both his eyes would soon shine in shades of purple and yellow, his competitive side had taken over. The first game had gone to Cody, Sophie, and Brandon. The second game to Hayden, Travis, and Amy. At some point between the two games both Amy and Brandon had taken a seat, putting a car's width between the pair of them as they watched stoically from the sidelines.

Cody and Sophie made a surprisingly good team. He wasn't sure where she had earned her baller stripes, and she certainly knew nothing about his old run-arounds on the courts back home, but that didn't stop them racking points. They drove up the court with impressive fluidity, each making space and passing at the right moments so the other could layup, or take the jump shot, and shine.

From the moment Hayden had charged Cody, Sophie guarded him, and Cody took Travis. Travis was swift, his ball-handling skills impressive. He had a way of pivoting fast and driving the ball up the court, though often his speed was to his detriment. A messy layup would see the ball bouncing off the backboard and away from the hoop, the point forfeited as Hayden scowled and Amy cheered naively from the bleachers.

"Don't fuck up now," Travis teased Cody from three feet away, his chestnut eyes locked onto Cody's own. Cody guarded the ball, holding it by his hip in both hands, keeping it out of reach of Travis' long arms. Travis' skin was peppered with sweat, his chest heaving from the exertion he hadn't realized he'd need in order to take on Cody and Sophie.

From the corner of his eye, Hayden and Sophie wrestled on the edge of the key. He had been soft on her, nowhere near as brutal as he had been with Cody, but she tested his limits now, pressing her shoulder against him and trying to knock him off balance.

One more shot... that's all we need.

"It all hangs on this." Travis grinned, a knowing look in his eye. "Make the shot, get the girl. You've seen the movies, right?"

Cody's ears burned. Each exhalation sent a small ream of condensation into the air. "Unlucky for you, all I care about is making the shot."

He shouted the last words, catching Travis off guard as he dropped his shoulder and carved around him. He made it to the edge of the key, looking up just long enough to see the feral look on Hayden's face as he realized that his teammate had failed him. It was down to one man versus two, and Hayden didn't like that one bit.

Hayden hurtled toward Cody, arms leading the way as he closed the gap between them. Cody planted both feet into the ground, twisted, then lobbed the ball over Hayden's head.

As Sophie lined up the shot, leaping off the floor and propelling the ball to the hoop, Cody side-stepped and spun away from Hayden's trajectory, already sensing the collision. Hayden's momentum carried him forward and, little to Cody's knowledge, straight into Travis, who had been streaming toward him from the opposite direction.

Hayden tried to slow himself, his fury melting to fear, but it was already too late. The pair of them skidded into each other, bashing shoulders before Travis toppled to the floor and Hayden pinwheeled his arms for balance, just managing to stay on his feet.

"Yes!" Sophie pumped her fist and laughed, jogging over to collect the ball. She cupped it in the crook of her arm then ran over to Cody, throwing one arm around his neck and pulling him into an embrace.

Too stunned to seize the moment, Cody patted a hand on her back, feeling the clamminess of sweat beneath her clothes, heat radiating from her collar.

"Foul!" Hayden cried, pointing at Travis. "Foul ball. No point."

Sophie rolled her eyes. "You're kidding. That was a legit pass and a legal move. Just because you two morons crashed into each other, doesn't mean the points don't count."

Travis cradled his elbow in the palm of his hand, eyes screwed tight in pain. "I think it's broken. Shit. It hurts."

"See! Broken limbs. That's our ball."

Sophie twisted away before Hayden could grab the ball. She passed the ball to Cody, putting some distance between Hayden and temptation. Amy climbed to her feet and jogged over to join them. "Foul ball. I saw it all."

"Ref's call." Hayden grinned.

"Since when was Amy assigned ref?" Sophie shot back. "We won, fair and square. Just pull up your big boy pants and take the loss."

Amy stood dutifully by Hayden's side, her fingers pawing at the loose folds of his clothing. A look of hurt crossed her face. "What's gotten into you?"

"What's gotten into me? First your boyfriend charges Cody for no reason, then he insists on a 'best of three' after he loses the first game, and now he's trying to claim that because he crashed into spaghetti limbs over there, we forfeit our winning point. Just accept the loss like a man and let's call it a night." She looked at Cody for help, her bright eyes keen.

Cody shrugged. When he spoke, he was embarrassed by how uncertain he sounded. "Yeah. We won. Fair and square." He bounced the ball, sending a loud elastic echo around the gymnasium. Brandon waited by the sidelines, huddled tightly in his jacket and insulated gear. His eyes were closed. Cody wondered if he'd fallen asleep.

Sophie caught Cody's eyes, a wry smile as they both turned in

Brandon's direction. "Your friend isn't really the adventurous type, is he?"

Cody smiled back, then rolled the ball at Brandon. When the ball touched the tip of his toes, Brandon jumped, startled from his snooze. "Come on, Trevors. We're heading home."

Cody made to reclaim his ball, but before he could get to it, something sped past him, knocking into his side before scooping the ball off the floor with nimble fingers. Travis smirked as he clutched the ball to his chest and wagged a finger at Cody. "I don't think so, new kid. Best of five."

He chest-passed the ball to Hayden who nodded his agreement, massaging his tender elbow after the throw. "That's the only way out of here. We win, or no one leaves."

Brandon climbed unsteadily to his feet. "Just like the NBA pros. Great sportsmanship."

"What was that?" Hayden snarled, eyes flashing.

Brandon's breath caught, eyes shying away from Hayden's. "Nothing."

Hayden tossed the ball back to Travis, eyes fixed on Brandon. He strode across the court, each step a thunderous clap as the sound raced in loops around the gymnasium. "Not 'nothing.' You got something to say, say it." He shoved Brandon firmly in the chest, sending him stumbling back into the lower row of bleachers.

"Hey, back off," Cody said, springing to his defense. "Brandon's done nothing wrong."

"He's certainly done nothing tonight," Amy muttered.

"You're one to talk." Sophie elicited a stunned look from Amy but refused to meet her gaze. She sped across the court, closing the gap between Hayden and Brandon, placing a hand on Hayden's chest. He glanced down at the whites of her fingers in disdain. "Look, we're all tired. We've had some fun, but let's quit now before something stupid happens. It's already," she looked at her watch, "nearly three in the morning, so let's pack up our gear and get out of here. Okay?"

Hayden's nostrils flared. His eyes darted to Brandon and then to Cody, now standing by Brandon's side. For a moment it looked as though he was going to press the issue, then he pointed a finger at Sophie and said, "No one hears about this. Got it?"

Sophie lowered her hand. "Fine."

She stood guard until Hayden moved away, following Travis to the pile of coats and gloves which they shrugged on in preparation for the cool elements. The temperature in the gymnasium had lost the edge of its chill thanks to their sweating session, but their breath still frosted before their eyes, and now that the heat of the game had worn off, their skin began to prickle.

Dressed and ready to call it a night, they made for the door. Brandon took the lead, the most eager of them to leave the gymnasium and get back into the warm cocoon of his bed. But, as they neared the door, they noticed that he was having difficulties pushing it open.

"What's the problem now?" Travis said.

"It won't budge." Brandon shoved his shoulder against the metal door. It held fast.

Hayden glared at Cody. "Your best friend is a pussy." He shoved Brandon indelicately out of the way. Placing both hands on the door, he dug his feet into the ground and shoved, his body quivering from the strain as he gave it everything he had. The door didn't move an inch.

Cody and Brandon exchanged a look, tried to hide their smiles.

"King, get your ass over here."

Travis joined Hayden's side, and together they pushed. Still, nothing happened. After another minute of straining, Hayden stepped back and shook his head. "Must be something blocking it."

"Need some help?" Sophie called out. There was a note of joy in her voice that didn't escape Hayden. He scowled as Sophie gathered Cody and Brandon, and even ushered Amy over to help.

"On the count of three," she said. "One. Two."

"Three!" Hayden finished, triggering them all to shove against the door. For the first time, there was some give. The double doors started to move, letting in a sharp, thin gust of cold that hurtled at Hayden's face, its edge keen and sharp. He grimaced against the blast, able to see the first hint of the darkness outside. The door opened another inch, and then held solidly in place.

Hayden growled. "Keep pushing!"

They did. The door wouldn't open any further.

Another minute passed before they gave up. Amy slumped against the door, wiping the back of her forehead with her glove as though this was the most strenuous activity she had ever been involved in. Brandon folded over, hands on his knees, back rising and falling in sharp bursts as he struggled for breath. Only Cody, Sophie, Hayden, and Travis had the energy left to step back and examine their work.

A two-inch gap allowed view of the world outside. Through the dark crack they could make out the drift of snow that had gathered against the door. It was piled up above their waists, easily three-feet high. Above the pure white section of snow was only darkness, interspersed with the fall of snow that, even now, continued to hurl its contents at the collecting drift in its attempt to cage them within the school.

"Shit," Brandon exclaimed, taking a step back from the door and blinking numbly.

Hayden rammed his shoulder against the door. "It's fine. Look, it's moving."

"No, it's not!"

"Yes, it is. See?" Travis joined Hayden and beat against the door, their shoulders bouncing straight back off as the door withstood their efforts. It may as well have been concrete for all the good of their efforts.

Cody's mouth hung open as he peered through the slit in the door. Already the chill had invaded what little warmth they'd generated, the darkness outside acting as a stark reminder that he was no longer safely nestled in Alex's home, but instead miles from the world he knew. The snow billowed with a ferocity that he had only glimpsed on one other occasion since his arrival here, and his thoughts began to roam to the question that was all beginning to dawn in their minds.

How were they going to get back?

Travis groaned, a look of desperation befalling his face. He took a few steps back, then sprinted at the door. The soles of his boots caught the flurry of ice that had fallen into the gym and slickened the laminate, and his feet slipped from beneath him. His arms flailed as he tried desperately to stop the crash, but it was too late. He toppled over and smashed into the door, his cheek and temple hitting the frozen metal. His eyes closed and he lay motionless as drifts of snowflakes settled on his face.

"Travis!" Hayden grabbed Travis' feet and dragged him away from the door, putting some distance between the invading snow and the unconscious body. He knelt to Travis' side and teased open his eyelid. Travis showed no sign of response.

"Holy fuck," Brandon muttered, unable to believe what he'd seen.

"What do we do?" Amy crouched beside Hayden, draping her arms around his shoulders and burying her face in the thick cloth of his collar.

Hayden shoved Amy with such ferocity that she landed in a pile beside him.

Sophie started toward her, "Hayden!"

His eyes flashed, not even bothering to look at Sophie, unsympathetic to the hurt displayed on Amy's face. Amy's mouth remained open in a perfect "O" as Hayden turned his attention back to Travis. A silent tear rolled down her cheek.

Sophie looked at Cody for help.

But Cody wasn't paying attention to any of this, his gaze fixed on the world outside, at the swirling tornadoes of snow finding their way through the small crack between the doors, their minute portal to the world outside. His skin began to prickle, and this time he wasn't certain that it was because of the cold. His eyes narrowed into the black void of darkness, a strange sense of discomfort burning inside his stomach.

Sophie helped Amy to her feet. "Are you alright?"

Amy shrugged Sophie off, patting down her sleeves and turning away. "I'm fine. God, it was nothing, okay?"

"There has to be another way out of here," Brandon breathed. "Another door? Can we get into the main school?"

"All the doors will be locked," Sophie said, eyes lingering on the back of Amy's head. "The only way we can get into the main school building is if this asshole is up for sharing his lock-picking skills with the rest of the group."

Hayden spun toward Sophie. "What did you just call me?"

"You heard me."

Amy glanced from Sophie to Hayden. To Sophie's surprise, it was Brandon that stepped between them this time, uncertainty shining in his glossy eyes. "This is not the time to turn on each other. We've got to find a way out of here before the snow builds up even more and we're trapped inside until the storm passes." He pointed to the far side of the hall where a wooden door led off into the farther reaches of the school. "If I know anything about storms and blizzards, the wind should have a dominant direction. The drift building against that door might just be the result of the wind blowing in one particular direction, meaning that if we can get out on the other side of the school—"

"The drift won't be as high," Sophie finished.

Brandon nodded, his cheeks flushing.

Hayden scowled from the floor, unimpressed that the fat kid had shown some kind of survivalist knowledge and was now leading the charge. "What about Travis, huh? He's out cold. Isn't it bad for you if you're moved when you get knocked unconscious?"

"You've already moved him," Sophie said.

Brandon approached Hayden and Travis as though he was entering a cage with a hungry predator. He knelt on the other side of Travis, pressing two fingers against his jugular. "He has a pulse, that's a good sign." He ran his fingers across the slick floor and dabbed his cold, wet fingertips against Travis' cheeks and lower eyelids. They flickered weakly. "Shit..."

"What?" Hayden asked.

Brandon met his gaze, but couldn't hold it. "We need to wake him.

If someone remains unconscious for too long, it can have serious long-lasting effects on their brain."

Hayden seized hold of Travis' shoulders and shook him violently, calling for him to wake up. Brandon shouted above him, urging him to stop. "No! Don't shake him. You could make things worse! We can't move him until he wakes."

"But you said he needs to wake up!" Hayden breathed heavily, that isolating darkness returning to his eyes as he leered at Brandon. "What are we supposed to do, Poindexter? One second you're saying we need to get the hell out of here, the next you're saying we can't go until King wakes. Which one is it?"

"Don't yell at him," Sophie said. "We need to calm down and think about this. All of us. Breathe and work through this." Sophie looked at each of them in turn, eyes lingering on Cody, still staring through the gap in the door, his face a sickly shade of white. "Cody? What's wrong?"

Cody heard her voice as a distant call. He didn't know how to explain what he was seeing, let alone how to activate his numbed vocal cords to put it into words. From the moment the figure had appeared in his field of view he had stood transfixed, unable to make out if this was some kind of strange dream he was stuck inside.

The figure spawned from the darkness, materializing like a specter. At first, he thought his mind was playing tricks on him. That perhaps his tired imagination was concocting monstrosities from nothing. But then he spotted the white of the skull hovering above the dark body. Empty sockets where eyes might once have been. Not human, not by any measure, but... something.

"Cody...?"

Cody raised an unsteady hand toward the door, unfurling his finger to point in the figure's direction. Sophie moved beside him, straining to see what he was drawing their attention to. Her face was next to his, cheeks almost touching. Her breath was warm.

"What the..."

The figure raised a cupped fist to its mouth.

Something shot through the gap in the door, a small black projectile, disturbing the air by Cody's cheek and finding its home in the wood of the bleachers. A second later, something heavy whacked against the doors, the metallic thud reverberating around the hall like the beating drums of some giant beast.

Amy screamed.

Sophie grabbed Cody's wrist and pulled him from his reverie as another resounding thump crashed against the door. It slammed shut with a sudden snap, bouncing off its frame to re-open again in the meager crack and get stuck in the snow.

Two heads peered through the gap, faces hidden by bone-white masks.

Brandon turned on his heels so suddenly that he almost slipped as he made a dash for the far side of the hall. Hayden glared forlornly at Travis, grabbed his ankle and started dragging him across the hall, both boys within just a few feet of the figures outside the door, whacking the metal, attempting to gain access inside.

Putting aside his reservations, Cody tore his wrist free from Sophie and ran to Hayden and Travis.

"Cody!"

He ignored Sophie, mind shrinking to tunnel vision as he grabbed Travis' other leg, doubling their speed, dragging him away from the doors and across the hall. Travis' head hung limply to one side as another thud exploded, and a second object flew through the air, missing them by feet this time thanks to the awkward angle granted by the doors.

A strange growl of frustration, followed the dying echoes of the banging thuds.

Cody dropped Travis' leg when they were ten feet from the door at the back of the hall. "Unlock it. Now."

Any remnant of Hayden's intimidation left in that moment as the weight of Cody's words sank in. Moving as if in a dream, Hayden fished out his lock-picking equipment. He began work on the heavy-duty padlock holding the thin wooden doors shut, the banging returning, growing ever more desperate with each beat.

"What the hell is that?" Sophie breathed, pressing her body

against the wall as though, if she could push hard enough, she might melt through the brickwork and fade from sight.

Cody stared at the small black slit on the other side of the hall, the vision of that thing filling his mind's eye as he slowly shook his head. The memory of the white of that skull hovering in the darkness.

10

KARL BOWMAN

K arl couldn't sleep. Not for one second had he kidded himself into believing that he would.

He sat upright, feet touching the bare wooden flooring at the side of his bed. Cadence slept soundly behind him, cocooned in the many folds of their marital bedsheets. Sheets her mother had woven for her to mark the occasion of their marriage. Sheets where they had consummated their nuptials and conceived their first and only child. Sheets which marked over a decade of love, arguments, joy, and misery.

Karl was tired of this shit.

He wore only his boxer briefs, his skin prickling with the first sign of cold from the storm outside. The streetlights shut off almost twenty minutes ago and cast the world in darkness. In his mind, he played a loop of the events which had taken place at Tori's house. The heat of the argument. The venom she had spewed. Karl's blood boiled at the memory of the tiny woman coming at him like a cornered Chihuahua, her feral mouth yapping her retorts and insults as he toyed with the opportunities that presented themselves: remain in a loveless marriage and raise his child, or throw it all away for a short-lived whirlwind of earth-shattering sex followed by the empty husk of a relationship that, deep down, he never truly wanted. That's all it had ever been to Karl, a way to pass the monotony of the ritualistic day-to-day of life in Denridge Hills. A way to add a modicum of adventure and excitement to the Groundhog Day that had become his existence. Sure, while he was out hunting, he could joke with the lads and forget it all as he plunged hooked and gleaming tools into the flesh of their catch, arterial spray slickening his grip as he fought with the tough hides, building their stock of meat for the townsfolk, only a set of tried-and-true rudimentary tools with which to hunt...

...but what happened after that? Return home, tune out the grating chatter of a relentless child, rest in the chair that was his, and his alone, grumble his responses to an ungrateful, complaining wife who no longer bore the mask of the woman he had fallen in love with, scorch his throat with scotch, sleep, repeat....

There was no place for love in Denridge.

Karl rose quietly, crossed to the window. He rested his palms on Cadence's vanity table, an old, carved thing which she had inherited from her grandmother. Another antique. Like everything here, sentimentality was at the top of the pecking order. It was sturdy, he had to give it that, but what he wouldn't give for something new. Some shiny object that would act as an intruding freckle on the unblemished, unremarkable virgin skin of his life in Denridge.

The snow fell endlessly from a darkened sky, ramping up its ferocity with every passing second. It had almost been enough to deter his return home. If he had left it any later, he might still be out there, struggling to trudge through the snowfall, shielding his eyes against the blizzard. By the time he had made it back, spotting the coned, pointed roof of the nearby chapel just down the road to his place, the drift in front of his door was only a few inches high. A swift tug with his muscular arms cleared the snow and he was inside.

Safe.

God, was there anything worse than being safe?

He sincerely thought he could love her at one point. In the early days of Karl and Tori's affair he had mistaken the excitement for love. The chemical pull that had him sneaking out of the house late at night and crossing the snow-covered town to find succor in the arms of her petite, supple body too overwhelming to resist. He'd listen to her rantings and ravings about comments she'd received from strangers on YouTube with eager ears, confused by the lingo, but happy to endure the drone until they fell into each other's arms again. Her life confused him, the computer plugged into the wall enough to somehow earn her cash that could be spent in the real world. Enough to give her cause to not involve herself in the traditions and occupations that Denridge Hills had honored for hundreds of years. Traditions that Karl and his family had held sacred for as far back as the lineage could tell.

Tori was beautiful. Tori was intelligent. But Tori was also vain and hooked her self-worth into the admirations of others. He soon learned that all he had to do was flutter a compliment into her ear once in a while and she would do things to him that Cadence never would. They had twisted into positions that he had never thought possible, tangled their bodies like wet spaghetti, and found new heights of pleasure in the fog of their ecstasy.

Now all of that was gone. He had made his choice, and now he was wedged between a rock and a hard place. At some point he would have to tell Cadence, because there was no way in hell that Tori was going to keep their affair secret. If he gleaned anything from the hurt in Tori's eyes that evening, he knew that things were already volatile. If it hadn't been for the blizzard, would she have stormed her way across town after him, ready to rant and rave and dish the truth to a sleep-drunk Cadence?

He would have to play these next few weeks carefully. *Hell hath no fury like a woman scorned.*

Hell hath met no man like Karl before.

The wind howled outside and in the wild whistling he imagined he could hear her now, calling out to the gusts, the storm carrying her message like an obedient servant. Her screams terrible, her rage a burning pyre, every fresh blow a desperate consonant toward a plea to claim Karl back.

Karl straightened, eyes narrowing out the window. He strained his ears, realizing that he wasn't imagining anything at all. Something *was* calling, a shrill cry of some kind of animal somewhere in the town. He loomed closer to the glass and could just make out three shapes moving along the edge of his vision, just beyond the cloak of the falling snow.

Wolves.

Karl furrowed his brow and stepped away from the vanity table. Sleep was never going to come now, he may as well find a use for himself. If the wolves came anywhere near his house, he'd find a good enough excuse to put a silver bullet between their eyes. Karl was a sharpshooter, and wolf skin was valuable. Three wolf pelts could be enough to help feed his family for a week.

If Tori doesn't step in the way and break my family, that is.

Karl shook his head, trying what he could to erase that irritating bubble of anger that broiled in his chest. In the dark recesses of his mind, a thought came to him. *Just kill her. As soon as the storm subsides, take her out. No one would have to know. Who does she have in her life who would miss her, anyway? It'd be easy.*

Karl's teeth sank into his lip. He blinked away the idea. Sure, Tori often made a point about the fact that she had little in the way of family left in the town, but that didn't rule them all out. If Karl remembered correctly, Tori's older sister lived on the outskirts of Denridge, right on the borders of the Drumtrie Forest. A lonely cabin, a kilometer or so from the farthest clusters of houses, stretched out into the tundra and standing sentinel beneath the midnight shadows of the great jack pines.

Make it look like an accident. Karl could do that. If there was one thing he had excelled at in his life, it was ending the lives of other creatures...

"No."

Karl grunted, suddenly aware that he had tramped through the house to his home armory without conscious thought. A wall of rifles, pistols, shotguns, and bows were on display, perfectly polished and regulated, most of them discharged and mere display items. However, he knew which weapons were locked and loaded and ready to go. He took down the .30-06 Springfield and examined the cartridges. From a nearby drawer, he took a long black silencer and screwed it to the rifle's mouth. Heart thumping, he suited up in his jacket and insulated trousers and headed out the back door.

He stuck close to the house, not wanting to risk losing himself in the blizzard. The wind buffeted his body. Snow whipped against the rosebuds of his cheeks, driving painful pins into his flesh. He skirted the house, finding his way onto the front porch. There he paused and examined the world.

The houses across the street had faded from view, lost in the belly of the blizzard. The world shrank around him, closing its walls so that he could only see a stone's throw into the distance at best. The hairs on the back of his neck prickled as another cry came from somewhere nearby.

Karl raised the scope to his eye, protected from some of the snowfall by the porch canopy. He hunted for the place where the shapes had appeared. One still remained. Just on the edges of his vision.

He licked his lips. His finger stroked the trigger as he lined up the shot, not quite able to make out what it was he was scoping. If only it would come a touch closer, he could confirm the kill and reap the rewards. The last thing he needed was to kill an innocent civilian.

Hypocrite... That's not what you were thinking a second ago.

He let out a small whistle, the wind tearing the sound from his mouth. The figure moved. Twitched. A moment later it started to grow larger, moving toward Karl's call.

"That's it, baby. Keep coming to daddy. A few steps more..."

The shape grew larger, turning from a fuzzy gray blob and stretching, taller now. It was long, almost as tall as a man, though he could still see no appendages or limbs which would identify which genus this creature belonged to.

The figure stopped. Karl's heart raced. He gave another whistle, hoping to coax the creature closer, but instead, a second whistle answered, followed by a searing pain above his left hip.

"Son of a bitch," he hissed, dropping the rifle. Something long and black stuck out of the material of his jacket. Although his coat was thick, the dart's needle was long enough to penetrate the cloth and break the skin.

"What the...?" Karl grimaced as he ripped out the dart. He searched in the storm for his attacker, but there was nothing out there. The world was white once more.

He pocketed the dart, making a note to examine the projectile in the shelter of his home, then picked up the rifle and aimed it in the direction the dart had come. He let off three shots in quick succession, hoping that one of them may blindly land, but if it did, there was no sign.

His hip throbbed. He sent one final shot in the direction of whatever had been out there, a strange nausea sweeping through his body and tickling his throat.

Resigning to defeat, he made his way toward the side door.

His back resting against the door, knees shaking beneath him, Karl fumbled for the lock with one hand, the other clutching the rapidly warming epicenter of his pain. Once inside, he worked quickly to remove his jacket and examine the site of the wound. His hands stretched out the bright red prick in his side, only inches above his hip bone. Small rivulets of blood trickled down to the waistband of his trousers, but blood shouldn't be that dark, should it? He touched a finger to the ichor and felt its tackiness. Remembering the dart, he dug through his jacket and held it at eye level. He examined its tip and found the same tar-like residue coating the long, thick needle. The dart itself was unremarkable. Carved wood with black feathers woven to the back. A few markings etched in black ink along the body.

But that residue...

A tidal wave of nausea crested, knocking Karl off balance. Eels swam in his throat. He wobbled on his feet and fought to stay upright. The edges of his vision swam. He tossed the dart onto a nearby unit where it rolled and fell to the floor.

Fighting his way through his house, he grabbed hold of anything his numb fingers could find to steady his passage toward Cadence and Alice. If whatever was out there had gotten to him, there was a chance that they could get to them, too. His *family*. He couldn't let that happen. Wouldn't. He was a protector. *The* alpha...

Karl was outside his bedroom. He blinked, not quite remembering the journey up the stairs or how he had gotten there. On his right, Alice's bedroom door stood ajar, the usual pink glow of her room cast by the nightlight now vanished in the wake of the power cut. Karl absently touched his hip, confused by the sudden surge of anger rising within. His throat, which had felt parched and dry only moments ago was now thick with his own saliva. He was hungry, but wasn't sure what—

Karl dizzied, moving a hand to his head as he wobbled on the spot. He was standing by his bed, no memory of entering the room. The bedsheets were scattered, shredded until the stuffing snowed its way over the room, some small flurries of fluff slowly raining still. The pillows were gone, cast haphazardly against the wall, the wooden headboard cracked, the vanity table turned on its side.

And the blood.

Oh, God, the blood.

Karl's breath caught as he followed the trail of blood and found the figure lying on the floor before him. He stood over Cadence's lifeless body, her frame twisted into unnatural angles. Her nightgown was nothing more than rags failing to hide her naked body. A lump of flesh had been torn from her neck, revealing the fragile wiring of her respiratory system beneath. Blood spurted from the wound like a freshly birthed geyser.

Karl let out a strange utterance that might have been a sob.

Movement by the bedroom door. Karl spun, his head concocting an image of his innocent daughter standing there in the darkness, discovering the haunting scene before them. Eyes wide, a scream on the horizon, cresting the hill...

But it wasn't Alice standing there at all. A naked man stood in the doorway.

No. Not a man...

The creature's flesh was far too pale for a man's, its limbs bracken-thin. Its rib cage was the widest part of his body, its stomach sinking grotesquely inward as though someone had stuck a nozzle down its throat and vacuumed out the innards. Its fingers, unnaturally long, were blackened and sharp, each breath accompanied by a dry rasp as of dead sticks brushed against a stone pavement.

Worse than all of that was the mask that he wore—for Karl could sense no sign of femininity on this creature. A juvenile stag's skull was fixed to the place where the head should be. Antlers as long as Karl's fingers jutted from the dome of its skull as the creature tilted his head to the side with childlike curiosity.

Karl stood frozen to the spot, the only sounds their breath and the sluicing of blood as it escaped Cadence's throat. His hands trembled, which was unusual for a man such as he who dealt with death and the harsh realities of this world on a daily basis.

"What did you do?" Anger surged within him, primal and untamed. An anger he had never known, overwhelming, all-consuming. He wanted—no, *needed*—to hurt *something*, and this creature had put himself in the line of fire. This creature had killed his wife, may have his daughter in his sights. Karl could not allow this, couldn't allow whatever the fuck this thing was to turn his life upside down any further, this grotesque, haunting visage of a man who...

The creature raised a hand, one long, black finger pointing at Karl. He was silent, head tilted in that whimsical way of a child examining an ant's nest for the first time, though if there was a childlike sparkle in his eye, Karl couldn't find it in the dark hollows of that mask.

Karl's eyebrows knitted together. He licked his lips. Tasted the tang of something warm and metallic on his tongue. He touched a finger to his lip, removed it, and found the tip frosted in dark residue.

Karl glanced down at his wife, at the wound in her neck, struggling to process and bring the pieces of the puzzle together. IT couldn't be...

It couldn't...

He turned back to the creature in his room. The clean, pristine being of bone and shadow. Face spotless. Not a drop of blood to be seen.

Dawning realization coursed through his veins.

Not just the agonizing, desperate realization that it was in fact he who had sunk his teeth through the soft tissue of his wife's flesh. Not the realization that this creature had somehow dispelled power over him to make him perform these heinous acts.

It was, in fact, the realization that Karl Bowman was still hungry.

Very hungry, indeed.

And, in the air, lingered the scent of a little girl's flesh.

EPISODE 2

BURIED

11

DENRIDGE HILLS

The blizzard raged on, the snow-laden clouds swollen and puffing to a magnitude that hadn't been witnessed—in this lifetime, at least. Grays turned to white turned to black, blocking the vista of the bleeding Aurora from sight, coveting it like the flesh protects the beating heart of life. Clouds roiled and fought, vying for space in the pregnant air as they vomited their torrents of snow upon the town.

They couldn't be called flakes any longer. Flakes suggested delicacy, a whisper from a stranger in a darkened room. These frozen snowballs barreled from the sky, stacking up on the ground, raising the height of the paths, barricading doors, and causing the ancient pines to groan under its weight. The wind roared, clutching and tearing at roof tiles, rattling windows. An old church, long abandoned after a fire raged in the pulpit almost thirty years prior, lost the last piece of the refuge which had held it together. The skeletal structure, with its flimsy, rotting walls and gaping holes, was the first true victim to the storm, long before they came.

But come they did.

Under the cloak of the storm they stalked. As promised. The lost remnants of the old world come to claim what was rightfully theirs.

Marching in the midst of the storm they came in their droves, undeterred by the raging weather.

Only a few were awake to witness their descent.

FOR TOMLIN LUDLOW, the first sign that something was wrong came in the form of a scream from the street outside. The haunting cry of a dying man. He had never heard anything so terrifying. Few could say that they knew with confidence the sounds a human could make when they stood upon the brink of death, but a primal, survival instinct is buried deep within us all, and Tomlin's instincts warned him that danger was nearby.

He sat up sharply, sweat peppering his brow. It had been a nightmare, of that he was almost certain. A foggy dream in which he had regressed forty years and his father had taken to him with his favorite weapon—a belt. With each bullwhip strike of leather against the pinkening flesh of his ass, the skin throbbed in fits of heat and pain. Nubs of concentrated hurt spiked as the belt whispered through the air and found its target. Tomlin was convinced this was no ordinary belt. Perhaps one of his mother's decorative pieces from her fleeting phase of listening to '80s glam rock and thinking that she was Joan Jett. Another whip, another stifled yelp, and there was no question that there was more to the belt than met the eye. A glance back confirmed this, showcasing a strip of metal studs which bit into his cheeks and ate the muscle and flesh beneath. Reams of blood sprayed his father's maniacal face as he drew back, the belt sucking to the mess of flesh and blood, clinging to the wet flesh with thousands of micro teeth as he scolded his son once again for something that was long buried in the past.

Although knowing that the dream had been ludicrous, Tomlin moved his hand to his rump and tentatively patted the skin. He expected pain to flare and spike at a simple touch but was glad to find that there was nothing wrong.

Nothing wrong at all.

Tomlin glanced at Rita, her eyelids fluttering as she lost herself in the throes of her dream. She looked so beautiful at night, skin lit by the glow of a single candle. So at peace. Her full lips were plump with color and her breathing was deep and full. The ghost of a smile traced his lips as his swollen heart beat its love for her.

Another cry.

Tomlin looked around, out of sorts and still a little lost in the clutches of his dream. He eased himself out of bed and trotted to the window. His podgy cheeks wobbled as he walked, and as he shifted the curtains, he was surprised at just how dark things had grown outside.

There hadn't been any sign of a storm before bed. Usually, the town would be warned of a coming storm, heralded to prepare and ensure that everyone had enough supplies to last out the worst of the extreme weather. The entire town depended on it. Ludlow's store would have been flooded with business before an approaching storm, customers ladening their cradled arms with more stock than they'd need, but today he had seen nothing more than the typical gaggle of "How do ya dos."

His breath fogged up the glass. Snow belted from the heavens, limiting his vision to no more than halfway across the street. In the boundaries of his vision, there was only storm. He would be forgiven for believing he'd stepped out of one dream and into another. Cast adrift. A lonely vessel tossed out to a white, frozen sea. The ghostly silhouettes of merpeople teasing the edges of his vision, never fully coalescing, but that ever-present feeling of being watched plaguing the back of his mind.

He tore his eyes from the window, seeking comfort in the form of his slumbering wife. He wondered what she was dreaming about, her fair face so at ease while his heart still raced in his chest and the ringing echoes of that scream resonated in his eardrums.

That scream... It had been so real. But who would be out in that weather at this time of night? He knew most of the town's residents by face, name, and heritage. No one would be that stupid.

He narrowed his eyes and searched for any sign of... anything in the street outside, but it was impossible. Perhaps it had been nothing more than the wind, funneling through the cracks and hollows of the town, creating a symphony of pain and protestation that he had heard. Perhaps he had still been dreaming when the scream had come, and that scream had actually been his own, calling his mother for help as his father tenderized his ass and flushed tears from a young Tomlin's eyes.

Tomlin shuddered, shaking away the visual. His father had been an asshole when he was alive. Years had passed since he had last thought of Christian Ludlow, and he wondered why the dream had come tonight, of all nights. Life had moved on. Everything was well. Business was booming and Rita was his world. They had even had kids, two of them, both grown and out in the town now, making their own way as they contributed to this one-of-a-kind community.

Tomlin pawed his eyes and debated going back to bed. Instead, he tiptoed across the room, triggering the protesting creaks of the floorboards until he was out of the room. Perhaps, when he was once a lighter man, he could have been more silent, but these days he was well-fed and well-loved, and that was alright, Jack.

The orange juice was cool on his throat, the sugary sharpness running its cool contents through his system. He stood in the solitary light of the fridge and drank straight from the carton, knowing that, if Rita caught him, he would receive one hell of a tongue-lashing. Feeling a little naughty that he didn't mind. She was pretty when she was mad. With his stomach satisfied, he closed the fridge door.

Something caught his eye.

A shadow had danced across the window, he was certain of it. A dark shape zooming past the house.

Tomlin screwed his fists in his tired eyes and looked again.

There was nothing there.

"You're driving yourself cuckoo, Tommy. Late nights, bad dreams, and a blizzard are a formula for paranoia. Stop shitting yourself up over every knock and groan." He chuckled, a vain attempt to shrug off the chills, and made his way toward the stairs.

He froze when the thud came on the door. A fist on wood. A

sound he had heard a thousand times, though never once had it forced him to swallow. With his eyes fixed on the upstairs landing, he debated turning around and acknowledging the sound. What would happen if he ignored it? If you don't look, you don't see, right?

Thump.

Tomlin gritted his eyes, his knuckles turning white on the banister. He had never considered himself a fearful man, but neither did he consider himself brave. There was a reason he had made his vocation among the townspeople while the stronger, bolder folk took to hunting. Tomlin was more at home handling change than handling a knife, and that showed in the quivering response of his body to the unseen visitor.

He muttered beneath his breath, annoyed that he was shaking so much. So what if there was a thud at the door? There's a storm raging outside. Any matter of objects could be caught in the winds and hurled against the house. It happens all the time, doesn't it?

Not like that, it doesn't.

Thump.

Tomlin took a steadying breath just as the upstairs light turned on. A buttery glow melted from the bedroom to the landing and Tomlin found himself wanting to shout for his wife to go back to their room. To bar herself inside a cupboard or under the bed and act as though she wasn't home. That instinctive tremble of caution shot down his spine like a shock of static. Another thump only fueled his urge to stop his wife from searching for him, but instead of anything useful spilling from his mouth, he let out a whimper, and warm urine flowed down his leg.

There was no more thumping after that. No more knocks on the door.

In place of the thumps, the door exploded off its hinges with ferocious gusto and the storm broke in. Torrents of frigid air pushed Tomlin onto the stairs, his flabby stomach the only cushioning protecting his body from its hard, wooden edges. Something growled and cried out in ecstatic rage, but he wouldn't give the invader the justice of acknowledging its existence. Even as his wife stood at the top of the stairs, screaming and scratching her nails down her face, leaving neat red lines, he closed his eyes and blamed the invasion on the storm. The heavy storm that pinned him to the stairs with strong, thin arms. The powerful storm that threw its weight onto his back and tore off his clothing. The Almighty storm that bit into his flesh and painted the stairs in his blood.

The wind was his killer. That's all that Tomlin would accept. The wind and its dozens of minions that scattered about his house and leaped over his dying body. To accept anything different would be ludicrous. The images his sleeping brain conjured were absurd, the dark shadows of twisted beings clambering over his rotund form to race toward his wife.

A groan from the wind, laced with orgasmic pleasure as its chilly teeth chomped into his back, its icicle tongue tasting his flesh as it sent him deep into the throes of the final abyss.

NOT HALF A MILE AWAY, Sheila Lawson lay face-down on the couch. Strings of saliva clung to the cavern of her mouth as she snored deeply. The wine glass was still in her hand, the final untasted dregs of the viscous red liquid teetering dangerously close to spilling onto the hand-stitched rug.

She was dreaming of nothing, as she so often did when she was inebriated—which had been increasingly often lately. After the not-so-distant death of her husband, Sheila had fallen into a rapid decline. The tiny things that Benjamin had once attended to were now colossal struggles, each tiny to-do vying for her attention—the upkeep and maintenance of the house, bill payments, keeping an eye on Amy, her ever-blossoming teenage daughter who seemed determined to tailspin into a hectic whirlwind of chaos and throw her life away before it had already begun. Life was tough, but escape was easy. As much as she struggled to afford a repairman to fix the hole in the roof, she always found bucketloads of cash to replenish the stock cupboards when she ran out of vino.

After wine, sleep was her secondary escape, and in escape Sheila was at peace. Occasionally her mind would coalesce something that might resemble a dream, but then it would blow away like smoke in a breeze, already safe in the knowledge that even if she did dream of something profound that may have the potential to change her life, she'd forget it the moment she opened her eyes and the internal drums of her hangover kicked in.

Sheila rolled to her side, the wine glass finally slipping from her fingers, staining the rug with the blood red of her chianti.

The ghost of a smile lined her face. A faint trace of happiness that was not reflective of the fact that in the last thirteen months she had become a widow and a single parent, nor from the fact that Amy was out in the town somewhere lost in the storm, gone without her knowledge. It would be difficult to say what that smile was for...

But what it was definitely *not* for, was the broken windows and the shattered doors. Nor was that smile for the dark figure that towered over her and licked its lips while she slept soundly on.

They gathered around her in the darkness, studying the middle-aged woman with the patience of a herd of hyenas closing in for their meal. Only one creature climbed onto her body, straddling her with the delicate poise of a lover ready to engage in the throes of coital passion. Had she been awake, she would have smelled the acrid scent of death on its breath. Would have marveled at its teeth, filed to needlelike points. The quivering excitement of its decrepit heart as it fluttered in its chest.

Sheila let out a soft laugh and weakly pushed at the creature's arms. Her iPad lay on the coffee table, the screen still dimly lit with an array of Scrabble tiles waiting to be placed into order. The word "librarian" left unconfirmed on the screen, barely able to scrape her eleven points.

She let out a gentle sigh.

In sleep we escape.

In death we sleep.

∾

IN THE FARTHEST reaches of town, under the shadow of the Drumtrie Forest, Naomi Oslow stared at the skull framed above her fireplace.

The thing was hideous, the rotten white skeletal structure of a human man. The eyes were dark voids from which Naomi spent most days in fear that beetles or some kind of scourge would scramble out from its depths and crawl into her living room. The remains of the human flesh that had once clung to the skull had been immaculately stripped, but little could be done to humanize what it had once been. The antlers had seen to that. Crude things imperfectly jabbed through the top of the skull, designed by its maker to twist the visage into the form of a grotesque hellbeast. Antlers which could have been taken from a buck in its prime, their reaches stretching across the entire width of the chimney column, as though the skull of her late husband had sprouted demonic wings and was attempting to fly back to its fire-born overlord.

A stark reminder of what had come before. A time when her darkest fears had been realized, and all that she had loved had been stolen. She had once believed that his alcohol dependency would be the undoing of their marriage, of their lives together. It turned out that the reality was far from that.

Naomi had been sitting downstairs in the isolated cabin ever since the Aurora had shed its colors and completed its metamorphosis. Her stomach broiled with discomfort, her gut lined with a potent acid that acted as though it had been activated by the Northern Lights. She sat on the couch, staring at the growing storm, cradling the rifle in one arm, a tumbler of Abraham's Nectar cupped in the steady hand of the other. Whisky she hadn't removed from their liquor cabinet since the day that Donavon had died, its glass bottle thick with a layer of dust that had gathered through the years. The scent of the drink kissed her nostrils like a gentle lover and in the darkness she saw him there, an inebriated ghost swaying unsteadily on his feet.

"You sure you remember how to use that thing?" His smirk was alarming, contrasting spectacularly against the grim aura that she felt in the air. "It's been a long time."

Naomi's face hardened. If she had once loved a man, it hadn't been this vision in front of her. Donavon had been kind, generous, dependable... until his fingers found the bottle again. The formative months of their son's life had been some of the most haunting she'd thought she'd ever experience.

Little did she know what was to come before Oscar was old enough to brace his legs and walk.

"I remember." Her voice was flat. Outside, the storm raged against the windows, thick flurries whipping across the side of the cabin. She had lost sight of the woods some time ago. The Drumtrie Forest. A constant reminder of their visit inside the columns of pines, all those years ago. "I remember a lot of things. I remember who you once were. What you became." Her eyes flickered to the skull on the wall.

"I was never that monster. You know me. I'd never leave you like that."

But did Naomi truly believe him? That was a question she had struggled with in the eleven years since his passing. As their beautiful son sprouted and grew before their eyes, her mistrust in their final days had never truly been shaken. She had woken up and he was gone. No explanation. No truth. No way to ever discover what had happened in the places where reality bent into the shadows and faded to darkness.

"You know I wouldn't leave you. I'd never leave you. I loved you too much."

But you fucking left! Naomi's internal scream was not reflected in the composed woman on the couch. She stared at her whisky. Took a long sip, wincing as the amber liquid burned her throat. "How the hell did you use to drink this stuff?"

"Practice. How the hell did you deliver us an angel?" Donavon stood by the framed picture of the three of them, a time in eons past. They were all so young, alive in a different lifetime. Oscar swaddled in his newborn blankets, Donavon with a virile glint in his eye and Naomi...

Naomi, before her hair had grayed and her innocence had abandoned her.

They stayed a while in silence, Naomi wondering how long it would be until the ghost decided to dissipate. She had seen him before, but only on those rare occasions where her grief revisited like an uninvited guest and tore open the closet where she had stuffed her feelings. On those occasions she had succumbed, forsaking the common sense of parenthood to disappear into her own bottles so that she could escape for just a few hours from the madness, sleep for less hours than she could count on one hand, and then wake to an energetic child who would never understand the hurt that weighed her down like tombstones strapped to her back.

A child who would never know what it meant to have a father.

"Why are you here?"

Donavon had taken to the large window which faced toward the woods, his fingers laced behind his back as though he were at the top of a skyscraper, looking out over the world. "Because the truth is coming, Naomi. The answers you've been seeking... they're here."

Naomi rose to her feet. She tried to pinch the tiredness from her eyes but failed. The rifle hung in one hand as she crossed the other tightly over her chest in a bid to cover the naked flesh spilling out of her gown. She loved her husband, but he was a stranger to her now. He deserved no part of her body.

She joined him at the window. He glanced at the sky. To the place where only a few hours ago the Aurora had pulsed in shimmering crimson. "The final cut has been made. The shackles broken. The lunatics will have their time running the asylum, and it's on you to ensure that you survive."

Naomi refused to look at Donavon, choosing instead to track the passage of the giant bullets of snow as they belted past the house and hit the window, each one feeling like a personal attack as they collided inches from her face. "This is a dream."

"You know that's not true."

"Then what's to come? You were never this cryptic in life."

Donavon's face hardened. "I promise you that I'll be with you, Naomi. Every step of this journey, I'll be here. The truth that you've been seeking has come right to your doorstep, and with their approach comes your answers."

"Who?"

Donavon remained silent.

Naomi shuddered, her eyes betraying her as tears pooled. The last delivery that had been signed with Donavon's name had been a disfigured skull on her doorstep—*his* disfigured skull. She glanced at the morbid art piece tacked above her mantelpiece and a sob escaped her lips. Over the years, friends and family had asked her the meaning behind its pride of place in the center of her house, and the only answer she'd ever been able to provide had been, "A reminder." But the truth was that she had never been sure of why she placed it up there. It just felt right, somehow. Silent forces moved in this world and sometimes you couldn't explain them, sometimes it was best to run with the wind and go where it may take you. That skull had marked something important, she just didn't know what. And now, as she stared at the skull and pondered her husband's words, she felt the time had finally come for the weight of the unknown to shift from her shoulders, and to finally embrace the truth.

She adjusted her grip on the rifle, the only thing she had handled since her husband's passing which offered any comfort. "You promise you'll be with me?"

Only silence.

Naomi turned back to Donavon, but all she found was her own haggard reflection staring back at her in the glass.

12

TORI ASPLIN

The glove that clamped over her mouth was the most warmth Tori had felt since she'd been forced from her home.

The material was soft and damp, resisting her efforts to bite through the cloth and inflict pain on her captor. She wrestled in their grip, thrashing her head around in a desperate attempt to escape this nightmare, growling and fighting back tears until a voice whispered in her ear.

"Shut the fuck up. You'll draw them right to you."

Tori softened at the sound of the voice. It was desperate, but there was a soothing quality to its tone.

"I'm going to remove my hand, now. Promise you'll keep calm."

Tori nodded.

The hand lifted. Tori turned and looked into the dark blue eyes of a man that she didn't recognize.

A stranger?

That nugget of information disturbed her the most, considering that she prided herself on her Guess-Who knowledge of every living and breathing man and woman in this town. Denridge Hills was a small town, and twenty-plus years living in this place was plenty of time to know most, if not all, by heart.

A rash of dark stubble leaked out from the material that covered the bottom half of the man's face. There were small wrinkles bunching at the corner of his eyes. An older man?

"Are you okay? You must be freezing."

"Those... Those things..." Tori managed, the weight of her attack and sudden flight overwhelming her now that she'd had a moment to stop. "They... Oh God... Stanley..."

A whimper escaped her lips. She sobbed and the gloved hand covered her mouth again. The Winchester rifle fell from her grasp and was claimed by the snow. She couldn't see the man through the blur of her tears, but she could feel affection there, and that was enough for her to let go. He cuddled her closely to his chest and let her ride out the tears until a cry came from somewhere nearby, another animal shriek of either triumph or despair. It was impossible to tell.

"We can't stay here," the man whispered, brushing her hair from her face. "Come on, we need to get you somewhere safe. Which direction did you come from?"

Tori thumbed over her shoulder, wiping the tears from her eyes. "That way. My house isn't too far from here."

"Shit."

"What?" she asked, her senses beginning to sharpen again as the snow and wind buffeted between the houses. "Wait, who the hell are you?"

"Alex. But, can we do full introductions later? If they're back where your house is, then we're fucking surrounded." He was exasperated, had clearly been unfortunate enough to deal with these creatures before. At least she was with someone who understood the monstrosities she'd witnessed spraying Stanley's blood across her couch. At least she wasn't alone anymore. "Come on. Someone around here must be able to take us in, have some weapons. Where'd your gun go?"

Tori patted herself, as though the firearm might be hiding on her person, then spotted the soft impression left in the snow. She dug down through the depths of fresh powder and retrieved her father's rifle. "Here."

Alex held out a gloved hand. "Would you mind?"

Tori clutched the rifle. In that moment, all that mattered was that *she* was safe, and in her bid for safety, the rifle was her ticket to freedom. If she yielded her weapon to this man... Alex... then what would she have to protect herself with?

But I'm so cold. I need my arms to warm my chest. What use is there in holding the one thing that can keep us both safe if my fingers are too numb to shoot?

Reading this debate in her eyes, Alex pulled off his gloves and offered them to Tori. "Here. Get warm. I'll keep us covered."

Another screech, closer this time.

"Let's get the hell out of this blizzard," Alex said. Tori didn't argue.

She remained close behind Alex, comforted by the residual warmth lingering in Alex's gloves as he teased his head around the corner and scanned for the creatures. Satisfied that none were nearby, he came around to the front of one of the houses and knocked on the door. Each knuckle rap sounded like a thunderclap to Tori who kept her eyes peeled on her limited view of the street around them, terrified of spotting a black shape approaching.

"Come on... Come on..." Alex muttered, but no answer came. Upstairs, a light switched off. "Sons of bitches are hiding."

"Can't say I blame them," Tori said.

They tried two more houses and met the same result. Each time Alex knocked on the door, there was no answer. A spike of fear ploughed through Tori. How sensitive were these creatures? Could they smell fear from a distance? She had read about monsters over the years, watched Netflix shows about werewolves, vampires, and ghosts, but never before had she encountered something like this. She had no frame of reference for the malnourished ice demons who broke through her windows. Her knees knocked together, her skin turned pink, her mouth ached from the constant chattering of her teeth.

"Fuck," Alex growled, his fists clenching to fight off the cold. He banged on the door with their fleshy underside, refusing to stop until someone answered. Another light switched off upstairs as the residents who lived in this home refused to acknowledge their noisy neighbors at this late hour.

Tori let out a soft moan. Concern grew in the depths of Alex's eyes as he spotted the pinks of her skin, noticed how much she was shivering. He shook his head, about to raise another fist to the door when it opened wide and a squat, balding man stood in front of them, a double-barreled shotgun in his hands as he stared down the sight at the pair of them.

"What's the meaning of this?" Harvey Dutton bellowed, his one open eye bloodshot and milky. "It's the middle of the goddamn…" He spun the gun from Alex to Tori, his rough demeanor melting at the sight of her. "Tori? Dear God, girl. What are you doing out in the middle of a blizzard dressed like that? You must be freezing."

Tori nodded, arms wrapped tightly around her. "I am, Mr Dutton. Please. Can we come inside?" She looked at him in earnest, feeling a sense of shame at disturbing his slumber. Harvey Dutton and his wife owned a clothing store a short distance across town, the one place which Tori frequented multiple times a week. In the past she had engaged in heated discussions with the pair, begging for the latest fashion trends to find their way to Denridge, working her way through almost every item of clothing they had so she could showcase them to her thousands of followers. Never in a million years would she imagine running into them like this, looking the mess that she did.

Harvey eyed Alex suspiciously, as though he had been the one to drag her out in these conditions, then ushered them inside. "If you could please keep it down, Damien is sleeping." He closed the door and the howling wind was shushed. Warmth flooded over Tori, her skin tingling as it began to thaw. "What the hell is going on out there? I hear wolves howling, people shouting. It's like there's a riot breaking out in the middle of a storm."

Alex opened his mouth to answer when Harvey's wife, Sherri, emerged at the top of the stairs, fingers fumbling with the loop of her gown. "Harvey, who's down there? What's going on?" Her eyes met Tori as she padded halfway down, her gaze lingering on the dark blood stains on her trousers. "Tori? What's happened to you? Is that... blood?"

Tori put a hand to her mouth to stifle her sob. Her knees gave and Alex moved to her side, holding her around the waist. He turned to Harvey, "Please, sir... madam... There are things out there in the snow. Strange things." He pulled the dart from his pocket. "They shot this at me, and I think they attacked Tori. I don't know what they are, or what they're here for, but..."

"A dart?" Harvey took the dart and studied it. "That's practically primitive. Who uses darts anymore?" He handed it back to Alex. "I haven't seen anything like this since I watched that documentary of natives in the Amazon. Jungle... something, it was called."

"Jungle Living," Sherri finished for him.

Tori let out a fresh wave of sobs. "They... They... Stan... Oh..." Harvey guided her to the couch where she sat and dabbed at her eyes with tissue offered by Sherri. When she calmed enough to speak, she said, "They killed Stanley. They did something to him. It's... They ripped out his chest and... They..." She took a calming breath, another burst of sobs threatening to take her as the horror of the situation hit her in full force. "They're monsters. They're not human. Not animal. I saw them. They broke into my house and they... ate Stanley."

"Ate?" Alex muttered.

Sherri put a hand to her chest. "Oh..."

Harvey shook his head. "Stanley Miller? No. Can't be. He's one of the toughest men we've got out there. It would take a hell of a beast to bring down someone like Stanley. I've seen him wrestle a moose with his bare hands and come out the victor."

Sherri shot him a look.

Tori rose to her feet, fear melting to anger. When had she last ridden a rollercoaster this intense? When had she last felt her emotions switch at the touch of a button? She pulled at her damp trousers, showcasing the blood that stained her leg. "This is *his* blood, Harvey. What, you think I'm making all this shit up? You think I'd be out there in that fucking blizzard because I fancied a midnight stroll? No. They *ate* him, dammit. Their mouths were stained with his blood, and they came for me, too. They came for me with hungry eyes and wanted a taste. I ran..." She collapsed back into the chair and fell into Alex. "I ran... I ran..."

Alex held her tightly. Harvey looked at him for confirmation. He shrugged. "I don't know what to tell you. Something's out there. I've seen them, but only through the snow. Not a clear look. They came for me, too. I didn't make that dart myself. I can't tell you what they are, but if you're hoping to survive the night, I suggest you arm yourselves."

As if to punctuate his point, a gunshot sounded in the distance.

Harvey sighed, only just accepting that he wasn't going to get any rest tonight. He handed the shotgun to his wife. "I've got a few more where that came from. Hold on, let me fetch the cavalry."

He left through a door at the back of the room as another gunshot echoed outside. A pregnant silence followed, with Sherri sitting upright and watching Alex with interest as he held Tori. "Is she going to be okay?"

Tori sat up. Rubbed her eyes dry. "Yes. Thank you, Sherri." She shuddered and wrapped her arms around herself again.

"You must still be freezing. Hold on, let me find you something fresh and dry." Sherri shuffled toward the stairs, hobbling on every other step, her arthritic knee buckling slightly. At the top of the stairs a young boy was waiting for her, his silhouette backlit by the soft flickering candlelight.

"Damien? What are you doing up?" she asked.

Damien stood in blue flannel pajamas, cuddling a blankie to his neck. "There are people outside making loud noises."

Sherri offered a maternal smile. "It's okay, honey. You go back to bed. There's nothing to worry about."

"Someone was below my bedroom window," Damien said softly. "Something hit the glass."

Sherri turned back to Tori and Alex who were already on their feet, the gun cocked and ready in Alex's hands.

13

CODY TREBECK

Hayden made it past the padlock, but now he fumbled with the door's main locking mechanism, his shaking hands barely able to hold his tools steady as he prodded inside the chamber. Cody, Sophie, Amy, and Brandon couldn't pull their eyes away from the door, the place where the creatures' hands fought and scrabbled to claw their way inside.

They had given up on their darts, unable to snatch the right angle to shoot their projectiles at the group, and now they clutched at the inch gap in the door, stretching fingers as black as night, as sharp as talons, straining to pull the gap wider and gain access inside.

Where Cody and the others had failed, they were succeeding.

"Hurry!" Sophie bellowed, her eyes fixed on the scrambling fingers, reaching through like the vines of inky plants. "Hayden, come on!"

Something clicked. Hayden let out a brief, triumphant cry as he struggled to his feet and turned the handle. He opened the door and was the first to dash through, forsaking even Amy as he bought distance from the creatures, tugging the unconscious body of Travis behind him.

Sophie waited for Cody to go, but he pushed her through. The last one to enter, he closed the door firmly behind them. "Hayden, you need to lock it back up, man."

"Are you kidding?" Hayden said. "We need to get as far away from those things as possible."

Brandon gripped a hand to his chest, his eyes screwed tight, hissing air through his teeth. "Lock it, Hayden. If they get in, we need to make it more difficult for them to follow."

"How are they going to get in? Nothing can move those doors. The snow is blocking it."

Cody, who could still see their fingers from where he stood, shook his head. Sure, Hayden hadn't paid his full attention to those... things, but they were certainly making progress. There was no doubt in his mind that they'd find a way through. Pretty soon they'd be able to fit their heads through that gap, and if their bodies were anywhere near as skinny as the one he'd witnessed through the snow, it wouldn't hold much of an obstacle to them. "Hayden. Please."

Hayden growled, before finally relenting. He ran to the door and drove a pick inside the lock. He cast a brief glance at the gymnasium's external door and what remained of his color drained from his face.

He battled with the lock, hands shaking, until there came another click. Running back to Travis, he indelicately picked up the leg he had been dragging.

"Is it done?" Cody asked.

"Fuck if I know. Maybe."

Something crashed in the hall. Cody ran to Travis' other leg and helped steer him through the corridor. It wasn't until they were halfway down the corridor that he noticed that one of their party was missing. "Where did Brandon go?"

Amy answered, deflated and quiet. "He ran off ahead. Said something about something. I don't know."

Cody leered at her, unable to believe her sullen demeanor. Just because her boyfriend had scolded her, that didn't mean she had to give—now, of all times. They were all in danger. They all needed to work together.

"Which way did he go?"

Amy pointed.

Another crash in the gymnasium. At this point Cody wasn't sure if all of this was real, or if he was imagining it. Either way, he knuckled down and got to walking as briskly as possible, Travis sliding smoothly along the tiled floors behind them. Sophie and Amy brought up the rear, casting furtive glances over their shoulders as they put distance between themselves and the creatures.

They came to a fork in the corridor. Brandon was some distance to the right, past a set of double doors, tugging on something they couldn't quite see. They opened the doors and could make out Brandon's desperate mutterings as he fought with a handle leading to the outside.

"Locked."

"Of course it is, fatty," Hayden said. "The whole place is locked tight. Did you think you were going to do without me? Barge your fat ass through?"

"Will you cut him some slack?" Sophie said. "He's doing his best."

"His best is going to get us killed."

Cody dropped Travis' leg and shoved Hayden, his patience wearing thin. His nose still throbbed from Hayden's attack and he was getting sick of the constant berating of Brandon. "Either help him or shut the fuck up."

Hayden glared at him. Shoved him back. "Don't you fucking touch me." He bore his weight at Cody, his power surprising as the cool touch of the wall pressed against Cody's back. Hayden's fist hovered inches from his face. "Don't get cocky, new kid. You're a long way from London. Remember that."

For a moment the two simply stared at each other.

Sophie stepped over Travis and shoved Hayden away from Cody. "Enough of the male bravado bullshit. Either help Brandon unlock the door or feed yourself to those things back there. I don't know about you, but I'd rather brave the blizzard than find out why they're trying to get to us."

Hayden, who now seemed to have found some of his former confidence, tutted. "Look at you guys, pissing yourself over a few spooks. We'll unlock this door and we'll be out and on the way home, no problem. Just you wait until the storm passes and we're back at school, I'll tell everyone how much of a pussy the new kid and his friend is."

Sophie bit back a retort. "Just open the door."

As Hayden knelt by the lock and worked with his tools, Sophie kept an eye on the corridor. Things had fallen eerily silent. Amy crossed her arms and leaned against the wall, her eyes glossy, bags hanging beneath them. Travis' breath was shallow, and Cody couldn't believe he had forsaken the safe confines of Alex's cabin for this... What? Adventure? For a game of basketball, miles from anywhere familiar, with a bunch of people he had only met a few weeks ago.

His thoughts turned to his parents, to the day that he had watched their coffins carried, making their final processions to their graves. Twin gravestones embossed with the names of the first super-heroes he had admired. What would they think of him now? Their own lives taken too early, a fragment of time glitching and snuffing their light. An "accident" they had called it, but to Cody it felt like more. What would they think of their boy, voluntarily putting himself in a situation where his life could be at risk? Even if those things out there in the storm weren't hostile—which Cody doubted greatly—the storm most certainly was. How long would he, a nobody kid from England, last in the midst of one of the planet's toughest elemental conditions?

Hot tears pricked the corner of his eyes as Hayden uttered a satisfied, "Okay," and stepped back. Brandon moved warily to his side as they pressed against the door. To all of their dismay, the snow had trapped them on this side, too.

Hayden took a few steps back, then leaped at the door, shoulder smashing into the metal. The door didn't budge. Another step back. Another leap. Then another, until he finally relented, crying out with a desperate, "Shit!"

He took a breather, hands resting on his knees as he stared at the floor. "What are you guys waiting for? A little help, please?"

Sophie passed by Cody, muttering quietly enough so that only he could hear, "That's the first time he's been polite all evening."

They gathered at the door, but Cody already knew it was pointless. The snow was piled high through the infinitesimal gap, measuring above their knees, and as much as they pushed, the wind blew back at them, the snow compacted, and the way ahead was barred.

Brandon clutched his chest again. "How is it possible that this side is blocked, too? The wind should have a dominant direction. It shouldn't—"

"Who cares about the shoulds and the shouldn'ts?" Hayden snapped. "We're fucking trapped."

"Cut it out," Sophie shot back. "Calm down, won't you? We won't get anywhere if we keep bickering like this."

"There has to be somewhere safe we can ride out the storm," Cody offered. "Somewhere where we can bar ourselves in until the storm passes." He glanced around, still not completely familiar with the layout of the school, particularly this building, which he had only been inside a handful of times. "Any ideas? Hey, Brandon, you okay?"

Brandon's eyes were screwed shut, his breath coming in short hitches. "I'm fine. Honestly, this happens sometimes." He placed his fingers behind his head, forcing a long breath through his nose. "There's a place. A basement. Davidson stores his cleaning equipment there. I've seen him go in there a couple of times as I've walked past."

Hayden raised an eyebrow. "You want to go to Davidson's pedo den? Are you insane?"

"That's just rumors."

"Not what I heard," Hayden said. "There's a reason people avoid that place."

"It's locked up tight because he has dangerous chemicals," Brandon retorted. "Bleach, acids, alkalis, all the things he needs to do his job. It needs to be locked away safely so that school kids can't break in and hurt themselves."

Hayden scoffed. "Well, that's perfect then."

"Where is it?" Sophie asked.

Just around the corner. Near the girl's locker rooms."

"No wonder he knows all about it, it's where he spends his time panty-sniffing."

Sophie bit back a retort and focused on Brandon. "Take us there. Hayden, you'll need to pick the lock—if you can. It's the only option we've got right now until the storm passes, and we can get the hell out of here."

With no better ideas offered, Hayden and Cody returned to Travis. They each took a leg and dragged him onward as Brandon took the lead. Cody watched Brandon carefully, his hands continuing to clutch his chest. He had seen it before, the pain of the heart. Once when his grandfather had shown the early stages of his third (and far from final) heart attack, and again when, what remained of his family, grieved at St Christopher's church as dirt was shoveled onto the twin graves.

Pain didn't always have to be physical. Cody had learned that the hard way.

"Guys, hold on," Amy said, surprising them all as she pointed. "It's Travis. Look."

Travis' head rolled from side to side, as if he was shaking off whatever dream he had fallen into. His eyelids fluttered, pupils struggling to connect with reality. He made a vague attempt to raise his head but could only manage an inch before it came back down again.

Hayden moved to his side. "King? King? You with us, buddy?"

Travis gave a weak groan, his tongue wetting his dry lips.

Cody eased Travis' leg down and waited impatiently. They would have time for a reunion later, there were more pressing matters at hand. Brandon seconded this notion with a silent nod at Cody.

Hayden let out a soft laugh. "Glad to see you're still with us."

"Not for long if you don't hurry your ass up," Sophie said, relaying what Cody and Brandon had been thinking.

As if in response, a clattering thud echoed down the halls, the sound reminiscent of the noise Hayden had made when he threw himself against the doors.

Sophie's face steeled. "Either get him walking or continue dragging. We're not out of the woods yet."

"Come on." Cody took Travis' leg and pulled.

Travis groaned. Another thud boomed back in the direction of the hall before Hayden took the other leg and helped Cody close the distance between them and Brandon. They rounded a corner, Brandon standing in front of a plain metal door with a bright yellow sticker which read: DANGER, KEEP OUT.

"Pedo cave," Hayden muttered.

"I thought it was 'pedo den,'" Cody said.

Sophie growled. "Whatever it is, just unlock it. Now!"

Hayden reluctantly got to work, shaking his head as he spotted the two independent locks on the door. "I don't know if I can do this."

Travis coughed. Spluttered. He raised his head with weary eyes. "The great Hayden Locklear. Beaten by a lock. Oh, the irony."

Hayden grinned, his brow furrowing. He fiddled with the picks until one of the mechanisms in the locks clicked.

He began work on the other, shaking his head as he listened closely to find the right part of the mechanism inside. The others watched with bated breath as the thudding grew more urgent, more frequent, bouncing its soundwaves along the vacated hallways.

"I can't..." Hayden threw the tools on the floor. "I just fucking can't."

A crash. Glass shattering.

"Fuck," Cody whispered.

A bone-shuddering screech made its way down the corridor, coupled with the urgent patter of footsteps racing rapidly toward them.

Without needing encouragement, Hayden retrieved his picks and battled with the mechanism. Somehow, impossibly, he managed to work the lock and he triumphantly booted the door in with a single kick.

Brandon and Sophie almost tumbled as they raced down the darkened staircase. Amy followed swiftly after, hand on the rail. Cody hooked his arms beneath Travis', struggling to lift and twist him by himself. Hayden watched with debating eyes as he struggled with the decision of whether to get himself to safety or help his friends. The creatures were advancing at a rapid pace. Their excited, gasping breaths accompanied the clattering of those long, blackened digits as they ran. Finally, Hayden dropped down and helped Cody pick Travis up, easing his arm around his shoulders as they made it through the door.

Cody spared a glance back at the haunting creatures barreling toward them. They were skeletal things, the white masks telling the tale of dead animals. A half dozen of them, at least, skidding into the walls as they fought to turn to their prey...

Cody had never seen anything like this.

Darkness closed about him. The door shut as Hayden grabbed his collar and pulled him through. Travis fell beside them as they worked the door's inner locks. It was tough. The darkness was total, and they blindly trusted their senses to do the rest of the work.

No sooner had they slid the locks into place than the thumping resumed. Immediate. Inches from their faces. Cold, hard fingers fought to gain entry and extract them, but as much as they tried, the door didn't budge.

"The fuck are they?" Hayden asked, breathless.

Cody didn't answer. He could barely hear him, even from just a foot away. He waited a few moments, making sure that the door wouldn't suddenly explode off its hinges, or that the monsters wouldn't somehow melt through. When he was satisfied, he took half of Travis' weight, and worked with Hayden to bring him down the stairs.

14

TORI ASPLIN

They sat in the darkness and listened to the world outside, Tori, Sherri, and Damien huddled close together on the couch while Alex and Harvey kept an eye on the world outside through the kitchen window.

"This is madness." Tori shook her head. "Complete madness."

Sherri drew her son tighter to her chest. Damien was eight years old and could do little to imagine the kinds of monstrosities she had seen. After his appearance on the stairs, Sherri brought him to the couch and cocooned him to sleep again. He dozed peacefully in her arms, sandy blond hair cropped neatly on his head. His pajamas thick and woolen.

Tori watched him snooze with a note of pity in her eyes. She was nervous, knowing what those things could do and how easily they could break into a house. While she felt safer having people around her, armed and ready, she still felt like they were sitting ducks. Every now and then a gunshot would sound somewhere in the town, followed by a shrill banshee scream that could have been either a human in pain or a creature in ecstasy.

It was hard to tell.

Alex and Harvey muttered softly to each other, guns readied in their hands. Tori wondered what experience Alex had with a firearm, recognizing his British accent almost immediately after he found her outside. She knew nothing about this stranger, but he had saved her. Had brought her in from the cold and found her shelter. There was a slim chance that she could be safe with him.

Who's keeping Naomi and Oscar safe?

She wished she had her phone with her. Sitting here in the dark, she craved the little illuminated device. Not even just because of the comfort of the thousands of eyes that kept watch over her, but because her phone was her only true connection with her sister. Even if the powerlines were down, even just having it in her hands may have brought her some comfort.

She flexed her fingers as Sherri stroked Damien's hair out of his face to check if he was asleep. She whispered, "Any idea what we're dealing with out there?"

Tori shook her head. "None. I've never seen anything like them before. They were... almost human. But there was something... wrong about them. It was as though they'd been left out in the sun to shrivel and wilt. They were naked, too. Not a shred of clothing."

Sherri's eyes sparkled with thought. "Do you think we're safe here?"

"No."

Alex appeared in the doorway, his voice soft and clipped. "There's a group of them outside. They appear to be roaming the streets but have no intention of coming this way. It's almost like they're setting up a guard, patrolling for any sign of movement inside a household."

"We heard gunshots," Sherri said.

Alex's face hardened. "I'm guessing that there's plenty more where that came from before the night's over. Doesn't your town have some protocol for times like this? Emergencies? Don't you have a guard or a police force or something? Shouldn't there be people out there shutting this crap down?"

Harvey spoke over his shoulder, staring out into the streets. "This *is* protocol, new blood. When a blizzard strikes, you bury your head in the snow and wait for it to pass. It'd be ludicrous to go outside and risk your life in the middle of a storm like this. The snow is piling higher by the minute, temperatures are enough to turn the blood in your system to thick slush, and visibility is atrocious."

Alex ran a hand through his dark hair, leaving a scruffy line in its wake. "We can't just sit here. What if they try to break in? Hypothetical scenario: what happens if a pack of wolves raids the town?"

Sherri answered. "On a normal day, we drive them out."

"In a blizzard, we lay low," Tori finished.

"Polar bears?" Alex asked.

"Same," Harvey replied. "We're not in London anymore, kid. Life in Denridge turns by a different set of rules. In all my life we've never had any animals break into a house and draw us out in the middle of the night—in the middle of a goddamn blizzard, no less. We're armed to the teeth, we're prepared, if they come for us, you best know that they're going to be kissing bullets."

Tori sipped from a cool glass of water, eyes not leaving Alex's. He gazed at her from across the darkened room, and a question came to Tori that hadn't occurred to her since all the madness had kicked off. "You were out there, too."

Sherri's face turned to Alex.

Tori continued, "Why were *you* out there in the blizzard? In the middle of the night?"

Alex's shoulders softened, he looked down at the floor. "My nephew—Cody... he snuck out at some point in the night. He must have left before the blizzard kicked in, but he's gone. I went to go find him before the storm grew too violent." He took a long breath. "I didn't get very far."

"I'm so sorry," Tori said, a flash of teeth and blood and batlike wingspans in her mind. "Do you have any idea where he might have gone?"

"My only guess is the school. His basketball wasn't in his room. It's the one thing he always keeps on him just in case he ever has a chance to play. I doubt he would have taken it if he didn't intend to play somewhere in town."

"And the only place to play is the school," Sherri said. "But that's got to be a mile away. Those things... What if they're out there, too?"

"Don't antagonize the man," Harvey called back. "You think he hasn't already thought of that?"

Alex's jaw clenched. "I have to get to him. I have to go out there and find him. He's just a kid."

"You're going nowhere until these things have shifted." Harvey turned away from the window and joined Alex in the doorway. "I can only make out so much of them, but they're parading up and down the streets as though they own the goddamn place. You want to get across town, you're going to have to go through a whole load of bad first. If you're up for that then fine. But we're staying put until the storm passes and something can be done about this. When the winds die down, the cops will be out in force, and this invasion will all be just a distant memory in tomorrow's Gazette."

Invasion. The word buzzed in Tori's ears like an insistent insect.

Harvey cracked his neck with a twist of his head and grunted. "Nope. That's not our plan. Remain quiet. Stay out of sight. We shoot if we need to, but shooting will only draw attention to ourselves." A series of gunshots sounded in the distance. They all glanced at the kitchen window where dark shapes streaked excitedly past. "See? The other idiots are drawing them away."

"That sounded like it came from Cali's house," Sherri said. "I hope they're okay."

Harvey rolled his eyes. "How the hell can you guess where that shot came from—"

Harvey cut short as something burst through the window. He grunted, hand moving to his neck as he grimaced in pain. He tugged at the foreign object, a slick wet sucking following as he produced a dart in his hand. The needle was thick with viscous goo. Sherri shot to her feet, alerting Damien who rolled across the couch toward Tori. He sat up and pawed his bleary eyes. "Mom?"

Harvey wiped a palm against his neck and found it slick with blood and the dark substance. There was a small hole in the window, spiderweb cracks trailing from its edges. A pale face with wispy white hair stared back at them, eyes composed of gleaming beetle shells. In her hand was a flute which she drew to her mouth as she prepared to fire a second projectile.

"Get down!" Alex shoved Harvey to the floor as the dart soared across the room, finding its mark in Sherri's chest. She let out a weak sob, breath catching in her throat. Tori grabbed her shoulders and pulled her down to her knees as Harvey twisted and let off his shotgun. The blast was deafening, smashing what remained of the window and sending the creature flying backward and out of sight. Wind and snow raced readily through the window, its desperate ferocity unnerving.

Alex dropped himself to his hands and knees and crept along the floor. Tori watched with dread as he crossed the kitchen and moved toward the window. All it would take was for one of those things to reach out and grab him, and he'd be gone, too. Her savior. She barely knew the man, but already he'd become a safety blanket to her. Someone she could rely on to help her through this twisted nightmare.

Alex placed his back against the cupboards and readied the borrowed rifle, listening for any commotion outside.

Only the storm spoke.

Alex maneuvered himself into a position where he could see over the counter. He peeked out his head at the storm. Snow pelted his face, chilling his skin and forcing him to blink rapidly, yet he could find no more sign of the creatures. He eased himself a little higher and could just about make out the shape of the creature Harvey had shot lying in the indentation in the snow. Already the storm was claiming her. In a few seconds, she'd be out of sight, and out of mind. Gone until the storm decided to relent and the snow melted to reveal the frozen husk beneath.

Alex closed the curtains, though they continued to flutter in the breeze. He returned to his sheltered position by the cupboards. Tori was the only person he could now see in the living room as she held her eye to the sight of the Winchester and covered him while he moved. When Alex made it back inside, he shut the door behind him.

A quick scan of the room brought him to the nearby mahogany storage unit, which he gripped with both hands in an attempt to drag it in front of the door. After a few seconds of struggling, Harvey came to his aid.

"You okay?" Alex asked when they were finished. With the door shut, the cold snap had been muted, too.

"I think so. Damn it to hell, what was that thing?"

Alex held out his dart. Harvey produced his own.

A perfect match.

"Hun? Something's wrong." Sherri sat on the couch, Tori beside her, examining the puncture wound which sat a short distance above her right breast. The entry was clean, leaving a dark hole-punch mark as thick blood seeped from inside, coagulated with the black ichor. Sherri's hands shook as she dabbed at the wound.

Harvey took a seat beside his wife. He winced at his own pain as he inspected her mark. He turned to Tori. "There's iodine in the bathroom cabinet. We need to clean this shit out before it infects the bloodstream."

"Harvey! Language."

Harvey's brows knitted together. "He has to learn. Tough words for tough situations." He grimaced as a fresh wave of pain throbbed through him.

Tori found the iodine, some bandages, and clean towels. She liberally poured the iodine onto Harvey and Sherry's wounds as Damien silently wept beside them. The orange-brown liquid stained their clothes but did the trick in cleaning the worst of the ichor and leaving nothing behind but a neat, round puncture mark.

When she was finished, Tori bandaged the wounds and perched herself on the edge of the coffee table. The whole time she worked they sat mostly in silence, with just Sherri whimpering, and Alex occasionally moving to the front windows to examine outside.

"Better?" Tori asked the pair.

"Thanks," Sherri said.

Harvey grunted. The bags beneath his eyes had grown darker, and a weariness washed over him. He struggled to keep his eyes open as he pushed himself to his feet, joining Alex at the window, hand clutching the bandages on his neck. "Any sign of them?"

"None."

"Why wouldn't they come after hearing the gunshot? They raced across the street when the others fired their weapons."

"I don't know." Alex peered through the curtain then closed it again. "I honestly don't. It doesn't make any sense to me."

"None of this makes sense," Tori added. "This whole fucking night doesn't make sense."

Sherri glared at Tori.

"Mommy? Are we going to be okay?" Damien's voice was soft, vulnerable. He scooted closer to Sherri as she wrapped an arm around him. "We're going to be fine, son. Everything's going to be fine. Whatever happens, you'll be okay."

Damien nestled into her, not wholly convinced.

Tori didn't blame him. Already something deep inside told her that this was all far from over. The storm was barely beginning, and already she had more questions than she had answers to.

She remained silent, watching Sherri with intense scrutiny as the older woman blinked sleepily in the darkened room and let out a yawn. Occasionally, Sherri would take a sharp intake of breath as her pain flared, then a moment of relief would follow as sleep washed over her and threatened to drag her into its clutches.

15

KARL BOWMAN

The tang of iron and copper lingered on Karl's tongue. Her flesh was tough, but not impossible to tear through. His masked sentinel watched without word as Karl tucked in, grinding his teeth and tugging against the stubborn gristle that clung to the bone, stretching the tendons until they snapped like broken elastic, pelting him in the face with wet strings.

He cried. He ate. He cried and ate. The two warring parts of Karl locked in their dispute. Karl was nothing more than a bystander to the debate. His body racked with tears at the disbelief that this could be happening, that he wasn't deep in the clutches of some fucked-up dream, triggered by the guilt and shame he felt at his half-year affair with Tori. Yet, on the other side was the deep satisfaction that came with each mouthful of flesh and blood. Every swallow swelled his appetite, each morsel invigorated his body, driving him onward, until all that he knew was hunger.

The masked figure was patient, standing silently in the dark. The stag's skull remained crooked in the darkness, the rest of the creature that Karl had begun to think of as the Masked One's body appearing as a frail composite of leather and bone. When Karl at last felt the first tease of satiety, he caught a glimpse of himself in the mirrored wardrobe and didn't recognize what he saw.

A beast, crouched on all fours, a bib of blood staining his front. What little remained of Cadence was a putrid mess of gristle and broken flesh. Except for the pale, severed hand which sparkled with the golden band that wrapped her second to last finger. Despite his delirious state, that was a detail that he couldn't stomach. A part of the flesh he couldn't defile, as if his vows in the eyes of God the Holy had placed an enchantment that ensured that at least that tiny part of humanity remained untouched. Unviolated.

Some rituals anchored themselves deeper in the spiritual, beyond the realms of human sacrilege.

The Masked One took a silent step forward, signaling for Karl to rise. He obeyed—what choice did he have?—his forehead peppered with sweat as the heat inside the house continued to rise. His clothes clung to him like wet paper, and he was suddenly, desperately aware that he was thirstier than he'd ever been.

"What's happening to me?"

The Masked One gave no response. Karl hadn't expected one. Instead, the being turned and swept out onto the landing. Karl's heart raced as the part of him that still held on to normality remembered the face of his daughter. Of Alice. The one bright star in his life who sprinted into their bedroom every morning and showered them with butterfly kisses. Whose giggles could thaw a frozen heart. Was she still here? Asleep and lined up to become his second course?

Karl followed, unable to stop himself from doing so. Wherever this thing was taking him, it would have answers, of that he was certain. The primal side of him that flicked his tongue across his teeth in a desperate bid to savor every last morsel of food overtook his delicate mind, causing his stomach to growl and his mouth to salivate.

There were more of them in the hallway. Karl had not expected that. A host of strange humanoid figures, each one clearly cast further down the pecking order than the Masked One. The others were a host of shriveled men and women, ages unknown, their bodies the sickly white of the dying, their limbs and digits unnaturally elongated. Their eyes were dark pools in their faces, and in that moment, Karl wished that they had all worn masks. Anything to cover the vapid hollows of the inky orbs watching his every move. Black circles that spoke of death and the shadows that lingered on the other side.

They were all silent, lined along one side of the hallway, a dozen of them leading down the stairs. One held the door open to Alice's bedroom, head bowing as the Masked One swept past her. He stopped beside the child's bed and waited for Karl to join his side.

Karl's throat constricted. The snow-white covers were pulled back and bunched at the base of the bed. The pillow still held the indent of her delicate head, a head he had cradled at birth, soft, careful, hardly large enough to fit in the palm of his hand. And there was Mrs Bunny—Alice's tattered and stained nighttime cuddle companion— flopped to one side, taking residency where the bed met the corners of the room.

There was no sign of Alice.

Relief mingled with disappointment, then curdled into nausea as Karl raised a hand to his mouth and fought back a sudden need to vomit. His beard scratched his sticky palms as another tear pooled in his cornea. When had been the last time Karl had cried? When had been the last time this beast of a man had allowed emotion to color his cheeks and wet his face?

The Masked One pointed a bony finger at the center of the bed. Karl was unnerved to find that, while the creatures in the hallway still sported some semblance of flesh over their fingers, now that he was closer to their leader, the skin around the Masked One's resembled tracing paper. Dry, thin, translucent skin that revealed the blackened bones beneath.

Karl fought back another heave. Where had Alice gone? It seemed that the Masked One was asking the same question.

"You can't have her." Karl mustered the words with great effort, fighting against the instinct inside him that demanded he find her and devour her whole. "You can't. Anyone but her."

The Masked One turned its head slowly, and in that moment Karl knew true fear. A wave of something lost to the world washed across him and it took all his strength to hold that empty stare. A stare where the ends of the Earth crumbled away and all that was known was the void. In the pits of the hollows of those eyes were the answers to everything, and the truth of nothing much at all. The pain of fire and the crackle of lightning. The hurt of the dying and the suffering of the sinners. Karl's skin prickled painfully and, as the Masked One presented a single black hair to Karl, his hunger returned, paining his stomach and forcing him to cripple over and clutch his sides. The stabbing demand of his appetite was overwhelming, the meager whiff of his daughter's scent cast onto that single hair powerful enough to send him out on the hunt like a beagle to a fox.

Karl groaned as a stream of thick bile rose from his stomach and expelled onto the floor. He took a couple of deep breaths and rose to his full height, a predatory grin on his face. He stared deep into the pits of the Masked One and gave a single nod, his nose twitching as he sniffed and began his hunt.

16

CODY TREBECK

"I'm thirsty."

They sat under the glow of a single flickering candle, the pulsing orange light barely strong enough to illuminate the many nooks and crannies of the janitor's storage closet. Rows upon rows of chemical bottles, plastic containers, and tools sat on metal racks, each one with stickers detailing the various hazards of the substances contained inside.

Hayden chuckled at Travis, glad to see that he was somewhat conscious, even if the most he could do was sit with his back to the bare stone wall and hang his head. "There's plenty in here to drink. What's your poison of choice?"

"That's not funny," Sophie said. Beside her sat Amy, arms folded and as silent as a specter since they had made it downstairs and the banging had stopped. Cody and Brandon sat across from them, with Hayden keeping Travis company across the far wall. "You'd think after all that happened up there, you'd have an ounce of concern for your so-called buddy."

"Shut your mouth, whore."

Amy's eyebrows rose, but her eyes didn't. Sophie flushed red. Cody sighed. "Is that really necessary? We're stuck down here together for who knows how long, can't we at least be civil?"

He briefly met Sophie's eyes. A silent "Thank you," passed between them.

"Fuck that," Hayden scoffed. "I should never have invited you guys out here. Much less fatty boy over there. If me and King were solo, we could've just run back before the shit hit the fan instead of worrying about you morons."

"Sure. Tell yourself that," Sophie said. "Whatever you need to believe."

Cody's eyes lingered on the metallic staircase, wondering what their next steps could be. The creatures banged relentlessly on that metal door for the best part of twenty minutes before they finally silenced. At one point it seemed as though there was enough power in their attack to break the door down but, by the grace of the divine, it held fast. It had now been almost an hour since their descent into the underground closet, and Cody had to admit that he was thirsty, too. What he wouldn't give for a glass of water.

Hayden rose to his feet and crossed to a wooden desk tucked in a crevice beneath the stairs. He rolled the office chair out, sat down, and pressed the power button of an ancient Windows computer. "Hey, this must be Davidson's computer. Reckon I can find a folder filled with all of his pedo porn?"

"He's not a pedo," Brandon said, mouth dry, voice cracking. His eyes barely open as he struggled to fight sleep.

"Me thinks the lady doth protest too much." Hayden spun toward Brandon. "How much has Davidson paid to keep you quiet, eh? How much does a fiddle cost these days?"

Sophie pushed herself to her feet, growling in frustration. "Jesus Christ, Hayden. I knew you were a dickhead before, but this is intolerable. Leave the poor guy alone, won't you? How about we play the quiet game and you shut your mouth until we can figure out what we're going to do to get out of here?"

Hayden's face twisted as he rolled over to Sophie. He stood up, looking down at her with the extra couple of inches his height allowed. "Why don't you sit down and behave, little girl, and let the grown-ups deal with this? Didn't your daddy ever teach you that good girls should be seen and not heard?"

Sophie slapped Hayden so suddenly that the room fell silent. Hayden held his hand to his face, eyes lighting up with rage. "You're going to fucking regret that, bitch."

He lashed out a fist, jabbing Sophie on the cheek. She took an uneven step backward, mouth falling open.

Cody's heart stopped, blood boiling.

"You hit me?" Sophie said, taken aback.

"You started it."

Cody rose to his feet, brow furrowed. "Guys! Come on. Calm down so we can figure this shit out, please? We won't be in here for long before the storm passes and someone comes down here to rescue us."

"What about those things out there?" Brandon said.

"They've gone silent. They're probably not even out there anymore."

Hayden pointed his chin at the stairs, a grin on his face. "Why don't you go up there and find out?"

"Maybe I will."

Sophie turned from Hayden to Cody. "No! That's stupid. We can last it out in here, right?"

Brandon shrugged. "Depends how long the storm goes on for."

Cody glanced down at Brandon, keeping Hayden locked in his peripherals. "What do you mean?"

"Storms in this town can last for days, Cody. My dad once told me of a storm back in '68 which lasted over two weeks. That's a fortnight of solid snow-build. If this storm is anything like that, then..."

"We're screwed." Sophie rubbed her cheek, glaring at Hayden. Hayden kept his fists tightly balled at his side.

"So, we need to work out a way to all get along, at least for the time being," Cody said, moving into the center of the room. "Come on, guys. Yes, we're in a shit position and we have no idea what the hell is out there, but that doesn't mean we can't deal with it. I don't know about you guys, but I've seen enough survival shows on Netflix to have picked up a few basics, at least."

Hayden chuckled. "Who made Mr Bean the leader of this voyage?"

Sophie gave an exasperated sigh. "Really? A Brit joke?"

Travis weakly raised his head. "Nice one."

"Cody's right." Brandon struggled to push himself from his nest on the floor. "We have to stick together. If we're going to make it out of this thing, we need to work out how we're going to eat, how we're going to drink." He pawed a fist at his eye. "We should probably catch up on sleep, too."

"Trust the fatty to think of food."

Sophie whirled on Hayden. "I swear to God."

Hayden raised his hands defensively, the smile not slipping from his face. "Fine. Fine." He sat back in the chair and turned to the computer. "Maybe we can log into pedo Davidson's emails and send a message from there. Internet might still be running, right? Could order a pizza or something."

"Doubt it," Brandon muttered.

"Worth a shot."

Brandon returned to his place on the floor and closed his eyes. His skin had paled, his hand still tight to his chest.

"Dude, are you okay?" Cody asked.

"It's nothing. I get it sometimes. Palpitations and stabbing pains when I'm stressed. It'll pass. I just need to breathe through it."

Cody looked at him with concern, then started pacing around the room. He stroked a hand across the cold stone of the walls and scanned the shelves for anything that might come in useful. "What do you think those things out there were?"

"Never seen anything like them," Sophie said.

"They're monsters." Amy pulled her legs toward her chest and folded her arms over her knees. "Monsters."

"Monsters don't exist," Hayden spat back, busy jimmying the mouse and attempting to guess Davidson's password.

Amy shut her eyes and whimpered into her sleeve, face laced with hurt. Sophie took a seat beside Amy and placed an arm over her shoulders. Amy closed her eyes and nestled into her.

"If they're not monsters, how do you explain what we saw?" Cody asked.

"I don't know what I saw," Hayden replied. "I was a little too busy getting King out of harm's reach and cracking locks in case you hadn't realized. The most I saw were people, sick people, trying to break in." He puffed out his chest and spun to the room. "In fact, if it hadn't been for me, you all would likely be captured or dead right now. And do I get a modicum of thanks for that? No. No I don't."

"Maybe if you weren't so much of an ass, we'd be thankful," Sophie said.

"They may not be monsters, but they're not human." Brandon stated, staring emptily into the center of the room.

"Of course, fatty has all the answers," Hayden scoffed.

Cody narrowed his eyes. "What do you mean? What do you think they are?"

Brandon's eyelids were barely parted. "I read a book once, a long time ago, about fabled creatures and monsters that have appeared in ancient texts across the world. Vampires, werewolves, ghosts, that kind of thing."

Hayden scoffed and returned to the computer. "Here we go."

"I found it interesting that most of those monsters appeared in Europe or Asia, halfway across the world. The most famous beings and creatures from stories never spawned from a region as isolated as Alaska or anywhere along the frozen belt of the north. It was always Transylvania, or Scandinavia, or Russia. But then I came across something that I almost couldn't believe."

"What was it?" Sophie asked.

"The Inuit..."

Hayden let out a sharp laugh. "Those primitive fuckers? This ought to be fascinating."

"Let him speak," Cody stated, not meeting Hayden's return glare.

Brandon coughed. Continued. "The Inuit who were once local to this region had their own set of gods and superstitions, unique to any other tribe or culture. Just one example I came across was an immortal being the Inuit know as 'Sedna.' Sedna was once a young girl who upset the tribe and was cast into the ocean by her father for penance. When she tried to climb back into the boat, her father severed her fingers and she fell back into the sea. The sea goddess witnessed this and turned Sedna into an immortal being who spends her days growing new fingers to replace the old ones. When a finger is fully formed, they wriggle free from her hand and become the walruses that populate the arctic seas."

Amy's lips curled. "Eww..."

"What's this got to do with those freaks that chased us?" Hayden asked.

"I'm just giving you a sample of how ludicrous I know this sounds." Brandon took a deep breath. "The Inuit also believed in a shadow race of their own people, a sub-branch of the Inuit population who, after a long winter in which food was scarce and times were desperate, were forced to resort to eating their own kind in order to survive the elements..."

"That's it! Fat boy is going to eat us. He just confessed."

"Hayden!" Sophie scolded.

Amy covered her ears, not wanting to hear any more.

"I'm just telling you what I know," Brandon said.

Cody, whose attention had been grabbed by Brandon's story, encouraged him to continue. In the back of his mind he saw the floating skull, imagined the creeping black fingers of something that certainly wasn't human as they sought refuge in the school and gave chase to the group. The hairs on the back of his neck stood to attention.

"When the storm passed, the Inuit who refused to eat the... well... you know... banished those who had partaken in the feast. But they were hit with a terrible curse. A hunger passed through the cannibalistic tribe and they became insatiable. Soon enough people were going missing every other day, found somewhere in the woods with their stomachs open and their insides eaten out.

"They called them wendigos," Brandon stated, drawing out the word slowly from his lips. "Beings who crave human flesh but can never satisfy their aching hunger for more. Creatures cursed to roam the world forever in search of human flesh. Never full. Always searching..."

A pregnant silence filled the room. Cody and Sophie exchanged a look.

"You're talking about fictional creatures," Cody said at last. "Monsters from fairy tales and myth. You don't seriously believe any of that, do you?"

Brandon gave a weak shrug. "I don't know. I didn't believe that I'd also see the Aurora bleed, but that all changed tonight. Something's going on in the world right now, and we'd be stupid to think otherwise. Forces are in effect that we may never understand."

"Fuck!" Hayden slammed his hand on the keyboard and threw the mouse. It stretched to the end of its wire then sprang back and clattered against the wood, swinging flaccidly against the desk drawers.

Sophie and Amy jumped out of their skin. "What the hell is your problem?"

"I can't figure out pedo's password."

Cody sighed. "You scared the shit out of us."

"What, because of Fatboy's fairy tale? Come on, you're not really buying any of that, are you?"

Sophie chewed her lip. "Honestly, I don't know if it's the tiredness of the adrenaline wearing off, but I don't know what to believe anymore."

"I'm with Soph," Cody said, avoiding her gaze but noticing a wry smile in his peripheries. "Until we know what's going on, we can only assume that every possibility is a reality and whittle them down from there."

Hayden slammed his hands on the desk. "Fine. You really want to see what those things are? Let's go have a look. Let's poke our heads out and see, shall we?" He marched to the stairs and ran up two at a time.

"What are you doing?" Sophie called after him. Amy sobbed and recoiled into her shell. Cody met her at the bottom of the stairs and gripped the handrail as they looked up at Hayden.

Hayden pressed his ear to the door, eyes wide with excitement. "See? Silence. Bet they're not even out there anymore. They got bored and moved on."

He eased the locks open. Gripped the handle tightly. He teased the door a centimeter, then an inch, then a few more, until he was able to peek through. After a heart-stopping minute, he let out a sigh of relief and laughed. "See? Nowhere to be—"

The screech was deafening. Something sped toward them and slammed into the door with such suddenness that Hayden screamed. If he hadn't been holding the handle, he would have been thrown clean down the stairs.

"Lock the damn door!" Cody shouted.

Hayden quickly obliged, spinning the locks into place. The beating fists pounded against the door again, the screams penetrating the walls and the metal, forcing Amy to clamp her hands to the sides of her head.

Hayden took a cautious step back, turning gingerly to Cody and Sophie below. "Don't you say a fucking word."

Cody didn't need to. He was certain the look in their eyes was reprimand enough. They stepped away as Hayden eased himself down the stairs, his legs visibly shaking. The color drained from his face as he returned to his seat at the desk and stared at the floor.

Cody and Sophie glanced to the pounding door, then returned to their own places, the group sitting once more in silence.

Hayden swung in the chair, knocking his knee against the desk. A flash of something, one of the desk drawers sliding open slightly. He opened it all the way, eyebrows rising, even as the creatures slammed themselves against the door.

Packets crinkled. In his hands he held a number of glittering silver snack bars. "On the plus side, I've found us some food."

17

ALEX GOINS

"We have to get out of here," Alex whispered, teasing the curtains open just a fraction. The permeating white of the snow, somehow glowing and bright even under the blackening sky, stung his tired eyes, yet still there was no sign of the creatures.

Tori stood beside him, the warmth returning to her body as she clung onto his arm and rested her head on his shoulder. If he felt tired, she looked worse. Her eyes were dark, and she could barely keep them open. Sherri and Harvey lay on the couch, dozing, heads together, Damien strewn across their laps, looking as though they'd just come back from a twenty-mile family hike and weariness had claimed them.

"We can't leave," Tori replied softly. "If we go out there, we're as good as dead."

"What about your sister? What happened to the Tori that was prepared to traipse through a blizzard to find her? She's still out there."

So is Cody.

Tori cast her eyes downward. "It was stupidity. She's on the other side of town. We'd never get there without being hunted by those...

animals, or we'd freeze to death. We have no choice but to remain here until this all passes over."

"Do you really want to do that?"

"No." A pause. A lip quiver. "We have to."

Alex remained unconvinced. Ever since they had cleaned the wounds of their hosts, he had noticed strange behaviors that set him on edge. Harvey had taken to standing sentinel beside him, for a short while, at least. Until he began to wobble unsteadily on his feet and had to hold on to Alex for support. There had been a brief moment in which something akin to the low growl of an angry pitbull had rumbled up Harvey's throat before Alex convinced him to take a seat beside his wife and rest. Harvey relented, his eyes unregistering as he slumped over to the couch and fell asleep almost instantly.

In those few seconds of movement, Alex was almost certain that the blue irises of Harvey's eyes had all but disappeared, his pupils so dilated that they were almost black.

"It's not just your sister out there, Tori," Alex said. "Cody is out there, too. If these things are working their way through town, who knows if the kid is safe. I need to get out there and find him. He's not prepared for this kind of situation."

"And you are?"

Alex was taken aback by the question. He glanced at Tori, brow furrowing.

"You're not from around here. You don't know what these kinds of storms can do. I've lived in this town my entire life, and these blizzards incapacitate the town. Harvey was right. We hide out in our homes until it's all passed over, that's just the way it is. Even our bravest hunters bunker down until it all blows over. There's a reason we hold reserves of food and have built an entire way of life around surviving inside our houses. Our summer clothes are insulated, we have curfews in the coldest months, even our cops won't come out when things are this bad. The cold is a killer. You think those monsters are a threat, wait until you step into the heart of a blizzard."

Tori looked up at him in earnest, eyes sparkling as she spoke. Alex eased himself away, an idea coming to him.

"Where are you going?"

Alex placed a finger over his lips and pointed to the snoozing family. He nodded to the rifle in Tori's hands and signaled that she should keep watch. Tori obeyed, but not without reserve.

Alex crept across the room and padded up the stairs as quietly as possible, finding a nearby room with the door ajar. Tori had mentioned the stores of food and clothing, and that ignited something in his brain. Tori may not be ready to step out into the cold with her current attire, but she had mentioned that Sherri and Harvey were the owners of a clothing store. Surely that would mean that...

Yes.

The walk-in wardrobe was packed to the brim with snowsuits and insulated gear at the far reaches of their silent bedroom. Alex rifled through the stores and produced items that he believed would stand them the best chance of fighting the elements. Although the Duttons had offered them hospitality and a chance to wait out the worst of the storm, Alex couldn't rest until he knew that Cody was safe with him. What timing was better than now, when the creatures were nowhere in sight, and they had an opening to sprint across the town and find him?

They're not creatures. You know what they are.

Alex shook the thought away. His research of this isolated region had taken him down some deep rabbit holes into Inuit lore and the myths, gods, and rituals they believed in in this part of the world, but he was not insane enough yet to forsake the power of science and worldly knowledge to open that floodgate and let himself believe.

He threw a host of items on the floor, then took a quick detour to the bedroom window. He looked out onto the street, both glad that there was no sign of them out there, but also concerned at their lack of presence. He had written enough books and seen enough movies to know that silence wasn't always as comforting as one would hope.

At the top of the stairs, Alex signaled Tori's attention. He waved her to him, and she reluctantly left her post.

"What are you doing?" Tori hissed, eyes lingering on the pile of clothes at his feet.

"Suit up. We're going."

Tori's eyes widened. "Are you crazy? What about the guys downstairs? What about those monsters outside?" She kicked at a neon-pink jacket strewn on the floor. "I wouldn't be seen dead in something like this." She crouched, investigating the logo. "She told me they didn't have any new imports! I knew they kept the best stuff for themselves."

"Those things have gone," Alex said, ignoring Tori's frustration. "We haven't seen one in almost an hour. If we don't seize our time now, we're going to lose it."

"But Harvey... Sherri..."

"They're at home with their family. They're armed and safely locked in the place they want to be. My nephew is somewhere out there, possibly freezing to death, or terrified and stuck, and I need to get to him. I dragged him a thousand miles away from home, and I made a promise, okay? I promised."

"Promised who?"

Alex fell silent, eyes imploring. "If you don't come with me, I'm going alone. You can't stop me, Tori. Didn't you say that your sister lived out there, too? Not all that far from the school?"

"I did." Her words were flat, a sudden weight bearing down on her shoulders.

"Then let's go together." Alex imagined Cody's face, a pale blue in color as he shivered alone somewhere outside the school building. Eyes unblinking, lips cracked, tongue black. He had no idea what condition he'd find his nephew in. Had Cody even made it to the school? Was he lost and freezing in the snow? Was he with a friend somewhere inside the school, cold and terrified? The idea of it made him sick. He promised Kathrin and Tom that he would take care of Cody. He thought that a trip away from the epicenter of their pain would be conducive for his grieving, granting him some time away from the constant reminders, but instead more pain had been inflicted. This time physical and life-threatening.

What the hell were you thinking, Cody?

Tori examined the clothing with heavy eyes, picking up a crisp white snow jacket still freshly sealed in a plastic case. "This is insanity."

"I know."

"What if we don't make it?"

"What if we do?"

Alex was taken aback as Tori wrapped her arms around his body and hugged him tightly, her head resting on his chest. She remained silent, as did he. As much as he wanted to find some words to comfort her, he wasn't sure what was going on in that moment. Was it a mistake to bring her along with him? Would she be a weight holding him back as he trudged across the town in search of Cody? Should he have found a way to sneak out there alone?

Tori took a steadying breath, the flow quivering as it passed her lips. "I'm glad you found me." Their eyes met and, in that moment, Alex saw a wellspring of hidden strength as determination replaced the vulnerability she had displayed in the wake of the madness. "Let's go find them."

They emerged at the top of the stairs a short while later, Tori sufficiently wrapped in clothing that held the faint smell of Sherri's perfume. There was room to spare inside her jacket and trousers, too. While Sherri easily had an extra hundred pounds or so, Tori's supple frame left enough of a gap that the warm air circulated inside the suit and provided her with an extra layer of comfort. She had to tie the strings as tightly as possible and, even then, they felt a little loose. Alex found a hat and gloves that were far warmer than the ones he had bought in England, and as they worked their way downstairs, they fought to remain quiet as the artificial material of their new attire rubbed and squeaked with each step.

Tori took the lead, turning back to Alex and stifling a laugh at the sounds. It seemed childish, but it was great to have something to smile about. A fleeting passage of respite. Alex pressed a finger to his lips, his cheeks rising above the high collar of his jacket which covered much of his mouth. It was only as they neared the bottom of the stairs that the smiles slipped from their faces.

Commotion from the couch. The groggy renderings of a child waking from sleep, mixed with the feral growls of wild animals.

Harvey and Sherri leered at each other from opposite ends of the couch, eyes narrowed as though they hardly recognized each other. Their teeth bared and eyes dark. They crouched with their arms raised, fingers curled into claws as Damien pawed at his tired eyes in the middle of them and let out a sleepy yawn.

Tori threw a glance back at Alex who slipped past her on the stairs and stopped a short distance from the back of the couch. "Harvey? Sherri? What are you doing?"

It was a pointless question, and one that was answered without words as Harvey whipped his head toward Alex and snapped his teeth. Sherri took this moment of distraction to pounce onto Damien, straddling his lap as she stared down hungrily at her son.

"Tori. Gun!"

Tori readied the rifle, all of the extra padding making it difficult to sufficiently bend her arms. She awkwardly brought the sight up to her eyes as she aimed the gun at Sherri's head. "Alex? What the hell is going on?"

Alex held Harvey's gaze, the pupils so dilated that there was no white left in his empty eyes. There was a sly grin on his face as he coiled back, preparing to strike. "It's got to be something in those darts. Harvey? Talk to me, buddy. Tell me what you're feeling."

Alex slowly brought his own gun up, nestling it into the crook of his shoulder as he lined up the sight between Harvey's eyes.

Harvey growled.

Sherri growled in reply, licking her lips as Damien struggled to surface to wakefulness. He wriggled beneath her, giggling, as though this was all one big, parental prank.

"Oh God," Tori muttered. "You don't think..."

Alex gave a slow nod, concerned that any sudden movements would trigger something he couldn't control. "I think we now know the reason why the others have left the area."

"What are you saying?"

Alex sighed. "I'm saying that maybe those darts breed more of these damn things. Why stick around when their new recruits will do their dirty work for them?"

Damien pushed against the couch, fighting to sit up properly. "Damn is a naughty word."

Sherri growled, her face moving closer to Damien, saliva pooling in the corner of her mouth and dripping onto her son's cheek.

"Mom? Mommy, what's wrong with you? Mom!" Damien finally exploded, a terrified scream coming from his innocent mouth as he kicked and flailed beneath her weight, realizing there was nowhere to run. This wasn't a game he wanted to play anymore.

The scream was the trigger Alex hadn't been hoping for. The first domino to set several things happening at once.

Harvey leaped at Alex in a way that he couldn't have imagined possible for a man of his age. Not the stunted, clunky movements of a fifty-year-old attempting to jump from the back of the couch, but with an animalistic grace that confounded Alex's brain and caused him to hesitate. Harvey's hands grabbed the rifle and deflected the shot as Alex's finger squeezed the trigger and sent a bullet careening into the ceiling. The weight of Harvey fell upon him. They crashed to the ground, the rifle pressed against Alex's throat with alarming strength.

Tori's scream joined Damien's as Harvey leaped, yet she kept her eyes fixed on Sherri whose open maw now bore down on her son. Damien cried for help, his head disappearing from view as Sherri's weight pressed down. Her twisted face disappeared behind a curtain of tangled gray hair.

Tori lowered the gun, finding she couldn't bring herself to shoot. Instead, she grabbed a fistful of Sherri's hair, pulling her away from Damien. Sherri growled and swiped a hand at Tori, only catching the thick material of her coat. Her eyes blazed as she lowered herself for another bite at her son.

Damien's cry filled the room as Sherri reared back, eyes lit with fury and pain at Damien's meager swipe. He wriggled and writhed beneath her, trying his best to escape.

"Tori!" Alex groaned from the floor. "Take her down. Get her off him!"

Tori turned between Alex and Harvey, and Sherri and Damien, uncertain of what to do. "But..."

"Now!"

Tori made her decision, spurred on by the young boy's cries. She leaped over the couch and came up behind the unaware Sherri, lost in her own thoughts of darkness. She wrapped her arms around Sherri's chest. and with a quick tug backward, Tori caught Sherri off balance and brought her crashing into the coffee table.

Alex twisted his head from side to side, avoiding the snapping jaws of Harvey. There was nothing left of the true Harvey that Alex could see. Whatever poison was pulsing through his veins, it had well and truly taken over, and all that was left was the attack.

Strings of saliva connected Harvey's lips to Alex's cheeks, and Alex's invasive, curious mind wondered if that acted as a kind of primal guidance system, drawing Harvey ever so slowly toward him.

Harvey snapped again, his teeth catching the slightest edge of Alex's lobe. For an awestruck moment, Alex felt the tug of his ear as Harvey threw his head back, but it wasn't enough to do much damage. A mere crumb, teasing the palate ahead of the feast.

It was enough for Alex to fight back. He drew his knee upward, catching Harvey in the one weak spot that all men share, causing his body to cripple momentarily as Harvey folded into a ball.

Alex shoved, sending Harvey rolling beside him as he scrambled to his feet and aimed for Tori and Damien.

Damien curled himself into a ball in the corner of the couch, a perfect mimic of his dear old dad, tears streaming down his cheeks. He yelled out in surprise as Alex scooped the boy in his arms and held him close. "Tori, let's go!"

Tori nodded her agreement and ran around to the back of the couch, bringing the gun once more to her eye to cover the others. Alex didn't bother waiting to see what was out there in the storm, all he knew was that they had to get out of there. Something had taken Harvey and Sherri, and that something wasn't going to relent until they were all dead.

Or worse.

The storm met them with its eager embrace, but the residual heat and adrenaline temporarily shielded them, if only for a moment. Damien clung delicate arms around his neck, his woolen pajamas already growing damp under the onslaught of the snow. Alex cast a glance over his shoulder to check that Tori was with him...

Which was when the report of the rifle exploded.

Alex covered Damien's eyes with a gloved hand, running blindly into the snow as Tori took aim at the man clawing at her feet, gripping onto the cuff of her trousers and desperately pulling her toward his snapping jaws. A second report rang, staining the open door with patches of blood and oil as Tori gasped, then turned on her heels and ran to catch up.

18

CODY TREBECK

Davidson's drawer was filled with a variety of snacks. All of them unhealthy, sugar-filled, and allowing a glimpse into the final puzzle pieces that explained why the school janitor had put on so much weight over the years, taking regular days and weeks off to attend his medical appointments at the Denridge surgery.

Still, Cody was thankful for the opportunity to provide his body with some form of nourishment, as were the others. Sophie and Hayden argued about the best ways to distribute what he had found but settled at last with a system that allowed them each two bars to enjoy, while they left the rest in the drawer to discuss later. The only downside of all of this being that there was nothing to drink to soothe their crumby throats.

"This is ludicrous," Cody chuckled, the delirium of exhaustion coupled with the rush of sugar sprinting through his system. "We're surrounded by snow. Snow is water, and we can't even drink that."

Travis lay on the hard, dusty ground, his head propped up by his thick hood. Beside him, Hayden sat with his back against the wall, chin resting on his chest as sleep finally took him. "You want a snow cone? Why don't you follow in Hayden's footsteps and try to get out of here? I'm sure those things aren't still waiting for us."

Cody didn't miss the sarcastic tone of his voice.

Sophie sat across from Cody, Amy resting her head on her shoulder as she slept. Her brow was furrowed as she studied Travis, concern in her eyes. "Why do you do that?"

"Do what?" Travis' eyes were glazed, unfocused, his voice croaky and weak.

"Act like an ass when he's around? I know you. I've seen you in the halls and around the gym. You're nice when he's not near you."

Travis blew air between his lips, then stifled a yawn. "I don't know what you're talking about. Hayden's my boy. I'm his. We got each other's backs."

Sophie debated arguing with Travis, then decided against it. She rested her head on the wall and stared at the slowly dwindling candle. The flame's reflection pooled in her eyes and made them glitter like stars.

Travis chuckled.

"What?" Cody asked.

"Ah, it's nothing. Just hilarious that she can't see how much you like her. If I had someone staring at me like a serial killer, you think I'd have noticed by now."

"Likes who?" Sophie said.

Cody shot Travis an intense look.

Travis waved a hand, then let it fall to the floor. "Nothing. As you were, Goldilocks."

Sophie sat up straighter, gently disturbing Amy who smacked her lips and adjusted her shoulders. "Who do you like, Cody?"

Cody's heart stopped, the breath sucked out of his body. He grew warm and cold at the same time as he struggled to meet Sophie's gaze. "Oh, no one. Well... Not no one."

"You can tell me," Sophie said, a soothing tone to her voice.

Cody struggled to find the words. He couldn't believe that Travis had put him in this position. He wasn't even sure he liked Sophie all that much, not really. How long had he even known her for? A month? Maybe two? It would be crazy to think that he could develop a crush on someone strongly enough to supersede the feelings he felt for Holly Marsh.

But he did, didn't he? If anything, the last few hours with Sophie had only strengthened that ache in the pit of his stomach that made him yearn for her. Before, she had been just a pretty girl in the upper year who had been nice to him on a couple of occasions. Now she was a pretty girl stranded in an underground room with him after proving she could hold her own on the basketball court, and who also had the guts to put an asshole like Hayden in his place when he stepped out of line.

His eyes flickered to the soft red mark on her cheek.

"Cody?"

She tilted her head at an angle that exposed the smooth skin of her porcelain neck. Her eyes were pools of beauty which dripped onto the rest of her body and made her skin glow. Cody wanted to tell her how he felt, considered letting the truth fall from his lips...

"Holly Marsh."

The words left his mouth before he could stop them. They flew away with the virility of a butterfly, desperate to find its place in the world, too late to ever be contained by Cody again. He lowered his eyes to his lap, tearing his gaze away with a sudden embarrassment that burned his insides.

"Oh..." Sophie muttered, yet there was something in that tone. Disappointment, perhaps? No... "Who's she?"

Cody directed a leer at Travis, but found that he was already fast asleep. His chest rose and fell peacefully while he left Cody to pick up the pieces of the bombshell he'd dropped into the room.

"A girl that I knew from home," Cody said, unsure what else to do but be honest. "In my year. She sits across from me in math, and we hang out at lunch sometimes. She's pretty and fun and smart."

"Sounds like a match made in heaven."

"She's a lot like you."

The faintest trace of a smile flickered across Sophie's face. "I'm not sure how to take that."

Cody let out a soft laugh, spurred on by that smile. "I'd take it as a hell of a compliment."

Sophie's smile only grew. Color rose to her cheeks and now it was her turn to look away.

They sat in silence for a long while, observing the sleeping group around them and unable to communicate the things rolling around in their heads. It was only when Brandon started snoring loudly, his body folded into a strange Z shape as he slipped from his seated position to a slump on the floor, that they both tried to stifle their laughs with their hands.

Sophie sighed. "Tell me honestly, Cody. Do you think we're going to be okay?"

"What do you mean? Of course we are," Cody said, not fully believing his own words. "Why are you asking?"

"I just mean that... I guess that people don't really realize how bad a situation is until it turns from bad to worse, right? We could hole ourselves up in here for as long as it takes for those things—those *wendigos*—to disappear or for people to find us, but what if they don't come? You heard Brandon, what if the storm outlasts us? How long is this food going to feed us for? We can't live on that. How long until we need to drink water, or one of us needs to go to the toilet?"

"I'm pretty sure I went when those things chased us."

Sophie laughed, that delicate hand covering her pink lips. "I'm serious. How long can we really survive down here? And if starvation, dehydration, or those monsters don't kill us, I'm pretty sure I'm going to be killing him at some point soon." She jerked a thumb at Hayden. "I mean, can you believe his attitude? It's like shacking up with a bratty child."

Cody's eyes bore into Hayden. "I know what you mean. Look, I'm not going to say that I have any answers. Nor do I know much about this town or how it works, but I've seen enough movies to know that the good guys always win. We're the good guys in this situation. As long as there are people out there looking for us, we'll be okay. All we've got to do is wait it out and they will come. They will come."

Sophie lowered her head.

"What's wrong?"

When she looked back at him her eyes were glossy with tears. "Thank you. I needed to hear that."

Cody smiled, his own cheeks flushing red. "I'm telling you, as long as there are people out there looking for us, we'll be okay." They stared at each other for a long moment. Finally, Cody said, "Grab some shut-eye. I'll stand watch a little longer. You need rest."

Sophie nodded and was soon closing her eyes and using Amy's head as her pillow. Cody leaned his head back against the chill, hard wall, the aches in his body already starting to irk him. He stood up and stretched, allowing his bones and muscles to crack and creak. The room was silent, even the hush from the storm unable to penetrate their little underground bunker. The creatures...

the wendigos

...had been silent for some time, but Cody knew better than to test the door as Hayden had some time ago.

Cody took his phone from his pocket and tapped the screen. 03:54. How had so much happened in the last three hours? He imagined himself back in the cold dark of his room, struggling to keep himself warm. Never in a million years could he have imagined that he'd find himself here, stuck in the janitorial room with Brandon, Sophie, and the others. He wondered what Alex would say when he woke up to find that Cody was gone. A storm outside shutting him into the house as he hunted frantically for Cody. What if those creatures...

the wendigos

...were out there, too? What if they had already gotten Alex? Who would be coming for him then?

He pocketed his phone and stared down at Sophie, his heart fluttering as her shallow breaths grew deeper. It hadn't taken many of them that long to fall asleep, and Cody was terrified that if they all clocked out of reality at the same time then it might open a hole for the monsters to come. Someone had to stay awake. Act as guard.

So, let it be him.

Cody yawned.

That's not a good start.

He paced the room, moving as quietly as possible despite the thick soles of his boots. He traced a finger across the metal shelves of the chemical racks as his mind concocted insane methods of escape that included creating concoctions of various chemicals that he had never handled before. Could they make a bomb, of sorts? Blow their way out of this hovel? He wandered to a box of tools at the back of the room, its lid open, revealing the contents inside. He teased a box cutter from the pile and pocketed it. Who knew when something like that might come in handy? Perhaps when the others were awake, they could all find something useful to wield. He let out a derisive laugh. Six kids, armed with blunt and rusted melee weapons. What hope did they have?

He passed by Hayden, then stepped across Travis to examine a deeper recess set around the corner of a wall at the back. There was a dark strip of shadow where the light from the candle refused to reach, and Cody found himself holding up his phone, the flashlight activated on the back as he explored the darkness and discovered only more large gray bricks—yet another wall blocking them inside.

Only... was it?

Something soft brushed his cheek. The delicate kiss of a frozen butterfly. His fingers touched his face and, sure enough, there it was again. Air...

Cody moved closer to the wall. A steady breeze was blowing through the tiny pores of the brick. He held the light closer and confirmed what he was feeling, a series of small porous holes decorating brickwork and allowing some of the light to slip through to the other side.

To a *beyond.*

Cody turned over his shoulder to check that the others were all asleep, then clamped his phone between his teeth and placed both palms on the brick closest to the stream of air. He gave a gentle nudge, and nothing happened. Undeterred, he pressed a little harder, and was surprised to find that the brick shifted, creating an inch-thick indentation in the wall.

Cody shone the light on the wall and inspected his work. He pocketed the phone, then shoved the brick again, this time with such force that it sent the brick clattering into the darkness beyond.

19

KARL BOWMAN

K arl had never known a hunger like this.

His stomach cramped with every step. Tiny, skeletal hands wrapped around his insides and squeezed, their long nails puncturing into the fleshy sack inside of him.

But he shouldn't be hungry, should he? Not after eating so much of the woman growing cold and stiff in his bedroom. That was how he thought of her now. The woman. No longer could he associate her with her name or imagine her on their wedding day, her dress as white as the snow around them. No more could he remember the incredible resilience and strength she had shown on the day she pushed out a living, breathing baby from between her legs and blessed him with a daughter. Nor could he hear the gentle squeaks and grunts which escaped from her lips as Cadence nuzzled into him in bed, her smile all the sign in the world that she was happy and content, something Karl had never been.

To do any of those things would be to humanize her and see her as more than a sack of meat bleeding into the fibers of their wolf-skin rug. If he ignored those things, he could picture her as a skinned buck or seal, the stomach sliced as their life force pooled on the stone floor, dripping hungrily into the waiting grates.

Oh, that hunger.

Karl turned the house over in his hunt. He gripped the bottom rungs of Alice's wooden bed and flipped the whole thing in one heroic toss, one part of him hoping to find her cowering in the crevices beneath, the other praying that she was long gone from this place. What would be worse for a seven-year-old? To be tossed into the embrace of the frigid storm, or to be torn limb from limb by her father?

For that's what he knew was coming. His body wasn't his anymore. His arms, as thick and hard as knotted rope, flexed and throbbed with his hunger and an anger he couldn't qualify. His peripheries had darkened, and it took all of his concentration to be able to focus on what was in front of him. The chest of drawers came tumbling down, the doors to the wardrobe ripped off their hinges with ease. By the time he was done with the bedroom it was as though the roof had blown clean off and a tornado had unleashed its wrath inside the house.

And still the sentinels watched.

They didn't move, not an inch. Standing in their strange formation as Karl swept from room to room, tossing furniture, shattering glass, traipsing to picture frames and relics that had once been carefully preserved for years before smashing them off the walls and countertops. When he reached the bathroom, he caught his reflection in the mirror and gripped the edge of the porcelain sink with shaking hands. His eyes were dark, glinting like obsidian crystals in their sockets, his hair a sweaty tangle on his head. His beard was dark and crusted, matted with blood, and a part of him wanted to wash himself clean, but his body wouldn't allow it. His knuckles whitened as he let out an almighty roar, his strength taking over as the sink buckled and the faucet snapped. A concentrated spray of freezing cold water shot toward him and caught his face and for a second, he could see clearly, could see what he'd become. The cold was like a sudden slap, but already, as he turned back to the doorway and found the Masked One waiting, the darkness crept back in. The respite gone from the madness.

Downstairs soon told the same tale of destruction as Karl tore the TV from the wall and threw the couch clean across the room. Every cupboard in the kitchen either lost its door or was left hanging on a single hinge. Karl checked the garage, the understairs cupboard, his trophy room of firearms, and still he came up empty. His stomach ached for another morsel, his senses overwhelmed by the satisfaction that would come from his next meal. Where the hell was she? She couldn't have gone far. She was a child for fuck's sake.

Where the hell was she?!

Karl returned to the living room, head slumped, shoulders rising and falling with each labored breath. A steady, rumbling growl purred from his throat as he found the Masked One waiting at the bottom of the stairs. His sentinels nothing more than ghostly decorations to his curious aura.

"She's gone," Karl said flatly between breaths. "She's not here."

Again, that curious head tilt as the Masked One lifted a bony finger and pointed to the front door, toward a small entry room with coats hanging on large golden hooks on one side. Ordinarily these were full, with Karl, Cadence, and Alice each accommodating one of the hooks with their coats.

One was missing.

Karl drifted closer, unable to control his feet as he made his way across the room to investigate further. Her boots were gone, too. The neon-pink snow boots which Karl and Cadence had bought her only three weeks ago, bright enough that she shouldn't get lost out there in the snow. Karl still remembered the love that he felt for her when they arrived home and placed those boots beside his and Cadence's, the tiny things looking so small and fragile beside their own monstrous sizes.

A trace of a smile came to Karl's lips. He flicked his tongue across them, catching the dregs of the crusted blood as realization washed over him.

If he were to go out there now, he would not return empty-handed. Karl was a hunter, and one of the town's best at that. If he couldn't fight off these creatures now, then what hope did he have out there, in their world? What hope did Alice have of survival if they triggered his primal instincts and set him to the catch?

Karl took a steadying breath, regretting it instantly as the sickening scent of copper and sweat tickled his nostrils. He turned toward the Masked One, alarmed to find the being already standing only a couple of feet from Karl. When had he moved? Its footsteps made no sound.

The Masked One's eyes were level with his own. Karl wasn't used to others reaching his height, with most of the town's residents easily half a foot or more shorter than him. Already he felt at a disadvantage as he stared into those vapid black sockets and searched for any semblance of humanity.

"I can't..." The words came out weaker than Karl could ever believe capable from his throat. Each thought was laborious, as he sought to fight against whatever poison they'd injected into his system. "You will not claim her. She is mine. I will not do this for you—"

Karl's throat closed, invisible hands squeezing it shut. The saliva and drool that had been a constant presence in his mouth since the dart clipped his hip dried instantly as the Masked One closed the gap between them and stopped but an inch from his face. An alien, piercing shriek burst from somewhere beneath the mask and an overwhelming stench of death poured from the cracks and crevices of the stag's skull.

Karl had never felt so cold. Standing in this thing's presence was akin to opening the door to an industrial freezer you hoped you would never find yourself trapped inside, but suddenly it's too late and the doors won't open. His skin prickled. He wanted to cry, but the tears hardened and froze inside of him, a torturous pressure behind his eyes.

The Masked One pressed closer, moving infinitesimally slowly now until his mask rested on Karl's forehead. The moment they made contact, the chill was confirmed, shooting from head to foot like a bolt of electricity, the static laced with icy needles. Karl gasped, eyes closing as all that he knew was ice and hunger, a primitive aching drive once buried deep inside the Neanderthals of old, those who had survived the ice age and fought to the ends of the Earth to continue their legacy. He saw generations pass in the blink of an eye, stars wheeling overhead, exploding like fireworks. Green teeth of a dark forest against a sky burning with the kaleidoscopic colors of the Aurora. The skeletal shape of the world beyond death, a gathering of ritualistic fervor as some danced in the flames and many tucked their blood-stained faces into the hollows of their human prey. A great beast at the edge of the clearing, towering above its flock, skeletal ribs like organic scaffolding as the greatest and largest skull of all watched on, cavernous eyes, titanic hands, horns as wide as the rising sun...

Karl's breath came back in a sudden, urgent whoosh of air as though surfacing from a long dive. He opened his eyes and the Masked One was gone. His sentinels were gone. The house was devoid of anything but himself, a heavy silence the only thing keeping him company.

For an unfounded moment, Karl wondered if it had all been a dream. If all that he had seen and done that night had been cast in the clutches of a terrible nightmare.

But if that were true, why did his house look this way? Why were his face and hands sticky and dark?

And why was there a solitary bear skull waiting for him by the back door?

Karl's stomach bit with a sharp and sudden vigor. He crumpled over, falling to one knee as though his body was forcing him to bow to the skull. He glanced into the empty hollows where the animal's eyes had once sat and understood what it was he must do. What task he must complete if he was to ever feel full again.

Karl licked his lips and smiled.

20

TORI ASPLIN

Tori was tired of running, but what else was there to do? Every time she stopped, some horrendous event poked its greasy tentacles through the cracks and spurred her onward. If it wasn't those things coming for Stanley, then it was the strange projectiles they fired at Sherri and Harvey, devouring their senses and turning them mad.

Snow pelted her face, but at least she had some protection now. The clothes she had taken from Sherri's closet were dry, and that was something at least. While the cold was bad, it didn't seem so terrible when she was actually wrapped up and prepared.

Not that anything prepared her legs for the energy she would have to exert just to traipse through the knee-high snow that blanketed the town.

"Just a little farther," Alex called back to her. His jacket was unzipped, Damien clinging to him like a koala bear. Alex stretched the fabric of his jacket around the boy, but he couldn't get it to close. Damien had stopped crying, but now he was silent, lethargic, the cold slowly freezing his system.

"Give the boy to me," Tori said for the third time since they'd set out. "I've got more room in here. Please. It'll be safer for him."

Alex had already expressed his concerns that Tori wouldn't be able to carry the boy while they trudged—at least not for any measurable distance. Her slight frame wasn't built for the heavy exertion of lugging around an eight-year-old while also tackling the snow. Still, as he looked into Damien's face, the skin taking on a sickly blue hue, he had no choice but to relent.

"We have to find somewhere to take a pitstop," Alex said as he passed the boy and helped Tori cocoon him inside. Sherri's extra weight and size allowed just enough room inside the jacket to allow Tori to zip it shut. It was a tight squeeze, but the snugness of the operation actually helped to cradle Damien inside the material and relieve some of the mass.

The boy shivered in her grasp.

They had gotten lucky so far, hadn't met any of the creatures along the way. Not that they would be able to tell if any of them were close or watching, the wind and snow limiting their vision to little more than a twenty-foot radius as Tori shouted directions and tried to navigate using the only landmarks that they could find in the fuzzy gloom. She estimated that they had to be at least halfway across town, now. Though it felt like it should be more than that. Each step sapped their strength as the storm did all it could to block their passage. She wondered what would happen if those things found them now. The creatures were far more equipped for padding across the snow. Was running even an option?

"Tori?"

"Yeah... Fine. We can't stop for long, though. If we keep this stop-start going, we're never going to make it to them."

Alex's jaw clenched as a powerful gust blasted them. "Agreed. Come on, let's make it a little further and see what we find."

Tori soon grew thankful that Alex had borne the brunt of the carrying. If she thought walking through the snow in a blizzard was difficult, it was nothing to the strain that came to her back and legs as she took the extra weight and attempted to keep the kid warm. Fire spurred in her thighs, her calves, her ass. On a couple of occasions, her thoughts strayed to abandonment, wondering if they could simply drop the kid off at someone's door, knock twice, then run. But as she passed more darkened houses, her thoughts drifted back to Sherri and Harvey, and the monsters they had somehow become. How many of the townsfolk had been converted? Which of these houses, if any, were truly safe tonight?

The only thing she could trust in the world right now was the stranger leading the way before her. He carved a path in the snow, offering some respite from what could have been an even more burdensome journey. A man whom she had never met but heard tell of from the townsfolk. A stranger to these lands who was giving everything he had to battle the monsters and the elements to find his nephew.

A man with honor and integrity.

Something she had never found in Karl. Had their relationship been flawed from the start? Had she been kidding herself all those months, imagining that infidelity would be the ideal fuel to start the fires of a real relationship? How stupid had she been?

They came to an intersection where the road widened. From where they stood it was all but impossible to make out any other houses across the street.

"Which way?" Alex asked.

Tori caught her breath. "Straight ahead should be St Mary's, then it's pretty much a downhill slope until you get to the school. Probably about another half mile or so. Naomi's isn't too far from there, either."

Tori groaned as a pang shot across the muscles in her lower back.

"Are you okay?"

She nodded, though the pain showed in the wrinkles of her brow. "Yeah. Let's go."

After a dozen steps the houses crept into view like a fleet of ships appearing through a foggy ocean. There was a ghostlike quality to them, the snow softening their corners and edges, the roof so laden with the white powder that it was impossible to see where the houses ended and the sky began.

"There." Tori pointed ahead. "St Mary's spire. That place is always open."

"Even during a blizzard?"

"The pastor has an open-house policy. He doesn't want religion to be constrained to business hours. We're a small town, remember? You're not going to get your London graffiti artists spray-painting the side of our places of worship."

"You have a low opinion of London."

"I need to sit down."

The church was a little farther ahead, accessible through a side street that passed between the town butchers and the only bar in Denridge with a commercial music license to play the latest world-wide hits (not that that stopped the others). On a sunny day, you might find the cobbled street leading you toward the quaint church, flowers blooming in wooden boxes on either side of the street, but for the majority of the year snow covered the pebbles and petals. They funneled along, the church coalescing before them as they grew closer. Large wooden doors beckoned to them like the warm smile of a friendly stranger.

"Will it be warm inside?" Alex asked. "It's all stone and brick."

"It will be warmer than outside." She glanced down at the tuft of hair sticking out of her collar. "Besides, I'm worried about the kid. We need to wrap him up properly and check he's okay. He's been through a lot..."

Alex moved a finger to his lips, his eyes widening as he listened out for something that Tori couldn't hear. A second later she heard it. Someone was stumbling through the snow, mumbling incoherently. The occasional grunt.

Alex pressed Tori against the wall, finding a small recess where they attempted to shield themselves from sight. Alex's back, however, was still well in view as the mumbling grew louder. It was a man's voice, talking and babbling to himself as he walked alone through the storm.

Tori peeked her head around the wall as the man came into sight. From this distance, it was difficult to make out particulars, but Tori's heart stopped as she recognized the man's gait, his broad shoulders, his mat of beard. Although she had been tricked earlier that night, there was something about the way he moved that confirmed who she was seeing.

"Karl..." she whispered.

Alex kept his eyes fixed on the man as he walked across the street, only a short distance away. Lost in his own world, he paid no heed to the trio hiding in the crevice of the nearby building.

"A friend of yours?"

Tori's heart ached. "It's complicated."

"Maybe he can help?" Alex suggested, until he noticed the strange object on his head. "What is he wearing?"

Tori narrowed her eyes. While his dark beard sprang from his lower jaw, something white decorated the top of his head and blended with the snow. There were two dark circles atop and...

"That's a skull..." Tori couldn't quite believe what she was seeing. "He's wearing a skull on his head?"

"Is that normal?"

Tori didn't answer. They watched with morbid fascination as Karl drunkenly shambled onward until he was out of sight. They waited a few minutes, wanting to be certain that he was gone before they broke cover.

Alex led them the final distance toward the ancient church.

EPISODE 3

BLACK ICE KILLS

21

CODY TREBECK

The bricks fell like dominoes. Once the first was knocked clear, the rest struggled to hold together, collapsing of their own volition, as if the passageway had been waiting to be discovered.

Cody stepped back, mouth agape, eyes monitoring the situation through a lens of fear, terrified that this simple act of curiosity, of nudging a brick, would cause the whole room to fold in on them. And then what? The monsters wouldn't matter anymore because Cody and his group would be crushed to death, buried under the weight of the walls and ceiling, lost in the darkness of pedo cave.

The top half caved first, the bricks clattering into the darkness, fading instantly from sight. It was loud, too. Loud enough to stir the others who pawed their eyes and looked dazedly around for the source of their disturbance. Sophie was on her feet first, Hayden joining her quickly after. Amy and Brandon were slower to rouse, the bags beneath their eyes saying all that needed to be said about their energy levels and mental state. Travis remained fast asleep.

Sophie approached with caution. A steady stream of frosted air entered their safe space. "Cody? What did you..."

Hayden wrapped his arms around his chest, the fresh influx of air knocking the temperature down several degrees in one quick snap.

His brows knitted together as he stood behind them both, staring ahead into the darkness. "A tunnel?"

"Seems that way." Cody glanced at his hands where a layer of brick dust coated his fingertips. He rubbed them together, letting the dust sprinkle to the floor. "I felt a breeze through the wall. The bricks... it was like they weren't properly put in place at all. Like this was all hastily built up, used to cover something up, but poorly done."

Sophie inched closer, craning her neck as if she'd be able to see further than the darkness would allow. "What do you think's down there?"

Hayden shoved his way between them, bringing his toes to what remained of the wall line, a three-brick-high layer below. He gave the bricks a nudge with his foot and finished the desecration. "Shine some light, then. Let's see what we've got."

Cody brought his phone to eye level, activating the torch and shining it into the darkness. While the light was weak, it was clear that the wall blocked a passageway that likely hadn't been accessed for some time. The cone of light illuminated the way for a distance of thirty feet before the darkness consumed the tunnel once more.

Hayden gasped, a realization dawning on him. "I was wrong! The room isn't pedo cave, pedo cave is through this tunnel."

Sophie rolled her eyes. "Will you let it go? You think Davidson's going to have his own private tunnel with an entrance that he rebuilds every time he's finished diddling kids? That's absurd."

Hayden shook his head. "I once read a story about a man who kept his wife in the basement of his house for fifteen years. Declared her publicly dead, arranged a funeral for her and everything. Had friends over for dinner, threw parties, celebrated New Year, all while she was locked up beneath the house. Fifteen years. You telling me that there's a zero per cent chance that Davidson could have led his victims down here and just rebuilt the wall when he needed to? It's not like the wall was well put together."

Brandon appeared behind them, warily eyeing the passageway. "There haven't been missing children reports for years. If Davidson was taking kids away, surely some of them would be declared missing?"

"I didn't say he *killed* them." Hayden's brow furrowed. "Man, use your imagination." He stepped across the threshold and into the tunnel.

"What are you doing?" Sophie asked.

"What does it look like I'm doing? Finding out where this thing leads. If this is our way out of here, then what are we standing around for? Those things up there are waiting until we're starving enough and thirsty enough to come out. So, while they wait, I'm heading in this direction." He thumbed ahead, then strode onward until his form disappeared beyond the reaches of the light.

Sophie leaned closer to Cody. "You think he remembers that his supposed best friend is incapacitated?"

Cody stared into the darkness, waiting for Hayden to reappear. After a minute, nothing came. He sidled past the others and crouched by Travis, gently nudging his shoulders.

Travis came groggily out of his stupor, eyes struggling to open as the reality of where they were set in. "Oh, man. I hoped it had all been a dream." He scanned the room. "Where's Hayden?"

"Are you okay to move? We've found a way out of here. Well, sort of. We need you walking."

"I don't know, my head is still a little foggy." He pressed a palm to his temple as he attempted to push himself into a sitting position. He struggled until Cody gave him a hand, easing him up. Travis grimaced and took a sharp intake of breath. "I wonder if this is what a hangover feels like."

"We need to be careful," Brandon warned, standing over the pair. "If there's internal damage somewhere, anything we do could exacerbate it. The best thing for Travis is to lie down and rest until someone comes for us."

"We've already dragged him halfway across the school. He's come down a flight of stairs for Christ's sake." Sophie folded her arms, eyes laced with a mixture of fear and concern. "What further damage could we do? He's fine. Let's go."

Brandon deflated. "We're not really going to follow Hayden down there, are we? We have no idea where that tunnel leads. For all we know, it could go straight toward a whole nest of those things." He turned to Cody for comfort, but none came his way.

"We've got to do something," Cody said. "If we wait here, we're just sitting ducks. At least that tunnel could take us to other people who could help. We're just kids, man. We can't do this alone."

Brandon rubbed a hand down his ashen face. Cody was pleased to see his heart had stopped giving him cause for concern, though Brandon's face twisted as though the pain was still there. "Cody..." His voice was pleading, a negotiator talking a suicidal man off a ledge. "You can't be serious. This isn't a movie. We're not heroes. You said it yourself, we're just kids. We need to rest. We're safe here."

"You were the one that said this storm could last for weeks! We may be safe for now, but what happens if—*when*—those things find a way in? And what about the people looking for us? They come to the school and those creatures are just going to let them walk straight on by? We've got to fight for our survival. We're on our own down here."

Cody blinked away the image of Alex fast asleep in his bed, a horde of those creatures closing in on him while he dozed. As much as he wanted to believe that Alex was out there looking for him, the chances were more than likely that he wasn't. If he wasn't still asleep, he'd already be mauled by those things.

Only if there are more of them.

Brandon shook his head. "I've got a bad feeling."

"You're with us," Sophie added, taking a stand next to Cody. Her hand brushed against his. His ears flushed red. "As long as we stick together, we'll be okay. Come on, we can do this."

Brandon fought with the decision, his face going through a kaleidoscope of emotions.

To all of their surprise, it was Amy's soft voice that broke the silence with a simple, "No."

Sophie frowned. "No?"

"I can't. I won't."

Cody couldn't believe the change that had come over Amy in so short a time. She was a puzzle undone, every minute removing a single component of her carefully put-together persona. Looking at her now was like looking at an entirely different person. The composed, well-to-do queen of the upper grade had been dismantled at first by Hayden, but now fear had broken her too. Her shoulders were tense, her whole demeanor withdrawn. Her perfectly combed hair now displayed tufts of bushy nests. Her eyes, usually keen and bright, were now shadowed and dark. Tiredness bruised her complexion, and she struggled to hold back tears.

"I'm staying." Her words no more than a whisper.

Sophie offered a reassuring smile. "Amy, it's okay. Come on, stick with me. We've been through loads of crap together. Before. Me and you. It'll be okay, I promise you."

Amy's lip quivered. "Those things... You knocked down the walls... The only thing protecting us from..." She sniffed loudly. "And Hayden. He... he hit you."

Cody turned his gaze to the floor as Sophie looked his way. On the one hand it was gratifying to see that Hayden's actions had consequences, and at some point along their journey even Amy had figured out that her toy-boy boyfriend was an asshole, but on the other hand, no one should have to witness their friend beaten by the one they were supposed to rely on the most.

"Bitch." Travis chuckled as he raised his head and rested it against the wall. "You have no idea how lucky you are."

"Zip it," Sophie snapped, accompanying her admonishment with a finger.

Cody grabbed Travis' arm and aided him to his feet. "Just keep it quiet, yeah? Now's not the time to jump to your boyfriend's defense."

Travis wobbled unsteadily, eyes glossing over as they fought to fix on Cody. Something wet and warm hit Cody's cheek, and it didn't take long to figure out that the phlegm had come from the very person Cody was trying to help up.

"I'm done." Cody let Travis fall back to his ass. Travis laughed drunkenly the whole way down. "I can't do this. You want to be an asshole like him, then fine. I've dragged you this far, you can stay here and wait for the cavalry, but I'm getting the hell out of here."

He wasn't sure where the sudden burst of emotion had come from. Whether it was the tiredness, the hunger, the thirst, or something else entirely. All he knew was that he was done trying to help two guys who couldn't give a shit about what happened to them. Travis sat in fits of giggles while Cody turned his back and fixed his gaze on Brandon. "Are you in or out?"

Brandon gave Cody a pleading look. "Cody…"

"In or out?" Cody barked, his words echoing around the room and down the tunnel, as if they were chasing Hayden.

Brandon's eyes flickered to Amy, then to the floor. "Out. I can't, Cody. This is safer."

"Fine." Cody marched past Brandon and paused at the threshold of the tunnel. He fought back the hurt that was creeping through him, a mixture of guilt, shame, and anger as he contemplated his journey into the darkness. Brandon had been good to him, had stuck up for him during all of this madness. It had been because of Brandon that they made it here, to safety.

And all of this because *he* had dragged Brandon out of his house.

He placed a hand against the wall to steady himself, a wave of dizziness washing over him. He glanced back at Brandon.

Brandon shook his head, taking a seat beside Amy who had slumped against the wall. Travis was still in the final throes of his laughing fit. "We'll come back for you. I promise."

Brandon nodded. "I know." Even Cody could tell he was unconvinced.

Sophie tore her gaze from Amy who merely stared at the floor, all motivation and hope lost from her eyes. She pulled her hood tightly about her head and huddled her knees to her chest.

Cody held out a hand for Sophie. She tentatively took it in her own as he held up the torch on his phone and pointed it into the darkness, no sign of Hayden remaining ahead.

"Wait," Travis announced just as they were about to cross the threshold. He pushed himself unsteadily to his feet, wobbling dangerously as he gripped the nearest shelf for support. The items rattled precariously, the unit threatening to topple. "I'm not staying behind with these pussies. I want out."

Cody sighed. "If you're in, you keep up." His eyes caught the box of tools. "You might want to grab something from the bucket, too. Who knows what we're going to encounter along the way?"

Sophie nodded her agreement and rifled through the tools. She settled for a long-handled claw hammer, while handing a flathead screwdriver to Travis. She offered another to Cody who shook his head and flicked out the blade of the boxcutter to show that he was already prepared. A strange look came over Sophie's face, but it didn't last long before she hooked Travis' arm around her shoulder and guided him to the threshold of the tunnel.

Cody took Travis' other side, already scornful at the fact that he wasn't walking beside Sophie. The ghost of her touch warmed his hand as he offered one final glance at his pale-faced friend, then headed into the darkness, convincing himself that it would be better this way. They could come back for the others. Brandon and Amy would slow them down if they fell, and they needed speed if they were to survive whatever monsters were lying in wait in the dark.

22

TORI ASPLIN

W hile the church offered a brief respite from the winds, it did little to provide any warmth or comfort.

Tori kept guard as Alex dug away at the snow that blocked the opening of the thick wooden doors. As the storm raged and snippets of the town's crying pain fluttered on the wind, Tori kept her eyes fixed on the white, hunting for any sign of Karl or the creatures. Her mind played away at the strange visage that she had seen, a creeping doubt sowing seeds that were already taking root. How could that have been Karl? Shouldn't he be at home with his wife? Was the storm once again playing tricks on her fragile state?

Yet, it wasn't enough to shake the certainty of what she had seen. His lumbering stride, his powerful build. It had to have been him. And, if it *was* him, the bear's skull perched across his head was a sure-fire sign that the worst had come, and Karl had been taken by those creatures. First Stanley, then Harvey and Sherri. How many of the town's civilians had they claimed?

Tori stared at the snowy blanket of white, a consistent niggle gnawing at her. It pained her to think the worst of him. To think that he could be one of the unlucky few under their influence.

In the days before the storm, a smoldering gaze from Karl would earn a completely different response from Tori. He could incapacitate her with one of his brooding stares. A simple hungry look would make her weak at the knees. Would make her mouth salivate. Would grease the crease between her legs. His mere presence was an aphrodisiac that had her bending to his every desire, Tori a willing participant, strapped into the rollercoaster of his carnal urges.

Now, that stare just felt wrong. Unfamiliar. Violating.

Her thoughts filled with the last moments before he had left. A lifetime ago, it seemed. The emptiness that painted his eyes as he donned his coat and left her behind, the storm claiming him like an empathetic friend, drawing him into its warm bosom as Tori was stranded in the doorway, tears turning to icicles.

All had changed on the turn of a dime. The world flipped upside down into a maelstrom of madness. It didn't matter what life was before, this was life in the present. Survival or death were the only cards to be dealt. Tori only wished she knew how the game would end.

"Okay." Alex's voice came from a distance as he opened the door and ushered them inside. Damien snored loudly inside her jacket. She was relieved to ease him down inside the dark church and take the weight off her back.

The scent of damp wood and extinguished candles lingered in the air. Each footstep echoed, a stark declaration of their presence in the house of worship. Alex cautiously investigated the space around them, looking up at the expansive ceiling, a balcony rimming the upper floors to accommodate the congregation that could crowd the place on days of celebration or ritualistic worship.

"Are you a man of God?" Tori asked, removing her jacket and cocooning the boy on the floor. He didn't flinch, merely snuggled more tightly into the nest while Tori shivered and hugged herself.

"No. Sometimes I wish I was, but I've never subscribed to the notion that there is much out there we don't know. I believed in science. Science was my God."

Alex strode on, eyes lingering around the darkened corners of the room. Tori could feel it, too. The threat of the unseen enemy. While the windows were intact and the place appeared vacant, who knew what lay hidden in the shadows.

"Believed?" Tori asked. "Past tense?"

Alex nodded solemnly, a grim expression staining his features. It wasn't unflattering. "Are you telling me that science can explain those creatures and their magic?"

Tori deliberated a response that Alex wasn't waiting for. He lapped the perimeter of the pews, sticking to the outside of the rows of wooden benches as he examined the stained-glass artwork on the windows. When he reached the pulpit, he took a step toward the altar and poked his head behind a length of heavy black curtains. Satisfied, he searched the other side of the building.

Tori sat on the cold floor beside Damien and ran a hand through his hair. Only a small portion of his skin was on display, and the part that she could see was as white as the snow. Bags that were far too heavy for a boy of his age were painted in a dark shade of blue, and his earlobes had turned an angry shade of crimson.

She pulled the hood tighter around his face, burying all but his eyes and nose.

"How's he doing?"

Tori shrugged. "I don't know. How would you be if you'd awoken to find your mom ready to munch on you and two strangers ripped you from your home to drag you through a blizzard?"

Alex took a seat beside her, Harvey's rifle lay in his lap, ready. He narrowed his eyes at Tori. "What happened back there?"

Tori swallowed dryly, eyes unblinking. "You know what happened."

Alex recoiled a little, surprised by Tori's abrupt tone. "Both of them?"

Tori shook her head, not wanting to remember their faces, but hardly having the choice. What else could she have done? Harvey and Sherri were coming for all three of them. They weren't themselves. In the heat of the moment, her body took over, and the rest was history.

"Tori...?"

Tori stared at the floor. "Harvey is dead."

"And Sherri?"

"I..." She took a long breath. "I don't know. I don't think so. It's all a blur. I... I hope not..."

They fell into a reverent silence, the only disturbance the relentless hush of the storm. The wind screed and the windows rattled, a steady thrum of drumbeats as the snow pelted the ancient glass. Tori put her head in her hands and cried, her body racking with sobs as she let it all out. Every step forward on her journey was a punctuation mark of misery, and she began to wonder when the end of the sentence would come.

Alex placed an arm around Tori. It was a comfort that she couldn't appreciate enough. Despite the increasing reach of the storm's frosty fingers, Alex remained a bonfire, glowing in the midst of the darkness. His warmth seeped through her top and took the edge off the goosebumps creeping along her flesh. She nestled into him and let the tears fall as they may.

When her tank was depleted and she eventually looked up once more, Alex's face was somber.

"We can't stay here long."

She could see his trouble in his eyes. She suddenly remembered Alex's personal quest. "Do you think he's still at the school?"

"I don't know. If you had asked me an hour ago, I would have said 'maybe,' but it looks as though there's no space in this town that those things can't penetrate. No ground is sacred here. If Cody is still at the school—and God, I hope he is—then we need to move quicker than this." He turned his head skyward. "It's like even this storm is a part of it all, pushing back against our efforts to unite. Trying to keep us separated so they can pick us off, one-by-one."

Tori offered a smile without humor, the idea of a sentient storm absurd to her.

Alex looked at her earnestly.

"You're serious?" she asked.

Alex half shrugged. "We can't rule it out. If the world is giving you all the signs it has that there are things that exist in the realms beyond our understanding and knowledge, then who are we to rule it out?"

"Alex... It's just a storm. A blizzard. You don't get it because you haven't lived here, but..."

"Look at the signs, Tori." Alex freed his arm from her and rose to his feet, gesturing to the thick plumes of white gathered on the window ledges. "There was no warning sign for this storm, no one was able to predict it coming. My first week here I was told by the pilot about your weather forecast warnings. It's the staple of your life here, a core function of your safety. When was the last time a storm crept up on you overnight and completely blanketed the town? It's half the reason that I brought the kid with me. I figured we'd be safe. You think I'd bring him to a town where this kind of shit could happen?"

Tori opened her mouth to answer, but Alex continued.

"And those creatures out there... Are you telling me it's a coincidence that we get buried in snow, and those things choose now to attack? It's like they're in cahoots. Symbiosis. Without the storm, there are no creatures. Without the creatures, there is no storm. Something big is happening here, Tori."

Tori placed her hands around Damien's ears, the boy beginning to shift as Alex's voice rose. "Stop. You're scaring me."

Alex cast a pitying glance her way, his hand rubbing his forehead as he struggled to process. His face softened at Tori's look of despair. "I'm not trying to scare you, I'm trying to be realistic. All my life I've focused my research on the strange and forgotten stories that span to the world's farthest corners. All my life I've investigated stories about situations like this, looking at strange legends and myths of creatures that vanished into the pages of fiction." He kneeled beside Tori, his eyes imploring. "Tori, I believe you, okay? Everything you've seen tonight, all that you've witnessed firsthand. This isn't some collective psychotic episode that we're all experiencing. We're not going to wake up tomorrow to sunshine and rainbows. Those creatures that you saw... I believe you. I just... I didn't really want to."

"Why not?" A strong gust whipped the snow loudly against the window. They both whipped their heads in its direction. After a moment of quiet, Alex returned his gaze to Tori.

"Are you aware of the Iñupiat tribe who live out by the frozen coast?"

"The primitive ones?" Tori asked, finding it difficult to imagine a way of life that didn't involve plug sockets, electricity, and an internet connection. "Of course. Everyone in town knows of them. They have their borders and we have ours. It was an agreement set up decades ago so they could preserve their way of life. Not that I understand why they would want to."

"Last week I went to visit them," Alex explained. "Research for my book."

"You're a writer?"

"I'm an author."

"What's the difference?"

Alex fixed Tori with a look.

"Right..." Tori said. "Sorry."

"I stayed with them overnight, managed to speak to some of the tribespeople. Their customs and way of life are a world away from what we know in the modern world. It's more than just hunting with their bare hands and braving the elements. It's seeing the world through a lens that the rest of the planet seems to have forgotten. The Northern Lights, for example."

Tori scoffed. "The Aurora?"

"Yes."

"Let me guess, they spoke of the spirits of their ancestors and how they ride the lights at night in the forms of their animal brethren?"

Alex furrowed his brow. Damien's eyelids fluttered as he let out a soft cough. "It's more than that. It's not just the dancing lights, it's the legends and folklore that they hold on to, that they refuse to let go. There was a fear among the tribe, an unease that even I could pick up on, even though I didn't speak the language. You could feel it in the air. It's the same unease that has pervaded the air ever since I discovered that Cody was missing."

"What is it?" Her curiosity was piqued. Although she had spent most of her life ignoring the primitive tribe that lived a few miles out into the wilderness, she couldn't help but feel drawn to them somehow. They were an ever-present force, even managing to take the lead role in some of her nightmares as a child. Fears of the wild ones coming into town and snatching her from her crib, forcing her to obey by the old ways and learn the crafts of the ancient tribe.

Another knock from outside the church. Alex turned his head, ears pricked for further disturbance. To Tori, it didn't sound anything like the knocks she had experienced at her home when the creatures had come. Rather, it sounded more like debris thrown by the wind.

After a moment, Alex continued. "They told me a story one night —Pana and Meriwa, the couple who granted us shelter. As we sat inside their igloo, stew cooking over a modest fire, they told me of their monsters, of the creatures who governed their kind, and the horrors that were taught to their children, the sole aim to prepare and protect them from the bad things that creep from the cracks in the world's planes."

Alex fixed his gaze on Tori, no hint of deception in those bright eyes. "Among the line-up of myths and legends they spoke of the wendigo. A creature who roamed the frozen tundra, ever hungry for food. As they regaled their stories, there was no hiding the glint of fear in their eyes. They truly believed. This creature was no joke to them."

Tori ran a hand through her hair. "A wendigo? I don't understand."

Alex stared at the window as he spoke, his eyes growing vacant. "The wendigo was a legend of old, a tale of an Inuit tribe struck by a particularly harsh winter. Food was scarce, hunger ravaged the tribes, and in the end, as their own kind fell like flies, they turned to the only food source nature had granted them."

Tori gasped, a coating of bile lining her throat as she foresaw where the story was heading.

"The first to feed sated their hunger... for a short while, at least. While a large portion of the tribes held out hope for cleaner food, meat not marred by corruption, those who had feasted on the flesh of their brethren soon found that the hunger could not be abated for long. Something bred inside them, cultured into an aching hunger that ate away at their own bodies. Members of their tribe went missing, found in the woods days later and torn to shreds. Those who were caught were banished by the tribes, but even as they continued their attack, their bodies ate away at itself until all that was left was skin and bones. Rib cages like xylophones. Hips like worn cotton stretched across bone. Stick-thin arms that should have less strength in them than a toddler, but with the ability to grip their victims and pull them in with ease." He turned to Tori. "Sound familiar?"

It did. Tori could picture the creature so clearly. The strange, stick-thin man-thing which had perched on her windowsill. Its arms like bracken, spread wide like a bat with no wings. A devilish desire for food in its dark eyes as it came for Stanley and devoured him from the inside out.

"Wendigo..." Tori whispered, the word tasting like mold on her tongue. "I can't believe this is where we are. I want to pinch myself and wake up."

"Me, too," Alex agreed. "I don't think that's an option right now." He paused, looking ready to say something else, unsure if he should.

"What is it?"

"There's more. I just don't know what it is, entirely. When I was with the Iñupiat, there was something else going on. Something secretive that they refused to discuss. My interpreter, Roark, he told me that the tribes would often allow visitors to grant a hello and well wishes to the village chieftains. However, when I pressed to see if it was possible to gain an audience with them, I was denied."

"That's not so unusual, is it? People of high positions have lots to attend to."

"It's more than that." Alex chewed his lip. "It was as though they were actively pushing me away from the request. After Roark raised this, they grew colder, more hostile. While they allowed us to stay the night, we were ushered away the next morning, with no chance to seek further counsel or even apologize."

"What are you saying?" Tori asked.

Alex sighed. "I'm saying they were hiding something. I don't know what, but something wasn't right. At the time I put it down to a clashing of cultures, but now... Now, I'm not so sure."

A thud against the window. This time Tori caught it out of the corner of her eye. A dark object thrown against the glass, its wings spread wide as it collided with the building and fell from sight. A delicate spray of blood stained the window.

Alex nodded down at Damien. "Take him behind the pulpit, tuck yourself away." He adjusted the rifle and trained it at the window. When Tori didn't move, he added, "Now."

Tori obeyed, her body slow to wake up and function. Sitting down had drained what remaining energy she had, and the cold was once more nipping at her skin. Alex stalked away as she picked Damien up, finding a nesting place in the cutout behind the pulpit. Damien groaned, eyes struggling to open. "Mom?"

Tori settled him on her lap and placed a finger over her lips. "Not now, Damien. We have to be quiet right now. Can you do that for me?"

Damien groggily nodded. Tori was glad to see movement from him. For a while, she wondered whether he had entered some kind of frost-induced coma. She patted her side and found the reassuring butt of her rifle. She brought it into sight, to a comfortable position where she could shoot, if necessary. Looking up, her eyes locked onto the intricate decorations of the church. Painting the walls around her were cutouts of the Lord and Savior, Jesus Christ. Ornaments and pictures of the man that so many of the world looked to as a beacon of hope. His gentle face watched over them, hands pinned to the far reaches of the crucifix with thick and bloody nails.

She wondered if any place was sacred from the creatures that hunted, and if there was even the slightest hint of truth behind Christ's legend. Just in case, she silently communicated with the inanimate objects, pleading that now would be a great time for the Savior to perform one of his miraculous interventions.

She didn't hold out for hope.

Nor was any given.

23

KARL BOWMAN

The storm embraced Karl with affectionate arms, swirling around his body in dizzying motes and eddies. Though he wore his usual jacket, designed to combat the chill and keep him warm in the frigid temperatures, his forehead was slick with sweat behind the bone mask, his breath coming in short bursts as his insides boiled and it all became too much to bear.

His nostrils flared as he sought her scent. His mouth hadn't stopped salivating since he had left the house, and he was certain he could detect her somewhere on the wind. A tantalizing sample of her flesh. If only the storm would relent a little, maybe he could speed up his journey through the snow and claim her.

Sate the hunger.

The town was beyond recognition. Karl had been in storms and blizzards before, but nothing in his waking memory compared to this. Nothing that had overtaken so quickly and was determined to blanket everything until all that was left was white. He passed houses with citizens tucked away inside that he might once have called neighbors, but never friends. He passed storefronts and statues and front yards buried under snow. As he passed by the church, he fancied that he might have detected Alice's scent, but as quickly as it had come, it was gone.

And where were the others who were supposedly aiding his purpose? Where were the sentinels and the Masked One who had gifted him this condition? Stirred up the famished frenzy in his hollow stomach and made him yearn for that which the world was determined to deny him? Where was he?

Nowhere, and everywhere, all at once.

Every sense was heightened. On the wind came the screams and cries of the townsfolk, melting under the thawing hand of his new brethren. Every drop of snow tickled his nerve endings and sent currents of electricity running through his system. His ability to smell their blood drove him crazy, he could still taste the lingering tang of metal on his tongue. Where the storm had once limited his vision, he could now see further, just able to make out the silhouettes of figures running for their lives. Some were the meal, and others were the bait. He knew that now, of course. Could understand more of the ecosystem which the Masked One had blessed him with. They were all connected, somehow. A single purpose to destroy, eat, and recruit as the storm wore on and granted them the cover they so desperately needed.

Without the storm, their adventures would be over. Time was a ticking clock, and no clock ran backward.

Karl's hands rose to the mask, the very act of wearing it on his head a claustrophobic experience. His breath misted the inside and heated up his face. It became unbearable. As he stalked through the snow, hunting for footprints and searching for his sweet darling daughter, he removed his jacket. Pleased by the drop in his own feverish body temperature. Beneath the jacket was a long-sleeved cotton shirt, a bib of crimson staining his front. The snow attacked the cotton until it was dripping wet and white and soon that layer too was gone.

To be shirtless was to be free. To be one with the storm was a blessing, each snowflake like the tongues of a thousand heated whores, attentive to each throb and desire that sprang to his imagination. Strolling in the snow was ecstasy, the chill becoming a part of his system as his skin turned white beneath the thick wires of dark hair that matted his chest. His shins felt none of the ice the snow had to offer, instead appearing to melt with each trudging step forward, allowing his passage through the worst of it.

A door opened up to his right, a man standing in its frame with a shotgun pointed his way. A familiar voice called, "Karl? Is that you? What are you doing out in the storm like that? Get inside, get warm. Come on in."

Karl obliged, accepting succor for the duration that it took to pin old Charlie Moxon up against the wall and crush his windpipe with one clenched fist. A young man who had inherited his father's house, Charlie lived alone, and that was a shame. As Karl sank his teeth into Charlie's neck and tore at the wiring of his biology, he only wished there would be a sweeter reward for his efforts. Charlie's blood gushed to the floor, pulsing like a broken faucet until Karl's arms were too slick to hold him airborne any longer. But the Masked One had prepared him for such, and to dine on all fours was a pleasure in itself. To bear down like the animals we once sprang from gifted Karl with an erection that pressed against the fibers of his trousers and made him ache with pain.

And then he was back out in the storm, free of all clothing. A stained trail of red in the snow that soon trailed away. He licked his lips and cleaned the last of the warm liquid from his face as his stomach digested the bits of Charlie that were chewy and nourishing.

Not that the nourishment and satisfaction would last for long. Only a minute later, his stomach ached again, longing for that which he could not find. Calling out for sustenance.

Karl growled, baring his teeth like a rabid jackal. The growl grew to a bark to a roar of rage. His muscles coiled as he belted his frustration at the storm, adding to the cacophony of torture sung around the town.

He roared until he was breathless, cried until he was hoarse, then doubled over and fell forward into the snow. His hands pressed into the fresh powder, sinking several feet, his face imprinting on its surface. The snow was wet and refreshing, but it didn't abate the gnawing sensation in his stomach. He pushed back onto his knees and was alarmed to notice that the thick padding of abdominal muscles he had earned from years of hunting and manual labor had shrunk, had diminished just a little, as if something was eating him from the inside out.

Panic set in as a glimpse of the reality of his situation called out to him. If he didn't eat, he would soon starve. If he didn't sustain his strength as he sought to find his prize, he would have no strength left to hunt and capture her. And then what would the Masked One say? What would he do?

He sniffed the air, closing his eyes to draw more attention to his senses. Something familiar swept along the current of the breeze, a tickle of something he had smelled before, but now struggled to identify.

Karl looked out at the white street behind him, a wicked grin growing on his face as he licked his lips and climbed to his feet.

24

CODY TREBECK

The good news was that, once they had made some progress through the tunnel, Travis seemed to find his legs. Instead of Cody and Sophie holding him upright, it wasn't long before Travis took his first independent step and lessened their load.

The bad news was that the tunnel was endless, and Hayden was still nowhere to be seen.

Cody's phone flashlight only stretched so far into the darkness, and those parts which did illuminate didn't fill them with much hope. A hundred feet into the tunnel the walls were cracked, ancient brick, slick with a thin layer of damp moss and lichen. Along the way, chunks of the wall were missing, revealing only dark, packed earth beyond. With every step the temperature dropped, increased the chill. All too soon they were well and truly removed from the pair they'd left behind.

Sophie and Cody hardly talked. With Travis acting as a social barrier between them, there was no opportunity to say what was on either of their minds. Cody still felt the soft warmth of her hand and only wished he could grasp it now, offer some semblance of comfort to her. The edges of her features caught the glow of the light, harsh and shadowed on one side, but even he could read that she was uncertain of their way ahead. The same question plaguing both of their minds: what if this road leads to nowhere?

Travis, meanwhile, muttered to himself, his limbs occasionally jerking in random spasms. It seemed that lack of food, and a heavy blow to the head occasionally removed Travis from the knowledge that he was walking in the company of others. "Never going back now. Nah-uh. Make it out of here. Find him first. Woop."

Cody did his best to ignore him, but the truth was that he was concerned. On the rare occasions Travis did look ahead, his eyes were glassy, pupils dilated. Something wasn't right, but what was he to do? None of them could do anything until they'd figured out a way out of here, and even then, what was waiting on the outside? How quickly could they bring Travis the medical attention he needed?

Twenty minutes into their walk, they came to a fork in the road. Here, the tunnel stretched wider, allowing them a little breathing room from the cloying closeness of the length they had traveled. When Cody and Sophie stopped to examine which route they might take, Travis continued ahead, acting as though he hadn't noticed either of them stop.

"Travis," Cody called. "Travis!"

Travis stopped, ears pricking up as though he had just woken from a dream. He whirled unsteadily and raised an arm to block the stream of light which attacked him and lit him up in white. "Dude, switch that thing off. I can't see."

"You won't be able to see anything at all with it off," Sophie said, moving to Cody's side and lowering his hand so that the beam pointed at the floor and softened the glare. "Are you okay, Travis? You don't look so hot."

"I'm fine. Just dandy." His eyes narrowed as he turned in a slow circle, hunting for something neither could see. "Where'd Hayden go?"

Cody and Sophie exchanged a look.

"Hayden went ahead," Cody replied. "Don't you remember?"

Travis raised an eyebrow and chuckled. "Don't be stupid. Hayden wouldn't leave me behind. We're best buds. He wouldn't." Although he protested, doubt plagued his eyes.

Sophie stepped cautiously forward. "Travis, I know you think you're feeling better, but you've got to take it easy. I'm worried about you."

"Worried?" Travis waved a hand and laughed. "Worried about what? That me and Hayden are going to save the day and you're both going to be nothing more than a footnote in our story of bravery? Seriously, where the hell is Hayden?"

"We don't know," Cody raised the torch at each of the tunnels. The smell of damp and rot was overwhelming, and it wasn't until he raised the torch to the ceiling that he saw why.

There was a hatch above them, square and wooden, the beams bent and sodden with damp. Mushrooms and moss grew in the cracks, and in certain areas they could make out the white of snow above.

"What do you think that is?" Cody asked. "A way out?"

Sophie brushed her hair from her eyes. "If it is, there's no way we can reach it. It's too high."

"Yeah, if you're a pussy." Travis laughed. "That can't be more than ten feet up. I've dunked that high before."

Sophie rolled her eyes. "I call bullshit."

"Oh yeah?" Travis said, eyes narrowing. He crossed to the wall and examined it, brushing a hand across the slick surface. "If that wall wasn't wet, I could use it to pop myself up and grab those beams."

Sophie folded her arms. "Well, the wall is wet, so what do you suggest instead?"

Travis chewed his lip, then took a step back.

"Don't even try it," Cody started, but before he could finish, Travis ran at the wall. He raised a foot and hooked it into a small crevice, using the traction to push up and gain extra height. His body rose, gaining enough distance that his fingertips scraped the beams. A moment later, he was plummeting to the ground.

Cody was there to catch him. He hooked his arms under Travis' armpits and supported him, the pair of them collapsing onto the floor, Cody landing on his ass, Travis landing on Cody's lap.

"Get off of me," Travis declared, rising quickly to his feet. His eyes drew slightly inward as he swayed, hand moving to his head as he fought to maintain his balance.

"Are you *trying* to kill yourself?" Sophie offered a hand to Cody and helped him up, handing him back the phone. Her eyes lingered on the display screen. "Your battery's nearly dead."

"I know."

"Which way do you think we should take?"

Cody cupped his hands around his mouth and spoke toward the center of the fork. "Hayden? If you're down there, let us know which way you went so we can go the other."

He paused. Listened. Nothing.

"Worth a shot."

Travis managed to stabilize himself, a drunken grin on his face. "Let's just pick already. No sense wasting time, is there? Not like we're getting there any faster by being hesitant." A look of confusion came over him as he stared intently at Cody.

"What is it?"

"Where's your ball?"

Cody looked down at his feet, as if the basketball was going to be there and waiting for him. A wave of sadness crested as he pictured his prize basketball somewhere in the school, left behind in their desperation to escape the creatures. It all seemed so long ago now. Another age.

Cody closed his eyes and composed himself. When he opened them, he walked past Travis, aiming for the right-hand tunnel. Sophie followed behind him, taking a moment to wave Travis ahead of her as they crept on further into the darkness.

As their footsteps clattered around the stone, the echoing sound masked the gentle steps that approached from somewhere in the tunnels.

25

ALEX GOINS

Alex stood by the door, ear pressed against the cold wood. Outside, the wind erased any real possibility of hearing oncoming danger, but he still wanted to be careful. The church had more entrances and exits than Harvey's house, and an ill-thought could leave them all vulnerable to predators.

For that's what he saw them as now. Predators. Hunters. Alex, Tori, Damien, anyone left alive and breathing in the town, they were simple fodder for these things. Nothing more than prey for...

...the wendigos.

Alex knew how crazy it sounded, and there was a part of him that was concerned for his fertile imagination. For years he had dreamed up fictional scenarios for characters, stretching the truth to suspend the disbelief of his readers, just so he could add a little entertainment to their vanilla lives. In each book, he made a point to explore the macabre, the forgotten, the wonderful, the extraordinary.

Which category did these creatures fall into?

His breath came in short bursts. As much as he maintained his composure around Tori and Damien, he was terrified. Alaska was a world away from England and, in that moment, he had never felt farther away from the familiar. He wished he was home. More than that, he wished he hadn't dragged Cody along on this journey with him. Everything would have been okay if they'd simply stayed put in the dreary landscape of foggy old London.

He teased open the door, glad to find little resistance from the snow. Beyond the door was a short entryway that blocked the worst of the slush from piling up and blocking him in. He closed the door behind him, then crept forward and pressed his back to the stone wall.

The place was deserted. A clean white postcard painting, reminding Alex of the time he had fallen asleep in class at school and woken to a full panorama of a blank sheet of A4 paper. To his left, the gray stone walls melted into white, but not before he could make out the odd dark shape in a soft bed of snow.

Keeping the rifle trained ahead, he strafed left, walking with determined purpose until he found the object. He breathed a sigh of relief, identifying the poor bird lying crooked and dead in the snow. A song sparrow, if he wasn't mistaken. Its beak was crushed, its neck bent at an odd angle. Its wings were spread wide, already clumped with the snow that showered from the sky. It wouldn't be long before the sparrow was just another creature buried and lost in the storm.

Alex cast a glance to the window, wondering what the bird had been doing out in the blizzard like this. To his knowledge, animals hid away when the elements were against them. With a freak storm like this, he would have imagined that they would be extra careful, their instincts tuning in to the primal protection frequencies that humans had lost long ago.

With a final sympathetic look down at the sparrow, Alex started back to the door. He kept his gaze on the horizon—what he could see of it, anyway—but no threat came.

From that direction at least.

When the scream came, it sounded from inside the church.

26

AMY LAWSON

E verywhere Amy turned, it was like looking through a tunnel of fog. The edges of her vision were framed in a haze of smoke, her exhaustion forcing her eyes closed while what remained of her common sense fought to stay awake.

She couldn't take a guess at what the time would be anymore. There was no way to know what the weather was like outside, or if anything had changed in the overworld since their descent into this cramped and uncomfortable underground bunker. Life existed in a vacuum, and she was only a witness to the horror that plagued her since they had arrived at the school.

She thought it would be different. She knew that she was taking a chance in dating a younger boy—one from the year below, no less. But Hayden was a shiny object, the king of the roost, and she knew that there was nothing those little bitches in her year could say to her that would make her change her mind. Amy thrived off rebellion. Her mother baked it into her blood. If her father was still around today, he might have a few words to say, but he wasn't, was he? So, what was the point in concerning herself with the disapproval of ghosts?

Life was hard and living at home only exacerbated the problem. There was no sense of control in Amy's life. No discipline, no real reason to try. While dating Hayden felt like an effective way to stick a middle finger up to the girls in her own grade, she soon found that she had fallen for him.

Fallen hard.

Hayden acted older than his age. He was a man among boys. Certain to be a future prom king. The cream of the crop.

And didn't Amy deserve the best? Hadn't her life been a hunt for premium? A desperate effort to keep the things that mattered close to her, no matter how material or expensive those items truly were, even if she couldn't afford them?

Amy knew she was conventionally pretty. Boys had fallen at her heels from the moment she looked into the bathroom mirror and saw the first sign of her breasts coming in. Small buds which had already matured to the point that the underwire of her bras were biting into her flesh. The other girls spoke behind their hands in envy, boys in the lower grades stared. It was all the attention that Amy craved, and she rode that theme park ride to the top of the hill. She played the game of high school, knowing which levers to pull and which pitfalls to dodge. If the big wide world beyond was just another high school, she'd be the triple letter signature at the top of the arcade's leader board. AMY. Three letters. Complete.

But life wasn't a high school, was it? She was learning that the hard way. In those precious moments where the world scrambles what is known and distorts the lens of your reality the truth breaks out without remorse. Hayden's true nature had been revealed, and it was grotesque and heart-breaking.

Initially, she had thought Hayden was playing around with his snappy remarks to Travis, Cody, and Brandon out in the snow. She figured that maybe things were just getting a little heated when Hayden headbutted Cody in the gymnasium.

She had no excuse for Hayden's behavior when he hit Sophie. Her dear friend Sophie. The only true friend she had. The one girl who listened when she was upset, and with whom she could trust with a secret. What had Hayden done to her? Where was she now?

When the monsters came, that had been the final shattering blow.

The glass floor cracked and fell away and all that Amy knew was fear as she fell. Nothing prepared her for this moment, to be trapped in a cold, dingy room with a boy she had hardly noticed in the halls, but yet here she was. Paralyzed, drained, and drifting into some far away land.

A land of the voices.

They whispered to her now in delicate croons, riding the gentle purring of the wind, softly tickling her eardrums with their sweet promise of succor. Voices she didn't recognize as human, yet could interpret their every syllable. They promised hope, spoke the words she so desperately craved to hear, promised Amy an out.

Brandon cleared his throat, head resting against the wall. His eyes were closed, head angled to the ceiling. Sleep would come soon. Sleep seemed to hit Brandon like a sledgehammer, and when his breathing turned to snores, maybe then she would try...

She couldn't pinpoint when the voices first came. All she could guess was that in the frenzy of their sprinting through the halls and the chaos at the top of the stairway they had broken through the barrier. When her eyes were closed, thoughts pervaded her dreams, visions plaguing her of simply walking out of this janitorial dungeon and into the school. Her mother would be waiting for her there, her online game of Scrabble forsaken, her iPad resting on the table beside her latest glass of vino. Brandon's mother would be there, too. Sophie's and Cody's beside her, Hayden's waiting by the door. They would be smiling, waiting with open arms to tell them the monsters were gone, and all would be okay.

All would be okay...

A single tear traced down Amy's cheek, her lips pursed together as she fought a fresh wave. Her eyes fixed to the highest point of the metal staircase. She didn't want to be here, couldn't stand being here a moment longer than she needed to be. She was thankful to have Brandon beside her but, more than anything, she wanted her freedom.

The walls closed in, claustrophobia squeezing its pressure on every part of her body. She choked from it, her tongue too large for her mouth, as though it was blocking the air from entering her throat. Her hands were clammy inside her gloves and as she pushed herself to her feet, she choked up a little, a strange guttural sob escaping her lips. Her head pounded, her eyes blurry.

She glanced down at Brandon, blood running cold as his eyes fixed on hers.

"Are you okay?"

Amy turned her gaze to the top of the stairs.

His eyes widened. "Are you crazy? Don't even think about it."

Amy took a step forward, eyes closing as Brandon clumsily stood. She swallowed loudly, then took a long breath.

"They're still out there. You know that, don't you?" Brandon's voice was soft, urgency in every syllable. "Whatever you're thinking right now, this is the safest place. If the others come back, they'll come with help. You're safe with me. Trust me. Please."

Amy took another step.

Brandon delicately touched her arm. "Amy..."

Amy couldn't tear her eyes away from the door. Now that she was closer, she knew that all it would take was a few bounding steps and she'd be out of here. She could outrun those things. They'd all done it once. Run to the door they had arrived through, sprint through the snow, make it home before morning crowed and her mother realized what had happened

Mom...

The voices confirmed her desire, tempting her with every line. Soft hisses speaking Shakespearean sonnets.

"Amy." Brandon's voice grew sharp. She hadn't noticed him walk in front of her, but now his rotund body filled her vision. "Sit down. Let's talk this through."

For a moment they simply stood, Brandon scanning Amy's face while Amy stared blankly ahead. Eventually, she broke, and Brandon guided her back to the wall where she slid down and took a seat, head tilted to the side, eyes staring vacantly at the floor.

Brandon rooted through the desk drawers and brought them both a snack bar. He offered Amy two, but she declined with a gentle shake of her head.

"You need to keep your strength up," Brandon said, munching away at his own bar. "We've both been through a lot. Food will help. Sleep will do better."

Amy reluctantly put the bar to her mouth. She bit down, but labored each chew, not gaining any joy in the flavor. What should have been a sugary delight turned to gray mush, she might as well have been eating ash.

"Talk me through how you're feeling."

Amy didn't reply. What was the point? He'd never understand.

"Amy, we're in this together, remember. You're not alone. I'm here with you. We'll get through this."

Brandon continued, but Amy wasn't listening. As her mouth robotically chewed the bar, her thoughts drifted off to better times. In her mind she was sitting on the couch, sharing a bottle of wine with her mother. Her father was off in the garage tinkering, as he so often did before his passing. The sun shone through the windows and the stereo played the blues. Her mother always loved the blues. She loved the saxophone. Amy always pictured herself falling in love with a saxophonist, dulcet tones soothing her to sleep each night.

Hayden couldn't play the saxophone.

Nowhere in Amy's vision was she trapped underground. Nowhere in this vision was she held hostage by a fat nobody who thought he knew what was best for her.

Nowhere in this vision was there a series of unidentified monsters waiting beyond the door.

Nowhere in this vision had Hayden broken her trust and attacked her best friend.

The door was a portal.

A portal to freedom.

And Amy was desperate to step inside.

27

TORI ASPLIN

From the moment Alex faded from view, Tori felt uneasy. He was her comfort blanket, her protector from the storm and its minions. Even just the mere notion of Alex disappearing from her line of sight put her on edge. How had she become so dependent on this stranger so quickly?

Damien shifted in her lap. He cuddled against her, affording her some of the warmth back from her jacket. She unzipped it and placed the jacket around them both once more, each body feeding what little warmth there was to the other.

"Excuse me?" Damien whispered, his voice barely audible.

Tori offered a reassuring smile. "Yeah?"

Damien considered his response, eyes sparkling with an intelligence that seemed beyond a boy of his age. "I think I had a bad dream. My mom and dad had..."

Tori swallowed dryly. "You can say it..."

"...turned to monsters."

Her stomach twisted into a painful knot. Since her talk with Alex about his visit with the Iñupiat tribe and the threat of the creatures they were facing, she had pushed back the memories of what had happened at Harvey's house. Now they came flooding back in high definition, the recoil of the rifle that jarred her arm as she aimed down at the floor and...

The boy read something in Tori's face and lowered his eyes. "Are we going to be okay?"

"I don't know. I honestly wish I could tell you different." She stroked his hair. "How are you feeling?"

"Tired. And cold. My feet hurt."

Tori adjusted so that Damien's feet were tucked inside his mother's spacious jacket. He was only wearing light socks, the cotton damp. It was no wonder they were hurting. If they weren't careful, it would only be a matter of time until the first signs of frostbite took hold.

"Are you going to hurt me?" Damien's eyes brimmed with tears.

Tori hugged the boy tightly to her chest and rocked him. "No. No, I'm not. As long as you're with us you're going to be okay. You believe that, don't you?"

Damien stared ahead, no suggestion of belief in his body language. "I suppose. Why's your boyfriend gone back out into the storm?"

Despite the fact that Damien wasn't even looking at her, she found herself blushing. "He's... He's not my boyfriend. He's a friend. Someone who we're incredibly lucky to have with us. As long as he's here, we're safe. As long as he's with us, we'll be okay. I promise."

"But he's not with us. He's outside."

The boy had smarts, she had to give it to him.

"Ain't that about the truth of it all?"

Tori didn't have time to turn before a blinding flash of white light bloomed in her vision and something smacked against the back of her head. The pain was both hot and cold at once, the force of it knocking both Tori and Damien onto their fronts. Tori had just enough time to put out her hands to stop her body squashing the boy inside the jacket before she rolled onto her side and spun to face her attacker.

What little color remained in Tori's face was lost the moment she looked into the cold dead eyes hiding behind the mask. If the beard wasn't a clear giveaway of who her attacker was, then it was his body. A body she had spent nights lusting after, now exposed and raw, no shade of discretion covering his flesh which had morphed into a sickly white as of wax melting from a candle.

Karl stared blankly through the eye holes of the bear's skull, the lower jaw missing and an upper row of sharp, predatory teeth hiding the majority of his features. He spoke in tones devoid of emotion. "Tori."

"Karl?" Tori was unable to believe what she was seeing. "What happened to you?" She spotted the crusted stains of something dark lingering around his maw, clumps of burgundy clinging to his beard. "They got to you, didn't they?"

Karl didn't answer. Instead, he crossed to Tori, moving faster than she could register until her hair was bundled in the grip of his fist. He pulled her from the floor, holding her up until she was almost suspended in the air. The tips of her toes scrabbled for the ground as pain throbbed in her head, clumps of hair slowly working free from the root.

Damien shifted in the jacket, hiding from sight, each tiny, shuffling movement sending spikes of pain through her scalp. She pirouetted indelicately until she was facing Karl, and that's when she let it out.

The scream was fueled by horror at the intention she found in Karl's eyes. She had only seen that look on documentary channels and corners of the darker side of the web, yet it was unmistakable. With his spare hand, Karl removed the bone helmet and freed his locks of dark hair. Her suspicions of blood were confirmed as she stared at his beard, the raw, animal smell seeping toward her and stinging her nostrils. He grinned, lips peeled back, eyes fixing to her neck, and it was in that moment that she understood his intent—Karl wanted to bite her. She had seen that same glare recently in the dark eyes of Harvey and Sherri Dutton, and it was a look that she wished she'd never learned.

She lashed a hand toward Karl, even as the scream poured from her throat. Desperation fueled the nightmarish screech, her fingernails catching Karl's cheek and digging a deep trench into his strangely cold flesh. The skin waxen and damp. Pink streaks appeared where she had scratched, welting with droplets of blood as her other hand attacked the right cheek. Damien cried out in fear, still hidden from view. Concentrated bubbles of pain burst on her scalp as the first hot droplets of blood freed along with each strand.

Karl pulled Tori closer and bashed his forehead against hers. White fireworks exploded in her vision, the world going hazy for a few disorientating seconds. Her scream cut off as pain took over.

Tori spun. Another full circle and he headbutted her again, waiting for Tori's eyes to connect with his. She let out a miserable moan, warm blood trickling from her nose. When she regained her bearings, feeling as though she were swimming up to the surface of dizzying waters, Karl's eyes were fixed on the red trail, a string of saliva pooling and dripping from the corner of his mouth.

"No. Karl, please..." she begged, wishing Damien would hold still. "You know me. You know me..."

But he didn't. Not anymore. He bared his teeth and hypnotically drew Tori toward him, holding her high from her hair like an edible puppet on a string. Tori grew desperate and let out another scream, wondering where Alex had gotten to. How could he not hear her? This monster was attacking her, and yet her savior was nowhere to be found. Had something gotten him, too?

Had Karl gotten Alex first?

She lashed out with everything she had, ignoring the thumping ache at the front of her skull. Her hands beat his flesh, her feet kicked at his legs, and yet he showed no sign of abating. The acrid scent of his breath—something that Karl had never suffered from in all those months of their romantic engagements—poured over her, her nose wrinkling in disgust. She screamed and kicked and writhed and fought, but it was all for naught. Karl reared his head back and, as Tori expected the blow to come to her head, it instead came to her shoulder.

His teeth clamped onto the material of her jacket. She was shocked by his strength as he tore a hole in the material. Another few efforts like that and he'd be at the flesh. In that moment it was impossible to believe that she had once loved this man. Had shared a bed with him. Had curled up by the fire, knitted her fingers into his chest hair and wished that he'd stay beside her forever.

What the hell happened to you?

Tori shut her eyes, failing to hold back tears as she kicked at Karl, this time catching her foot between his legs. For the first time, he registered a sign of pain as he doubled over, the air knocked from his lungs.

Tori dropped to her feet.

Damien spilled out of the bottom of the jacket and landed in a pile on the floor.

Karl looked up, attention suddenly drawn to the wriggling mass at Tori's feet. She massaged her head, eyes growing wide. "Karl, no." She fought to open the jacket, the place where the boy had been safe and unseen, unsure what else to do in that moment. "Damien, back inside. Now."

But Damien wasn't listening. Already, he was scrambling up, the boy vulnerable and innocent in his flannel pajamas as his damp feet padded across the church. He leaped down the alter stairs, struggled to find his balance as he skidded. He found his footing, headed toward the pews, and ran.

A wry smile crept onto Karl's face at the prospect of the hunt. He took a keen step forward, about to give chase to the boy when something exploded behind his head, a plaster casting of Christ obliterated as the bullet tore into the wall.

Karl and Tori turned in the direction of the gunshot. Alex stood in the doorway. For a fleeting moment, Tori's heart lifted. However, when Karl grabbed her from behind and pulled her to his muscular chest, she knew that things wouldn't be so easy.

"Gun down!" Karl bellowed, surprising Tori with the force of his voice. Despite his massive size, he crouched behind her, lips dangerously close to the soft groove of her neck. His breath tickled the skin, a sensation that had previously made her weak at the knees, but now only filled her with a creeping sense of dread. Her skin broke out in gooseflesh, her eyes closing as she wished she was anywhere but there.

"Let her go," Alex commanded, easing around the doorway the moment he spotted that Karl was weaponless. The rifle led the way, his steps painstakingly slow.

His finger flexed on the trigger.

"I see it didn't take long for you to move on," Karl whispered into Tori's ear. "I could crush him in one hand. You know that, don't you?"

Tori gulped, nausea rising in her throat.

Alex closed the gap between them, stopping at the base of the altar. At this distance, Tori knew there was very little margin for error if Alex were to shoot now. One half an inch in the wrong direction, and it would be bye-bye for good. Although he had been a good omen to her so far, how much could she truly trust Alex, a man who hailed from a country where firearms were all but banned except to farmers, to take an accurate shot?

"Please," Tori managed. "Karl, let me go."

"You know this man?" Alex asked.

"Oh, I'd say it was more than that, wasn't it, sweetheart?" There was a hint of sadistic glee in Karl's voice, an animation she hadn't heard before. He had always been so brooding, so cool. Now, he was dizzy in his madness, some force deep down in the well of his stomach finding delight in destruction. "Tori was my little fuck toy. My piece on the side. My secret affair." A broad grin broke across his face, dark eyes glinting. "You were my sack of sex, weren't you, babe? Ready and willing to do whatever it was that I asked, just so you could get your kicks. A vessel for my seed..."

"Stop it!" Tori cried, pained by his words. The wound was still too fresh. It had only been a few hours since he had shattered her heart and left the pieces scattered on the floor. "Stop..."

Karl laughed, filling the church with his demonic echoes. Tori's eyes glanced at the many statues, her silent mind praying for that miracle to come any time soon.

"Is the truth still too raw for you, Tori?" Karl jeered. "You had no idea that you were nothing more than a hobby for me? Entertainment. A piece of sport. Who else would be dumb enough to fall head over heels for a married man? Especially in this shit-heap town. Who else would be so naive and ignorant, so self-involved that they couldn't see the truth? You couldn't see past your fucking phone, could you? Couldn't look past all your devoted admirers? I was never going to leave Cadence and Alice." At the mention of their names he closed his eyes, licking his lips hungrily as a wave of pleasure ran through him. "They were my loves. They were the ones I went home to at the end of a hard day. You were a pounding bag, no more use to me than a fucking blow-up doll—"

"Enough!" Alex fired a warning shot past Tori's head, another plaster ornament erupting into powder. Tori could barely see him through the blur of her tears. "Release her, or the next one will be for you."

Karl roared with laughter, his grip tightening around Tori's throat. He pressed against her back, something rigid and unwanted poking into the crevice between her ass cheeks. He sniffed deeply of her hair, then licked the back of her neck. Tori shuddered at the cold trail that it left behind, then let out a banshee shriek as his teeth grazed her skin.

The next thing she knew, Karl had taken his first bite.

28

ALEX GOINS

The scream was enough to spur Alex on. The man was a brute, a giant, but he was lacking the one thing that would give him the true advantage—a weapon.

Alex rushed forward, unable to process the reality of what he was seeing as Karl's head reared back from Tori's neck and a spray of red mist followed. There was something fleshy and pink between his teeth, an orgasmic look on his face as he chewed and savored the taste of her skin.

"Tori! Duck!"

It was a risky maneuver, but despite her anguish, Tori heard his cry and sank to her knees. Karl's hand loosened around her throat, the streak of blood slickening his grip, her head moving out of the range of fire.

Unfortunately, Karl ducked, too.

The bullet whizzed over both of their heads, finding its bed in the walls. Alex lined up another shot, but there was no time to find a mark, since Tori was now careening toward him.

Her body drove into him at full force, catching him off guard. Desperate to escape, she clung to him with all she had. They fell in a heap on the floor. Karl rose from his crouch, mouth decorated in blood, eyebrows furrowed as he stalked toward them. The man was a mountain. From their position down low, Karl towered over both of them, shoulders like boulders, hands like anvils. Alex wrestled Tori indelicately off him, his gun fallen out of his hand and landing a foot out of reach. Tori moaned in pain at the shove, but Alex already knew that the only way to end this man's attack was to incapacitate him—whatever that took.

Alex crawled on his front, hands clawing for the gun, but a sudden weight on the center of his back stopped him in his tracks. He didn't need to turn to know that Karl was pinning him to the ground, bearing his weight into the center of Alex's spine. The pressure grew. Something popped loudly. Alex grunted, hoping that the increasing weight would stop.

But it didn't.

Karl gave a throaty laugh and, as Alex turned his head, his heart sank. Tori's hair was back in Karl's grasp, the mammoth man managing to take them both in his control. Tori's face was a mask of suffering. As she rotated, Alex was witness to the chunk of flesh missing from her neck. Blood pooled around the wound and trickled into the folds of her jacket, staining the material crimson. Another few pounds of pressure on his back, and Alex understood that he was dangerously close to his spine breaking.

A strange sound came from Karl, a raucous gurgling from the pit of his stomach. A hungry stomach rumble processed through a megaphone.

Karl's eyes closed as the pain of it washed over him. He held his grip on Tori, maintained his pressure on Alex, but something was upsetting him. Based on what Alex had heard from the Iñupiat, he believed he knew what it was. If Karl was slowly transforming into one of them, then his hunger would only grow. Painfully so.

They needed to escape. Fast.

Karl licked his lips, black eyes fixating on Tori as he dragged her closer to him. His sickly flesh was impossibly peppered in a greasy layer of sweat, the dark coils of his body hair matted into wet clumps. She kicked at him again, but this time he was prepared. He threw his head forward with such force that Alex was convinced he'd caved in her skull. There was a sickening crunch. Drops of blood splatted on the cold, hard floor. When Karl pulled away, Tori's eyes were closed, head drooping, limbs limp, skin split in the center of her forehead.

Karl growled. "So much for miss popular and her army of digital followers. Where are they now? Not here to save you, are they? Maybe you should have spent more time making real friends instead of chasing pixels." He spat on the floor, white drool tinged with pink.

Karl opened his maw, set to take another bite of her flesh, when Alex exploded into a raging cry. He pressed his hands against the floor and pushed as hard as he could, adrenaline surging through his body. While he was no physical match for Karl, the sudden act of moving while Karl was distracted knocked the brute off balance and granted Alex a moment of grace in which he slid forward on his stomach and crossed the final distance to the rifle.

Karl's eyes flashed. His teeth bared. He discarded Tori with a flick of the wrist, sending her crashing into the pews as though she were a used napkin.

Alex grabbed the rifle.

Karl barreled toward him.

Alex scrambled to line up the gun.

His palms were sweaty, his finger unable to find the trigger.

Karl loomed over him, rearing back his leg for the kick. A concrete pillar of power coming straight for Alex's head. Nowhere to turn.

Gunfire.

Karl's bicep exploded in a spray of viscera, blood, and tissue. His mouth hung open in surprise.

Another shot.

The bullet grazed Karl's hip.

A third.

Wood exploded in the pews behind Tori, dangerously close to her chest.

A final bullet ricocheted off the floor at Karl's feet.

Karl let out a frustrated growl as he clutched at his wounds, darkness swamping his features. With a ferocious swipe, he grabbed a fistful of the unconscious Tori's hair and dragged her along with him as he turned on his heels and ran across the church. He dropped his shoulder, crashed through the wooden side door, and vanished into the storm.

The church fell quiet.

Alex stared down at the rifle in his hands, the barrel cold and impotent. He couldn't understand what just happened. Had he fired the gun? He had no memory of it. Had that all been him, without his knowledge? His body working instinctively for him.

Gentle footsteps down the aisle of the church.

Damien cautiously approached, the Winchester comically large in his delicate hands. He trembled from head to foot, silvery tears trailing down his cheeks. His lips quivered. There was a dark stain around the crotch of his pajamas.

"I did it..." he stuttered between racking sobs. "The bad man is gone... He's... He's gone..."

Alex sat, frozen and not quite able to comprehend what had happened. Tori... She was...

"Did I do a bad thing?" Damien's voice trembled. The rifle slipped from his fingers as he dissolved into a fit of tears.

Alex broke from his reverie. He pushed himself to his feet, crossed to the boy, and wrapped his arms tightly around him, fingers running through his hair, pulling him into an embrace that was comforting and necessary for them both.

While Damien sobbed into Alex's shoulder, Alex couldn't tear his eyes away from the door, a hollow space appearing in his chest as he tried to imagine what hell that beast could inflict on Tori if he didn't retrieve her, and what kind of trouble Cody would be in if he delayed his journey to the school much longer.

29

BRANDON TREVORS

B randon Trevors dreamed of home.

His exhausted mind conjured images of all the stuff that he cherished the most. His handwoven blanket created by his late grandmother and passed down through generations of Trevors, patterns stitched of moose and bison and bear. His personal home computer, a clunky, blocky thing fished straight from the late '90s during a time when computer monitors had yet to melt and thin under the compact pressure of time. His signed posters of NBA champions through the years, a testament to the true feats of strength that his heroes held in their fields. Heights that Brandon never truly believed he could reach himself. His R2-D2 bedside clock, the red LEDs broadcasting the time on the ceiling, the familiar whistles and beeps which rang in each morning echoing through his slumbering mind.

Brandon was a boy of comfort and simplicity. In his years of existence on this planet, Brandon had asked for little and received just as much. He knew his place. While other boys and girls sought popularity and won their sporting trophies, Brandon kept his nose in his books and saw through each year with solid, but not overwhelming grades. He'd watch heroes and villains on TV, read about historical figures throughout the ages, and wish he could one day amount to something.

Anything.

Yet, the cards you're dealt are rarely the cards that you wish for.

But now, somehow, Brandon was cast into the leading role of his story. He had stayed awake with Amy for as long as he could, terrified that she would submit to whatever desires were rattling around inside her head. He couldn't understand her fixation with the door. Why her eyes kept darting to the stairs. Her sudden selective mutism. Despite how much Brandon encouraged Amy to talk through what she was feeling, the girl remained silent. Oh, there was thought swimming in the pools behind her eyes, but they were for her own private viewing. Brandon wasn't privy to the secrets of the fairer sex, and after some time he too chose to cease his chatter.

And so they sat, cold and alone.

Quiet and hungry.

Tired and pained.

There was no comfort to be gleaned from that room, particularly now the tunnel yawned at them both, breathing its steady breeze of cold. When the wall had been standing, at least they had each other to feed their heat from. Now there was nothing.

Nothing, except Brandon and the most popular girl in the grade above.

He sat close enough to her that it offered him comfort, and he hoped it offered some comfort in return, but not so close that she could misinterpret any of his actions. That's what life was in high school, every decision, every minor action a play in the grander game of power among the grades. One wrong move could see you fall from the grace of popularity and straight into the mud pits with the socially inept and the unfortunately blessed. Kids with warts and acne and braces and weight problems, minor blemishes that were no true fault of their own but determined their social standing among the unspoken laws of puberty.

Fuck, Brandon hated it all. If only his classmates could see him now, the only lucid survivor in that room. Him—Brandon Trevors—looking after Amy Lawson in the middle of a freak storm.

They don't teach you about this in your classrooms.

Brandon's head slumped, leaning a little to one side. His neck ruffled as his chins multiplied their number. His gentle snores were rhythmic. Beneath his closed eyelids his eyes juddered in all directions, caught in the throes of REM sleep as his dream-self ran down the stairs and engaged in an early morning breakfast with his mother and father—something that he lamented would never happen again. On the menu were fried eggs, a slab of venison steak, and garden peas, each mouthful as delicious as the last as he lapped it up and swallowed it almost whole, his father laughing at his fervor, a great chunk of cooked meat balancing on his fork.

"You're a bottomless pit," his father jested before jamming the meat into his own mouth. He spoke between chews. "You'd be better off just bringing the animal straight in here and letting him eat it raw."

Brandon's mother stood by the sink, washing the dishes. She half turned, a smile that lit up the room. "That can be arranged."

The dream morphed in the way that dreams do, and as Brandon tucked into another bite, the table and the plates melted away. Stable stink stung his nostrils. Flies buzzed around his ears. Inches from his face was a mass of brown fur, coarse and short. He didn't question it, he merely chomped into the flank of the creature, relishing in the pulsating gushes of its blood as it spilled viscous juices which splattered on the wooden floors. The moose craned its head to watch, chewing cud and acting as if each bite was only the nibble of a nuisance insect. Brandon's hunger surged through him, his face disappearing into the creature's side as the hole grew larger. His hands tangled into the hair on either side to further aid his feast, pig-squeal grunts of excitement with each bite, his father's laughter warped and echoing somewhere outside of the shell of the grandiose beast. He chomped with urgency, chewed without pause. Brandon's teeth jarred on the thick white bones of the moose's ribcage, and still the creature showed no sign of care. It was warm and sticky. The meat was delicious. His stomach craved more, wanted more, each bite only driving his hunger until he at last came up for air, sucking in lungfuls of air as though he had just breached the surface of a red sea...

The world was white. Brandon was alone. His bare feet frozen in the blood-stained snow, only the impression of the moose's hooves remaining. Snowflakes danced lazily and it was then that he realized he was naked. He folded his arms across his protruding stomach, its flesh stretched and swollen from the bloody meal as he cried out into the dark... Called for help from... Someone. Anyone. A stark feeling of isolation colder than the wind that pricked his skin and...

Something cool licked his cheek.

Brandon moved a lazy arm to his face, his eyes shut tight, mind grappling with reality. Caught between two worlds.

Another cool chill, a steady stream of cold air. His groggy mind fought to surface from the dream, and as his eyelids fluttered to wakefulness, he wished he had never come out of his stupor.

Clanging.

Foot on metal.

Feet on the staircase.

He reached an arm to his left. Swiped.

Nothing.

Amy was no longer beside him.

"Amy! No!"

Brandon struggled to gain his footing, one leg numb from sleeping on the cold, hard floor. He grimaced as he hobbled across the room, relying heavily on the shelves for support as they wobbled and protested, threatening to spill their hazardous contents as he closed the gap.

Amy's clothes were strewn across the floor. Brandon's foot caught up in her thick jacket and he almost fell. In front of the jacket were trousers, socks, shoes, and...

The last item was thrown casually over her shoulder, as though Amy was playing a game that Brandon had only ever dreamed of playing. He paused at the bottom of the staircase, staring up at Amy's naked flesh, the crease of her butt elegantly shifting side-to-side with each step. Her back was smooth, her dark hair cascading between her shoulder blades like a chocolate waterfall.

Brandon's mouth went dry. He wasn't sure if he should look away. A knee-jerk reaction for a socially shy kid. Sure, he had seen naked women before in late-night Google searches and the back of magazines with phone numbers attached to their profile, but he had never seen a girl as beautiful as Amy stripped down to nothing more than the flesh God had blessed her with.

The temperature suddenly rose. Brandon tugged his collar from his neck, wanting more air. Then, as Amy reached forward for the lock on the door, Brandon's sensibilities returned.

"Amy! What are you doing?" He used the rail to propel himself up the stairs. He was a large kid, not built for this kind of exercise. Couple that with the lingering fear of the monsters and the naked girl in front of him, and his heart pains came back in full force. Total overwhelm racked his body as he fought his way through a coming shockwave. He clutched his chest with one hand, teeth gritted as he forced himself onward. By the time he was halfway up, the lock had already clicked.

Amy's pants were a hot pink and lay at his feet. Brandon's breath came in sharp bursts. Tears glazed his vision as she eased the door open, waiting expectantly, as though she were simply awaiting the postman's arrival.

Brandon doubled over. Groaned in pain. He rested his hands on his knees and craned his head to the doorway.

They had waited patiently. Brooding figures of monstrous proportions. The urgency from their attack had faded, but their menace blew over them like a storm cloud, darkening the already gloomy room.

"Close the door..." Brandon muttered, the pain taking him, his heart beating so wildly in his chest that he wondered why it hadn't broken his ribs and exploded out of his body. "Close it..."

If Amy could hear, she paid no attention. She stood in the center of the doorway, arms spread, head raised to the ceiling as though she were mimicking a figure from a movie before they dived off the edge of the world. He supposed that she was. Somehow, in her mind, she was there.

The closest two monstrosities crept toward her, long black fingers pulling her into their embrace as needled teeth opened wide and took their first bites. They groaned in delight as they dined, bodies bucking with ecstasy, strings of tendon and tissue pulling away from the body as they reared their heads back and tugged until an elasticated snap accompanied the spray of blood.

Another bite and they both stopped at once. Brandon took a few steady steps back as a shadow loomed down the hallway wall, stretching and darkening until another figure parted the two blood-stained monsters and stopped before Amy.

There was no sign of her pain. No registering of anything that might have suggested that several chunks of flesh were absent from her shoulders. Blood ran in rivers, staining her virgin flesh. If she was in fact dreaming, Brandon wished he could be in it too. At least in a world far from here he wouldn't have to watch. He wouldn't have to suffer, too.

The figure stood as silent as a specter. Brandon feared this one most of all. Not simply because of its overwhelming height, nor the fact that its frame was more withered and skeletal than the others, the only substance to its body coming in the form of a ribcage which protruded from the neckline then caved into nothing where a stomach should have been. Nor was it because of the leathery flesh that was draped carelessly over the bone. It wasn't even because of the long arms which almost scraped along the floor, Neanderthalic and hideously thin, bristling with dark, coarse hair.

No.

The reason that Brandon feared this being the most was because of the mask that covered its face. The great dome of an adult stag, horns reaching out like grasping fingers of bone. The eyes within were nothing more than dark pools of onyx. Brandon had a feeling that behind that mask was something that no human eyes should ever feast on. An unholiness that defied the realms of science and progression and would cause the onlooker to go mad. That mask was a part of the being, had merged with what had once been flesh. The two were one, and the one was something powerful.

The Masked One.

The name came unbidden, sneaking into his mind on the whispers of shadows. A name plucked from the realms of time and the broiling cauldron of magic. Brandon knew the being could do things that were simply impossible, if measured by the realms of the mortal.

In the next moment, The Masked One proved it.

It reached up with dexterous dead fingers, each one a hooked, narrow scythe, placing the tip of its digits on either side of Amy's temples. She gave an urgent gasp, followed by an unholy screech as she buckled to her knees, fingers tearing out her hair in violent bursts, the skin of her supple frame stretching and revealing the nodules of her spine as her scream stretched for what felt like an eternity.

It was enough to snap Brandon from his hypnotic state, the boy once rooted to the ground, paralyzed in awed fear, now spun on his heels and fled. His mind was not with him, the room listing like a ship tossed by unfriendly seas. A shelving unit crashed to the ground, plastic and glass tubs of hazardous liquids that cracked and gave off a foul reek as they bubbled and crept along the floor. When Brandon passed another shelf, he pulled with intention this time, hoping against hope that perhaps those creatures couldn't cross a floor laden with acids and alkalis. Maybe it would slow them down. Give Brandon a chance to escape. It was his only hope. He knew that much, at least.

The floor is lava! Brandon laughed without humor as he careened around the corner, sparing a final glance back at the staircase before disappearing into the tunnel.

Amy had stopped screaming.

Amy was gone, only parts remaining.

Blinking back hot tears, Brandon ran into the darkness.

30

CODY TREBECK

"Shit."

Cody shone the light at the end of the passageway, his throat constricting as a nervous wave of fear crept through him. Bricks and lumps of stone were piled up high, blocking the way ahead. The stones and rubble must have been standing for quite some time, given the moss and mushrooms that decorated and plugged the gaps and hollows.

"We've got to turn back," Sophie said, voicing what Cody was refusing to come to terms with.

Travis leaned haphazardly against the wall, struggling to prop himself up. In the faint glow of Cody's flashlight his skin was ashen, his eyes barely open. To Cody, he looked like his Uncle Jimmy had at the end of many of their family gatherings, elbow propped against the piano as he fought back the urge to vomit, none of that stopping him from pounding his tenth tequila and telling Aunt Gilly to go to hell as he slapped the offered glass of water from her wrinkled hands. Cody and Sophie exchanged a look, her worry reflected back at him.

"No!" Travis barked, half raising a hand. The very effort of it a monumental feat. "We've walked for hours through this mole hole. We're not turning back now. Nope. No way. Not doing it." He hiccupped and stumbled, grasping the wall for support. "You've got to be high as a kite, my friend. Nuh-uh."

Cody's shoulders softened. "We've got no choice. I don't like it either, but we can't dig our way out of here. We should've gone the other way."

Sophie placed a hand on his arm. "We couldn't have known."

"Hayden clearly did." Cody placed his hand on hers, still unable to look her directly in the eye while they were touching. He hated it, that feeling that broiled in his stomach that told him he wasn't worthy, that he was just imagining the connection between the pair of them. Why couldn't he lean into it? Why couldn't he just grab her hand and be close to her? Why was he waiting for her to make the first move?

Because you're trapped down here. One wrong move and you not only piss her off, but you break the magic. Isn't it better to live with the unconfirmed possibility that it could happen, rather than to know for sure that's it? Besides...What's your plan here? Make out in a cold, dank tunnel while you try to avoid capture from those creatures? Are you forgetting that Travis is here, too? A kid who probably shouldn't be left to support himself right now, even if you know you can't carry him? A kid who is undoubtedly in need of medical attention.

Travis' elbow slipped, his head coming dangerously close to hitting the wall. He collected himself, threw them both a goofy smile, then folded over and unleashed a torrent of vomit onto the floor.

Sophie sighed. She crossed to Travis and rubbed his back. Travis gave a pitiful whimper as another wave of bile expelled from between his lips.

"Are you okay?" Cody asked, knowing the answer already, his keen eyes not missing the strings of red in the yellowed bile.

"Oh, fine. Just dandy," Travis managed, wiping his mouth with the back of his sleeve. "I feel like a million dollars."

Cody resisted countering his sarcasm, instead choosing to join Sophie at his side, avoiding the pool of vomit on the floor. "We need to carry you."

"How?" Sophie asked. "We're already exhausted. Carrying him is going to take three times as long to retrace our steps and find the other tunnel. And even if we do get there, we have no idea what's on the other side. It could be another dead end."

"We have to try. Besides, the other tunnel must lead somewhere. It just has to."

"How can you be so sure?"

"Because Hayden hasn't shown his fugly mug. If the other way was blocked too, we'd have seen him by now." Cody screwed up his fists in frustration. "Can you believe that guy? Leaving us two to look out for his so-called best friend."

"Hayden is a prick," Travis said weakly, gathering his breath as his nausea subsided.

Cody and Sophie exchanged a look over the top of the bent over Travis.

"I really thought he'd be back by now." Travis' body shuddered as a couple of tears dropped to the floor. "Guys, I'm scared."

Sophie delicately patted his back. "I know. We are, too."

Cody straightened, shining his flashlight back the way they had come. He froze, certain that, for half a second, he had seen something moving down the tunnel. The shape of... something on the edge of the darkness, retreating as the cone of the flashlight did its best to fight the shadows.

"Cody?"

Cody shrugged it off, certain that the darkness was playing tricks on him. If it was one of those things, they'd have come straight at him, surely? The last thing he wanted to do was alarm anyone further. Besides, they had no choice but to go ahead, the other arm of the tunnel the only possible solace from what would remain the most haunting and exhausting night of his life.

"Let's go." Cody's hand wrapped around the box cutter, his mind drifting to Brandon and Amy, hoping that at least they were okay together.

At least they were keeping each other safe.

~

THE STRANGE SOMETHING that lingered on the edge of the darkness materialized and faded on a number of occasions as they made the laborious trek back. While Travis had been exaggerating, stating that the first part of their journey had taken them hours, their way back certainly felt that way to Cody. Travis was a challenge to carry on his back. Despite his lean, slight frame, he weighed considerably more than Cody predicted. Though he gripped weakly around Cody's shoulders, occasionally granting him a break from Cody having to bolster his full mass, the high school athlete kept fading in and out of consciousness, and with each fade, his grip weakened and he slid back, arms tugging at Cody's throat and forcing him to gasp for air.

Cody's legs throbbed with exhaustion, his knees pulsed painfully with each step. The extra exertion kept him warm, but it did little to ease his apprehension as the figure danced on the edges of his vision. Each time, it would appear as a gray blur on a black background, and each time they caught up to where it had appeared, the figure would melt into the shape of a large rock or outcrop of the wall.

Is this what delirium feels like? Is this the encroaching madness? You're seeing things, Cody. It's happening. You're going insane.

Sophie strode alongside Cody, occasionally helping him adjust Travis to a better position. On one occasion she took the weight of him, but only managed a short distance before she had to switch back. "We should've stocked up on some of Davidson's nutrition bars. Why didn't we think of food?"

"Because we're kids," Cody replied, having already had the same thought on multiple occasions. "I'm thirsty."

"Lick the walls?" Sophie laughed, the sound hollow as it reverberated down the tunnel.

Cody grinned, too tired to laugh. He took Travis' weight once again from Sophie and marched onward, a renewed vigor from the simple act of her laughing. Such a normal sound punctuating an abnormal situation. Normalcy felt good.

When they finally returned to the fork, Cody gave a sigh of relief and eased Travis to the side of the tunnel. Cody rested his hands on his thighs, recuperating his breath as he tried to ignore the burning in his legs. He wasn't sure how much longer he could go on, he only knew that he must.

Sophie crouched beside Travis, now fast asleep on the damp, cold floor. She held her ear to his lips and felt his forehead. "He's burning up, but at least he's breathing."

"What do we do?"

Sophie let out a long breath. "I don't know. There are few outward signs of damage, but there's something seriously wrong with him. Brandon was right, we should never have moved him."

"Are you saying we should have left him for those things?"

"No. We could have... Well... What if we'd..." She sighed. "I don't know..."

Cody crouched beside Sophie. The rise and fall of Travis' chest was shallow, hardly noticeable between his layers of clothing. At a distance, it'd be easy to assume him dead. "Fuck."

Sophie nodded empathetically.

"He's right, you know," Sophie said.

"About what?"

"Hayden is a massive prick."

"And you're just coming to that conclusion?"

Sophie chewed her lip. "It seems like *you* are. Tell me honestly, why did you even come out with Hayden tonight? If a teenage boy showed up at my house in the middle of the night, you best believe that I'd know what he wanted."

"Sex?" Cody said, the words jumping from his lips.

"No!" Sophie shoved him playfully. "Is that all you guys think about?"

Cody blushed.

Sophie chuckled. "I mean... Probably the stuff leading up to that at least. It's never an innocent visit, is it? But you... I'm failing to see why you would leave your uncle's house to go out in the middle of the night just to play basketball. You must have known that Hayden had a reputation?"

"I knew he could be... difficult. But he was my chaperone. He was good to me, at least for a few weeks. He showed me around, helped me get my bearings. I felt lucky... to be in with the popular crowd from the start. American schools are different to the English ones, I've seen your TV shows. You think I wanted to isolate myself by not going along with the fun? Become a social outcast?" Cody cast his eyes to Travis' serene face. "Besides, sometimes you do stupid things to forget the ghosts that haunt you... if only for a moment."

Sophie stared intently at Cody, his cheeks burning under her gaze. "Cody..." Her voice was soft. "What happened? What aren't you telling me?"

"I..." Cody's throat closed, teeth biting into his lip as he suddenly warmed.

Sophie drew closer, a tender hand on his shoulder. "You can tell me. It's okay..."

Cody's eyes stung as he fought back tears. It came on so suddenly that he was defenseless to it. He turned away, ashamed to cry in front of Sophie, unable to stop himself as the ghosts of his mother and father stood not ten feet away in the shadows. He closed his eyes, and they followed, the weight of it all suddenly more than he could take. He tried to answer Sophie as she wrapped an arm around his shoulders and held him close, but instead, all he could do was let the tears fall. His stomach gurgled with hunger, his muscles ached, his body screamed for rest, but in that moment, it felt good to let go. Good to submit to the natural commands of his body. The grief he had pent up which exploded unexpectedly like a geyser plugged with bravado surged now, racking his body with relentless sobs as she held him tight. Her perfume was long gone, replaced instead with the musty scent of her sweat. Not unpleasant. Familiar. As though, deep down, once you scrape away all the layers of pretense and artificiality that we paint ourselves with, we're all just the same. All capable of being haunted and scarred by the world, all just manufactured cardboard cutouts of a species that loves and laughs and cries just the same. When stripped to the necessary urges to survive, when banished from the ability to prosper and rank ourselves, we find what is truly common among our kind.

Blood and flesh and bone.

Cody cried until he couldn't, face buried in Sophie's collar. When his tank was empty, he remained there for an unknown length of time, his grief morphing to fear of what he would find when he raised his head and looked into her eyes. He had just expelled his tears onto the girl his heart yearned for. A girl so strong of will, and so empowered in her own self value that she would, without doubt, mock the silly little boy sobbing on her shoulder. He screwed his eyes shut and hid until she shifted beneath him, but soon he had no choice but to move.

A delicate finger on his chin. Soft lips brushed his. A moment of tender confusion.

Cody teased his eyes open, his breath stolen as Sophie's lips pressed against his. Her eyes were closed, her movements delicate. Her lips were warm, wet. He kissed back, losing himself in the moment. His breath quickened, body reacting to her touch, the world falling away until all that remained was Sophie...

It could have been fleeting, it might have lasted forever. When Sophie pulled away, a coy grin lay on her lips, Cody chuckled, eyes drifting down to the floor. "Thanks."

Sophie tilted her head, her smile enchanting, accentuating the delicate lips he had just kissed. "It felt like you needed it."

Cody smirked, his tongue swollen in his mouth, unsure what else to say. Luckily, Sophie spared him the pain. "Come on. We've got to keep moving. No point going through all of this if we're just going to stop and rot down here."

Cody nodded, accepting Sophie's help as he raised the sleeping Travis over his shoulders. He bore him in a fireman's lift, finding this method a little easier to carry, the weight distributed more evenly and less dependent on Travis' input.

They turned toward the fork not yet traveled and started their journey again. The tunnel was dark. Water dripped and echoed. The light wore down. Unspoken thoughts lingered between them.

They had only trekked a short distance, when a bone-chilling scream exploded in the darkness.

31

ALEX GOINS

The storm pressed in on all sides, the concept of a dominant wind direction falling by the wayside as the storm battered every inch of Alex's body.

The decision had been a painful one, and something that he fought to justify with every step he trudged into the snow. Cody was his charge, his reason for being, the very reason he had even entered the storm in the first place, but now he was directionless and lost. Muddled and stolen by the storm. A compass with no polar magnetism.

It had become apparent from the moment he had wrapped Damien in a series of blankets stolen from an abandoned cupboard at the rear of the church. Thick pieces of cloth left for some unknown purpose which morphed into a safe cocoon of warmth for the young kid. Alex worked the material into a papoose and fixed it to his back, fashioning the device in the way he had observed of the tribal women of Mongolia during his visit to the rainforests. A technique handed down from generation to generation which allowed women the opportunity of continuing their work while children snoozed on their backs. A fitting solution to a problem that Alex never foresaw. From the moment the bonds were secure, and the door to the church was opened, Alex understood that he was lost.

Until that moment, he hadn't realized how much he was relying on Tori, not only for her company in the midst of this madness, but for a solid idea of direction. Together, they had a plan. They each had an end goal. And now both had been snatched from their quests, driven off course, shoved off track by a monstrous beast taken over by the wendigos.

Alex wondered what the true nature of their relationship had been. The man—Karl—had been perverse, but was that just a symptom of the substance crawling through his veins? Could she really have been involved in a carnal relationship with that man? What did that say about her? Someone of his size would destroy her, surely?

There was no time to find an answer. Alex knew he had to move fast to find her again. Which would have been impossible had it not been for one minor saving grace: the tracks in the white.

Thanks to the weight of Tori's unconscious body, deep grooves carved their mark in the snow. While the storm was doing all that it could to claim the track and throw him off course, he had a path. He had a trail. While Karl's footprints may already have been lost, the snow was slower to claim the smooth hollow of the tracks that Tori's body left behind.

And that was where Alex began.

The wind was relentless, the snow hurting with each tiny pellet it threw. Alex's nose grew sore, then numb, then sore some more. He could only guess at the temperature, but he had never felt anything like this. He thought that the heat in the Egyptian deserts was more than he could bare, but what he wouldn't give right now for a break in the flurry of cloud cover, even if it meant being watched by the eye of the crimson Aurora.

Alex shuddered, his thoughts straying to the sky beyond the clouds, wondering if it was all somehow connected. Certain that it had to be, somehow. A sky that bled. A town that bled.

And so, Tori bled.

Damien was silent, for the most part. Occasionally he would shift in the papoose, fighting for comfort. With each movement, Alex reminded the boy that his fidgeting was slowing them both down. He couldn't believe the willpower on this kid, the fact that Damien had found the inner strength to fire the rifle at Karl. Even if his aim had been poor, Alex knew for certain that he had a lot to thank Damien for. He had spared all their lives—if only for a little bit longer, at least.

Assuming that Tori was, indeed, still breathing.

Time passed slowly, Alex unable to shake the feeling that he was being watched. Figures appeared in the farthest reaches of the storm, watching like sentinels, or so it appeared. Perhaps his overactive mind was playing tricks on him. Perhaps it was telling the truth. All that he knew was that he had to believe the worst, which was getting easier all the time, especially now that the tracks were beginning to fade.

How fast had Karl been moving through the snow? How rapid had his descent into madness been if he was already loping around as one of them, naked and unaffected by the snow? Alex dug down deeper into his strength reserves and tailed after the trail, but it wasn't enough. While he passed buildings he vaguely recognized, all too soon the trail vanished, and Alex was left with no indication of where they had gone.

Or where he and Damien had come from.

Their own trail was already gone. The footprints faded like snowflakes melting on the surface of a puddle.

For the first time since he had set forth into the storm, Alex gave a primal cry of frustration. The wind battered his face, slipped between his lips and froze his throat, but it couldn't stop the heat of rage that exploded from within. In that moment, he didn't care if those things could hear him, he didn't care if they came for him now. He had his weapons and he was prepared for the attack. He'd find her, no matter what it took.

A shape in the distance. Dark and lean, no more than a silhouette. He aimed the rifle into the storm and set to pull the trigger when the wind abated, just a touch, and he discovered that he was aiming his intent at a mailbox. A solitary mailbox. Not a wendigo. Not a corrupt townsperson filled with malevolent purpose. Such an ordinary thing. A fucking mailbox.

Alex scanned his surroundings, hating to stop the momentum he had built. Damien poked out his head from the papoose, eyes squinting against the brunt of the blizzard. "Why have we stopped?"

Because we're lost, Alex wanted to say, but couldn't find the courage to tell the boy. He was a beacon of hope, for the kid. Someone the boy could count on. He wasn't going to let him down now.

"I just needed a breather. Hunker on down, we're almost there."

Damien obeyed. Alex put one foot in front of the other, the snow piling up around his knees, hungrily nibbling away at what little energy remained.

32

HAYDEN LOCKLEAR

Hayden's stomach rumbled. His ankle throbbed painfully. He gritted his teeth and strode into the dark.

As the shadows claimed him, they made him their own. At first, when he had drawn free of the group, it had merely been an act of boyish bravado. An act of play. Ever since their arrival at the school that night, he had been snubbed by Sophie and Cody, made a mockery of as he attempted to prove who the king alpha was. It was him, of course. Who else would have had the courage to unite the group and bring them to the school? Who else had the balls to break in and play a game of ball in the middle of the night? Who else had the wherewithal to attract the hottest girl in the upper grades and claim her as his own?

Hayden Locklear, that's who.

Over the last few years, Hayden had worked tirelessly to make the school his bitch. Sure, he was blessed with good looks and an athletic constitution to be envied, but it was backed up with his charm and his ability to coerce and manipulate those around him, often without their knowledge that he had done anything at all. He knew every inch of what made him popular, and he flaunted it in the best way he could.

Take Amy, for example. He could see from a mile away that she was an insecure bitch. His father had beaten that lesson into him from an early age, informed Hayden that the women who were the prettiest were often the loneliest. Everyone was scared to ask the Amy Lawsons of the world to prom, or to speak to them in the halls, which is why they latched onto any attention they could get.

And boy, did he shower her with attention.

Matthew Malone had been his primary competition, but even that kid couldn't hold a candle to Hayden. Matthew was good-looking, but he was also a fucking nerd. He'd stare at Amy in class, but he'd never act upon his urges. He could have had his grubby mitts on Amy any time he liked, but did he take advantage of that? No. He left the door wide open for Hayden to walk in and claim Amy for his own.

Hayden rained compliments, showered affections, and bought his way to her heart. It was easy. All Hayden had to do was occasionally say something nice, show up when he told her he would, and she'd be putty in his hands. Her own father was out of the picture, so it was only natural she'd take to another male figure in her life.

If only she'd let him fuck her.

That had been a sticking point, and part of the reason he had invited her out tonight. His pocket was lined with condoms, his mind fixed on the magic moment finally happening. As much of a so-called rebel Amy was, she would never come out without her safety blanket — a safety blanket named Sophie. She was often hesitant to hang out with Hayden one-on-one, knowing how quickly rumors fly around Denridge. And so it had been tonight that he planned to have her. Something more than a kiss. Anything more than a fucking kiss.

So why the fuck was he here?

It was Cody's fault. Cody and that spoiled little whore, Sophie. They had helped to show his true colors, so what then was the point in hiding? Tempers flare under stress, and Hayden had never been one to be conservative when shit hit the fan. The slap he had bequeathed upon Sophie felt great, made his heart race in his chest. The sensation of Cody's nose buckling under his forehead was incredible. The blood was the perfect sizzle to the steak. Even if those fuckers tried to gang up on him, what did it matter now to him? Hayden was unleashed, unbound. The one true link holding him back had been in the protection of his best friend, but even that had been stolen now. Whipped away by the kindness of those two love-birds, prized from his hands before he had a chance to sneak up on them and startle them. To jump out and cry "goose."

He had hung around in edges of the darkness, able to see them a mile away in their sphere of light. Their whispers traveled down the tunnel, finding unfiltered clarity in his ears as Sophie and Cody voiced their true feelings for Hayden. Hayden had been ready to jump out at them, scare them out of their skin and delight in their fear when Travis confirmed the one true fear that Hayden had.

"Hayden is a prick."

Hayden's face fell. His demonic grin faded as the words pene-trated his cold exterior. Along the way, Travis had been the only companion he genuinely cared about. The one who had stuck by him through thick and thin. He knew that Travis would be okay in their hands, would afford him time to plot his prank...

But now those bastards had manipulated him, too.

It was then that Cody looked up and met Hayden's eyes. Hayden slunk back into the darkness, unsure if he had been spotted, then turned on his heels and faded, traveling back down to the other tunnel where he would creep ahead and find his way out alone, if that's what it took. Anything to get out of there and away from those assholes. Anything to find freedom and barricade their escape. Maybe they would all die that night, he didn't care. All he wanted was to find a way out. A way for him to be safe.

He stumbled in the darkness, feeling his way with tentative fingers. He tripped on more than one occasion, his vivid imagination turning innocent rocks into the desecrated corpses of victims trapped in the tunnel, victims of years long past. He could swear he heard rats. Water dripped. The pads of his fingers grew numb and bled as they scratched across the rough rock walls while he hunted for his escape.

He was too preoccupied when the scream came. It was too far in the distance, its ferocity lost in the reaches of where Hayden resided. His breath muted to all else but the immediacy of his vicinity. He wondered what the purpose of this tunnel had been, when it would end. He walked, then ran, then walked, then ran, his feet growing cold and sodden as he splashed in puddles. Another trip. A blow to his head and knees. He pushed himself back up, uncertain if he was even going forward anymore, feeling sick and confused and alone and...

A light, up ahead.

Hayden paused, unable to believe what he was seeing. From the ceiling came a muted shaft of light. Not artificial. Not made by electricity, but in the darkness of that underground tunnel, anything that wasn't black glowed like a campfire in the gloom.

Hayden turned back to the darkness, commotion sounding from far away. His thoughts strayed to Travis, then to Cody. A hot rage burned inside as he faced the shaft of light, and walked ahead.

33

TORI ASPLIN

In starlit skies and stormy seas
Your grace and love will shelter me
A love for you that burns so true
In light and dark, my love shines through

T he ghost of a smile crept on Tori's lips. The melody soft, the voice one that she recognized from the womb.

Her mother had always been an amazing singer, though it was lost on her, as much as Tori tried to convince her that it was true. As much as she implored her mother to start a social media profile and share her gift with the world, months before Tori found her own fame. Days on end, Tori would listen in the other room, captivated by the haunting melodies her mother sang. As a child, her singing had been all she had known.

In starlit skies and stormy seas...

Tori listened to her now, her favorite song, the gentle rocking motion fixing her into a trance.

She lay on a bed of fresh linens, a steady stream of sunlight filtering through the embroidered mesh curtains. Her mother's face hovered above, larger than it should have been, her smile stretching from one side of the world to the next. Her father pottered around somewhere, his tools clanging as he sought to repair some junked-up piece of furniture he could later sell to the townsfolk. In another room, Naomi clapped her toys together, mimicking the sound of an airplane between her lips.

... your grace and love will shelter me...

When had life last been like this? So blissful. So quiet and carefree? The sun was warm, but not scalding. Her mother's rocking soothed every part of her, easing the aches she had once felt, erasing the troubles from the world. As a kid, her mother had been her everything. As an adult, life had stolen her away. Her mother absorbed pain. Her absence allowed the mileage she had collected from years of parental protection to seep back out into the world, like water saturated in a sponge. There was only so much anyone could protect the ones they loved. Bills, taxes, internet trolls, unfriendly giants, they were all a part of Tori's reality, now.

But not in this moment.

... a love for you that burns so true...

Tori laughed, a juvenile chuckle. It surprised her. Her mature womanly tone replaced with the innocence of the babe she had once been. Her vision blurred, her tiny hands unable to hold anything with sufficient grip. Her mother rubbed a thumb around her lips and she sucked it, her aching stomach longing for food, but pacified by its tip.

Tori closed her eyes. Yawned. In the moment she opened her eyes she became aware of a dampness around her crotch. A cloying moistness as she relieved herself and the diaper absorbed its contents. Her mother laughed between phrases, the act of Tori pissing herself not enough to slow her down.

...in light and dark, my love shines through.

I love you too, Mom. More than you can ever know.

Her mother placed a warm kiss on her forehead. Tori closed her eyes, a giggle rising within her. Warmed and comforted by this simple act of love. An oasis of relief among a landscape of—

White.

All the world was white.

She gasped, pain igniting as something yanked her already protesting scalp, dragging Tori through the snow as the storm swirled overhead. Her body was numb, even beneath the layers of her thick clothing. She couldn't feel her lips. It hurt to blink. Her vision was tinged with red.

They stopped. Her head flopped unkindly to the ground, sinking into a bed of snow. It bunched around her, a good portion of it caving onto her face. She shook her head and cleared it away, trying to press herself to a sitting position, but struggling with a world that shifted and spun beneath her.

Mom? Where did you go?

"I have one for you." The voice was gruff, tired. For a fleeting moment she felt sorry for Karl, as her recollection of her last few hours hit her like an avalanche. "A gift to give you in her stead."

Tori managed to sit upright, using her arms to prop her up. Her breath caught as the figures came into sight, gathered around them in a tight circle, each one more terrifying than the last. Tall figures, not unlike the ones she had witnessed in her window, but unlike them all the same. Their arms were long and thin, their bodies malnourished. They were all naked except for the rough tufts of coarse dark hair now flecked with snow. Only, where the creatures she had encountered before held some kind of semblance of humanity, these had none remaining.

The difference came in the masks. Each of them wore a cleanly picked mask of bone over their faces. Some were of great stags, others of bears and moose. She couldn't see beyond the mask, but she knew that none of them were human. Not anymore, at least. And they all stared reverently at Karl.

"I can't..." Karl exclaimed, answering a question that Tori hadn't heard. One particular devil stood before him, closer than the others, unflinching in the chill of the snow.

Karl fell to his knees. Blood stained his hip. His bicep was shredded to pieces, barely clinging onto the bone. Tori wondered what had happened to him. What were these creatures doing?

"Take her," Karl begged. "In place of the other. Please. I need—"

Karl's hands clamped to his ears as his scream rent the night. She couldn't believe a sound like that could come out of his mouth. She had heard him laugh, heard him cry, heard him reach climax, but never could she imagine this.

Karl collapsed forward, hands pressed against the floor. The creature—the *wendigo*, she reminded herself—remained still, no indication that anything had happened at all.

Karl nodded, returning to his kneeling position, a dog shocked by the collar and reminded who was alpha. He glanced over his shoulder at Tori, eye's darker than the pits of hell, and nodded. Resignation laced his tone. "As you wish."

Karl climbed to his feet, intention etched in unfaltering clarity on his face. Tori tried to move, but found herself weak and frozen, her pounding head unable to process the mass of man coming for her. The most she could do was pat her side and hunt for a gun that was no longer there.

Tori shook her head, mouth dropping open as she begged Karl for mercy, cried for him to stay away. In the distant reaches of her consciousness, she rocked gently in the sunshine, basked in the warmth of her mother's bosom, her mind taking control and wresting her away to another place.

Another world.

Anywhere but here.

And so, her mother sang.

EPISODE 4

MASKS OF BONE

34

CODY TREBECK

The scream rang for an impossible stretch of time, the urgency and horror communicated in rapid sound waves reverberating toward them.

Cody swallowed dryly, Travis hanging around his neck for support. "What was..."

"Amy!" Sophie took a step in that direction. "Cody, that was Amy."

"How do you—"

"I know it was her. She's my best friend. I've heard her laugh, I've heard her cry, I've..." Her hands shot to her mouth. "Oh, God. Does that mean...?"

"I don't know. But I'm not about to wait around and find out."

Cody helped Travis onward several steps, but Sophie didn't follow. "Soph?"

"We have to go back." Her face determined as she took another step toward the fading scream. "What if they've got Hayden? Or Brandon, too? What if they're doing something unspeakable to them?"

Cody took Sophie's hand and eased her away. The scream was fading, but the memory of it echoed in their minds.

Sophie resisted.

"Sophie, come on." Cody grew desperate. Something heavy

clanged, followed by crashing metal on concrete. The sounds were so clear, as though it was all happening just outside the reaches of the light. Did the tunnel magnify sound, or had he, Sophie, and Travis barely put any distance between themselves and the dingy walls of pedo den? How futile had been their efforts at escape, if the world was determined to push them back at every turn? "Let's go."

"Why isn't Brandon screaming?" Sophie asked. "If Amy is hurt, why isn't Brandon?" Her eyes widened. "What if *he* hurt her?"

"Brandon wouldn't." Cody pulled, harder this time. Sophie yielded, moving a few feet his way. She shot him a reproachful look that stood in stark contrast to her affections given just a few moments ago. "Sophie, please. I'm scared."

The words echoed in the tunnel until they were swallowed by another sound. Footsteps. Loud, thumping feet tearing up the tunnel. Sweat beaded Cody's forehead as they stood rooted to the spot. They couldn't turn away if they tried. The sound had them paralyzed, a mixture of curiosity and terror as the tunnel filled with the cacophonous clang, magnified by the echoes until it sounded more like an army of a thousand than an individual pair of shoes.

And then he sprang from the darkness. There was no coalescing of his rotund body, no melting from the shadows. One minute he wasn't, and then he was. The darkness spat him out in one disgusted spurt and Brandon skidded across the floor, finding Cody and Travis and clutching onto them for support. His face was red, eyes streaming with tears. Sweat dripped off every available surface. He grimaced, every breath a struggle.

"Brandon?" Cody held Brandon in his arms. "Talk to me, buddy. What's going on down there? Where's Amy?"

Sophie stood on the edge of the darkness, peering into nothing. Her fingers threaded in her hair as she waited for someone... Waited for Amy to join them.

Brandon wheezed, a hand pinned to his chest, every breath painful. He pointed the way he had come. "Dark... They... Amy... Oh, God... Cody... Run... Please..."

There was no noise behind them, no continuation of the scream.

Sophie continued staring, silently crying at something that had yet to be confirmed or denied.

"Brandon, breathe. What happened back there? What was that scream?"

Brandon looked into Cody's eyes, his own shimmering with tears. He uttered a single word that told Sophie, Cody, and Travis all that they needed to know.

"Wen... wendigo."

Cody turned over his shoulder, only now realizing that Travis had broken free and was using the wall for support. He leaned haphazardly against the stone, one shoulder slumped, eyes half closed. In the faint glow cast from Cody's dying flashlight, he almost looked like one of them. The shadows played games with his features, adding darkness where there should be none. His eyes glinted like inky pools, cheeks gaunt. Travis wobbled unsteadily, his own breath coming in sparing hitches.

Cody left Brandon to recover his breath as he stood by Sophie's side. He took her hand in his, but there was no return. Sophie's attention was drilled on the darkness, her lower lip quivering, eyes unblinking.

Cody gave a gentle tug of encouragement, wanting nothing more than to just sprint and get out of there. But he couldn't, not without Sophie. They had come this far. She had held him when he needed it. This was his chance to save *her*, to return the favor.

Sophie resisted.

"Sophie... She's gone," Cody said, hating the way the words tasted on his tongue. "We have to go—"

Sophie tore her hand from Cody's and took a step toward the darkness. "No! I can't. She's... What if she's..."

"What if she's what?" Travis barked, appearing so suddenly beside them that they both jumped. "What if fatso managed to outrun her and she's still back there?" For the first time since the scream, Sophie tore her eyes away from the darkness, Travis' gaze waiting for her, surprisingly lucid. "We've already seen what those things are, how fast they can move. Amy is dead, Soph. Pull your shit together and let's get the fuck out of here. What the hell are you waiting for?"

Cody couldn't comprehend the clarity in Travis' words and demeanor. He was thankful for the help, but Sophie still resisted.

"But... Amy..."

Travis strode toward her, leg buckling on every other step. He placed his hands on her shoulders, half to support himself, half to try and break through to her. "I know what it's like to lose a best friend. Don't get yourself killed because you can't accept the truth."

Sophie shook her head. "Hayden's not dead."

"Where is he, then?" Travis returned. "He sure as hell ain't here."

Sophie protested. "She's not dead. She's not..." She finally turned to Brandon. "Is she...?"

Brandon was doubled over, his face beetroot red. He gave a resigned nod. "She's gone..."

Then came the second scream, this one more painful than Cody could have imagined. Sophie fell to her knees, losing her head in her hands as she let it all out, the piercing shriek raced along the tunnel like a Japanese bullet train.

Cody was only dimly aware of Brandon's babbling as he crouched beside her. He held Sophie, pulled her close to his chest, allowing themselves a single moment of respite as Sophie tackled with the truth. Amy was gone.

Amy was gone...

Which meant that those things could only be what Brandon said they were...

Which meant...

They didn't hear them approaching. The wendigos didn't sprint or scrabble along the tunnels as they had when they chased them through the hallways.

The first sign that Cody had of the wendigos was as he glanced up from Sophie's shoulder and saw a single face hovering in the darkness. The same face he had witnessed through the thin crack in the gymnasium doorway.

A mask of bone, its white turned gray in the shadows, head

cocked with the fascinated curiosity of a bird eyeing up its prey, antlers sprouting from the top of the dome.

Cody's breath caught. He tapped Sophie's shoulder. She faced the monster.

Sophie screamed.

Brandon sobbed.

Travis roared.

The flashlight died.

35

KARL BOWMAN

She was so small. So frail. A baby bird dropped from her nest and left to fend for herself.

It was all so clear in that moment. The Masked Ones—for they were many, and they were beyond number—directed the call, plunged Karl's mind into an oasis of its own, far removed from the blizzard, far detached from the taste of his wife's pulsating life force on his lips, a thousand years gone from the sex-crazed nights of passion that he and Tori had once shared.

For she wasn't Tori anymore.

Karl blinked in the dazzling sunshine, his massive hand not enough to dampen its shine. The air was crisp, the sky a brilliant azure, the likes of which he hadn't seen in years. Somewhere nearby, the ocean played its melody, a gentle hushing against the glacier as the moon and the sun wrestled for its control.

Something wet smacked nearby. His colleagues, Stanley and Turner, straddled the lifeless body of the walrus as their blades dived into the blubber and parted the skin. The blades were keen, honed in preparation of their daily duties, and so the skin yielded readily, as if the knife held a magic that could simply unzip the coat that nature had given the creature.

Their hands were stained red. The ice was painted pink. Across a small break in the ice, out of reach across the waters, an island of walruses watched on with indifference, just glad that it hadn't been them this time. One of their own had died, but nature was cruel, and so the circle of life spun on its axis.

"You gonna give us a hand, or no?" Stanley called over, a smile on his lips. "We've saved you your favorite—the head."

The incisions were crude, but tactical. While Stanley worked the lower third, Turner worked the rotund stomach, wrangling the spilling organs. Nearby, more workers were busy assembling the sacks and equipment to transport the individual sections of the beast. The kill would be divided among the teams, the dogs given solace in not having to haul the bulk of the one-and-a-half-ton monster of the sea. They had tried in the past, and it had almost killed their dogs. More could be bred, in Karl's opinion, but apparently the township didn't agree.

The world was changing.

Karl turned back to the ocean, unsure what that niggle of discomfort was in his stomach. A minor fault in the world that tugged at his very fibers. In the distance, he thought he could hear something calling him. A faint whisper on the breeze. Stanley and Turner continued their dissection, a strange hunger in their eyes as the longest slice unleashed the bulk of the beast's innards in one foul eruption, intestines and kidneys and liver bursting from the seams like an overstuffed teddy, the walrus deflating as though, beyond the blood and guts, it were made of nothing more than air, squeezed between the hands of a vengeful child.

And still that call rose on the winds.

Turner called to Karl this time. Karl waved a dismissive hand. His voice wasn't with him. He couldn't access it, and he didn't need it. He walked away, following the coastline and leaving his tracks in the snow. Somewhere far off, a polar bear growled, and the scars that decorated Karl's chest puckered and throbbed in response. Karl gripped his knife as the trees came into view. A copse of pines, a dozen or so in a strange cluster, emancipated from the reaches of the forest a half kilometer in the other direction. The sound grew louder as he approached. He wondered how the roots of the trees could grip into the ice, for he was sure that the coastline could be composed of only frozen water, far from the nutrient-rich soil that they usually demanded.

Dogs barked, the sound far away. The strange siren grew louder. An urgent plea. Help. Desperation. Weakness.

He passed beneath the arms of the trees and found it. A small brown dollop of blubber, clapping its flippers against the ground as it spun in circles. Its milky, bloodshot eyes searched frantically, its nose raised to the air to smell the stranger to its nest.

Karl stood for a moment and watched its pitiful form. At just three-months-old, the walrus calf was near useless in the wild. It could swim, but without the protection of its mother and pack, it was open to attack from all kinds of predators. Its tusks hadn't grown in and still it relied on its mother's milk for sustenance.

The calf detected Karl and paused, their eyes meeting, though he was unsure if the baby could truly see him. It shuddered, then padded closer, its curiosity drawing it toward the hulking man. Karl bent to one knee and extended a hand. The skin, while glossy and appearing as though it should be damp or wet, was dry to the bone. It felt... wrong, somehow. Like the flesh should have belonged to a human. The tough rubber exterior of its mother hadn't yet formed, and so, instead, here lay this pathetic excuse for a creature.

The calf nestled into the cup of his hand. He stroked its head, feeling coarse strands of hair that shouldn't exist. He raised his hands and invisible strands knotted in his fingers. He pulled and the pup squealed, the poor baby blinking in pain and betrayal.

Karl lowered to his other knee. Stanley and Turner were lost to memory, Karl only existing in the shade of the woods. The trees grew closer. They shouldn't have been able to, but they did, nonetheless. Every time Karl looked up, they closed in on him. The calf cooed beneath his palm.

And then it bit him.

Karl's body surged with red-hot anger, his emotions twisting on a dime. His hand found the hilt of his knife. He gripped it with both hands, a white-hot pain throbbing in his right shoulder, not that he could understand why. Perhaps he'd pulled a muscle on the hunt? Letting his right arm hang limply, he raised the knife above his head, ready to drive down and puncture the poor fucker's skull. No infant would best him, cause him more pain than he had a right to feel. There wasn't a creature alive that could best Karl Bowman, the greatest hunter that Denridge Hills had to—

The report exploded. Bark erupted from the trees, splinters of wood spraying in all directions. One of the pines toppled, creaking with a voice that had to be human as it fell back and crashed to the ground.

Another report. Another tree down.

Karl spun in disarray, hunting for the source of the chaos. A third shot, and Karl was knocked to the ground, pain searing in the place where his shoulder had given him grief. This time, when he looked down, his arm was gone. In its place was a neat stump, healed over and clean. A nub where the arm had once been.

Karl raised an eyebrow in confusion, the knife still gripped in a white-knuckle clench in his other hand. He glanced down at the calf, surprised to see a woman staring back at him, her mouth agape, her lips painted in blood.

His blood.

Another tree toppled. Shrieks rent the night. As the fourth pine came down and collided with the snow, the visage faded, the jack pine morphing into the body of the Masked One. The skull shattered.

And that's when she came.

36

TORI ASPLIN

T he snow encased them both in a frigid cocoon. The visage of Tori's dream slipped away, the echoing coo of her mother's song fading into the distance and stopping abruptly as Karl towered over her, leaving little else to see.

His eyes were dark. There was no humanity left in them. He swayed gently, gaze vacant, a hypnotized drone. Wherever his mind was, it wasn't here. Tori envied that. Karl's spell hadn't broken, while hers had. For a brief moment her mother had been her savior, her guardian. For a brief moment she had been home.

A home that hadn't existed for years. And now death faced her.

She always wondered what her final moments would be like. She wondered at the possibility of following in her parents' footsteps and falling victim to illness at an early age. Or possibly developing a fatal drinking addiction and drowning in the bottom of a bottle like her brother-in-law, Donavon. Perhaps she would one day just get lost in the woods, and nature would take care of her, her body opening itself up under the claws and snarls of a predatory beast.

But never, not once in her lifetime, had she imagined her final moments to be anything like this.

The wind punctured her skin with icy needles. Her head dizzied, blood coagulating in the split on her forehead. The world rocked and keeled. Karl was on his knees now, staring pitifully into her face as her body refused to react. Fear, exhaustion, lethargy, it all amounted to the same thing. She was frozen. The elements and the world working against her, determined to have her die under the blade of her former lover. One last final bout of penetration to secure the rocky relationship they once had. Rutting in blood and surrounded by supernatural voyeurs.

Something she could never have written herself.

Her lips parted, but no sound escaped. Karl cupped her cheek and stared emptily into her eyes. He tugged at her hair and elicited a pained scream from her lips.

Tori bit him.

Karl growled and raised his knife into the air. In the place where his bicep had been, she could see his muscles and tendons trying to work together and aid his effort, as though he had all but forgotten that he was injured. He flinched. Grimaced. A flicker of humanity crossed his eyes, then they darkened again.

She wanted to scream at him. She wanted to punch him in the chest. She wanted to deal damage. She wanted to run. She wanted to get the fuck out of there.

And yet, somewhere amidst all the confusion of her body, she wanted to kiss him. His lips were on their way to turning blue, his body cast in a sickly hue. If this were a movie, all Karl would need would be a princess. A kiss to wake him up and shatter the spell. If this were a movie, she could—

This isn't a fucking movie.

Despite it all, she wanted to help him. She let out a small sigh, but the wind tore it away. The Masked Ones stood on the edge of their circle, half lost in the blizzard, but present enough to remind Tori of this fucked-up situation she found herself in. To kiss, or not to kiss before her prince stabbed her to death.

A fitting end to a fairy-tale story.

Karl dropped his pained arm and held the knife steady. The moment had come, and all Tori could do was bear it. There was no escape. Alex was gone. She was alone, and these creatures would take the town. That's all there was to it. Life wasn't a movie. Life was a cyclical current of hopes and misery. An ebb and flow of joy and despair. Every day, the world over, the miracle of new life was offset by the inevitability of death. She supposed both were blessings in their own right.

When the first shot sounded, Tori couldn't comprehend what was happening. She looked to the sky, expecting a lightning strike to accompany the thunder. But that wasn't how storms worked, was it? Lightning came first. So, where had the sound come from?

Shrieking from behind. Tori whirled as one of the Masked Ones buckled and folded into a pile of bones and tattered flesh. The others in their masks turned as one to the source of the report.

Another gunshot struck another creature. The bullet tore through what remained of the stomach and left a hole in its wake. The creature stood, unmarred and unaffected, before a follow-up shot broke the supporting spinal column and the creature met the same end. The bone mask of the polar bear nesting on top of the brittle pile.

Karl roared as the next shot found the remainder of his arm. Tori yelped, the bullet passing so close to her cheek that the wake of the bullet rippled the air. Blood splattered her face and entered her mouth, thick and sour. She spat reflexively, her body rejecting the poison that had been in Karl's veins.

Karl bowed forward, staring at his bloody stump with curiosity. He showed no sign of pain at the loss of his limb, merely examining the wound like a child staring at the spatchcocked form of a frog in a biology class.

A figure came into view. Tori could just about make out the stranger as they came through the snow. The figure approached from behind Karl, walking with a gait that was human, yet decorated with a skull that was unlike her brethren. While the creatures sported skulls from animals, Tori was almost certain that this skull was an amalgamation of human and creature. Familiar. So, so familiar...

In the figure's hands was a rifle, a scope fitted to the top, but they didn't use the scope to improve their aim. They were too close for that. Somehow this stranger had approached without the knowledge of the masked, and now they were...

What? What were they doing?

Another pull of the trigger and the creature nearest to them gave a shrill banshee cry. The bullet shattered the bone mask, momentarily revealing the shriveled, rotten head of the creature beneath before it exploded like a ripe fruit beneath the flat head of the hammer.

The woman—for Tori could now make out her lean body and womanly curves—ran ahead, eliciting a stir among the remaining Masked Ones. Karl turned at her approach and received the butt end of the rifle in his face as the woman extended a hand to Tori. "Get up. Now. Come."

For a moment, Tori remained still. Another impossible development in an obscene situation. She had prepared herself for death, but she hadn't prepared herself to be saved. The story had been written. Tori was ready to close the book.

Who was this mystery writer who wished to add more chapters?

"Now!" the woman screamed and, in that moment, Tori thought she recognized something in that tone. A flashback to years gone by and memories locked safely in the vaults of the past. It was enough to garner her attention. Tori grabbed the offered wrist. She wobbled unsteadily, the latent effects of her concussion doing its best to drag her back down. The woman steadied her, wrapped Tori's arm around her shoulder and let off two shots in quick succession. The creatures were rattled, but they did not attack. They passively watched on, allowing the woman behind the mask to perform her act. Maybe after the show's interval they would get involved, but at this point the theatrics of this performance were too great to abandon, even if it had wiped out half their number.

They walked backward, the woman kicking Karl's hand away as he reached for Tori's ankle. Bile rose in Tori's throat as they passed over one of the piles of bone. Vomit dribbled from between her lips, stained her jacket. The woman held her steady, Tori submitting to her guidance. Each step was a battle through the snow, but soon the creatures were out of sight. Soon the creatures were gone.

Or, at least, Tori hoped. She cast a look back, and still the wendigos stood on the edge of her vision, Karl on his knees between them. The only sign of recognition of the events which had just taken place were the eyes which trailed them into the storm.

Eyes that marked her. Eyes that she felt on her body long after they were gone.

"Let's get you somewhere safe," the woman said, the gun now strapped across her shoulder.

Tori shook her head, fighting back tears. "Nowhere is safe. It's over. It's all gone. Every bit of it."

"No, Tori. It's not."

Tori stopped in her tracks, fighting against the woman, now. The mention of Tori's name surprised her and brought back the flooding of memories she had experienced in the heat of the battle. "Naomi?"

The woman reached to the muzzle of the human skull and raised it above her eyeline. Naomi Oslow was haggard, her eyes weary, her lips thin and pressed into a white line.

Tori didn't know whether to laugh or cry.

"Sis?"

Naomi gave a stern nod.

"I don't... What is..." Tori stared at the skull. "That's..."

Naomi lowered the skull over her eyes once more, taking a firm hold on Tori. "We don't have time for this now. Let's get you out of this storm. We can discuss all of this when we're away from those... things."

As if to illustrate her point, the sound of Karl's pained cries carried on the wind. Finally, after all that had happened, his dream had shattered, and his agonizing reality had finally caught up with him.

37

ALEX GOINS

The white was endless.

Sky bled into ground into sky into ground. The oppressive white stung his eyes. It turned his mind to mush. He wasn't sure if he was going forward or backward. He wasn't sure if he was simply walking directly into a white and endless pit. Every step burned, but the storm soon sorted that with a chilly blast of menace. Damien stilled in his cocoon, and Alex wondered if he was even still breathing. Past blurred into present into future, no defining edges to the world which he could hold on to for support.

The town had faded some time ago. The last of the ghostly houses were absorbed by the storm, and then there was no more... anything.

At first, he thought that they may have just hit a brief recess in the line of houses, a large gap of white between streets. Now he was certain they had breached the town limits and Denridge had been left far behind. The idea of turning and heading back irked him, a possibility he couldn't stomach. It took all that he had to keep moving forward. Like an automated machine burning low on gas, if he stopped, he knew he was done for.

He couldn't feel his eyelids anymore. He hardly blinked. Ice crusted his corneas and blurred his vision. The storm threw minia-ture daggers at his flesh, but he couldn't feel that anymore. Somehow, despite it all, his skin was warm.

And that wasn't a good sign.

In his studies of frostbite—for Alex rarely set off to a new climate without doing his research—Alex had studied every stage of the disease. He was smart to the ways of the body, knew that every part of his biological makeup was currently preoccupied with staving away the pain and preserving his internal systems. What little energy remained filtered into protecting his extremities from permanently damaging themselves in the cold. It was a clever system, but that didn't make it efficient. Soon all of the warmth would retreat to his vital organs. His skin would blacken, and the outer epidermal layers would rot. His nose and ears would be the first to go. His cheeks would blush with gray, forcing him to resemble a necrotic Santa Claus. All too soon, there would be no coming back from this. Snow burned. Wasn't that the biggest irony of all?

Alex's heart spiked his chest. In the distance he saw shapes of things he knew couldn't be possible. He saw Tori, smiling and waving, beckoning him forward. He saw Tom and Kathrin standing side by side, their bodies intact and healthy. Strange patterns whirled around them, spraying them with the iridescent colors of the Aurora, before it had been tainted. Greens and blues and oranges and purples. No reds. Nothing akin to the bleeding stain the Aurora had displayed earlier that night. This was wholesome magic, the forgotten gods casting their spell and playing with his fragile mind.

Alex was parched. His throat was scratchy and dry. He placed one foot in front of the other until he had nothing else to give. After an indeterminate amount of time, just as it seemed that he would soon reach the ghosts of his past, he collapsed in the snow.

The powder was damp, and that was something. Flurries entered his mouth and melted on his tongue. He sipped from the snow, but it wasn't enough. It would never be enough. The machine had broken down. The gas had run dry. Even the boy wriggling beneath his stomach was not enough of a motivation to climb back up and finish the journey.

He was done. Alex had failed. He had failed his publisher. He had failed his agent. He had failed his book. He had failed his sister and brother-in-law. He had failed Tori.

More than all of that, he had failed Cody.

He lay there, the snow piling on top of him. It claimed him greedily, burying the evidence of his existence with eager shovels. In just minutes he would be done. No Viking funeral, no cremation, no fanfare. Alex would be gone. The kid with him.

If only Damien would stop struggling.

It was uncomfortable, each movement an additional dagger in Alex's dying body. He rolled to the side and allowed Damien to exit. The boy birthed himself like a mole gaining entry from the earth. Dark hair came first, then a rosy-cheeked face, a parasite drawing on Alex's remaining warmth and leaving nothing in return.

"What's going on?" Damien asked, writhing free and pushing himself to his feet. "Why have we stopped?" In seconds he was forced to wrap his arms around his chest. His teeth chattered.

Alex found no answer.

"Come on..." Damien urged. "Get up. Please... I don't want to die."

Alex tried to close his eyes, found that he couldn't. "We all die someday. You can't fight the inevitable."

A strained sob escaped Damien's throat. He tore his eyes from Alex and scanned the white, teeth clapping with the cold. He paused, fixing on something in the distance.

Alex raised his head and opened his jacket. "Kid, just climb inside. Get comfortable. We can make this easy. I promise. It won't hurt a bit."

Guilt twisted Alex's stomach. Wasn't that what you were meant to do with children? Lie? Tell them that they had everything special to offer the world and that life would be easy? Fill their head with hope and ambitions until the day they head out into the world by themselves and all their dreams shatter under the unbearable weight of reality? Why stop now. Lie until you're blue in the face.

Or black.

Damien ignored Alex, a hand rising to shield his eyes.

"Damien?"

Damien pointed.

"Kid... Come on..."

"There."

"Don't make it harder than it has to be—"

"Just look!" Damien cried.

Alex sighed, his lungs shrunken and frozen to a third of their capacity. He fought to push himself off the ground, unable to believe what he was seeing.

There, in the distance, the faint outline of the school loomed over them like a Lovecraftian titan rising from the depths. Their shape was almost indistinct, but they were there. The school's cluster of buildings. A little way ahead.

Somewhere safe.

Somewhere warm?

Alex sat upright, battling his protesting body. It took longer than he'd ever expect to get himself to his feet but, once he was up, his resolve returned. He leaned on the kid as they both stared at the school.

"We made it," Damien breathed.

Alex's jaw clenched. He pictured Cody somewhere inside, remembered the wendigos and their haunting attacks on the town. "Not yet we haven't."

WHEN THEY REACHED the fence bordering the school's perimeter, Alex found that a hole had already been cut to allow entry.

His heart lifted. If the hole was here, that might mean that he was on the right path.

Damien followed a few steps behind, now draped in Alex's jacket. Alex could barely feel his limbs as it was, what did it matter if his internal body temperature dropped a few extra degrees?

They found their way to the nearest door, a large padlock clasped around a chain. Alex tried the handle, knowing it would do nothing. He groaned and shivered before taking a step back and spotting a nearby window, glass thick and covered in a frozen layer of condensation.

The bullet tore through the glass with ease. The report was swallowed by the storm.

Damien held his hands over his ears, eyes clamped shut. Alex borrowed the jacket and used it to dust off the remaining fragments around the window's edge, then heaved himself inside. He returned to the window, leaned out, and offered Damien a hand. It was only then that he noticed a shard lodged in the center of his palm. Thick, dark blood was the only indicator. There was no pain.

Lifting the boy the final distance was a struggle but they soon managed. For a moment, they both waited and collected their breath, reveling in the stale classroom air. Alex couldn't believe the impact that being out of the storm had on him. The temperature was no different, but they were shielded from the wind and the snow. That in itself was a victory.

"Are we safe, now?" Damien asked, his voice timid and broken.

Alex plucked the shard of glass from his hand with little resistance. His nerves were frozen. He tried to flex his fingers. The tips of each digit were blue, despite having been inside his gloves. He focused on just moving his thumb. After a minute of experimentation and thawing, he managed it. He rubbed his hands together, wiped the stain of blood on his trousers, then turned his attention to the classroom door.

"Are we safe?" Damien repeated.

Alex tested the handle, unsurprised to find that it was locked. "I honestly don't know. I don't have any answers for you."

Damien's face creased in pained concentration. "There are more of them, aren't there? Those monsters. They're everywhere."

Alex glanced down at the boy, sorrow in his eyes. "I don't know what to tell you." It was an honest response, and somehow the boy understood. "We need to get out of this cold. How well do you know this school?"

Damien tucked his hands beneath his armpits. "I don't know this building. Third grade is across the quad. We're not allowed this way. That's for the bigger kids."

Alex studied the door. He gave it a gentle nudge. It rocked in its frame. "Do you know the teachers here?"

"No. Why?"

Alex took a step back. "I just don't want you grassing on me for what I'm about to do."

"What's grassing—"

Damien shrank, ears covered as Alex kicked at the door. The first kick was weak, his aching legs barely able to gather their strength. By the fourth kick, a splinter of a crack appeared near the latch. The glass panel located in the center of the door shattered. Alex kicked twice more before the door finally swung open.

He stepped back and examined his handiwork. "Not bad. Not as dramatic as it is in the films. Was kind of hoping the door would come away first time, fall backward, hit the ground."

Damien unfurled, scared and concerned. "Mom says that's vandalism."

Alex bit back his retort—*mama ain't around no more.* He offered a hand to Damien who took it readily. "Look, Damien. I can't promise you that I'm going to be able to protect you from anything we find inside this place. But if you stick with me and do exactly as I say, we may just be able to make it out of this alive. Do you understand?"

Damien looked to the darkened corridor. "Do you really think your boy is hiding somewhere in the school?"

Alex considered this. He cocked an ear, listening for any sign of movement or company. "I have to, kid. I have to."

38

CODY TREBECK

They lost themselves in the darkness, ghosts of the monstrosities left behind in the afterburn of the lost light.

Sophie, Travis, Brandon, and Cody called out for each other, their voices mingling in the dark. Somewhere in that cacophonous din was the shrieking hiss of the creatures in the tunnel. Cody found Sophie's hand and pulled her away, his other hand shoving the phone in his pocket and finding Davidson's box cutter. It felt good to have something sharp, something *deadly*, though with their vision compromised there was no way of knowing which way to turn to escape. Already, he had lost his sense of direction as he urged Brandon and Travis to run after them.

Sophie screamed, loud enough for his eardrums to pop. Something grabbed his collar and pulled him back and, for the slightest of moments, skeletal fingers scratched his neck. He spun, slashed with the box cutter. The blade notched onto something hard. Sophie urged him away. Brandon's heaving breaths followed.

Another screech, unmistakably made by the creatures. No human could make that sound. Cody traced his fingers along the wall, using the cold, damp surface to guide him. Occasionally they'd stumbled over fallen debris, but it seemed that they were at least giving the creatures a run for their money and gaining ground.

Something heavy fell. A meaty thwack against the stone. Lungs extinguishing breath. "Keep going!" Travis called, voice laced with pain. "Go!"

Cody slowed, facing behind them as he jogged backward. "Keep running, Travis!"

Sophie, undeterred, tugged Cody forward. Brandon bowled into Cody, sending them sprawling to the ground.

"Come at me, fuckers!" Travis bellowed amidst the chaos, followed swiftly by the thudding of something metal striking bone.

It was then that Cody remembered the hammer Sophie had selected from the pile. She clutched at his clothes and dragged him to his feet, then patted her pockets. "Son of a bitch stole my hammer."

Travis laughed, the tunnel broadcasting each note of mania that laced his words. He was gone now, lost in the moment, his anger turning to humor, transforming to determination as he fought the beasts in the dark. Cody tried to imagine him spinning with the hammer, whirling around and embedding the metal into their skulls.

Another screech.

"Let's go," Cody hissed. He found Brandon's hand and helped him to his feet. The three sprinted away from the din, listening for anything that might be following. Cloaked by the darkness, there would be no way to tell what was behind or what was in front of them. The creatures had approached without their knowledge, snuck up on them without giving away their position. If they could do it once, they could do it again.

"Bet that one hurt, you bastards!" Travis sang. "Eat steel, bitches!"

The tunnel was endless. Travis' cries rang out as he held the creatures at bay. Cody wished that he could see it. Wished he could watch Travis' final stand as he barricaded the creatures from pursuing.

He would fail, of course. Cody had no doubt. The night had yet to grant them any reprieve from the horrors, and he was sure that there were many surprises left in store. All Cody needed to do was to keep running, to get out of these stinking tunnels and find a way to hide from the beasts. That was his one objective now: to get Sophie and Brandon to safety—whatever it took.

The darkness absorbed them. Travis exchanged his words for grunts. Soon the madness stilled, and they all knew then that Travis was gone. There was no crowning glory, no final moment of power granted to him. One minute he was standing, the next he was lying dead on the floor. Even in the darkness they knew that much.

Sophie gave a muted sob.

They kept running.

They ran for what felt like hours. There was no way to tell how far they'd come, or if they were even making any progress. They could have been running in circles for all they knew. There was no sign of the creatures anymore, no sound, no intimation that they were in pursuit.

And that was the worst of it all. They knew that if they stopped, they'd only increase their chances of capture, but who knew what these things could do in the dark? Who knew the unholy powers granted to them by the shadows? Cody's chest hurt, and he could only imagine what Brandon was going through—Brandon, who was falling behind them with every step.

"There's got to be a way out," Sophie huffed. "There's got to be..."

Cody didn't answer. His attention had been drawn by the tiniest speck of something in the distance. A break in the darkness. After another stretch of uneven ground covered, the speck grew to a dull light in his vision. "Are you seeing what I'm seeing?"

Sophie confirmed that she was. They doubled their pace, Cody so focused on the light that he didn't realize that Brandon was no longer with them. The tunnel silent behind them both.

The light grew brighter with every step. Not a blinding light like that given from the fluorescents of bulbs, but a vast contrast to the enveloping darkness from which they sought their escape. Next to the shaft of light was an iron ladder, the edges and rungs sporting patches of rust and corrosion. Without waiting to test it, Cody nudged Sophie ahead and she scaled the ladder with ease. She reached toward the light and shoved against the hatch. The hinges creaked and the thick wooden trap swung open.

The light stung their eyes, but Sophie climbed out without hesitation. Cody followed swiftly after, not taking in their surroundings as they stared into the square of black darkness, only then realizing that one of their team was missing.

"Brandon!" Cody cried. "Brandon, come on!"

There was no reply. His fingers gripped the edge of the hatch while Sophie's hands pulled at his waist. There was no sign that anything else was down there. Their own echoes had faded, and all that greeted them was darkness.

"Fuck," Cody muttered. "Brandon!"

"He's gone," Sophie said, her words dry and hollow. "Close it. Help me block them. He's gone."

Cody remained at the edge of the hatch while Sophie found something to plug the hole. Heavy wooden feet dragged across the floor. There was a thud. Sophie uttered, "Shit."

With difficulty, Cody pulled his eyes from the darkness. The wooden display cabinet was far too heavy for one person to drag toward the hole, its insides no longer displaying glassware and pottery, but instead coated with a thick layer of dust.

The unit caught against a thick bundle of cloth on the floor. Cody shifted the cloth, then helped Sophie drag the mammoth piece of furniture the remaining distance.

As they neared the hatch, Sophie told Cody to close the entry back up. Cody stared down into the darkness, unable to bring himself to do so. Sealing the tunnel would mean accepting that Brandon was gone. Hammering the final nail in the coffin.

"Cody... Please. Before they come."

Cody sighed. He crouched, was halfway to closing the lid when a voice barked at them from somewhere in the darkness. "No! Please! Wait!"

The footsteps were explosive, hammering in beats against the stone tunnel. Cody found it impossible to believe that they hadn't been able to hear them a moment ago, and he wondered if there was maybe some magic at play here. That the creatures might have been able to absorb the sound and play with their senses.

"Cody!"

"Brandon!" Cody called, falling onto the flat of his stomach. He lay at the edge of the hatch and reached down a hand. Brandon came into sight, staggering toward the ladder. He gripped the rungs, his sweating palms struggling to find purchase, iron creaking beneath his weight, but soon Cody had him. Cody inched him to the top, and soon Brandon was free. He flopped face-first to the ground and crawled away from the hatch, scrambling to a nearby wall.

Cody made for the hatch lid, when a pale white arm with dark fingers shot out from the shadows and grabbed his wrist. The creature yanked him forward, his body slipping back into the hole.

Sophie caught his ankle.

Cody cried out, the grip on his wrist painful, a frozen vice. The fingers were slender and long, able to easily wrap twice around his hands. Each twitching digit was like papier-mâché, or the delicate, brittle structure of a wasp's nest after the colony has flown, yet had a strength that could not be described.

Sophie called for Brandon's aid, but Cody had no idea if he was coming. The wendigo's arm stretched into pure darkness, not even the light from the hatch enough to shed illumination on the creature. The bone mask hovered in the darkness, only a foot or so from his face. The fetid stench of rot and death worked its way to him, and he knew in that moment that he had to act.

Cody reached into his pocket and found the box cutter. He flicked out the blade and slashed at the wendigo's arm. The blade caught against the creature's bony arm, only managing to form a small notch.

Undeterred, Cody tried again. He slipped another inch into the darkness. Somehow, he knew that he was surrounded now, and all the minions were waiting. He could sense them in the darkness, waiting for their master to complete the work. He hacked again, a strange rattling cry coming from the creature's throat.

He slipped another inch.

"Nooo!" Cody cried, this time stabbing the tip of the blade into the hand which clutched him. The blade embedded in the bone and, with a sharp twist of the box cutter, the bone fractured. Another wrenching turn in the other direction, and something cracked. The finger broke free.

The wendigo loosened its grip.

It all happened so fast that Cody was still pushing down on the blade when the wendigo retreated. The box cutter drove into his forearm, gouging a wide gash in the meaty flesh. He grunted, then pushed against the ladder as Sophie pulled his legs, both doing whatever they could to help bring him back to the surface.

A haunting shriek. The minions appeared from the darkness, coming for Cody. He made it out of the hole and grabbed the hatch lid on his way out, slamming it shut as they thudded against the wood. He pushed himself away, relieved to find that Brandon was already helping Sophie push the unit the final few feet it needed to cover the hatch.

The creatures thumped against the wood.

They squealed.

They screeched.

The unit covered the hole.

They stood back and stared at the floor, each waiting in silent trepidation for the next terrible thing to happen. The edge of the hatch could be seen beneath the unit. Tiny holes allowed the frustrated cries of the wendigo to escape. Holding his chest and grimacing, Brandon dropped to his knees. His nose wrinkled. From his pocket he drew a bottle of something that Cody couldn't identify. He poured the contents through the tiny pores until the bottle was empty. He discarded the bottle, then produced a lighter from inside his jacket.

"Stand back," he gasped, eyes struggling to focus. He ignited the lighter and touched the ember to the liquid.

A surge of flame rushed into existence with an audible *whoosh* as the liquid caught alight. Orange and yellow light danced from the holes as the shrieks and cries increased in urgency, filling the room with their pain. Heat flooded toward them, granting them a moment's respite as they sat in haunted silence, listening to the pained chorus of the masked.

Brandon patted his sleeve, the only part of him which had caught the fire. He shuffled back until he found the wall, resting his head against the stone, eyes fixed on the hole.

Sophie looked at Cody, then Brandon, her own chest rising and falling. "Did we get them? Is it over?"

Cody chewed his lip, unsure what to say.

Brandon, however, shook his head. "I don't think so. I think it's only just beginning."

He clutched his chest as a fresh wave of pain took over.

39

NAOMI OSLOW

T he house was quiet. Naomi liked that.

She helped Tori through the front door, the same door where Tori had stood and waited to be let in by her sister on innumerable occasions, but never once imagined it might be under these circumstances.

Tori was a mess. There was a welt on her head, her nose was busted, her neck was stained red, and blood crusted in her hair. Her eyes struggled to focus, and over the last few hundred meters of their trek through the blizzard, Naomi wondered if she'd be able to carry her the final stretch.

What are big sisters for, if not for times like these?

She eased Tori onto the couch, propping her head up on a pillow before making her way around the house and checking that everything was as it should be. All of the windows were intact, the doors were still locked and, most importantly, Oscar was still asleep.

She stood in his doorway, for a moment simply watching the rise and fall of her darling boy's chest beneath the covers. He had always reminded her of Donavon. That was the best thing he had left behind, a reminder of the man that Donavon had once been. Before the drinking. Long before the...

She lowered her head and turned from the room. Downstairs, she was surprised to find Tori sitting upright on the couch, watching her as she approached. She silently passed Tori and poured herself a drink of whisky—Abraham's Nectar.

Donavon watched from the bottom of the stairwell. A silent specter. Arms folded, a lopsided crooked smirk.

"Are you going to take that thing off?" Tori asked.

Naomi hadn't even realized the skull was still on her head. She placed her drink down and carefully eased the mask off. She suddenly felt naked. Exposed.

She examined the mask, taking in the contours of the skull. Once, this had been her husband's head. Once, she had seen those teeth nestled behind lips she would kiss every morning. Once, he had sat across from her at the dinner table, laughed as she admonished him for the flake of spinach caught between those molars.

"Naomi?"

Naomi placed the skull back on its hook on the wall. For a moment, it swung precariously, finding its equilibrium. The empty hollows of the eyes watched them.

Naomi took a sip of her drink and sat on the arm of the couch, eyes downcast, lost in thought.

"Naomi?"

Tori's gaze was intense. Demanded answers. Yet, Naomi was happy to wait for a question.

"What was that back there? Those... things..."

"Wendigos," Naomi clarified, catching Tori off balance.

"Right. The wendigos. How did you know to come? How did you know to find me?"

Naomi sipped from her drink, in no hurry to answer. The amber liquid burned her esophagus, warming the parts of her insides that the minimal heat of the house couldn't reach. She could see why Donavon had so easily lost himself to this vice.

The specter that was her husband leaned against the banister. Waved.

"It's... complicated."

"More complicated than this?" Tori rose sharply, wobbling a little as her hand moved to her head. Her voice rose in volume, the results of the past few hours tumbling out from between her lips. "I want to know what the fuck is going on, Naomi. I've been attacked in my own goddamn home by freakish creatures from another dimension. I've had a man die in my living room, eaten from the inside out. I've traipsed through a fucking blizzard, saved by a man I'd never met before, only to think we'd found safety and get attacked all over again. Not only that, but the man who I thought would eventually leave his wife and go steady with me decides to end things and then hunts me down in the middle of the storm to drag me back like some Neanderthalic Tarzan so that he can parade me around to his colony of fucked-up bone creatures and celebrate the spoils. Next thing I know, my own fucking sister appears, wearing a *human skull*, and blasts half of the creatures into oblivion. Do they chase her? No. They don't. Yet, for some reason they won't leave *me* the fuck alone." Tori fell to her knees, eyes red and puffy. There were no more tears left to spill. "So, please tell me. What the fuck is going on out there?"

Naomi placed her drink on the coffee table and kneeled before her sister. She embraced her, holding her until the wracking sobs faded. The storm raged outside, showing no signs of abating.

Naomi eased Tori back and held her shoulders, staring deeply into her eyes. Behind Tori, Donavon shifted his weight to the other foot, eyes sparkling. "You wouldn't even begin to believe me if I told you."

Tori laughed, sawed a hand across her nose, then winced. A string of pink snot trailed the back of her hand. "Try me. I've seen some crazy shit tonight. Weren't you just listening?"

"Mine's crazier."

"I doubt that."

"Just you wait," Naomi said.

Tori cleared her throat, eyes darting to Naomi's drink.

Naomi offered a weak smile. "Let me fix you something to wet the windpipe, first. You look like you've been dragged through the Drumtrie backwards."

She poured Tori a glass of water which she drained in seconds. Laughing, she went to grab her another, offering her something to nibble on, too. Tori refused, stating that, as hungry as she was, her stomach wouldn't be able to take it, yet.

Finally, Naomi returned to her seat. "I hardly know where to begin."

"The start?"

Tori smiled, but this time Naomi didn't. She chewed her lip, then started at the only place she could think of. The week her entire reality had flipped upside down.

40

TORI ASPLIN

Tori knew better than most of the rocky relationship her sister and her brother-in-law had shared.

Donavon Oslow had always been the independent sort and thrived on being able to provide for his family. When he and Naomi first met, Tori was thrilled to bits. Donavon was cool, he was resourceful, he was funny. At the time she had only been in her early teens, but she could still remember the fun they all shared together. When Donavon and Naomi came over to her parent's house for dinner, Donavon would have the family howling with laughter, offering to help with the dishes and giving her father advice on the best ways to hunt and cure game. When plates were emptied, Donavon would be the first to offer to clean up.

As most relationships do, the dynamic changed slowly. After the pair married, they found their little house on the borders of the Drumtrie Forest. An abandoned building that was in dire need of a spruce-up. Donavon worked tirelessly to turn the shack into the dream home they'd always wanted, slaving away into the late hours with their father, and when Naomi finally fell pregnant with their first (and last) child, no one could be happier

Pregnancy was tough. Naomi and Donavon grew ever more withdrawn. With less time to donate to family, they instead focused on their own relationship. At the time, that seemed normal enough, although it didn't help Tori and Naomi's relationship. Tori was struggling through her high school hormone phase, and needed an older sister to lean on. Naomi only had time for the soon-to-be baby, and so their bond began to sour.

There was a brief respite on the day that Oscar was born. A chunky baby boy. Eight pounds and thirteen ounces, full of life. The boy came out screaming, and it seemed that his lungs carried no lack of oxygen. From that fateful day, Oscar's cries had been the soundtrack to every visit, and on Tori's third time seeing the baby, when Oscar was just eight days old, she offered to watch him while Naomi and Donavon caught a few hours of rest.

For three hours she tried to settle the baby, catching only short glimpses of silence when Oscar wore himself out and finally shut his eyes. Tori would chance making a drink or attending to her bladder, but the slightest of sounds would trigger him, and the screams would fire up all over again.

Naomi and Donavon gleaned no sleep, despite their family's help. After a couple of weeks, they stopped requesting assistance and broke contact with the family altogether. Tori wondered what it must have been like, constantly on alert and at the beck and call of a demanding infant. Did they have any time to themselves at all? Was it just a phase that Oscar was going through?

Naomi called, on occasion. Always, the backing track to their conversation was a despairing Donavon and a screaming child. Even when Naomi went to the opposite end of the house, it wasn't far enough to silence the din. They could both be heard shouting and screaming. Naomi put on a brave face and sounded positive enough, but it was always clear to Tori that something was wrong, even if her sister never stated it at the time.

Alcoholism. The demon that slipped through the door, shielded and invisible beyond the dark curtain of baby cries and restless slumber. Donavon had been a drinker on and off for years, yet it was only in the wake of his death that Naomi ever told Tori her version of the truth. While Naomi coped with her son's endless demand for attention by staring into his shining blue eyes and drawing gratitude and inspiration to protect and watch over her squishy, pink miracle, no matter how tough parenthood proved to be, Donavon made his peace by drinking until he was numb and passing out where he lay.

The demon took over. Donavon changed. He drew insular. Naomi shared with Tori the moments in which she detected the hatred in her husband's eyes. A deep resentment that a child could claw at every corner of his life and claim it for his own. She tried to pacify Donavon, explain that this was parenthood, and that they would work through it together. But over time the bottles emptied, and the lion's share of the work fell on Naomi.

Tori didn't see Naomi for months. On the rare occasions that Tori called her sister, Naomi's voice grew ever more strained and cracked. Then, one day, as Tori was running downstairs to pack her bag and get ready for school, she could hear Naomi's tinny, distorted screams through the telephone receiver. Her mom held the phone at arm's length, her father lowered his paper with interest.

They never did find Donavon's body. Naomi only managed to track him so far into the woods. His footprints led in, but they never led out. The town performed a rudimentary search of the borders of the Drumtrie Forest, but even the local authorities hardly dared to tread further inside than necessary. Superstition was rife in Denridge, and it was believed that dark magic lay in the beating heart of the dense pines. Those who entered never returned. It was just a way of life.

Tori and her parents helped Naomi through her grief as best they could. How could you console a broken mother and a weeping infant after such a loss? Naomi told the family of Donavon's drinking, explained the dark spin his life had taken, spoke something about a tale of a white stag and Donavon's obsession with his "Death Hunt," but that all fell on deaf ears. Tori was young, swallowed by her own grief. She had grown close to Donavon and had never experienced a loss so close to her inner circle.

A few years, and the loss of her parents, would change that.

That had been the story as Tori knew it. It had never explained the strange appearance of the mutant man-stag skull that appeared over Naomi's hearth, but since the arrival of that skull, her sister had found some semblance of peace. It was a strange ornament, looking as though it belonged in a museum of medical marvels more than as a decorative piece to display on the mantel, but Tori didn't press her sister on the subject. The grief-stricken work through their process, and it's for no one else to understand. The best you can do as an outsider is support and provide a shoulder to lean on when asked. Grief is a solitary journey, made harder for a widow and her newborn child.

Now, Tori listened with morbid eagerness as Naomi regaled her tale, taking the existing narrative and twisting and bending it into shapes that Tori couldn't comprehend. She remained tight-lipped as Naomi spoke of those final months again, turning over the story of Donavon and his drinking, matching the mantra line for line until she came to the day that she discovered that he was gone.

"He was obsessed with hunting that stag. A huge white thing. I wasn't even convinced existed, it just seemed like a figment of his imagination. Something that he hooked onto and couldn't let go. No matter how much I tried to keep our life moving forward, he couldn't let go."

She told Tori of her and Donavon's trip into the Drumtrie Forest to gather wood, the long, invisible hook drawing him deeper into its heart. She had dragged him home. Thought she could keep him safe, curb his obsession...

That night proved her wrong.

"I woke up and he was gone. He didn't make a peep, which was unusual, he wasn't the quietest riser. But he wasn't there. He just wasn't. When I went downstairs, the back door was open, a chill running through the house. I remember thinking that the chill should have woken Oscar—hell, everything woke Oscar back then— but he was sound asleep, as if the world was conspiring to help him vanish."

Footsteps trailed into the forest. Naomi sprinted toward the borders, the weight of the monolithic trees towering above her an oppressive force. Somewhere in the darkness she fancied she heard laughter, deep, menacing laughter, but it was soon replaced by Oscar's cries.

Tori knew all of this—well, near enough. It was the next part that had Tori sitting up straight, the remaining water in her glass shaking in her hands.

"You know what came next. The search party. No body. No sign of Donavon. The police chief—Sanders, I think his name was, back then—he wrote it off as an unsolved mystery. Closed the books and called it a day. But that wasn't the end for me."

A smile played on Naomi's lips, no trace of mirth in them, just a shrug of nostalgia. "I remember finding the whole thing impossible to believe. I couldn't cry because I couldn't accept that it had happened. One day Donavon would return from the woods, maybe a little disheveled, maybe a little worse-for-wear, but he'd come back to me. Through it all, he'd always come back to me."

Naomi looked past Tori and to the stairs—not for the first time.

"And then it happened."

Tori reached forward and touched Naomi's hand. "It's okay."

Naomi nodded. "Four days later... it was... something that I haven't shared with anyone since that day." She took a steadying breath. "It was the middle of the night when I woke up and... felt something strange. Oscar needed a feed and so I obliged, taking him into my bosom until he was full. When I laid him back in his crib, milk-drunk and satisfied, I heard a knock on the door downstairs. My heart skipped. Already, I allowed myself to believe that it would be Donavon standing there, ready to greet me and apologize and I'd forgive him—of course, I would —and we could put all of this stupidity behind us. My love, returning from a booze-addled binge, but I could fix him. We'd make it right."

Naomi's eyes grew glossy. "I went downstairs and stood in front of the door, scared to open it. What if it wasn't him? What if it was whoever took him from me, come to claim what Donavon had left behind?"

Tori swallowed dryly.

"I was right on both accounts, I suppose. No one standing there. The world was empty and cold, and whoever had knocked was long gone." Naomi's brows knitted together as she met Tori's gaze. "Donavon was there, though. He was home."

It was Tori's turn to frown. "You just said no one was standing there?"

Naomi bit her lip to try and stop it wobbling. "He wasn't standing. He was... He was..." She closed her eyes, unable to say the rest, but Tori wouldn't let it go. Not now. She needed to understand.

"Was what, Naomi? Was what?"

Naomi glanced over Tori's shoulder. Tori turned and found nothing there, just an empty room. When she turned back, Naomi was staring up at the skull on the mantel, a strange sob stuck in her throat.

It took Tori a moment before she connected the dots and, when she did, her breath caught. She strode toward the skull, as if in a dream. She shook her head, taking her first proper look at the mask of bone, imagining what it might look like with a layer of flesh covering its surface, threaded with nerves and muscle and tissue and gelatinous fat, two eyeballs rolling around in the hollow sockets and a head of dark hair.

"It... It can't be."

Naomi joined her side. "It's him."

Tori's mouth gaped. The skull stared back at her with an intelligence it shouldn't hold. The shadows in those hollows looked out at her with the same dead-eyed stare of the wendigos. It was an unnerving thought, the wendigos burying themselves in her sister's life and watching her with every passing day.

Tori felt for the couch, her legs losing what little strength remained. "I don't understand any of this. What is happening to this town?"

Naomi continued to stare at the skull. "That's a big question. I'm not sure anyone has the answer."

"But you found me out there. You rescued me. How did you know to come for me? Why did the wendigos leave you alone?"

Naomi let out a soft sigh. "If there's one thing you've learned tonight it's that there are things in this world which cannot be explained. Am I right?"

Tori narrowed her eyes. "Yeah..."

"There's a higher power to this world, a plane of existence that we will never truly know or understand. The Iñupiat have known it for years, it's what they base their entire culture around, right? Their beliefs, their rituals, it's all bound in the unknown forces of this world. They worship the gods and ask for forgiveness. They cherish the beating hearts of Nature's creatures, even though they stuff their stomachs with their meat. The Aurora..." Naomi scoffed. "Magnetism and lights? Give me a break. It's a phenomenon that is otherworldly. The one true constant that remained in my bubble of the world... it broke tonight. The green and blue lights... They changed. They were tarnished. Did you see it?"

"I did." Tori saw the strange crimson glow in her mind, shining through her window as Karl pulled on his clothes and left the house, what seemed like a lifetime ago. She hadn't given it much thought until then, but could it all be connected? Was there something in the air that these creatures were drawing their power from? Alex had spoken of the Iñupiat too, had discussed the strange goings on in their tribes and their belief in the wendigo. Could it all somehow be one?

Tori's shoulders slumped. "This is crazy. Will this night never end?"

"There's more." Naomi poured herself another drink, this time draining it in one gulp. "You asked how I knew where to find you. How the wendigos let me be?"

Tori nodded.

"I can give you the answer to the first question, though you won't believe me."

"Try me."

Naomi let out a steady breath. "Donavon showed me."

Tori's brow creased. "I'm sorry?" She pointed at the wall. "The skull showed you?"

Naomi shook her head, eyes darting back to the staircase. "No. *He* did. Donavon. I don't know how to explain it, but he's back. He's here." She chuckled, as though she hardly believed it herself.

Tori turned over her shoulder, finding nothing of note behind her. "I don't understand what you're talking about. Donavon died over a decade ago. What do you mean he was here?"

"No, Tori. *Is* here. Right there."

Again, she pointed to the stairwell. Again, Tori saw nothing.

Tori fixed Naomi with a concerned stare. "You're crazy."

"Am I?" Naomi asked. "I struggled to come to terms with it, too. But he's here. It's real. He came to me tonight. I woke up, that same discomfort in the pit of my stomach that came on the night that I woke to find him missing. There's something in the air, Tori. Something *big*. I fought to discredit what I was seeing, came up with a thousand reasons as to why it couldn't be true. But there he stands, and if it hadn't been for Donavon, I would never have found you. Would never have known you were in trouble. He guided me through the storm. Showed me the way back. You don't owe your life to me. You owe your life to him."

"To a dead man?"

"He's not dead!"

Tori threw her hands in the air. "Don't you hear yourself? This is insanity. Donavon is dead. Ghosts don't exist. This is all—"

"Then you explain it," Naomi barked. Tears sparkled in her eyes. "Explain why I can see him standing there. Explain why I can hear his voice. Explain how my innate GPS system guided me straight to you. You can't, can you? You said it yourself. You saw those fucking things out there. When I found you, there were half a dozen of them and some brute who had been possessed by their power. There's magic at play, Tori. I don't have all the fucking answers, but I know what I know." She pointed to the stairs. "Turn around and thank him. Thank my fucking husband for saving your ass. You don't owe me shit, but you owe him everything."

Tori turned slowly to the stairs. Her eyes lingered in the place where her sister claimed her late husband stood. There was nothing out of place there, nothing out of the ordinary. No sign to give credit to her sister's claim.

"Naomi, I don't see…"

"Go on."

Tori closed her eyes and tried to imagine him there. Her brother-in-law, in his prime, beaming back at her, a smile that could light up a room. And, as she imagined him there, an image coalesced in her mind. When she spoke, the words were soft, wrapped in cotton wool, a deep appreciation set into the inside like a sticky nougat treat. "Thank you."

A shadow appeared at the bottom of the stairs. Tori's eyes narrowed, her heart beating faster. In the place where she had imagined Donavon, the shadows took his shape, swelling and growing until they accommodated his size and figure. Tori gasped, unable to process what she was—

"Mom?" Oscar's voice trailed down the stairs. His bare feet appeared as he padded down the wooden steps, and it was then that Tori realized the shadow had been his, cast by what little light leaked from somewhere upstairs as Oscar eavesdropped on their conversation.

Naomi poured herself a drink and nursed it in her hand. "Yes, baby?"

Oscar stopped halfway down the stairs, resting his head on the railing. He was the spitting image of his father. The same keen eyes, a dark crop of hair in a scruffy mess, sticking out on one side from where he had been sleeping. "Is everything okay? I heard shouting." His eyes found Tori, lingering on the dark stains of blood around her nose. "Aunt Tori? Are you okay?"

Naomi was silent, pondering her response. Tori hated to think it, but she had aged considerably in the years since Donavon's disappearance. Her sister, once lithe and filled with vigor, was now a ghost of what she once had been. Not that that diminished the inner sparkle she saw in her tonight.

"Mom?"

"Everything's okay..." Tori started, until Naomi cut across her, head shaking.

"Everything's not okay. Don't even pretend that it is." Her words were keen, sharpened. "Oscar, you should know that something has happened tonight. Something terrible is taking place in the town, and as much as I believe that we might be safe here, we have to be prepared for what might happen if that doesn't turn out to be the case. Can you do that for me?"

Oscar's back straightened. He puffed out his chest. A real mini man of the house. "What is it? What's going on?"

"Go to your father's store and select one of his guns," Naomi instructed. "Pick something that you know you can handle. None of that rifle bullshit, get yourself a handgun. Maybe a .38. You've been practicing with that one, haven't you?"

Oscar nodded and ran down the stairs, disappearing through a door at the back of the room. They heard him rummaging around as Tori opened her mouth in disbelief. "I thought you didn't want to lie to him?"

"I'm not."

"You told him things might be okay. You told him that this house might be safe. That's a downright lie, as far as I'm concerned."

Naomi shot Tori an intense glare that was alien on her face. Oscar returned with a gleaming Colt Super .38 as he played with the chamber and checked the ammunition.

"Got it!" There was a sense of pride in his eyes. Even at eleven-years-old he seemed to understand the severity of the situation. "What are we hunting, Ma? Is it the storm? Has it brought more wolves?"

"Yeah," Tori added, shooting Naomi an accusatory look. "What are we hunting?"

Naomi sipped her drink. Placed it on the counter. "I'll show you."

She led them upstairs, Tori allowing Oscar to follow directly after his mother. She marveled at the paintings on the walls, the decorative pieces of furniture, all items that bookmarked the year of Donavon's passing. Streaks of dust and dirt lined every surface, and there were mud tracks on the carpet that looked as though they had been there for some time.

A widow finds their own way to grieve. Their own way to manage.

They passed Oscar's bedroom as Naomi led them to the landing window, a wide strip of glass that, on a sunny day, gave them an unobstructed view of Drumtrie Forest.

Naomi drew the curtain.

They stood either side of Naomi—Oscar on her left, Tori to the right. Their breath fogged the glass, clouding the view ahead. Tori cocked her head, wondering if she could sense the storm easing up a little. For the first time that night she could see beyond the reach of her arm as the snow came down in gentle flakes. The ground outside was virgin white. Her eyes trailed as far as the snow would allow as a hand slowly rose to her lips.

"Some things can't be explained," Naomi whispered. "I'm yet to determine what this means... I fear the answer."

Standing on the borderline of their field of view were over a dozen of the pale white creatures, arranged in a uniform line that formed a perimeter between the house and the forest. They stood as silent sentinels, each one unflinching as snowflakes gathered on their shoulders and the crowns of their heads. They wore no masks, their faces gaunt and drawn, giving the haunting appearance of skulls balancing atop their bodies. Already the snow had mounted up to their ankles.

Oscar reached for his mother's arm. "What are they?"

Tori's face hardened. She remembered Alex's words, his visit to the Iñupiat, the name he had given them as they sought shelter in the heart of St. David's church. The same name that had fallen from Naomi's lips. She wondered where Alex was now, if he had finally found a way back to his nephew. Was Damien okay, too? Were they even alive right now, or had the creatures gotten to them?

Her eyes stung with tears as she took a long breath, fearing that saying their name might trigger them into action. "Wendigos, Oscar. They're wendigos."

Oscar raised an eyebrow. "What are they doing?"

"Watching," his mother said simply. "And waiting."

"Waiting for what?"

The two sisters stared out at the wendigos, the answer to Oscar's question on both their lips. Neither one of them brave enough to admit the truth.

We don't know, Oscar. We don't know.

From somewhere deep in the heart of the Drumtrie, the forest rumbled.

41

ALEX GOINS

E very shadow was an enemy. Every suggestion of sound an invader.

With Damien in tow, Alex led the way, approaching every classroom, office, bathroom, and closet as though a thousand wendigos might be waiting to pounce. There was no sign of intrusion in the building they entered through, and the maps and signs on the walls only further confused him. The room number system was shoddy and outdated, and in many cases the signs were faded and barely legible. How kids managed to make their way to class every day was beyond him.

The only sounds were their own footsteps as their boots clapped against the linoleum, and the ever-present hush of the raging storm. Damien was silent, for the most part, finding his voice only when they'd stop and Alex would scratch his head trying to figure if he was heading in the right direction to the gymnasium. In the beginning, he had sought the outdoor courts, until a raging howl of wind reminded him that no man or woman would be able to play basketball in these conditions, which meant only one possibility remained.

It was all hypothetical, of course. Alex questioned how kids would be able to break into the school to access its facilities. Those locks were monstrous, and he was certain that Cody wouldn't befriend kids who carried rifles and shot through the glass just so they could steal some bonus recreational time.

But what did he truly know anymore? Hadn't this night proven to him that he had grossly underestimated the limits of Cody's rebellion, let alone the types of activities that kids in this area of the world engaged in? He was in a foreign land, far from home, caught in the storm of a lifetime. Didn't he have to be open to all possibilities?

When they reached a set of external fire doors, their search of this side of the school turning up nothing, they braced themselves to momentarily re-enter the storm.

"You ready?" Alex asked, eliciting a firm nod from Damien. They ran to the next building, shriveling in the snow and gritting their teeth. Alex shot the window, cleared the glass, helped the kid up, then climbed in after him.

He shook the snow free from his hair. Blood and dexterity had returned to his extremities, but there was a warm throb in his earlobes which concerned him. His nose was sore and raw to touch, and if he strained to look down at its tip it was darker in color.

I hope it's not too late.

Their journey had taken them to the teacher's lounge. Couches formed a square around a central coffee table. Papers lined the walls, fluttering gently against a cork board as the wind explored the room. A coffee machine sat against a countertop and a faucet dripped idly over the sink.

Damien wandered over to the wall, heavy bags hanging beneath his eyes. He reached for a piece of paper, holding it steady, a smile on his face.

"What have you found?"

Damien traced his finger along the paper's surface. "It's Courtney, Ewan, and Trey. They're on the teacher's bad behavior list."

Alex stood behind him, examining the faces of the three young children. While it wasn't exactly a list of kids to watch out for, there were notes scribbled on the page. Red lettering in a scrawl that was barely legible, but the overall tone was clear. The teachers were working together to figure out what to do with these kids. Alex wondered how that would fit into teaching practices in the wider world. If kids should be singled out and viewed as bandits once were to a Western town. "Reward $500." Not that it mattered at all here. In this tiny town, who would even take the mantel of regulating teaching practices? What rules applied in the forgotten towns of the north?

"Come on." Alex placed a hand on Damien's shoulder and nudged him away. The paper slipped from the kid's fingers, but he remained still. "What is it?"

"I'm hungry."

Alex laughed, the sound taking him by surprise. It seemed so ordinary, yet unusual, too. Hunger. A simple thing, forgotten under the stress and trauma.

His stomach rumbled, responding to the call. "Me, too."

"Got any food?" Damien held no hint of irony to his face. His eyes wide and bright.

"No. I haven't. I didn't think to pack a lunch before I came out."

"Mom always had food," Damien said, resting against the back of the couch. "Better to be safe than sorry, she'd always say. Always had packets in her pockets. Snacks for every occasion." His face darkened. "I miss her."

Alex frowned, his shoulders slumping. He crouched in front of the kid. "When this is all over, we'll make you the biggest meal you can think of. Anything you want. Me and you. We'll load our plates and eat until we throw it all back up again. How's that?"

Damien laughed, the sound refreshing and uplifting.

"What's your favorite?"

Damien screwed his face in thought. "I like beef jerky."

"We can get you beef jerky."

"And reindeer dogs?" Damien's eyes lit up.

Alex cocked his head. "Reindeer dogs?"

"Yeah, like dogs in a bun."

"Hot dogs?"

"Sure, I like them hot."

Alex chuckled. "Anything else?"

"Ice cream?" Damien's excitement grew. "All the flavors of ice cream. Chocolate, and strawberry, and mint, and the blue one."

"Bubblegum?"

"Mom puts them all in a bowl and I mix it."

"You do?"

"It's like a rainbow in a bowl." Damien hopped to his feet, mimicking stirring a spoon in a gigantic bowl. "It goes around and around and around, until it's all wet and melted."

"Sounds magical."

"It is. Until it goes an icky gray color."

Alex pushed himself to his feet. "We can get you ice cream, hot dogs, jerky, all that stuff. Anything you like once this is all over. Think you've got a little bit more in you to keep going? I reckon we're close."

Damien walked past Alex and stopped at the door. He looked back over his shoulder, confusion on his face.

"What're you thinking?"

"You didn't say Cody. When you said we were going to eat lots of food together. You said me and you. You didn't say Cody." The mirth dissolved from his face, eyes lowering to the floor. "My mom is dead, isn't she?"

Alex's face hardened, the reality of their situation returning in spades. "I don't know."

"And my dad, too."

Alex closed the distance between them. "I wish I could tell you, Damien. I honestly don't know."

Damien chewed his lip, eyes brimming with tears. "When will we know?"

"When this is over."

"When will that be?"

Before Alex had the chance to answer, they both flinched at a sudden crash coming from somewhere down the hallway.

"What was that?" Damien breathed.

Alex placed a finger to his lips. He leaned against the door and pressed his ear to the wood. There was something moving out there. Uneven footsteps and the scratch of something solid and sharp.

He reached for the lock and twisted. Damien pressed against him. "Under that table," Alex whispered, pointing to the coffee table. It wouldn't provide a lot of cover, but it would do to hide him for a moment.

Damien obeyed, disappearing into a ball beneath the table. The disturbance grew louder, accompanied by a sound that forced Alex to imagine an asthmatic trying to scream.

He teased the door open a crack, eyes widening at the creature flailing around the halls. It was a wendigo, no question. Its gaunt, malnourished body spasmed, its hands pinned to its head. Ivory toenails scratched across the linoleum, and every now and then an arm would reach to the wall for support. It searched and scrabbled in a frenzied state as though it had been blinded. Scorch marks stained the remaining bone, some of the leathery flesh burned and singed around the edges of its empty wounds, waving like tattered ribbon.

Alex edged the door open and sidled through. He approached slowly, rifle trained in front of him, waiting to get a proper look at the damage. Burned meat tinged the air. The wendigo flailed, bashed into a set of lockers, fell to the ground, pushed itself back to its feet. So preoccupied in its own struggle it hardly noticed Alex standing there.

Alex took aim, eye held to the sight. He readied his finger on the trigger, exhaled.

Shot.

The rifle kicked back against his shoulder, but the shot was true. The bullet found its way into what remained of the wendigo's head. Thick splatters of gore and flesh sprayed the walls as the wendigo was put out of its misery. It folded, crumpled on the floor, limbs at impossible angles. Alex adjusted the rifle and crept forward. Although the creature was down, he remained on his guard. These were creatures from another realm, he had no guarantee that bullets would kill the magic at work here.

He stood over the wendigo and shot again. Bullets were precious, but so was his life. The wendigo bucked, then lay still. There was no animal skull to protect the creature's head. Nothing there to guard the shrunken, shriveled mess that may once have held a human face. The nose sunken in, the lips non-existent. What remained of the head was nothing more than a prune left to dry in the sun, the features almost faded entirely.

No longer human.

Not of this world.

A creature. Nothing more.

A door creaked. Alex whirled. Damien gave a weak cry and shied back. Alex lowered the gun. "It's okay. It's gone. Come out."

Damien ran to Alex and threw his arms around his waist. "I thought you were dead."

"Now, why would you think that?"

"Because everyone's dying tonight."

Alex cupped the boy's head and pressed him closer, offering a small modicum of comfort. They both studied the creature, its limbs stretched out, beyond human length. Those arms were primitive, the creature so gaunt that Alex was sure there would be no medical explanation as to how this creature had once lived and breathed.

"What is it?" Damien asked softly.

"A monster."

"Where did it come from?"

Alex glanced down the hallway. "That way. Come on, if there was one, there may be more."

"And that's where you'll find Cody?"

Alex sighed. "I hope not."

42

CODY TREBECK

Cody knelt beside Brandon, holding a cold compress to his forehead. Sophie had salvaged it, finding an old scrap of stained cloth somewhere in the depths of the ancient cupboards. She had fought to open the window, wrestling enough of a gap to hold the rag out into the storm until it was sodden and cold. It was all they could think to do, and judging by Brandon's condition, it wasn't enough.

Cody frowned. "Talk to me, Brandon. What's going through your head?"

His breath came in sharp hitches. From the moment the fires faded in the tunnel and the screeches ground to a halt, Brandon slumped against the wall, hand clutching his chest. Despite the cold, his forehead was sticky with sweat. Cody and Sophie worked to ease him out of his jacket, finding dark patches beneath the armpits of his undershirt, as well as a generous puddle of sweat gathered around the folds of fat that circled his midriff. They both knew it wasn't a good sign. A fever in a blizzard demanded medical attention.

Brandon gasped for air, each hollow intake a death rattle. His eyes were clamped shut, mouth open, lips dry. Cody remembered the day his father had taken him fishing, years back, with high promises of hooking a catch large enough to put Jaws to shame. On that baking summer day, with the leaves in the trees still and the lake's surface smooth as silk, Cody had caught his prize. A forty-pound carp that writhed and wriggled, heavy enough that his father came to his aid to help him reel the carp to the shore.

Cody posed for a picture, gripping the fish tightly. It couldn't have been out of the water for longer than three minutes, but that was all it took for the fish to suffer.

"Great job. That's one for the photo albums," his father beamed, presenting the small window of the digital camera. "Wait until your mom sees this."

But Cody wasn't listening. The carp looked up at him imploringly, gills opening and closing with strained effort. Mouth hung open as it gasped for oxygen. Starved of water. Unable to do anything but lie there at the mercy of the kid holding him tightly in his arms.

His father gently took the carp from Cody. "I think that's time enough, don't you?" His voice was friendly, soothing. "Fish need water like we need air. Fishing may be fun for us, but only so long as we put them back when we're done. They don't deserve our cruelty."

Cody had been certain the carp was dead. By the time his father eased the fish to the lake's surface, it had long fallen still. Eyes blank. Yet, at the moment contact with the lake was made, the carp sprang to life, kicking off a small splash of water at Cody's shirt, his father reeling with laughter.

The carp swam a circle, then vanished into the mirky greens. Cody couldn't stop smiling.

But this wasn't a hot summer day, and Brandon wasn't a carp, even if he did sport that same lifeless look on his face. Peace subbing in for the pain as thick lips desperately sought what his oxygen-starved body lacked.

"Brandon?"

Cody shook him violently. Sophie said something that didn't penetrate Cody's bubble. Brandon's head lolled on his shoulders. Chin rested on his chest. A string of drool snaked from his lips and wet his shirt.

"Cody!" Sophie pulled him back, freeing Brandon from his clutches. Cody's eyes widened as his bubble popped and the dawning of his desperation hit him. Sophie eased Brandon's head back and rested it against the wall. "We've got to be careful. We don't know what could make him worse."

"We need to make him better," Cody replied. "We can't just leave him like this."

Sophie nodded. "I know. But this isn't the way. We've already lost Hayden, Travis and…" She exhaled slowly and composed herself. "We've lost too many already. This isn't the way. He needs medical attention. We can't just shake him back to health."

Brandon grunted, eyes flickering beneath closed lids.

"We don't know that Hayden is dead."

"How can he not be?" Sophie retorted.

Cody's lips pressed into a thin line. "What do we do, then? We can't just sit here. We can't."

Sophie sighed. "I don't know. Wherever this place is, it's far from anywhere." She looked around the room. A door stood ajar in the corner, still open from Sophie's exploration around the tiny shack. Cody had sat with Brandon while Sophie searched the house, able to find only one other room on the ground floor, and a set of stairs which led to an open space upstairs that had once been a bedroom. The shack was empty, clear of other people. Holes as wide as bears dotted the walls upstairs, allowing the storm to sweep through and freeze the barren wood planks. When Sophie returned to the others, she had been wide-eyed and shivering.

At least this room was properly sheltered.

"What even is this place?" Cody asked.

"It makes no sense. Maybe it was one of the earlier houses in the town? Could be a false start from when the first settlers founded Denridge."

"That doesn't explain why there's a tunnel connecting it to the school." Cody rose from Brandon, happy to leave him with Sophie as he crossed to the window. Outside, all was white. No landmarks or signs to mark their compass by. "Where the hell are we?"

Sophie placed the compress to Brandon's forehead. A relieved smile played on his lips. Goofy, crooked. Brandon coughed, then shuffled uncomfortably, fingers tightening on his heart.

Cody gave him a pitied look. "He's the smart one. He'd know what to do, that's the bitch of it. He knew about Travis and his concussion. If we could get him to talk now, he could help us out of this situation. He could tell us how to fix him."

"He's not a doctor, Cody."

"No. He's a friend."

Sophie's eyes glittered, tears threatening to spill. "I think the answer would lie in not being chased by wendigos through a rotting tunnel, much less having to sprint when you're overweight, too." She placed her head in her hands. "Fuck, Cody. What the hell were we thinking tonight?"

Cody rested his back to the wall, all thoughts of rebellion and basketball and girls cycling around his head in a sour mess. "I don't know. I guess..." He chewed his lip, unsure whether to say what was on his mind.

Sophie helped him out. Her skin was tainted with dirt and grease, her hair out of sorts. However bad she looked, Cody was certain he looked worse. "I hate to get morbid, but I'm pretty sure there's a real possibility we could die tonight. Whatever you've got to say, just say it."

Cody's eyes grew glassy. Sophie was an arm's reach from him. He traced his toes along the ground, creating small, clean grooves in the dust. "I guess... I just wanted to spend time with you."

Sophie smiled, her own eyes misty with tears. She leaned forward and placed her lips on Cody's and once again he was transported. For a brief moment they were gone from this world to a private plane where all that existed was Cody and Sophie. His hands cupped her cheeks. She tasted of earth and dust. Her hands found his lower back. Their tongues danced. What little breath remained in his lungs vanished as they claimed their moment—possibly their last —together.

When Sophie pulled away, they struggled to meet each other's eyes. "We have to get out of this."

Cody gave a short, derisive snort. "But what do we do? Where do we go?"

Sophie looked to the window. "I don't know. But we can't wait here. This shack is no protection if the wendigos come."

"When..."

"When," Sophie confirmed.

"Fuck." Cody's hands balled into fists. No matter which way he turned, it all amounted to the same. They were trapped. It all boiled down to two simple choices: hide in the hollows of this shack until the monsters came, or chance a deadly blizzard in the hope of finding safety out there, in the white. One way or another, the most likely scenario was death.

Cody took Sophie's hands. "We've got to go out there."

"But, Cody..."

"Not far," Cody assured her. "Enough to see if anything is nearby. It's the best option we have." He took a long breath and zipped up his jacket. He brought his hood over his head. "Keep an eye on Brandon. If I'm not back in fifteen minutes..."

"What?"

"I don't know. Stay here. Come for me. I don't know..."

Sophie's face twisted in frustration, but she didn't argue. She knew that Cody was right. His mind was set. She nodded, then ran swiftly from the room. A moment later she returned with a long coil of rope in her hands. "I found this in the other room. It's a little worse for wear, but it might be enough to tie to create an anchor point at the house and to make sure you don't get lost in the storm."

"I'll find my way back."

Sophie's face hardened. "I'm not taking any chances. If you lose sight of this house, the blizzard will take you. I'm sure of it. In case you hadn't noticed, the storm... the *Aurora*, is working against us, too."

Cody reached for the rope. Sophie pulled away, looking at him earnestly. "Make sure you come back. I can't lose you, too. I... I need you, Cody."

Cody flushed.

The storm belted its frozen breath the moment he opened the front door. It belched its snow and battered his body even as he knotted the rope around the bottom bar of the stairway banisters and secured the other end around his waist. Sophie checked the knotting at either end, then kissed his lips once more. "Good luck. Don't be long."

"I don't plan to."

Her hand rose to his cheek. "I'm not sure they care all that much for our plans today."

Cody offered a weak smile before turning to face the white.

One foot after another, he entered the storm, Sophie closing the door quickly behind.

43

HAYDEN LOCKLEAR

The floorboards creaked beneath him. They sagged and flexed with each infinitesimal movement, but at least from up here he could keep watch. He could keep safe.

They had made it safely out of the tunnel. Well, Sophie had, at least. Through the missing knot in the wooden floorboards he watched over her as she examined the upstairs room of the shitty little shack. She wouldn't find anything of value. Hayden had already searched every nook and cranny of this place. Had time to peruse the house and determine that there was nothing around to help his cause. Nothing there to fight the monsters and guide them home. Not downstairs, at least. Not that they cared. All of them were conspiring against him. They hated him, and he hated them back. Tit for tat.

He wondered how Travis was doing; if Sophie had left the poor guy downstairs while she searched the house. He had already been in bad shape when he melted into the darkness, stairs wouldn't help anything there. Travis was going to be a goner soon. They all were. Hayden had been certain that he had reached his end. One look out of the window offered no sign of relief. They were in the ass end of nowhere, and those creatures would get them.

Or, so he had begun to think.

The hatch to the attic avoided him at first. It wasn't until he'd climbed inside the closet and searched amongst the moth-bitten jackets and clothing that a creak drew his attention to the ceiling. He squinted in the darkness, noticing a thin break in the gloom, and with that he climbed. The old clothing rail bowed in protest, but still he climbed, finding his way into the attic.

It was cold up here, but that didn't matter none. It wasn't as cold as the room below, and that was enough.

Boxes littered the space, most of them filled with rotten shit that had decayed over time. Crates and cardboard now bent and warped, filled with the ghosts of forgotten times and better years. Dust itched his nostrils and stung his eyes. Yet, amidst it all, in a rectangular chest, cushioned on a bed of velvet...

A revolver.

Somehow, despite the passage of time since the gun had last been handled, it was in near mint condition. Hayden had only ever handled his father's rifle, but he could glean enough and extrapolate the information to work out how to use a revolver. It was loaded. It was ready. Four bullets nestled in the chamber. Would the gunpowder still ignite? Would the damn thing fire? Hell if Hayden knew, but dammit did he feel powerful.

The tables have turned, fuckers. Now it's time to play by my rules.

Knowing that they would eventually end up in Hayden's little corner of the world, he had bided his time. Laid low. Shivered. Napped. Conserved his energy. Lying in wait...

And now they were here.

When Sophie disappeared from sight, Hayden counted the seconds, waiting to see if the others would come upstairs. After half an hour, he pushed himself to his knees and grinned in the darkness. He weighed the gun in his hand, flexed his finger on the trigger. How would it feel to shoot a human? Would it be a far cry to the birds and moose he had taken down with his father? Would they scream and beg for mercy in the end?

Hayden crawled toward the hatch, taking his time, not wanting to do anything that might alert the unsuspecting victims. He teased open the edge of the hatch and was about to lower himself down when something caught his attention. He was almost certain he'd heard a cough.

A cough?

You're going crazy, my friend.

Still, he glanced back into the dark, the shadows playing tricks with his mind. Visions of wendigos danced in the black, one small figure drawing his focus as it stood there and trembled.

"Please don't go..."

Hayden started, unable to comprehend what he was hearing. The voice was gentle, innocent. He shook his head, wriggled his finger in his ear. It couldn't be.

The girl stepped forward, fingers laced in front of her body. She was tiny, dark hair covered one side of her face. As she stepped out from behind a box, her neon-pink snow boots drew his focus.

"Are you... real?" he asked.

"I'm lost," the girl said. "Please, can you help me?"

Hayden eased the hatch shut and faced the girl, sitting on his ass. The gun hung loosely in his hand. "Is this your house?"

The girl shook her head.

"What are you doing here? Are you one of them?"

"One of what?"

Hayden considered his reply. "You're alone?"

The girl nodded. "I ran. There are monsters out there." She stated the words as casually as a news reporter reeling off the death count from a plane crash.

"I know."

"Are you a monster?"

"No. I'm Hayden. Who are you?"

"Alice," the little girl replied. "Can you keep me safe?"

Hayden glanced down at the gun in his hand. Thoughts raced through his mind of the horrors they'd seen tonight. Those creatures were out there, hunting them down. His friends had abandoned him. It was every man for himself, and now here was a little girl, asking him to protect her. To act as some kind of guardian.

Didn't she realize that Hayden Locklear was no one's hero?

He brought the gun to his eye and aimed it at Alice's chest. If she felt any fear, she showed no sign. He pulled back the hammer and took a slow breath, finger tensing on the trigger.

"What are you doing?"

"Sparing you the pain, Alice. Saving you from the monsters. Just like you asked."

There came a disturbance from downstairs. A door opening and the rushing howl of wind. Hayden looked over his shoulder at the hatch, wondering what the hell they were doing down there.

In his moment of distraction, the girl came for him. She swung the small metal box at his head, the corners colliding with his temple. Hayden's eyes rolled into the back of his head as the attic faded to darkness.

44

ALEX GOINS

I t was the only door that had been left open, and blood pooled at the threshold.

Alex knew they were in the right place. The awkward wall signs told him to continue to the gymnasium, but the sight of the crimson puddle veered him toward its coppery scent. Blood meant life. Life meant people.

Blood means more than that, though. You know this, Alex.

Corrugated metal stairs led into a downstairs room, but all that Alex could focus on was the dead girl.

Or, what was left of her.

"Damien, stay back," he said, without turning away. It was no use, Damien had already seen the body. What would Alex have done with it, anyway? Covered it with a blanket and told the kid the floor was slick with cherry juice?

Damien took Alex's hand. "Cody?"

Alex's eyes trailed down the metal staircase, following the tributaries of blood as they continued to drip and slither to the bottom. A pair of hot pink panties drank the blood halfway down the stairs. A couple of bones had been discarded and lay haphazardly, obstacles to their descent. A hunk of naked flesh lay against the wall, bite marks gouged along the creases of remaining skin.

Alex shook his head. "Watch your step and stay close." He started on the staircase, the soles of his shoes fighting for friction as the sticky lubricant slicked each step. He gripped the metal railing for support and encouraged Damien to follow by example. When they reached the bottom, Alex was prepared to find the bodies of more children but was relieved to discover that there was no trace. There were, however, a mix of corrosive chemicals puddled on the floor. Shelving units were toppled, the whole room more like a trap from a mad scientist's lab than a functional workspace.

"They had to have been here," he said, more to himself. Empty silver wrappers confirmed his belief, as well as a strange stream of air which blew through the room, though he couldn't locate its source.

He glanced warily at the puddles on the floor. In patches around the concrete basement, the liquid bubbled and baked the stone black. Yellow hazard labels flashed their warnings.

"Climb onto my back."

The boy didn't argue. Alex helped him, hands cradling his feet and growing sticky with the tacky residue of the girl's blood. He cupped his hands together beneath the back of Damien's thighs and started across the room, raising his own legs high enough to avoid tripping on the metal shelving structures, and avoiding the patches where acids consumed the stone flooring. When he reached the back wall, the air called his attention, and a quick look to his left found a gaping hole in the recess of the room.

He stood there for a minute, wondering if his eyes were playing tricks on him. What kind of kids could smash through a wall? Had this place been the birth of the Kool Aid man? He turned back to the stairwell, wondering if he was just making assumptions. Maybe Cody was elsewhere. Maybe he was hiding in a classroom. One dead body didn't prove they had come this way.

Then why was something deep down in his gut pulling him in that direction? Why was a nearby candle burned down to the wick?

A faint sizzling hiss rose from below. Alex looked down, the leather of his thick soles bubbling in the clear liquids. He marched away, turning to the tunnel's entrance as he stepped across the threshold and stared into the darkness.

"You got a light?" Alex asked Damien.

"Nope. Dad won't let me have a phone."

"Damn..."

"That's a bad word."

"Get ready for many more of them." Alex stared into the darkness, trepidation feathering his breath. He turned back to the room, finding a bucket of tools near the tunnel's entrance. He checked the floor before placing Damien down in a dry patch, then tore a section of his jacket off and wrapped it around the long handle of a hammer. He found a dull knife and examined the blade before sliding it roughly along the stone.

Meager sparks glowed in its wake.

"Interesting..." Alex thought back to the research he underwent when writing his desert thriller. His protagonist, Archie Taylor, had been trapped in the catacombs of the Egyptian pyramids, in dire need of a light source. Alex had pored over the internet for hours, hunting for means and methods to provide illumination to the guy, hating the idea of going back several chapters to rewrite what he had already spent days laboring over. At the time, the research had been painful, and the block in his writing had taken almost a week to pass. Now, though, he was thankful for the block.

"Let's see if this works in practice..." Alex touched the rag to the nearest puddle. He then held the damp cloth next to the stone and hacked at the wall with the knife until the metal grew hot and another show of sparks flashed. A few more urgent scrapes and a spark caught the material, the cloth bursting into life with a warm, orange flame.

Damien tugged his waist, hungry for the warmth. Alex held the torch toward them both as they allowed themselves just a moment to bask in its heat. Alex brought his finger to the tip of his nose, dismayed that he couldn't feel its touch.

Worry about frostbite when this is over. There's little you can do about it now.

Holding the torch high, they stared down the stone tunnel and into the gloom. The flames flickered, catching the notches and crevices in the crude construction of the passageway. There was a green stain of moss on the walls, interspersed with white clusters of fungus. The ground was soft in patches, with stone interwoven with the dirt. The dancing shadows caused the tunnel to wobble, reminding Alex of a distant carnival ride that made him queasy.

He offered a hand to Damien, then remembered his rifle hanging over his arm. He guided Damien's hand to his side and told him to hold on tight. Without a word, Alex started walking, torch in one hand, rifle ready in the other.

Their footsteps beat the soundtrack to their march. The tunnel was endless, infinite. They passed no landmarks or unique points of interest until they arrived at a fork in the tunnel.

"Which way?" Damien asked, bulblike eyes glancing between the two.

Alex examined both entrances. He studied the ground, looking for footprints, but found nothing of note. It wasn't until he neared the left entrance and saw something on the edge of the torch's reach that he took another few steps forward.

Another one. Broken and burned and lying in a heap on the floor. A pile of blackened bones and ashen skin. This one sported no mask, either, but it didn't need one. The face was the only part left intact, and this one had the decency to at least try to appear human. The skin was a sickly hue, eyes wide and lifeless. The cheeks sunken in, lips peeled back, receded until all that showed were teeth and gums. But it was still human, at least in part. Alex wondered about that. About the stages of deterioration of the wendigo and the pecking order of the creatures. In most packs and groups there was a hierarchy. How many academics had had the chance to study this? To work out the order of the wendigo and preach it to the world. Could this be Alex's greatest project?

Wishful thinking.

First, he had to survive.

"This way," Alex said.

Damien hurried, momentarily separated from his guide. Alex stepped around the wendigo, and Damien followed. A few meters ahead, another body. This one human. A teen. A boy. There was a welt on his head and a peaceful smile on his face which stood in stark contrast to the bite marks and holes that littered his body. They had feasted, even as the boy had made his last stand. A hammer lay in the cup of his limp hand.

Bile rose in Alex's throat. He turned away, took a steadying breath, then walked on.

They came across more of them the further into the tunnel they trod. Three of them were dead and dealt with, and that gave Alex confidence. The one thing he was sure of now was that these things, no matter what fucked-up genetic makeup lay in their DNA, could be killed. Fire, steel, and gunpowder could destroy them. If they could die, there was a chance the others could survive.

Body number four was bordering on death. They heard it up ahead, a long time before it came into view, the tunnel magnifying its pitied efforts to crawl to safety. It dragged its shattered body with determined fingers, mouth still flapping, teeth clapping as it pulled itself away. There were no legs, only a torso, arms, and half a face. The other half had somehow caved in.

Alex debated using his rifle, until he found a nearby rock and used that, instead. Damien covered his eyes as Alex bashed in the creature's skull, a wet smack with every rise and fall until the body shuddered and fell still.

Alex discarded the rock with a loud clatter. He resumed his grip on the gun. Continued into the dark.

He wasn't sure how long they had walked for, but it was clear that Damien was beat. His feet dragged behind him, his shoulders slumped. The torch kept them warm and that made Damien drowsy. His eyelids fluttered, half-shut as he staggered onward, and it was just as Alex thought the kid might fold over and collapse that he spotted the pile of bodies ahead. He couldn't count how many there were. All that remained were blackened bones and charred walls. In the center of the bodies, an ember still burned, billowing out a sour smell that landed on Alex's tongue and made him wretch.

Damien continued walking, unfazed by this latest development. It wasn't until Alex was about to reach out and pull him back that he spotted the ladder. Alex held the flame higher, gaze drawn to the hatch in the ceiling.

His mind was bombarded with calculations and deductions, his heart fluttering as he tried to understand what he was seeing. There was a way out. Something had burned these creatures, fought them back. Could that mean what he thought it meant? That Cody was through that hatch? Whatever survivors there were to this hell-ridden path, they were through there?

Cody? Could it truly be?

Alex ran past Damien and scaled the ladder. He pushed the hatch but found no give. He climbed higher, throwing his shoulder against the ceiling, finding the tiniest bit of give on the hatch. Somewhere above, he was certain he heard voices muttering. "Cody! Cody! It's me. It's Alex! Let me in. Please! Let me in!" Damien stood at the bottom of the ladder, eyes fixed on Alex as his frenzy grew.

"Cody! If you can hear me, let me in! I'm here! It's me!"

Alex pounded his fist against the hatch, the sounds echoing along the tunnel. All his focus set on breaking this goddamn door down and closing the distance between them.

For the first time since Alex left his house that night, he allowed himself to hope.

45

SOPHIE PEARCE

I t all happened at once. The moment Sophie closed the door to preserve what little heat remained, colossal thuds rang out in the room where Brandon sat.

She froze, back to the door, wondering if Cody had heard. By the time she opened the door and called out to him, Cody was gone. Lost in the white. The wind stole her words and left her alone. The rope uncoiling around her feet as her thoughts turned from Cody to Brandon.

Oh God, she thought, remembering the way the unit had threatened to topple from the hatch before they had ignited the beasts. *They've come back. There are more of them. They're coming.*

She trailed her eyes up the stairs, sure that she had heard something from up there too, until another thud came from nearby. She ran toward the sound, skidding to a halt. Brandon sat against the wall, eyes closed. She couldn't tell whether he was breathing anymore. Both his hands were limp by his sides, his head resting on his chest, legs spread like a forgotten teddy bear. Another thud from the hatch beneath the unit and Sophie cried out in surprise.

She reached into her pocket, momentarily forgetting that Travis had stolen her weapon in the tunnels. Her hammer had been used in his last stand and now she was defenseless. What was she to do? She glanced at the hatch, expecting slender black fingers to poke through, the ghost of a bone mask staring through tiny holes.

"Cody! Cody! It's me. It's Alex! Let me in. Please! Let me in!"

Sophie's mouth fell open. It was a voice. A *human* voice. Someone had finally come to their rescue.

She stood there, stunned. Another few thuds against the hatch. Another surge of cries. "Cody! If you can hear me, let me in! I'm here! It's me!"

Cody. He said "Cody." Could it be...?

"Hold on!" Sophie cried, pressing herself against the unit and shoving with all her might. The unit shuffled a few inches. The hatch thudded beneath her feet. The unit caught on a groove in the floor. The voice cried out. Sophie shoved desperately, trying to undo what they had so recently done. She bent her knees, using her back, now. Her feet digging into the floor as the unit shifted.

And then the hatch was clear. Sophie had just enough time to jump clear when it burst open. A man's face appeared from the darkness, a rash of stubble and scruffy dark hair. In his hand was a flaming torch. The stink of charred meat and barbecue met her nostrils. He climbed free of the hole and stood in the room, looking wildly around. "Cody? Where's Cody?"

Sophie stood back, wary of the wild-eyed man and his gun. "Are you..."

"Alex," he stated. "Cody's my nephew. Where is he?"

Sophie broke into a run, launching at Alex and wrapping her arms around his waist. He was at least a foot taller than she was. He stank of sweat and fire. She closed her eyes and buried her head in his stomach, tears spilling from her eyes as relief overwhelmed her. A *grown-up*. A responsible adult. Someone who could finally help them out of this mess. She couldn't believe it. Help had finally arrived.

Alex eased Sophie back and crouched before her. He brushed a lock of hair from her face. "Are you okay? Were you with him? Where's Cody?" He looked past her, finding Brandon's body slumped against the wall. "Oh, God. He's not..."

Sophie shook her head. "No. Cody is fine. He's alive."

"Where is he?" The man's eyes took on a sense of urgency. "Please, just tell me where he is. I want to see him."

Sophie turned to the front door, just visible at the end of the room. The rope stretched to its full length, the line taught and anchored beneath the crook of the door. "He went out to see what was nearby." She looked up into Alex's face. "I can get him. I can bring him back. Please, just fix our friend first." She pointed to Brandon. Alex's face hardened.

"Deal. Just go get him, okay?" Sophie gave a resolute nod. But before she could get up, he added, "What's your name?"

"Sophie."

"Nice to meet you, Sophie." His smile was warm. Contagious. The corners of her own lips piqued.

Shuffling and huffing drew her attention to a young boy climbing out of the tunnel. His face was dirty and there was blood on his hands and legs. "Long story. We'll explain later. Please, get Cody."

As Alex busied himself with searching for what remained of Brandon's pulse and teasing his eyelids open to examine his pupils, Sophie made her way to the door. The rope was tight. That was a good sign. It would either mean that Cody was at the end of the rope and searching their perimeter, or he was using the rope to find his way back.

She opened the door, met by a blast of chill air that sucked the breath from her lungs. She stared into the white but could barely see her hand in front of her face.

She tugged at the rope, hoping to encourage Cody toward her, or at least warn him that something was happening... that he needed to come back.

However, when she tugged the line, all tension ceased. The rope went slack, limp in the palm of her hands. As she reeled in the line, fist over fist, her hope began to dwindle. By the time she found its end, her blood froze.

The end of the rope had frayed. Cody was gone.

EPISODE 5

INTO THE WHITE

46

CODY TREBECK

T here was only white.

The relentless brunt of the storm numbed Cody's face. He had forgotten what it was like to be out here, in the belly of the beast, having been safely sheltered in the nurturing womb of the school and the tunnels. Now, he was birthed into a mad world, a world dominated by only one color and an unbending will to end his life and bury him beneath the white.

The white.

It was all about the white.

The ancient, fraying rope was his single anchor to the known world, an umbilical cord that acted as his one remaining lifeline in this virgin landscape. He wondered if this was Heaven or Hell, for the stories had told him that Heaven was the white counterpart of the afterlife—clouds and beds of white.

But Heaven wouldn't batter his body like this. Barrage him with thousands upon thousands of pellets of ice, designed to bruise and tenderize his form, to weaken his will and turn him to mush.

Into white...

Sight was useless. There were no landmarks, no houses, no trees, no hills, no shadows, no shade, no protection from the white. For the first stretch of exploration, Cody held the rope with one hand, relying on the rope as a man with a broken foot bears his crutch. His footprints were rapidly swallowed up by a storm that felt increasingly sentient and angry with his presence in its bosom. A storm created by an unforgiving god, cast to punish him for a crime he didn't commit.

Cody wept, but the wind froze his tears. If he couldn't go back to the house with good news, then it was all over. They were trapped. On one side of them was a tunnel littered with the remains of the wendigos, their corpses burned and charred, and who knew if more were coming? Who knew if, even now, an army of the damned were racing toward Sophie and Brandon, smashing against the unit that blocked the hatch as they vied for entry?

And then there was the storm. A blizzard which assaulted their senses and granted no respite, no possible peek at the world around them. He could be just twenty feet away from help for all he knew, but the storm wouldn't show him its secrets. Oh, no. The storm wanted Cody's body. It fed off the pain and misery of the town as it gave the wendigos permission to continue their attack.

Cody relinquished his grip on the rope, walking ahead until it grew taught and tugged against the back of his jacket, reminding him that he was safe. As long as the rope was a part of him, he was a part of the house. He was a part of his friends. Of Sophie...

He brought his hand up to block the stinging snow as he strafed to his right, using the rope as an anchor point to the house so he could explore the perimeter. He imagined the reaction he'd elicit from Sophie when he headed back inside empty-handed.

"Hey Cody, what did you see out there?"

"Oh, nothing at all. Looks like everything outside is white. Ha!"

"Oh, never mind. I guess we're just trapped here until the storm blows over. Ha ha ha!"

"Ha!"

"*HA!*"

No matter which side of the house Cody examined, no matter which direction he faced—if direction was even a relevant metric anymore—there was only white. The wind pulled at his clothing from all angles, even going so far as to jar against the rope and tug against him as he doggedly continued. By the time he estimated himself to be halfway around the house, he knew something was wrong.

The tugging on the rope persisted. It pulled against his back, yanking so hard that he was forced back a couple of steps. He pulled the rope a few times to test it, staring at the point where the thin line of discolored cord disappeared into the white. By the time he knew that something had gone badly awry, it was too late.

The rope quivered in his hand, then went slack. The straight, measured line fell limp and collapsed like a string of wet spaghetti. His heart jarred as he pulled the rope toward him and one frayed end came into sight.

Oh no...

Cody scanned for the meddler, knowing that the wind itself could not have bitten through the rope. That was a trick he couldn't allow himself to believe of the wind. Not that. Not a storm that lives and breathes and cuts.

His mind filled with a thousand possibilities, thoughts of the wendigos craftily isolating him from the pack, picking them off one by one. His throat constricted, his breathing growing shallow as he prepared to run in the direction of the rope, terrified of not being able to make his way back to the house. A single knock off course and he'd be lost, guessing his way in this Neverland of snow.

He'd taken all of four steps before the thing streaked toward him, knocking into the side of his thigh. It sped by, losing itself in the white before Cody had a chance to get a proper look. Cody yelped, trying to process what he had just seen.

But he hadn't seen anything. Not really. Just felt the force of it.

Heart performing a drum roll in his chest, he set off again, only to be met with the snarling growl of the beast as it leaped at his back, this time knocking him face-first into the powder. Cody bit his lip, a droplet of blood falling into the snow, the only stain on an otherwise flawless world.

The growls rumbled from somewhere in the distance. Cody

scanned for the creature. Ahead, he fancied he could see the faint silhouette of the house. But could he, really? Could he believe it would all be that simple?

Another rumbling growl from behind as the creature caught his leg, daggerlike teeth sinking into the puffy material of his trouser. It pulled at him, dragging him backward as its head shook side to side, snarling and determined. Cody turned over his shoulder and could hardly make out what he was seeing. Two dark eyes buried into the white. A black nose turned gray from the battering snow. Indeterminate features floating in the snow.

Cody kicked out at the creature, emitting a pained howl as it spun and sprinted back into the white, vanishing the moment he could no longer see its eyes. The white of its furry body lost in the white of the storm.

Furry?

Cody pounded an angry fist into the ground, tired of it all. The rope trailed behind him, flaccid and useless. He pushed to his feet, stumbling a little at the pain that spiked his ankle. The teeth had clipped the skin, and something grew warm down there. Still, with a slight test, Cody found that he could walk. The shadow of the house was ahead, a beacon in the mist that called to him. A siren song of sailors lost at sea, and he, the stray captain hunting for land, if only he could cross the final stretch of ocean and find his way there.

A hundred meters or so of running and the house faded from sight. He expected the shadow to grow, for the house to materialize through the storm, but instead it trailed away and vanished. He'd had dreams like this before, dreams of running along an open motorway, racing toward his parent's car, screaming to warn them of their impending collision with the semi-truck, the beast swaying haphazardly as it took the on-ramp with too much speed and worked toward its inevitable jack-knife. Arms pumping, feet hitting the tarmac, yet gaining no ground, working the hallucinogenic treadmill of his mind to no avail.

Watching the crash in slow motion.

Breathless and sweating in the folds of his clothes, Cody pulled to a stop. He gasped at the air, trying to suck in oxygen but only succeeding in swallowing pellets of frozen water. He spun, knowing already that he was lost. That whatever that thing was that had been sent to waylay him had won. A creature, unlike those he had already encountered, something that appeared like a fuzzy blip in the coming storm of a migraine—and it had succeeded.

It had won.

Cody was the fool for believing he could act the hero. For believing he could save himself and his friends. A kid playing a game designed for grown-ups, out of his depth and stuck in his own failings.

There was nothing more for it. Cody picked a direction at random, knowing that there was a 359:1 chance that he was heading further off course, but what else was there to do? To reman still in this blizzard would be suicide. Inaction would lead to death. At least in walking he could hope to keep his engine warm and eventually find something. Anything.

Yeah, right. That's exactly what the world wants to give you. A goddamn break. That's why the world stole your parents when they were still in their prime. That's why you shipped out thousands of miles from home to live with an uncle who couldn't care enough to come and find you. That's why those monsters have killed your friends. That's why Hayden and Amy, and probably now Brandon, are all dead. That's why you're out here alone, lost in the heart of the blizzard. Because the world wants to cut you some slack. Because life is kind enough to give you just about enough that you open your heart to the idea of hope, only to have it ripped away again. This is it, Cody. This is the world you're living in, a world that would rather play games with your existence than let you sail a steady sea and find your destiny. When are you going to grow up and learn that life isn't about thriving? It's about survival. Get out of this one now, jackass. See if you can do it. I dare you.

Cody's thumb traced his lip, the ghost of Sophie's kiss still with him, though her scent was long gone. He thought of London, of the daily post-school ritual where his parents probed him for information on his day across the dinner table, the smell of roast potatoes and gravy hanging in the air. How his father only raised his voice at football games and his mother hugged him like he was still a six-year-old when she was drunk. Cody wanted nothing more than to cry, to fall onto his knees and submit. He didn't know what he was fighting for anymore. Life had stolen all meaning, and in its wake, it had left one thing.

The white.

Is this what it all meant? Was this the end that was spoken of in films and fairy tales? Was Cody just now being faced with the reality of death, walking into the white—*the light*—and that was the eternal walk? The final stretch of life that would bring him to the precipice? The place where time and space bind into a singularity and all that is known collects in the Never?

Cody stumbled, back hunched, arms draped like useless appendages. He staggered onward, the cold finding its way into his crevices, bringing him back to his bedroom and the cracks and grooves that whistled and howled and seeped the cold into his room, finding a bed in the marrow of his bones.

The howling winds...

The howls...

The howl.

A single, hollow note broke the white, striking the air from dead ahead. Cody paused, skin breaking out in gooseflesh as his dry tongue stuck to the roof of his mouth. It was back. Those two dark eyes, like the coal peepers of a snowman, the only break in the eternal white of the storm. Eyes ringed with the color of wedding bands and dripping honey.

The eyes grew larger as the creature approached, its entire body a pristine white that blended with the snow. Cody had no idea how large or small this creature may be, all he knew was that the eyes bore into his, and in their gaze was a plea for help.

Cody remained frozen and stunned as the creature came closer, stopping a short distance in front of him. It perched on its hinds and cocked its head, an obedient wolf quizzing the intentions of its master, asking for clarification, and yet only one question plagued Cody's mind.

Was this the same being that had attacked him just a few moments ago?

"Hello?" Cody's voice was cracked, soft, barely audible.

The wolf emitted a single, pitched bark, its maw showing a row of sharp, stubby teeth. It turned and padded away, once more fading as the blacks of its eyes were cast from sight. Cody waited, rooted to the spot, until the wolf looked over its shoulder and barked thrice more.

Was the creature telling Cody to follow it? It waited patiently, staring at Cody until he began his walk. A walk that would prove to be near impossible, considering that every time the wolf turned, he was lost from view.

47

ALEX GOINS

Alex's rudimentary examination revealed little more than they already knew. The boy was fading in and out of consciousness, struggling to get the oxygen he needed to his lungs. A faint sheen of sweat coated his brow, and with every attempt to breathe, the result was a shallow puff and wheeze.

Alex eased him onto the cold floor. The kid offered no resistance, his heavy frame aiding his fall, his head hitting the bare wood with a dull thud. He unzipped his jacket, working to get closer to the flesh so that he could examine what was going on inside. As he chipped away at the layers, Damien's shadow appeared behind him, the young boy watching his every move with a strange fascination.

"Is he dead?"

"No. If he was dead, he wouldn't be breathing." He managed to expose the boy's flesh and leaned down, placing an ear on his chest. "There's a rhythm there, though it's weak. Understandable, given all they've gone through and the nature of his body shape."

Damien leaned over Alex's shoulder. "What body shape?"

Alex didn't want to have to say it. There weren't many polite ways to voice it. Instead, he ignored the boy's question, looking around the room to try and work out what he could do to improve his condition.

Although he was by no means a medical expert, Alex had taken enough first aid courses and workshops to understand the mechanics of assisting a fallen patient with their breathing. It had been a fundamental part of writing the realism that carried the narrative in his books, understanding the basic functionality of modern medicine so that his characters could work their way out of any scrapes they found themselves in. Knowing when and how to apply a tourniquet, the best ways to treat a third-degree burn, and placing someone in the recovery position were things that had all come in handy with his catalogue of protagonists and side characters.

Still, if this kid was in arrhythmia or had gone into anaphylactic shock, then what was he to do? There was no medicine nearby, no tools, nothing to ease him from his discomfort. The house had been abandoned for years, what little was left was stripped bare or rotten. For the first time, Alex wondered what this place was and why they were here.

He lifted the kid's chin into the air, eliminating the threat of him choking on his own tongue. With some difficulty, he shifted his hips until his body rested on its side. He raised one leg at an angle, then sat back, hoping that this would somehow aid the boy's struggles and open up his airway. Only time would tell. There was no question that this kid's time was short. Even in the few seconds since he had listened to his chest, his breaths had grown quieter and more infrequent.

Damien tilted his head. "Is that it? Is he okay?"

"I don't know." Alex frowned at the doorway. "What's taking her so long?"

"I'll check," Damien said, eager to contribute. He trotted to the door, but before he could reach for the handle, Sophie swept into the room.

Before she spoke, Alex could already tell that something was wrong. "What is it?

Sophie revealed a length of rope, the other end trailing into the hall. She unfurled its remaining length, stopping when the rope ran out, holding up a frayed end.

Alex stood. "He's... gone?"

Sophie whimpered, her hand clamping her mouth.

Indelicately shoving Sophie aside, Alex rushed to the front door. He yanked it open, the full brunt of the storm hitting him in the chest, stinging his eyes, taking his breath. Outside, there was nothing but white, the ground, the air, the sky, all was lost in that singular color where the world had once been. He scanned the ground for footprints, any sign of a trail that might indicate that Cody had once been here, but all was lost.

The hope that had flooded his heart at finding the kids in the house melted and pooled around his feet. His fingers gripped the doorjamb, knuckles turning as white as the world outside as he slammed the door and closed off the blizzard. The storm beat against the door with icy fists, shouting its protest as Alex ran his hands through his hair and tried to think clearly about the next step ahead. In his periphery Sophie tried to hold in her anguish, the faint pulsing sobs of her misery leaking through the cracks of her fingers. Damien sat beside the dying kid, staring at Alex with that same curious expression that had become a staple on his young face.

The rope trailed on the ground, a dead, anorexic snake, its head blown off and left as wet strings of viscera in the wake of the shotgun shell. Not thinking, he wrapped it around his waist and secured the knot. There was still considerable length left, perhaps it could be enough to reach him out there.

He was out of the door before the others could react. Sophie's shouts formed the soundtrack to his exit as he ran into the snow until the rope pulled taught and snapped him back. He was thrown onto his ass, sinking into layers of powder.

Back on his feet. He scanned, searching in all directions for signs of Cody. When none came, he ran around the house, using the rope as his anchor point, mimicking what Cody should have been able to do with ease until the rope had snapped...

Snapped?

Alex stopped. He tugged at the rope, the only fixed point in this world of neutrality. The rope was strong—strong enough to bear Alex's weight as he had recoiled at the end of its tether.

So how had it split?

The storm picked up its fervor, hurling its contents at Alex in an effort to distract him from its wrath. He folded over himself, shielded the frayed piece of rope bound around his waist to examine the fine strings. Something had to have cut the rope. Something had to have interfered, severed it without Cody's knowledge.

So, what could it have been? What else was out there in the storm? The wendigos? Tori's ex-lover? What other secrets could the storm be holding? Waiting until the endgame to reveal its full hand of winning cards to reap the spoils.

Alex took a calming breath and reeled himself back to the house. It was useless. Even if there was a sign that Cody was nearby, he'd never find it. Not now. Not like this. The odds slimmer than finding a snowflake fallen into a bowl of warm water.

With every step, Alex expected the rope to go slack in his hands. Yet, after a minute of working his way along its taught length, the house came into sight. A mixture of relief and sadness flooded his body as he thought of Cody, wishing that he had been able to get back as easily and safely as Alex had.

Sophie stood waiting in the doorway, the front of her body jeweled in snow. She made way for Alex as he crossed the threshold, the weight he bore on his shoulders heavier than it had ever been. He had been so close. So damn close to finding his nephew...

"Did you...?" Sophie's voice trailed away, understanding it was worthless to ask.

Alex shook off the excess snow, leaving a small pile of damp in front of the door. He untied the rope and studied its end once more. "Something cut him loose."

Tears pricked Sophie's eyes. "How can you be sure?"

Alex ran the frayed threads across his gloved hand. "This is a strong rope. I'd be surprised if it broke of its own accord. Something was out there with him. They hacked away at the rope without him knowing. He's out there with them now, I'm sure of it."

"Is he...?" Sophie failed once more to finish her sentence.

Alex's eyes grew dark as he lost himself in dreary thought. A cough came from the other room, the sound of a geriatric, life-long smoker fighting the build-up of tar in his respiratory system. Alex gritted his teeth, allowing helplessness to take him.

Sophie surprised Alex by wrapping her arms around his waist. She pressed herself into his chest and cried. "I'm scared."

Alex cocooned Sophie in his arms. He looked over the top of her head to where Damien hovered near the big kid. Alex's collective tribe of misfits. How had it come to this? A man who had spent most of his growing years avoiding the shackles of parenthood, choosing instead to invest his time in creation, travel, and friends, now the sole guardian of two teens and a child—one teen clinging onto the brink of life in the heart of the storm...

"Me, too." He sighed. "Me, too..."

A creak from above, followed by a soft thud. Unmistakable. He glanced up the stairs.

Alex encouraged Sophie to head into the other room, teasing her arms from around his waist. He took the rifle from his shoulder.

"What is it? Is it one of them?" Sophie asked.

"Close the door," Alex said. "Wait with your friend. If you hear anything other than a gunshot, run."

"Run? Run where?"

Alex started his ascent, the wooden planks bowing beneath his weight. Each step protested, groaning loudly as he took the next.

Upstairs had fallen strangely quiet, and now each step he took alerted possible intruders of his position. There was no way to remain silent, but he didn't need silence with a rifle in his hands. He only needed to discover the source of the noise, which he was certain had been more than the architectural vocals of the shack.

Shadows danced ahead of him. A single room without a door. It may once have been a bedroom, but it had been a long time since anyone had slept here. A four-poster bed collapsed in on itself, only one post remaining. The floorboards were swollen and uneven, moth-bitten curtains flitting in the steady breeze created by large holes in the walls. It was a wonder that any of the glass remained, considering the spider-web cracks that littered their surface.

Alex swept the rifle around the room, preparing himself for the worst. In his mind he saw wendigos and vampires and werewolves, denizens of the night and of myth, coiled and ready to spring at the new arrival. Instead, he found nothing. Just an abandoned room, without even the trace of the ghosts of its former owners.

Alex shook his head, wondering if he had been hearing things. The night had been full of stresses, and he was no stranger to what this kind of stress, adrenaline, and a tired mind could do to its host. He wandered over to the bed and peeked beneath, emulating the fearful child he had once been, terrified of finding the Bogeyman or some multi-limbed creature eager to gnaw at his foot as it hung limply outside the safety of the covers. In his infantile mind he had once sworn to his parents that he had seen the beast wink at him, two orbs of colossal size in the darkness like jaundice moons staring back from infinite space. One eclipse becoming the intelligent wink that snatched his sleep for the next ten nights.

But Alex was older now, long past those prepubescent years of imagination and devilish wonder. Beneath the bed he could make out the shapes of decaying boxes and reams of cobwebs. Nothing moved down there, nothing shifted—unless you counted the gentle vibrations of his breath on the dusty gossamer.

A click from behind. Alex spun, staring into the face of a young girl, as pale as a lily, tinged with a hint of ice-blue. The unblinking eye of the barrel of the gun pointed directly at him.

"Are you a monster?"

Her voice was as soft as petals blown by a summer wind. Alex was taken aback by this sudden apparition, unable to comprehend where the girl had come from. She seemed so out of place here, her bright neon-pink boots attempting to draw the eye from the imminent threat of her pistol.

"No. I'm not a monster."

"Are you a friend?"

"I'd say I'm a stranger in this situation." Alex matched the girl's volume, fearful of drawing attention to the kids downstairs in case they rushed to his rescue and scared the tender doe.

"Mommy said not to talk to strangers. She calls it 'stranger danger.'"

"I bet your mommy also told you not to go wandering through the streets at night. Where are your parents?"

"I don't know." The gun lowered, a little.

"Are they here? Do they live in this house with you?"

The little girl shook her head, her curtain of dark hair falling over her face. "I'm Alice."

"I'm Alex."

Alice giggled softly. "They sound the same."

"They do." Alex shared none of her mirth. "Alice... Please put the gun down. There's nothing to be afraid of here. I'm not going to hurt you."

Alice considered this, the smile fading from her face. "But *you* have one."

Alex glanced down at the rifle clutched limply in his hand. He placed it flat on the floor and held up placating hands. "Not anymore. See?"

Alice allowed the pistol to slip from her grip and thump on the wooden floorboards. Her eyes lowered. "Alex...?"

"Yes, Alice?"

"I don't want to die."

The sadness in her eyes brought a dull ache in his heart. No girl her age should know that level of pain.

"Are you alone in this house?"

Alice sawed her nose with the back of her arm, eyes flickering momentarily to the ceiling. "Yes."

"Is this your house?" Alex felt he knew the answer but didn't want to presume. Alice confirmed his suspicions with a shake of her head.

"Where are your parents?"

Tiny pink boots kicked at the floor. She couldn't meet his eye. "The monsters came."

Alex swallowed, trying not to push the girl further than she was comfortable. "And how did you find your way to this house? How did you make it through the storm alone?"

"I walked."

Alice offered no other explanation, yet her words gave Alex hope. If a little girl could walk across Denridge and find her way to... wherever this place was... then wouldn't that mean they could all walk back together? If a... six-year-old? could survive the journey then, surely, they could too?

"Do you remember which direction you came from?" Alex shuffled closer, forcing her to look at him. "Do you remember how you got here?"

"No." She stared into Alex's eyes. "I heard voices downstairs."

Alex's eyes narrowed. Yes, there were people downstairs. But how would Alice react to the state of the dying kid? Should he expose a teen on the brink of death to a girl barely old enough to pick out her own clothes?

He reached for the pistol by Alice's boot and took it before she could realize what he was doing. By the time it was in his hands, she had taken a step back, eyes growing wide in fear. "No! I'm sorry... Please, no!"

Alex shoved the pistol hastily in his pocket and raised his hands. "Hey, it's okay. I'm not going to hurt you, I promise, okay? Alice... Calm down."

Alice stumbled backward, her face a mask of fear. Alex didn't know what to do. He could hardly chase her, could he? He took a tentative step toward her, thankful when a friendly face appeared in the doorway.

Sophie looked between Alex and Alice, brow furrowed as she examined the girl cowering against the wall.

"Where did she come from?" There was a hint of accusation in her voice.

"I don't know," Alex said. "But she's here now, and she's one of us... aren't you, Alice?"

Alice stared at Alex for a long moment, eyes unblinking.

"Alice?" Sophie took a tentative step forward. "That's a pretty name. Why don't you come a little closer so we can say a proper hello? I don't bite."

Alice's shoulders softened.

She took another step.

"What's your name?" Alice asked.

"Sophie. Are you alone, Alice?"

Alice nodded.

"She doesn't know where her parents are," Alex said. "She says the monsters came for them."

Sophie's face hardened. "I'm sorry to hear that. We've had loved ones taken by the monsters, too. Why don't you come downstairs with the rest of us and tell us all about it? We can all help each other get out of this mess together."

Alex's jaw clenched. "We don't have time for talking. Cody is…"

Sophie shot Alex a glare that screamed, "Shut up for one second."

Alex silenced.

She placed her arm around Alice's shoulder and guided her to the staircase. "We can all work together and figure this out, can't we? You don't have to be alone anymore."

As she walked, Alice's eyes trailed to the ceiling. Alex stayed where he was, watching the pair descend the stairs until they were out of sight. When they were gone, he examined the rest of the bedroom, only pausing for a moment to stare up into a curious hole he discovered in the ceiling of the walk-in closet. He reached a hand up, then pulled it back as he heard the voices of Damien and Alice downstairs.

"Alex?" Sophie called up the stairs. "It's Brandon…"

You're being stupid, Alex. There's no way a monster could comfortably climb up or down into the hole without making some kind of racket…

"Alex?"

"Okay, I'm coming." Alex peeled his eyes from the hatch and headed downstairs.

48

TORI ASPLIN

Tori returned to the window. The same place that had consumed her attention ever since Naomi had shown her the bizarre spectacle outside.

It was enchanting, the neat line of wendigos standing in formation as though they were waiting for something, creating their barrier to the forest. On either side of the line the snow fell at its full force yet, where the wendigos stood, the powder came in gentle drifts, forming a wide gulley where, for the first time that night, Tori could see a modest distance. At the farthest reaches of her vision, the first of the forest's jack pines loomed.

She nursed the coffee that warmed her hands, taking advantage of its heat between sips. Naomi and Oscar bustled around downstairs, raiding Donavon's stores for more equipment to arm themselves with. By the sounds of what Naomi was declaring, they were going to war.

Tori didn't feel the same fire in her stomach that Naomi did. Tiredness had caught up with her, and she wished she could curl up in the nearest bedroom and sleep. Just close her eyes and wait until all of this was over.

But how could she? This night was far from done. As she studied the pale white sentinels in turn, her mind replayed each of the incidents where they had played the starring role. She had seen the insides of a man tonight, had seen the product of their work. They had claimed Karl and turned him into one of their own, an obedient slave to their hidden agendas. She had bowed before the hypnotized Karl, surrounded by the ones who bore the masks of bone, cowering in fear as her mind prepared her for the end. She couldn't understand it, couldn't work out what they wanted or how to make it stop. All that she knew was that stepping outside the four walls of this house meant destruction and, as long as they remained under this roof, at least for now, they appeared to be safe.

One of the sentinel's knees buckled. Under the weight of the gathering snow, it folded to one knee, then the other. Not too long after, it collapsed onto its front, unmoving.

The others showed no sign of recognition nor care for their fallen brethren. Instead, a curious thing happened. As if they had known that such a fall was to come, another unmasked wendigo—one resembling more of a human form than that which had fallen—strode from the forest, tracked through the snow, and took the wendigo's position.

Tori blew the rising vapor from her drink, digesting this information as an ornithologist might study a parakeet. It seemed so surreal, the whole notion of what she was seeing was impossible.

But was it?

"Are you ready?" Naomi stood at the top of the stairs, face steeled, Donavon's tampered skull hooked under one arm.

Tori shook her head. Sipped her coffee. "No. You?"

Naomi's lips thinned, as if the very idea of showing an ounce of fear was blasphemous. "We have to try."

Tori turned back to the window, another wendigo beginning to show its first sign of weakness. *I suppose that's true*, she thought.

I suppose that's true...

49

CODY TREBECK

Following the wolf was as impossible as following the trail of a catfish in the depths of a mirky swamp. Occasionally the canine would turn and show those amber-ringed eyes, but for a long stretch of time, Cody simply walked into a sheet of white, hoping for the best.

And what was it all for? He had no idea. For all he knew, the wolf could have been leading him into the arms of the wendigos, to their den of misery and death. It seemed that every part of the night had been employed by the wendigos for their malevolent purpose, so what was one more step into this vacuous hole of pain and destruction?

The white stretched indefinitely, and soon Cody could go no further. His legs ached from sludging through the snow, the frigid winds ravaged his exhausted body and turned his exposed skin blue, and if his teeth didn't stop chattering soon, he wondered if they might just shatter in the frozen bed of his gums.

After what had been the longest stretch of time without seeing hide nor hair of the wolf, Cody folded his arms and bellowed into the void. He screamed and cried and shouted his disgust and agonizing pain into the elements, venting every last ounce of frustration contained within. He cursed the wendigos, he cursed the wolf, he cursed Alex and Sophie, his mom and his dad, all the gods that he didn't believe in, and still it wasn't enough. He dropped to his knees, snot already turning to ice as it thickened and attempted to trail from his nose, the skin of his eyelids scratched and raw from pawing his gloves across his face to clear the frozen pellets of ice. His shouting match with the storm was futile. The storm's lungs were infinite. The storm had more volume.

The storm had more *life.*

Cody lowered his head, gasping to refill his depleted lungs. He would end things here. Born from the white and lost to the white. Even when he closed his eyes, the white was all he could see. The white and—

The musty scent of animal filled his nostrils. Something rough and wet traced along his chin. He opened his eyes to find the wolf licking eagerly at his face. Their eyes connected, and somewhere deep in the well of those amber-ringed pits was an intelligence that Cody couldn't fathom. In that moment he found it laughable that he could have ever been afraid of such a creature.

The wolf nuzzled the dome of its head against Cody's chin and pushed upward, as if trying to encourage Cody to stand. Its thick fur was sodden, and as Cody rose to his feet, he noticed that the wolf was, in fact, no wolf at all. Wolflike in many ways, but a stone's throw from the breed he had suspected.

Cody had seen enough of them on the lawns of Greenwich Park to know a husky when he saw one up close. A friendly dog, fiercely loyal to their owner, and filled with bottomless energy. Though he had never seen one quite so white as this.

Born of the white...

The husky barked at Cody's feet, much of its height lost in the snow. It excitedly reared back on its haunches and ran a tight circle around his legs. Cody laughed, a stark contrast to the infinite frustration that had plagued him just moments before. When it had completed its loop, it nodded its head into the white and barked again.

"That way?"

The husky barked its response.

Cody squinted ahead, only able to see white until the faintest of shapes coalesced in the distance. He shielded his eyes from the snow with one gloved hand. *What was out there?*

The husky ran a few meters, then stopped and waited for Cody. When Cody caught up, it took off again, following the same game of catch and run. The faint shape in the distance grew darker with each step, and after a short while Cody understood that there was no foul play at work here, no trick of the mind, no hallucination. Something was dead ahead, and Cody wanted a piece of it.

He broke into a sprint, terrified that the shape might slip through his fingers. Soon the shape took a form that he recognized, something that he had only seen firsthand in books and magazines and films.

An igloo.

The dog passed Cody and paused by the igloo's entrance. It barked three times before digging through the narrow entrance and vanishing inside.

Cody looked over his shoulder, making certain that no one was following him, no further surprises to be had. Satisfied he was alone, he crouched and took his first look inside, a steady spill of orange heat warming his face as he gasped.

50

KARL BOWMAN

The warm richness of blood coated Karl's tongue. He lapped greedily, savoring the flavor, the texture, the viscosity.

The life.

He wasn't sure whose blood it was, and he didn't really care. All that mattered was that he was alive, and the Masked Ones had shown the true extent of their kindness. They relished him with meat, caressed him with bone, coddled him with flesh.

Karl didn't deserve their affection.

They should have killed him then and there. He knew that. He had let them down, allowed the bitch to escape and run off into the night. If Karl had only done his job properly, Tori would be in their bellies instead of in their storm, and all would be right in the world. He'd be somewhere off in the night, hunting for his sweet little girl to deliver to his frozen masters. Finding the innocent child so they may do unto her what they will.

Whatever that may be.

One of the Masked Ones—the one who bore the bear—ladled the blood one delicious scoopful at a time. It sloshed in a clay pot, aged and thick with the crusted remains of previous dinners, adding to the flavors that sparked and blossomed on Karl's tongue. His arm throbbed, throwing splinters of pain into his system, but the Masked Ones took care of that, too. Although only one arm remained, it would be all that he needed to complete his purpose. They had healed him, taken care of him, proved that he was one of their own and he was valued among the tribe. The blessed Masked Ones with all their compassion and drive and purpose... How could Karl be in safer hands than these?

Even the snow didn't bother him anymore. They had left the storm behind some time ago, the Masked Ones flanking Karl as they stalked away from the location of their conflict with Tori and the mystery woman, leading Karl toward destinations unknown. For a while, all had been white. The houses had vanished, and the storm cloaked them in its protective bubble. They touched him without physical connection, spurring power into him which removed the aches that plagued his body. He was stunned, stupefied, following blindly in the direction in which they guided, because what could be worse than not being in the presence of his masters? What could be worse than their abandonment, to go back to the life he had once called living?

Pines had risen like daggers ahead, the fallen lower jaw of some colossal beast buried in the snow. The Masked Ones appeared to float across the ground, leaving only gentle footprints in their wake which the storm dutifully covered. As they passed through the trees, the snow came to a sudden stop, and walking into the forest felt like arriving home.

Karl knew he shouldn't have been able to see in the darkness that unfurled around them, but as he continued alongside the Masked Ones, the forest opened ahead of him in shades of black, gray, and white. Columns of wood and bark littered the way ahead, and it seemed impossible that anyone should know their direction in a place such as this but, of course, they did. The Masked Ones were unfaltering as they slipped through the darkness, their white masks floating like dying stars in the eternal void.

The forest reached out fingertips of delight, caressing Karl as he walked. His naked body warmed in the absence of snow. The wound of his stump knitted neatly, deep scar lines melting into smooth, leathery skin. Rivulets of blood ceased their descent down his body, and the pain that had once racked from the impact of the bullet faded into nothingness.

Nothingness.

That was all that was left in this world. When the world shrinks around you, and all you can see is its true components, what else is there? Nothingness...

...and the Masked Ones.

Karl's skin tingled. Pine needles caressed the arches of his feet. Fallen roots slithered away to allow him access through the tangles, and he became suddenly aware of a hot red burning as his penis stiffened with the fervid excitement of what lay ahead.

A titanic growl, the groan of a steel girder bending under tremendous weight. The aching sigh of a tired machine from somewhere in the gloom. A goofy grin crept onto Karl's pale cheeks, stained and crusted with the remnants of dried blood as they drew ever closer to a presence that Karl couldn't even begin to comprehend, but which he felt somewhere deep in the disconnected wiring of his ancestors.

When the clearing appeared ahead, the Masked Ones slowed, coming to a stop in its center. Stones were gathered in a circle, leaving traces of ash from a fire that had long-since died. A stretch of cotton canvas that might once have been the canvas roof of a primitive tent flapped lazily in the steady breeze, two of its corners pinched beneath the weight of a dozen rocks. What appeared to be a woven basket, shredded, raided, and torn, hung from one handle on the stubby branches of a nearby pine.

The Masked Ones gathered around Karl, forming a tight circle that, to many, would have been constricting, but to Karl it felt like love. He cried, tears of endless joy salting his lips as they laid him on a bed of dry pine needles and coaxed his eyes closed with just their thoughts. They truly were beautiful, born of the raw elements of the Earth. Their bracken-thin arms cradled him and eased his descent, the breath that seeped from their masks smelled like familial history, the darkest corners of an attic left unexplored for generations. With each infinitesimal touch his penis ached, throbbed, twitched, until it was almost painful.

Was this what Heaven felt like?

When the blood coated his lips, ecstasy took over, throwing his mind into psychedelic waves of appreciation that could not have been experienced by another human being in history. While the others stood and cast their gaze at Karl, the bear ladled the blood and fed him the flesh, each mouthful like the first time he had tasted sugar and candy. His hunger sated for mere moments before his aching stomach demanded more, and they provided. Readily, willingly, fattening him up, only for his newfound biology to burn the calories and demand more. More. Always more. Through dazed eyes he glanced at his bearers' forms and couldn't understand how they'd worked themselves so thin, so frail, yet held the strength they did. Only when he craned his neck and looked at his own body did he realize that he was not all that different from them.

His stomach was sunken. The first traces of his ribs were displayed like gentle waves rippling on an ocean. It had been years since he had seen his ribs, his impressive pectorals and six-pack abs doing much of the work in hiding them from view. Now they were there for everyone to see.

And Karl was thankful. He was one step closer to becoming one of their own, and that was all that he could hope for as something cold and wet slipped down his throat in one easy swallow.

That mechanical, groaning complaint sounded again, echoing throughout the hollow, vibrating the marrow of Karl's bones. He experienced the rumble as one might a thumping bass line of a Marshall amplifier at a concert, and for the first time since they had escaped the storm, he was afraid.

Not because the Masked Ones couldn't protect him from what lay ahead—Karl was certain that his new guardians had his best interests at heart, hadn't they led him this far?—but because, in that most primal of calls, there came a fluttering sensation of something ancient that Karl couldn't comprehend. The awakening of a piece of his circuitry that had otherwise remained hidden since the dawning of time. A defunct segment of genealogy that bristled his hairs and caused his frozen heart to race.

In that groan there was power, and in power there came fear. The ground softly rumbled beneath his firm bed of pines, and as the Masked Ones tended to his wounds, filled his stomach, and worked their magic, Karl found himself caught in the chasm that spanned between two worlds.

51

TORI ASPLIN

"Are you ready?" Although there was a slight quiver to Oscar's words, there was also strength. Strength that Tori admired, and which reflected the internal resolve his father had once harnessed.

Naomi gripped the door handle, the bone mask of her late husband secured on her head. The sight of it was disturbing, a stark reminder of what they were setting out to do. They had no idea if this would work, all they could do was try. Something was beyond the barrier of wendigos, and that something had to be stopped.

Tori gave a curt nod and sighed.

Oscar adjusted his grip on the rifle—the same rifle Naomi had so recently used to free Tori from Karl and the Masked Ones. He looked absurd, such a young lad holding the weapon of older men. Still, as long as he could point and shoot, that was all that they needed.

Naomi opened the door.

Tori expected an icy blast to greet them, but none came. The power of the storm that she had come to expect was muted on this side of the house, and in that muting was a welcome break. She could almost cry, not realizing that her thoughts had turned so dark as to believe that this storm would never end. That it was all she would know. She had almost died in the arms of the blizzard, but now it was like walking into the first sprinkle of winter. Snowflakes idly drifted like leaves scattered on an autumn wind. The air, while chilly, was fresh, and the density of the oppressing storm was lost. She could breathe out here in the land where footprints faded at a normal rate and you could see beyond the reach of your arm. The snow glittered around them as they took their first tentative steps toward the blockade of creatures.

Naomi took point, skull donned on her head, appearing eerily as one of the wendigo's own as they broke out into the open. There was a strange quiet that set Tori on edge, a feeling that was only magnified as the wendigos simultaneously pivoted their heads to turn in their direction, drawn to the newcomers like moths to a vibrant flame.

Oscar brought his father's rifle to his eyeline. Tori rested a hand on top of the barrel and lowered it, terrified that any sudden movement or sign of threat could break this pregnant quiet. "Wait..." she soothed.

The rifle trembled in his grip.

Naomi scanned the wendigos, then took another step forward. She held up an arm behind her without turning, indicating that the others should stay put. Maintaining equidistant from the blockade, she stalked in one direction, then the other, tracing along the deep groove she created with her feet in the snow. It was then that Tori realized that they weren't following the group at all, their attention was fixed solely on Naomi.

She watched with fascination as Naomi repeated her pattern, ensuring that her theory was true. The heads swiveled mechanically, unfaltering as they tracked Naomi's movements. Bodies frozen still. When Naomi made it back to the others, her words were muffled through the mask. "Stay close. Do *not* turn your back on them."

They moved closer to Naomi. Oscar's breath quickened, his skin grown pale. Tori couldn't blame him. This would be the first time he'd come face to face with the ghastly creatures. An experience she would never wish upon anyone as fleeting images of the batlike invasion of wendigos flickered through her mind.

For the first time since she had been cast from her house, she thought back to her old life. Back to her life as an online celebrity, showered by fans and admirers the world over. How had it come to this? To become so detached from the world she had once known, alone in the fight for her life.

Not alone. With family.

But where is your legion of followers? Where are your digi-pals now?

They stopped just ten feet shy from the center of the barrier. The wendigos were unblinking, empty in their stares. In their frozen state, Tori's eyes were drawn to the imperfections of their bodies—which were many—each wendigo displaying a unique pattern of scars, bruises, and chunks of flesh which had been hollowed from their bodies with bite marks and scratches. While many were in various states of decomposition, a small number appeared freshly inducted into the wendigo family, more akin to a regular human than Tori would care to admit. The only things that they all held in common, were the pale white of their skins, the long, thin blackness of their extremities, and the absence of the masks their masters wore.

Naomi held up a hand again, issuing silent instructions like a commander in the throes of a recon mission. She took a steady step closer. Tori readied her rifle, giving a small nod to Oscar to do the same. They took aim on the wendigos closest to Naomi as she readied to cross the threshold, set to pull the trigger if necessary.

God, I hope it isn't necessary.

Naomi was within arm's reach, now. With ease, the wendigos could extend their malnourished arms and grip her throat, scratch her body, draw her toward them. Flashes of a darkened room, a screaming Stanley, the metallic scent of blood as her vision filled with throbbing organs, slick with—

But they didn't touch her. They remained still.

Emboldened, Naomi took another step, now standing between

the two wendigos, just inches from both. She turned her gaze between the two, staring into their blank eyes as she made the final step across the threshold.

She turned her back to the forest, continually looking between the silent pair as she stalked backward.

"Mom...?" Oscar trained his sight to the forest's edge where a single wendigo was working its way toward them. A moment later, another appeared through the trees, then a third.

Tori's tongue swelled in her mouth. In her periphery, something moved, and in that moment, she allowed panic to take her. She swung the rifle toward the wendigo and fired, catching it square in its beady head as it collapsed and flopped into the snow. A strange black ichor painted the ground where blood should have been. She swept her rifle back and forth, palms slick on the handle. When another wendigo twitched and fell, it was Oscar who had taken aim and fired. His aim was impressive, though it fell just short of true. He hit the wendigo a little off-center to her chest and forced her away from its position where she, too, was lost in the white.

The shots were like thunderclaps in the muted quiet and dread overcame Tori. In her mind, she saw the wendigos breaking formation and rushing toward Naomi, gripping their talons into her flesh, splitting her skin, feasting on her sister's meat as they had with Stanley in her home—on her *couch*. Oscar's report sang again as a third wendigo twitched and became the next victim in their showdown. Naomi took a fighting stance, preparing for an attack that never came.

Oscar readied another shot when Tori called for him to stop. She could already see what had happened, even if his juvenile brain hadn't yet processed it. The wendigos that had broken from the trees now stood in the place of their forebears, resuming the holes in the broken line, standing patiently with their eyes locked onto Naomi.

It's like they know... Like they can see the future...

Tori called to Naomi. "Get out of there. It's too dangerous. Come back."

Beneath the mask, Naomi's face hardened, her eyes turning dark as she shook her head. "No. This ends tonight."

"There has to be another way," Tori replied, already seeing the intent in Naomi's eyes. "We can get reinforcements. Find more people to help. Naomi, going into that forest alone is suicide."

Naomi answered with her body, turning her back to Tori and Oscar. She strolled confidently toward the edge of the forest. Its shadows absorbed her, welcoming her into its embrace as she drew closer to the trees.

Another surge of panic rose through Tori. She had seen what the wendigos were capable of, even if her sister had not. Her sister's informant was a dead husband who, even though Tori questioned his existence, could hardly be ignored in his plight of guiding Naomi to Tori in the nick of time. Whereas Tori's knowledge came from a firsthand, near-death experience with the creatures. Somehow she knew that, if Naomi were to enter those trees, she would never return.

Yet, that dogged determination had taken her. Naomi didn't spare a second glance as she advanced on the forest, the branches of her antlers making her appear larger than Tori knew her to be. Tori gritted her teeth, tightened the grip on her rifle, and ran for her sister. "Naomi! Stop!"

She doubled over and sprinted toward her sister, aiming for the gap between the wendigos. Not noticing that they had stopped watching Naomi, and instead looked straight ahead, as if satisfied that their target had been delivered, and there was nothing more to concern themselves with. That wasn't necessarily true, and as Tori broke across the threshold, arms shot out from either side and locked her in icy grips, fingers as strong as steel vices preventing her advance toward her sister.

"Naomi!" Tori screamed.

Naomi was gone.

Oscar cried out from behind her. Tori couldn't decipher his words. They floated on the wind, came to her in a sea of panic, muting their clarity as the wendigos on either side broke their ranks and tussled to claim their payment of flesh. Their wanting mouths salivated and chomped in her direction. Tori tried to wrestle free, but it was futile. Ahead of her, two more wendigos appeared from the darkness and started toward her, not with the steady calm that their predecessors carried, but sprinting with their full force, streaming at a terrified Tori who could only scream and shout to a sister who was already lost in another world, gone and embraced by the cloth of darkness the forest wore.

An explosion of gunfire. A second. The wendigos' grip on Tori broke and, for a second, she had control of her body. Her teeth clenched as the remaining wendigos filed toward her, offended by her brazen act of breaking into their territory, occupying their space. Something tugged on her back and she whirled, swinging the rifle around to destroy whatever force had caught her. When Oscar's face spun into view, she gasped as he pulled her away from the threshold and back toward the house.

They ran twenty feet away from the wendigos before Oscar spared a glance over his shoulder and slowed. "Aunt Tori... Look..."

Tori did. She felt sick. The wendigos shuffled around in their group, working themselves back into the formation they had previously held before Tori crossed the threshold. Forming the invisible barrier between worlds.

"They're blocking us out." The idea of it sounded absurd coming from her lips. "They let Naomi right through, but they're blocking us out. Somehow she's a part of this."

"What do you mean?" Oscar's brow creased, the rifle falling limply beside him. "Why would they let Mom through and not us? Aunt Tori, what do we do?"

Tori knew the answer, she just didn't understand its rationale. It was all linked somehow. The mask that Naomi wore—the gift once left on her doorstep over a decade ago—it sheltered her. Formed some kind of protection. Made her one with the wendigos in a way that she couldn't decipher. The wendigos allowed her through because that was what they wanted. Not these two human strangers, but one of their own. A family reunion of flesh and bone.

"What's going to happen to her?" Oscar asked, a slight tremble on his lip.

"I don't know," Tori answered truthfully. "Whatever happens, we have to find a way inside before there's no way out."

As if listening to her thoughts, the forest called out its response, a tremendous grumble rippling through the trees.

52

ALEX GOINS

"Something's out there..."

Alex squinted into the white, peeking through a thin gap in the front door as the grumbles rang faintly in the distance. To him, they sounded like distant gunshots, morphed and translated by the storm. In reality, they could have been anything.

"What is it?" Sophie asked, her back to the wall near the window as she reached a hand outside and allowed snow to warm on her fingers. She lapped the melting residue greedily, finding a strange comfort in the cool liquid as it rolled down her throat. Damien sat beside Brandon, guarding him like a faithful Labrador as Brandon's breathing hitched and faded. Alice wandered around the room, seemingly energized by being around others.

"I don't know. But it's something, and I'm pretty sure it came from that direction." He pointed into the white, but already the memory of the noise was fading. Not for the first time that night he wondered how much of it was real, and how much of it was his tired imagination hunting for solutions to their problems. Brandon was dying. There was no way to sugarcoat that fact. With each passing second the color drained from his face and his breath grew shallower. Now, his chest hardly rose, and it appeared as though it never would again

— which was a bad enough situation to face yet, coupled with the fact that two of his charges were under the age of ten and had, presumably, never encountered a dead person in their life, Alex's urgency grew in fervor. What kind of guardian would he be if he allowed this to take place under his watch? How could their parents ever forgive him?

If they ever see their parents again...

Alex made a decision. There was no other way around it. "Get up. Everyone. Now. Up."

Alice frowned. "I am up."

"You. Sophie. Damien. Get up. We've got to go."

"Why?" Damien asked, hopeful. "Is someone coming?"

"No one's coming. If we're going to survive this, we've got to figure this thing out for ourselves. All those heroes that you watch on TV and read about in books, they don't sit on their ass and wait for help to come, do they? They make their own destiny. They find their own solutions. If we want to survive this damn thing, we've got to get out of here, whatever it takes."

Sophie was the only one to remain where she sat. "But... the storm. How are we going to survive out there if we get lost? And what about those creatures? Something stole Cody, and you want to go out there and risk us getting taken, too?"

For a moment, Alex saw red, frustration rising at the aching knowledge of how close he had been to reuniting with his nephew. "You should never have sent Cody out there by himself! What were you thinking, sending a kid out into a fucking blizzard without any weaponry or navigation? Don't blame me for what happened to him, it's because of the stupidity of children like you that he's somewhere out there in the storm, lost and, very possibly, dead. If you had been thinking, maybe you could have come up with a better plan than to dangle a snack out there on a length of rope for those creatures to find."

Silence followed Alex's words. His ears throbbed with heat. He towered over the teenage girl, chest heaving with each breath. She glanced up, wide eyes sparkling with tears, before lowering them to her lap and sobbing. Breath hitching. "I know... I'm sorry. It's all my fault. It's all..."

Alex's anger dissipated in a heartbeat. He stepped away, placing his head in his hands as he fought to recompose himself. Damien shuffled awkwardly, hands in his pocket. "You should say sorry."

Alex turned to the boy.

"You should say sorry," Damien insisted. "You hurt her feelings."

Alice nodded. "Yep."

Alex softened. He crouched in front of Sophie. "I didn't mean it. It's just... this night has been hard on all of us. No one is to blame, because no one asked for any of this to happen. I... I'm just trying to keep it all together and keep us moving. We have to work together to survive this, okay?" He leaned closer. "And I need you. You're the second oldest here, and that puts you second in command. I need you, you got that?"

Sophie let out a long exhale and looked up at the ceiling. "I shouldn't have let him go out there alone, but I couldn't stop him. Cody is stubborn. He wouldn't take no for an answer."

Alex offered a sad smile. "That sounds like Cody."

Sophie pawed at her eyes. "Do we really need to go out there?"

"Yes."

"What about Brandon?"

Alex's smile faltered. That had been the question he hadn't wanted to answer, but now there came no other option but to say it. "He stays here. There's nothing any of us can do for him, now. The best we can offer is to find someone to help and bring them back here as soon as we can."

Sophie cast her eyes at Brandon. When she spoke, Alex strained to hear. "He's dead, isn't he?"

Alex lowered his gaze.

Sophie's lips pressed together. She took a couple of deep breaths, then pushed herself to her feet. Wiping away her tears, she clapped her hands together. "Come on, then. Let's go find help."

Damien trotted to Alex's side and took his hand. Alex offered his jacket to Damien, allowing the boy to get lost in its warmth as they readied themselves for the chill outside. "You should stop saying naughty words," Damien said.

"Hmm?"

"To Sophie. You were bad."

Alex couldn't help but laugh. Sophie joined him. "I warned you, didn't I?" He wrapped an arm around Damien's shoulder. "Come on, let's get going. For all we know, in a few minutes we'll be safe in the warmth of a log cabin with a fire burning and marshmallows roasting on sticks."

"Do you really believe that?" Sophie asked.

Alex pointed her gaze in the direction of the two children. Sophie closed her mouth.

At the doorway, Damien fixed his gaze on Brandon. "We're leaving him to die, aren't we?"

Alex's jaw clenched as he chewed over the correct response. Sophie saved him. "No. We're leaving him so we can find someone to help him live."

Alex could see her battling with the lie, but it was enough to get the kids back out into the storm. They huddled closely, the four of them, winds blasting in their direction as they began their journey into the white. Alex made an educated guess at the direction of the rumbles, and led them onward, the house soon disappearing as the storm welcomed them back with frozen arms.

53

HAYDEN LOCKLEAR

He could have had them then and there. The four of them, lined up in his sight. It could have been easy. It *should* have been easy. All he needed was the pistol.

But the pistol had been taken.

Hayden cursed himself for losing focus and allowing the girl the chance to escape. How could a girl of such a young age have so much resolve in her that she could attack a boy more than double her size?

Now, they had found help. A relative of Cody's, it seemed, if the mumbles from downstairs were anything to go by. Hayden's eyes stung, his head pounded, his body groaned, and he was tired of this shit. Tired of being left behind and forgotten. Tired of being a fucking afterthought in this shitstorm.

He scratched his head, sticky residue clotting on his scalp.

Hayden had rooted through the attic in the wake of his attack, hunting for something that could have been of use. In a far-off box he found a letter opener. Its blade was dulled, but it still held some of its bite. He tested its edge by stabbing it into a nearby teddy bear, one button eye dangling on a length of string and an explosion of stuffing spilling from the crook of its arm. The blade punctured the bear easily enough, and that was good enough for Hayden.

He would make them all suffer. The pricks who thought they were better than him, those who would oust him to his peers and tarnish his credibility when all of this was over—if all of this ended. If he played his cards right, he could be the survivor. He could be the hero. History was written by the victors, after all.

They opened the door and a cool shunt of air found its way upstairs. Hayden gritted his teeth, wanting to just leap down and take one of them with him. The little girl, perhaps. Maybe even Sophie. Anything to feel like he had some kind of control again. He deserved to be at the top of the food chain. What the fuck was he waiting for?

His attention was pulled to the man's rifle. Now *that* was something that could come in handy. Fuck the pistol, that rifle packed the real heat. Imagine the power of a bullet barreling from that chamber. You could shut a man up before he had a chance to beg for mercy...

He tracked them in silence as they sidled out the front door and into the storm. They wouldn't last long out there—let's be real—and in their demise, he could take their weapons and regain the power he had lost. All he had to do was remain out of sight for a little bit longer.

And didn't that sound like the easiest part of it all?

54

CODY TREBECK

O n any other day, even just the igloo would have been a marvel to behold.

It was truly a testament to its creator, the solid dome of compacted snow that granted Cody respite from the storm. There wasn't a single exposed crevice or crack, no hiss or whistle of the wind running through the holes he'd struggled to become accustomed to in his rented shack. Cody couldn't understand how Alex's house—a complicated construction built from the knowledge of so-called "smarter" men—could howl and groan and sing its song beneath the strain of the elements, while this simple shelter could deflect it all, snuggle him in the warmth of its embrace and keep him cozied in the heart of the storm.

The fire crackled, which seemed impossible, too. The great gift of heat having no impact on the walls of ice surrounding it. Smoke ribboned through a thin shaft in the ceiling, but all of that was still nothing compared to the woman hunched against the igloo walls.

At first, Cody hadn't been certain that she was alive. The great bundle of clothing appearing as though it was waiting for its owner to return, a great mass of animal skin and fur simply dumped in the igloo and left for a later occasion. It wasn't until the husky nuzzled its nose into the folds of the clothing and a weak cough was emitted that Cody knew better.

The woman was as old as time itself. Her skin pruned and wrinkled with bountiful craters, her skin thick and leathered. Her eyes peeped out from the depths of her folds, a cobalt blue and dazzling with a vibrant intelligence. She shuffled until her back was straight and her head rose above her jacket, revealing gray hair tied back into messy pigtails. Her mouth was a thin scar beneath her prominent nose.

Cody was hesitant to advance further, holding his place in the entrance of the igloo. If this night had taught him anything, it was that danger could come from every direction, and this woman had yet to prove her innocence.

"Come. Sit."

Cody remained where he was.

"I don't ask twice."

Although there was authority in her voice, Cody couldn't detect malice. He eased himself into the igloo, eyes fixed on her with every move as he took a seat as far across the fire as the space allowed.

The husky padded up beside him and sniffed at his body. It found the place where its teeth had nipped at Cody's ankle and offered a few affectionate licks before curling up beside him and closing its eyes.

"Kazu doesn't make friends so easy." The woman peered through narrowed eyes, her face stern. "There must be something about you, boy."

"Cody."

The woman nodded. "Cody..."

"Who are you?"

The woman stared hard at Cody, and he wondered if she was going to answer. Her stare was invasive, as though she could see through the layers of Cody's clothing and straight into his soul. He wondered how old this woman was. His great aunt Hilda had been one of the lucky few in his family to make it to the golden age of ninety-six, but she passed away several years ago. Hilda had looked old in her time, but she was nothing compared to this woman.

"In our tribe, a boy only speaks when spoken to."

Cody blinked.

A faint grin appeared on the woman's lips. More of a twitch than a true smile. "My people call me many names."

"But you have to have one? One that you were born with?"

"Chikuk."

"Cody."

"You have said this."

"I'm scared."

Cody blushed. He narrowed his eyes, realizing for the first time that, as Chikuk spoke, her lips hardly moved—if they moved at all.

Chikuk coughed into the ring of her fist, wiping the residual saliva on her jacket. "You have come a long way, Cody. I can see that in you. There is much further to go."

"Where are you from?" Cody glanced around the igloo. "Where are we?"

"In the end game, should the winds turn in your favor."

Kazu nestled into Cody, resting his head on his lap. Cody absent-mindedly stroked his fur.

"You know what's out there?"

"I know what plagues this land."

"What are they?"

The woman coughed. Or maybe she laughed. It was impossible to tell. Her face creased in pain as she leaned forward and dug through a leather pouch, taking a scoopful of black powder and tossing it into the flames.

At first, the fire hissed. Then it crackled. When Cody thought that nothing more would occur, the flames changed color, morphing into a shade of crimson which was instantly recognizable, an image from earlier that evening, plaguing the Aurora pulsing across the night sky.

"My people have lived in this region for centuries," Chikuk explained, her words labored and slow. Each syllable laced with emotion, spoken more with her eyes than her lips. Although there was a thickness to her accent, he could understand every word as though they were spoken with crystal clarity inside his own head. "There isn't a time in living memory in which the Iñupiat tribe didn't once roam these lands, living off the livestock and resources the world has to offer. Once, our existence was simple, bound on a turntable that continued to spin, granting us the ability to prosper and thrive in the frigid elements of the north."

Cody's fingers combed through Kazu's fur, his eyes unblinking, unable to pull away from the fire.

"Among the Iñupiat tribe there have always been chiefs and their brides—commanders and rulers of the Iñupiat people—assigned with the role as guardian, steward, and ruler. In the primitive days, there always existed an alpha, and the chieftain was selected through a fierce physical competition, in which many died attempting to claim the throne."

The flames flickered and, to Cody's surprise, he fancied he could make out the shapes of the figures she spoke of, fighting in the fire. Dark silhouettes of men with sticks and weapons scrapping through the flames.

"The strongest and the first in recorded memory to claim the role as chief was a man of great girth and heart. His name was Nukilik, meaning 'one who is strong.' Nukilik once led our people to peace, settling the disruptions of the early tribesmen and allowing our people to thrive. With each generation born from Nukilik's seed came the successors to the Iñupiat throne. Aklaq—my spouse—commanded this tribe for nigh on seventy years, ruling with an iron fist and commanding the Iñupiat people into a new era, one of westernization and the plague of modern man. Aklaq was a direct descendent of Nukilik, the spawn of a bloodline spanning seven generations, each with their own tales to tell, and their own wisdom to impart."

The fire died suddenly, as if a gust of wind had extinguished it in one blow. Cody looked in confusion at Chikuk, his throat dry as he asked, "You are the wife of an Inuit chieftain?"

"Spouse," Chikuk corrected, face souring. "We do not adopt your Western rituals."

Cody furrowed his brow. "But, why are you telling me this? What have your people got to do with what's out there? The creatures and the storm?"

Chikuk smiled—a real smile this time—breaking her face into a thousand memories and tales. "Everything."

She reached for another pouch and tossed a slip of meat to Kazu. The organ was slimy and dark, but Kazu readily ate it down. Cody stared at the dying embers of the fire and was about to ask another question, when Chikuk clapped her hands and the fire blossomed once more, this time alight with a sickly green hue.

"There is magic in this world, boy. A magic that your people could never embrace, but which my kin have lived beside for millennia. While the stone cities grew and your connection with the natural world was lost, tribes such as mine maintained our connection with Mother Earth, blessing the gods and choosing to respect the unseen powers. We have our rituals, designed to appease the gods and grant us peace, but there are those in the world whose corrupt hearts have the power to stain those around them."

The flames danced, turning through a kaleidoscopic display of color as first the Aurora came, and then the forms of eagles, bear, and fish swam through the fire. The souls and majesty of the natural world pirouetting in wonder before a dark spill of shadow erased them from existence.

"I know this story," Cody said softly, furrowing his brow. Brandon had once told them, in an age long, long ago. A time where he shared a room with his peers, Brandon's head resting on the stone wall, explaining to Cody and the others the origin of the wendigo legend. "Your people were starving, hit with a harsh winter. Some of you turned to cannibalism, and from there the wendigos were born?"

Chikuk gave a curt nod. Her face wobbled through the fire, mouth unmoving, the words without distortion in his head. "That is indeed how they were birthed, a tale which one would never wish to tell another. A dark time for the Iñupiat people, and one that has caused untold misery for generation after generation.

"The wendigo are the ever-hungry. The gods punished them,

casting the curse of eternal famine as recourse for their sin. They will never be satisfied, as long as they exist on this planet their stomachs will never be full. The first to taste the flesh of man was one called Tulimaq. A man so foul that it was a wonder no one saw it coming. Tulimaq saw deceit and pain as a means of life and that pained my great-great-grandfather, Tulok. Story tells that, when the great winter hit, Tulimaq lured children away from the camp to sample at their flesh. Reports came of the missing ones, and a great hunt was set forth. They found ragged shreds of Tulimaq's clothing stained with blood beside the half-buried corpses of the fallen. They tried to kill him, hunting him down like the monster he was, but he found a means to escape."

Chikuk took a few recovering breaths, the fire resuming its normal hue and casting eerie shadows across her face.

"Are you okay?" Cody asked. "Do you need some water? Some food?"

Chikuk held up a hand. "Over the next few months, Tulimaq lived on the borders of discovery, recruiting contributions for his tribe. He brought the meek and suffering to the dark side. It was said that a parasite had found its way into his body, a tapeworm unlike the world had known. But we knew better. We knew the gods were enraged and that Tulimaq was paying the price. What we didn't know was how far he would push them, just how far he would degenerate and fade from the man he had once been."

Cody tried to imagine it, the transformation from man to creature. The wendigos were disturbing enough without trying to imagine the metamorphosis. As Chikuk spoke, he struggled to understand how any of this could be real, could it really be that he had simply been shielded from the impossible by Western civilization? Could the stories of ghosts and monsters running around London's streets have any grain of truth to them? What lay on the other side of the "known?"

He truly didn't know anymore.

"You're distracted."

Chikuk's stare was intense.

"I'm tired."

"Here." Chikuk drew some jerky from her bag and tossed it to Cody. He rolled it over in his hand and sniffed at the meat. "Don't worry. It's not human."

Cody wanted to laugh, but nothing came. He nibbled the edge of the dark purple strip, a tang of salt teasing his tongue. His next bite was more enthusiastic, and after that he ate the whole thing without thought.

"There's more if you'd like."

Cody was desperate for more, but he was also terrified. All this talk of human flesh and the wrath of the gods unsettled his stomach and made him long for home more than ever.

"What happened to Talamak?"

"Tulimaq," Chikuk said. "What many of your historical records won't tell you is that the Iñupiat tribe were on the brink of civil war. Tulimaq and his band of devourers continued to pick off our tribe one by one, until our people could take no more losses. Some of our people they killed, while others they converted, and in the heart of one wintry night Tulok saw his brother, a stick-thin shadow sneaking into the camp for his next meal.

"The stories tell of his sickness, his body turning inward on itself as it ate away at his own flesh. Eyes dark as the void, teeth stained purple from their diet of meat and flesh. At that point it was clear that something larger was at play. Tulok drove Tulimaq and his followers into the forest, and it is there that they hid away, biding their time before their next attack as they regained strength."

"It sounds awful," Cody breathed, fingers locked into Kazu's damp fur.

Chikuk nodded solemnly, eyes glazing. The fire swelled, increasing its heat inside the igloo. For the first time since he had set forth that night with Hayden, Cody was satisfied with his internal temperature. Parts of him that he didn't know were frozen thawed out and he grew drowsy in comfort. Chikuk faded across the flames of the fire, her form turning into an illusion as great as the shapes cast into the conflagration.

"We were forced to turn our hands to the gods."

The igloo melted around them. He could hear the roars of battle, the groans of the dead. His mind's eye shaped and manifested the dense forest and tracked the shapes of Iñupiat and wendigo alike.

"Tulok chased his brother into the woods, fighting the wendigos as he went. The chieftains of the Iñupiat people are great warriors, and his strength was put to the test. He battled valiantly, Tulok and his band of fighters eventually making their way into the hollows of the Drumtrie Forest."

Chikuk sighed. "It should have ended that night..."

Cody's eyelids grew heavy as waves of heat washed over him. Colossal trees surrounded him, great monoliths of nature pressing in from all sides. Ahead, a broad-shouldered warrior approached the clearing.

"They were waiting for him. At least two dozen strong, their bodies like paper skeletons, their cheeks gaunt, their eyes keen. Tulimaq stood among them, and it was then that Tulok discovered the truth behind the creature that had once been his brother. The dark gods had intervened and bestowed onto Tulimaq an unholy power. As the Aurora pulsed and glowed in colors of green and blue above them, they faced off, a span of eternity stretching between the two worlds. It is said that Tulimaq had grown, standing double the size of his brethren. His arms stretched to the floor, the skull placed on his head was the size of no creature they had ever seen, antlers stretching from tree to tree. A desperate bloodlust formed a cloud around them and the Iñupiat people trembled."

Cody saw it all, the terrifying creature with his army flanking his sides. No longer human in any way other than his bipedal state. Fingers as long as scythes, hunched over his own anatomy as the skull leered at his brother through the gloom.

Warm tears slicked Cody's cheeks as the vision rumbled and warped before him. "How did they escape?"

"Tulok made a pact with the gods. Under the glow of the Aurora, he drew a captured wendigo into his grasp and spilled its blood on the hollow. The wendigos watched with gleeful curiosity, not understanding the magic at play in their own home. The blood darkened the grass, and as Tulok chanted and pleaded to the gods, the Aurora morphed above them, turning from its vibrant hues to a deep crimson. Tulimaq grew afraid and came for Tulok, finding that he could not cross the bloody barrier. The other wendigos tried to scatter but found they could not leave the hollow. They were bound in blood, and there they would lie.

"Or so it was thought."

The wendigos panicked as the Iñupiat stalked out of the clearing and into the trees. The howls and screams of rage ensued, a mind-bending din that caused the Aurora to pulse and dance.

"Peace reigned in the years following the wendigo's imprisonment, and all was thought to be right. It would be thirty years later that the truth would reveal itself. For, though the gods are kind, they also speak balance, and light cannot exist without darkness."

A trail of drool fell from Cody's lips. His breath deepened.

"On the eve of Tulok's death, after forty-three years of reign, the sky signaled the coming attack. Shamans and herbalists knelt at Tulok's bedside, his skin stretched tight, his face pale. Each labored breath rattled in his throat as the sky above shifted and morphed. The Aurora bled. A storm brewed on the horizon."

Visions flashed in Cody's mind. Wendigos leaping from the forest. A blizzard clothing their arrival. Blood staining the snow. Dozens of creatures using the storm for their cloak, feasting hungrily on the flesh of their kin. A furious frenzied feast as the wendigo were unleashed.

Cody grimaced, his head lolling on his neck as he fought away the images. "Make it stop. Please... Make it stop..."

Chikuk's face swallowed his vision, her floating head taking up every inch of space inside the igloo, her wrinkles and folds wobbling in the unbearable heat. "There is no end. The wendigo curse lies upon our people. Generation after generation has fought and lost, and it is there that this tale ends. What occurs tonight is nothing but the way of things. The truth that those who call themselves 'modern' ignore. The storm claims. The wendigos come. For one full turn of the moon and sun, the world is theirs, and that is the reward for their patience. Our father, and his father before him, and his father before, all have learned that, upon the night of the passing of the great chiefs, they come. We feed them, and we cower in our homes. It is only in the coming of your Western blood that you have placed yourselves in harm's way. The wendigo feast, and you have chosen to settle in the crossfire, mere inches from the forest's edge. You have no idea what you have awoken, for my spouse's reign stretched for the longest in recorded history of our people. He kept the threat at bay while you all grew comfortable, thinking you could brave the elements and make a home where you were not wanted..."

The woman was terrifying, imposing. The weight of her visage pressed down on him, consuming all that Cody knew. He babbled, pleading his innocence, "I'm not from this place. I don't know what you're talking about. I just want to go home..."

He became aware that he'd wet himself, his pants clinging to his leg. He shrank against the walls of the igloo while Kazu barked noisily, a wet tongue occasionally licking his cheek. Chikuk bore down on him, eyes lit with fire as she melted into the spectacle of the Aurora.

"There has to be a way to end this..." Cody bit his lip. Warm blood filled his mouth. "There has to..."

The Aurora shifted, its colors turning into autumn as it took the shape of a great eagle. It swooped across the sky, leaving a trail of fire and gold in its wake. The spectacle consumed Cody's vision until it didn't, and the hollow of the Drumtrie Forest came into view.

The forest was dark. The world fell silent. Cody took a step and the crack of dry bracken rang through the trees. There was something nearby, without seeing it he knew, he just couldn't tell what it was. He squinted, barely able to breathe in this constricting dark. A great mound lay before him, and it took him some time to realize it was gently rising and falling.

Another step. Another crack.

A great white eye snapped open.

Cody lost himself, falling into the great orb of white, dropped from the enormity of the universe and pulled into its gravity. Nothing existed in that moment but the white, and as he tumbled in the forever, the forever stretched like taffy, until time was nothing and life was futile. Head over heels, swirling and swallowed by the infinite stretch of white, taking him back to the storm, to the womb, to the moments before death when all that is known is a singularity of virgin snow, the purest forms of light when all other colors merge their rainbow, and what was once known is lost.

Cody fell.

Until he didn't.

55

NAOMI OSLOW

T he woods were exactly how she remembered them.

They had played a starring role in her dreams over the years, the towering jack pines surrounding her like dark monoliths. While she fought through the grieving process in the wake of her husband's passing and raised an infant son on her own, her sleep was plagued with the memories of her time spent in here. Though her visits had been brief, they left a permanent scar on her mind. It was in here that Donavon collected firewood, clinging to the edges of the forest to evade the dense unknown within. It had been here that she and Donavon had kissed and reconnected, Naomi finally finding herself in a position where she could forgive Donavon for the vice of his drinking and almost killing their infant son, picturing a future that was eternally brighter than it had previously been.

It was in here that her husband had disappeared, never to be seen alive again.

The forest held an enchantment, she felt it from the moment they had chosen to live on the outskirts of the city. She had never been a believer before, ignoring the tales of the other townsfolk of monsters and creatures and the supernatural. To her, the forest was misunderstood. There are many dark, unexplored places of this world, and all it took was one brave voyager to shine a light on what was previously unknown. Look how they'd ended up here, for example. Denridge Hills was built in the frozen unknown, in one of the farthest reaches of the planet. At one point a region such as this would have kicked out some horror stories. Tales of bears and wolves and uncivilized strangers in thick hoods made from animal skin and fur.

But now the world knew better, and with each mesmerized step she became aware of the ancient timespan of these trees. She reached out a hand, stroking the rough bark as she passed, realizing then that she was touching history. These pines were of an age unknown, likely stretching back hundreds—maybe even thousands—of years. These trees had their secrets, and they whispered them to each other in a language Naomi could never interpret. A language born of the Earth...

The language of the gods.

She sloped through the trees, walking in a singular direction that called out to her. Her mind was consumed by the darkness, her skin prickling at the warmth of the shadows that embraced her. All she knew was that she must go forward, and in going forward she would find the answers. The forest would speak to her, and she would listen. The constant whispers and niggles of darkness would fade, and she'd find peace at the end.

Pine needles and fallen twigs crackled underfoot, yet the sound was soft around the edges as the forest warped her reality. There was no sign of animal life, and no sign of the storm. No snow fell, no wind howled, nothing existed except for Naomi and the trees.

The bone mask irritated her face, the tough contours that had once shaped her husband's beautiful head rubbed at her skin. It was warm in the mask, but she feared its removal. The mask had offered her protection from the wendigos, and she was lax to abandon the enchantment. A pang of guilt gnawed at her for leaving Oscar with Tori, their gunshots and screams rattling around her head, but she knew he would be okay in her hands. Tori loved Oscar, even if Naomi had withdrawn over the last few years and contact with her sister had ceased. Should anything happen to Naomi, Tori would do what was right, and that was enough.

The strangest part of her trajectory through the forest was that Donavon was nowhere to be seen. The ghost of her late husband had been by her side through most of that night, and now he was gone. While she mounted her mask and set off into the storm to rescue Tori, he had remained at home. When she returned, he met her with grinning lips, a faithful shadow that offered her some comfort.

Maybe Donavon couldn't leave the house? Wasn't that what she had heard once? That ghosts were bound to a singular location for eternity, doomed to remain in the confines of their perimeter until their final business was done.

Or... Naomi thought, noting that Donavon faded every time she put on the mask. *Perhaps he is linked to the bones...*

She walked for what felt like a lifetime. Halfway through the forest she stripped off her jacket, the heat overwhelming, her clothes cloying her skin. An impulse told her to remove her shoes. She obeyed. The needles felt good on her bare feet. Soon her trousers came off, then her top, until all that was left was underwear.

And the mask. She couldn't forget the mask.

The trees started opening up as the ground rumbled beneath her feet. The space between the trunks widened and in the twilight gloom shapes coalesced from the shadows. They weren't much taller than her, but their forms were thin. Although she couldn't make out what they were, she could guess. Dozens of them, lining the forest around her, forming an alley through which she was already treading without their encouragement. With each step she took, the alley closed in, until she could just make out the dark glints of their eyes. Something growled in the distance, much louder than it should have been, as though a giant from a kid's fairy tale was waking from their slumber.

Naomi reached back and unclasped her bra. The forest's breath tickled her skin. She slipped out of her panties, and pulled to a stop, unsure why until the figure appeared before her.

She recognized the man, although he was a far cry from what she had once known. She hadn't had the chance to look at him properly earlier, but with all the time in the world to examine now, she saw him for who he was. A man once witnessed on occasional journeys through the town to collect supplies, and sometimes spoken about when Tori came to her house.

Karl Bowman stood before Naomi, as naked as she was.

He was a mess. His beard was a thicket of tangles, crusted with a substance that she could only presume was blood. His dark eyes winked in her direction, hip bones protruding like pan handles, his once-famous muscular arms now shrunken and without definition. He had aged a lifetime in a single night, his knees knobby like a deer's, his feet flat. The most disconcerting sight was the erection that stood to attention like a raised flag and pointed straight at her.

They stared at each other for a long while, neither party in need of haste. The crowd of wendigos watched on with endless patience. Naomi swallowed, the bone mask irritating the bridge of her nose, the eye sockets limiting her vision to what lay before her.

Something moved behind Karl. Four figures appeared through the shadows, each with their own masks. They remained a small distance behind Karl, and in that moment, Naomi fancied she could hear the whispers of their thoughts inside her head. Karl cocked his head as if listening in, too, and it was then that he stumbled a few steps forward.

Naomi raised a hand, palm outward. Karl stopped, a crooked grin splitting his face. "Your time has come."

Naomi waited for more, but Karl fell silent.

"I have come to claim back my husband," Naomi spoke at last. "No matter what the outcome, I will not stop until I rest in the peace that you stole from us."

A sudden, shrill shriek filled the forest, piercing Naomi's eardrums. She clamped her hands to the side of her head, screaming in agony, falling to one knee as she fought against the all-encompassing cry, realizing then that it wasn't coming from the forest at all, but from inside her own head. Even with her hands scrambling to mute the shriek, it was everywhere, and there was nothing she could do. She screwed her eyes shut. She bit her tongue, warm blood filling her mouth. Somewhere in the mix of it all another screamed. When she peeled an eye open, Karl was on the floor, mouth stretched open in pain as he writhed and covered his ears.

The sound stretched on, and a warmth trickled into Naomi's hand. She was almost certain that her ears were bleeding, but she couldn't risk checking. She folded over, visibly shaking as tears spilled to the ground and her brain bordered on exploding into mush inside her skull.

In a desperate bid to end her distress, she removed the mask, realizing that she had been unable to fully cover her ears with the bone blocking her.

The second she removed the mask, the world fell silent. It was unnerving, how all-encompassing it had been and how absent it was now. For a moment, she wondered if she'd gone deaf, until she found the Masked Ones towering over her, mere feet from where she crouched.

When had they moved?

The bed of detritus rustled under their skeletal feet. They hooked a hand beneath the crook of her arms, their touch like death, each point of contact a searing white-hot pain on her naked skin. To her dismay, where they touched, her skin turned black, the darkness spreading across her pale flesh.

She struggled against them, throwing an elbow and catching one of the creatures in the chest. It reared back, grip loosening. Naomi kicked as she was lifted off the ground. Each connection with her feet on their bodies was like trying to shift an iceberg. Still, she thrashed and tossed herself around, desperate to be free.

Somewhere beyond the creatures, Donavon appeared, his face a mask of neutrality. In the blur of her frantic movements she saw him and, as if commanding her from afar, she stilled. She cried out to him in her mind, eyes wide as the Masked Ones prepared to carry her deeper into the forest. Donavon smiled, that old familiar twinkle in his eye through which she still drew strength.

She bided her time, waiting until their defenses were lowered before fighting again. She gave one final urgent kick, she threw another elbow. Impossibly, one of them let go of her arm.

It was enough. Naomi dipped toward the ground and scooped up Donavon's skull. She clumsily placed it on her head, and immediately the Masked Ones let go, withdrawing as though she had burst into flame and scorched their fingers.

Their shrieks filled her head again, drawn into her mind as though the skull picked up a radio frequency no mortal should hear. Naomi looked for Donavon, but he was no longer there. She opened her mouth and screamed in response, shrieking to match their shrieks, crying to match their cries, a race to the threshold of their pains and, somehow, she already knew she'd lose.

When their shrieks stopped, Naomi's throat was scratched and dry. She'd yelled herself hoarse, and there was little remaining if she needed to combat them again. Karl was still on his knees, facing away from Naomi, hands outstretched as if thanking the Earth for its bounty. The Masked Ones stood either side. They, too, looking away.

And that's when she saw it. Rising like some titanic piece of fiction, a being that she had never believed would ever exist across any corner of the Earth. A being of flesh, bone, blood—

—*and myth.*

Naomi steeled herself, knowing deep down that this is what she came for.

Little knowing just what kind of strength it would take to bring down a creature unborn from this world.

56

ALEX GOINS

They trailed through the snow, in a direction that seemed to constantly shift.

With no frame of reference to guide them, they could have been heading anywhere. On several occasions, Alex truly let himself believe that the nightmare would subside, and in its place would be revealed the monuments of familiar life. Through the sheets of white would come the London Bridge, the Houses of Parliament, maybe even the Leaning Tower of Pisa.

He was their shepherd, and they were his flock. The author guarding the lives of three children. Sophie, Damien, and Alice, all huddled together as they trekked into the unknown and searched for landmarks.

They each were led astray by feverish minds, taking turns to point to shapes that turned out to be nothing more than rises and falls in the terrain. Alex carried Damien, realizing quickly after they had set off that he wouldn't last long without his jacket. It made the trek harder, but at least they were making progress. Sophie folded her arms and gritted her teeth against the chill, and Alice...

Well, Alice wouldn't stop talking.

"Is all this snow going to be gone when the sun rises?"

"Sure." Alex had stopped elaborating on his answers, choosing instead to conserve his energy and concentration.

"But where does it go? Mom says it turns into water, but we're not in the ocean, are we?"

"No."

"Can you breathe underwater in the ocean?"

"No."

"Not even if you're a super good swimmer?"

"No."

"I bet it's too cold to swim, anyway." Her face screwed up in thought. "Why isn't the ocean frozen?"

"Some of it is."

"Why not all of it?"

"Because."

"Is ice colder than water?"

"Yes."

"So, we're swimming in snow?" Alice giggled and looked up at Sophie. "Why are you so quiet?"

Sophie didn't answer.

As Alice trailed on, Alex narrowed his focus ahead. Like the others, his mind, so desperate to find something tactile that he could aim toward, kept creating visions in the white. Only on one occasion so far had he been right, and in the middle of nowhere they had found a juvenile sapling springing from the ground. Five feet in height, a sad, anorexic thing, undergoing its own battle with the elements. Despite his questioning the others, no one could claim they'd seen this tree before, and the more they walked, the stranger it seemed that it was out here alone, in the middle of nowhere, as though it was marking something that was long lost to the pages of time.

"I hope they don't hurt my daddy..."

Alex tuned in to the sadness in Alice's voice. He exchanged a look with Sophie and paused their trek. "Whatever happens, you'll be safe with us. Do you understand that?"

Alice nodded brightly, though she glanced at the ground. The snow was eating up to her waist and would have been an issue if she wasn't following in Alex's tracks. "I just hope he's okay."

"Me too, kid."

Alex scrambled for something else to say. He was highly aware that anything he said wouldn't just be absorbed by one kid but would resonate with all three. He had to be the leader, the one who held it together, the beacon of hope that guided these three bright lights across the black seas of—

"There."

Sophie's words, while flat and shallow, held conviction. Alice looked past Alex and followed the stretch of Sophie's arm. There was something out there, a shape on the cusp of their vision. Alex moved in front of the group and swept them behind his arm. He shuffled Damien to his other arm and secured the butt of the rifle to his shoulder with one hand. Something jabbed his hip then fell into the snow. He glanced down, not seeing what it was through the fast-fading impression. Fixing his gaze ahead, he stalked closer, more than prepared for the shape to vanish as all the others did, but it remained where it was.

It was stick-thin, each step bringing its fuzzy edges into sight. Alex's breath caught as he waited for the antlers to coalesce, the limbs to stretch to either side, and for the wendigo to charge at them, help-less and lost in the snow. Another few steps and he let out a choking sob, relief flooding his body as the item came into view.

A wooden sign. A thick beam of timber, with arrows pointing in several directions. On the wooden arrows were carvings of locations and their approximate distances.

Alex broke into a run, eager to read each arrow. The kids called from behind and he waved them over. Sophie took Alice's hand as they followed in Alex's wake.

Denridge Proper = 2 miles.
Drumtrie Forest = 0.2 miles.
Coastal Path = 3 miles.

ALEX GRINNED up at the sign, so thankful that he could almost kiss the ground. He was so taken by the sign and its promise of direction —of *civilization*—that he didn't notice what lay beyond until Alice clapped her gloved hands. "There! There! There!"

A large shape loomed before them. Alex's grin stretched wider as he shifted Damien into a more comfortable position and encouraged the group onward. They followed in reverent silence, each one of them eager to get out of the storm and into the large wooden house that looked oh so inviting.

57

HAYDEN LOCKLEAR

The storm was tricksy, the storm was unkind.

In the beginning, following their tracks was easy. With four of them marking the way ahead, all Hayden had to do was follow the grooves in the snow and hover just far enough behind that they couldn't see him.

He could hear them occasionally, as the wind stole snippets from the little girl and threw them to him, he heard. After some time, the talking stopped, and the trail faded from sight, the eager storm covering their tracks and working against him, too. Everyone working against Hayden, even the fucking weather. He picked up his pace and managed to latch onto the failing ends of the trail...

His foot struck something solid.

He crouched in the snow.

Fished a hand.

Found the gun.

Alice's gun.

Alex's gun.

Hayden's gun.

. . .

THE SAME PISTOL he had found in the attic, however long ago that had been. The same object which had stolen his consciousness and left him alone and vulnerable in the confines of the loft space. Somehow it was there, a small black wink of an eye in the snow, and it was there that he grabbed it. His grin spread from ear to ear, even as he shivered on the spot. He examined the pistol, checked the chamber, ensured that it was loaded and ready. Maybe it had slipped through their numb fingers. Maybe they had discarded it deliberately. Perhaps something had attacked them and, in their panic, they had left it behind.

Whatever it was, it was power. And power made Hayden very happy indeed.

If only the storm hadn't benefitted from Hayden's distraction, and the trail hadn't vanished from sight...

EPISODE 6

WINTER COMES

58

DENRIDGE HILLS

The world took a slow breath. Raging clouds halted their assault for a precious few moments, slowing to a soft flurry in apprehension of all that was to follow. The tiny town of Denridge Hills counted their dead, wept, and barricaded themselves inside.

The ravaged town shook, gently at first. Townsfolk who were quick to respond to the sudden threats of the night staggered about in their houses, cleaning up the mess made by the raiders, the air thick with gunpowder and the iron scent of blood. Windows were shattered, sheets were torn, living rooms and kitchens and bedrooms were overturned, the delicate items of luxury and memory lying scattered in pieces across the floorboards. Trinkets and treasures of loved ones, now nothing more than shards and fragments.

Few remained in their beds beyond those who had been slaughtered where they lay. Heavy pieces of furniture stood in front of gaping holes, trying to grant the citizens the grace of warmth and protection from the combined efforts of the storm and the wendigos. Dark creatures flitted about excitedly, running through the streets, darting from house to house as squeals and cries of delight rang in the air. Somewhere along Trampton Lane the cries of an abandoned child called for attention, the infant's mother lying dead at his crib side, his father trapped in a cocoon of destruction as the desperate reports from his shotgun, coupled with the wendigos' fury, caved the ceiling and trapped him under the weight of thick timbers.

A shot rang out.

Another would follow soon.

In the Emerson's family home, a congregation collected, composed of survivors from the onslaught. Windows and doors were boarded, peepholes left between planks of wood for the sentries to keep an eye on the external world of white. Their collective body warmth was a gift little appreciated as the vulnerable and the terrified shivered in fear. Barney Emerson—the eldest of the three Emerson brothers—stood upon an upturned pail and bellowed his rallying cry, disheartened at the tepid response from the others. He wanted scout patrols to set forth into the storm and gather survivors. Paul and Garrett Emerson argued that it was too soon. The only thing waiting beyond their door was death.

A gunshot took their attention before they could argue further.

Half a mile away, Daisy Crawley gathered the shattered pieces of her collection of ornamental quartz, her top stained with splatters of crimson. Her mother stood by her bedroom door, firing hushed whispers of annoyance as the frenzied teenager sobbed and clattered about. Downstairs dark things moved in the shadows and made themselves known with indelicate passage. Daisy and Francine would be lucky if they lasted the next few minutes, let alone the night.

Officer Turner Highgarde, the only policeman working in the office that night, fought against the station doors. Great drifts of snow closed around the building, and though the wendigo tramped across the roofs and tried to enter, even they found themselves struggling to break their snowy barriers and snatch their prize. Officer Highgarde shivered in the frozen office, papers scattered, coffee soaking into the pages of his latest case filings from where he had awoken sharply at the animalistic cries of the wendigo. A dark stain on his shirt matched those on the papers.

Shots fired. Four, five, six.

Turner sprinted through the dark, toward the sound of their invasion. Reaching the farthest office, he saw them. Dark, famished hands reaching inside, black in color, clawing at the air, mouths and tongues darting hungrily between the iron bars. Those at the front were shoved forward by their kin until their cheeks scraped the metal and left rough patches of dead, frozen skin behind.

Seven, eight, nine shots, and three more bodies were added to the death toll. Officer Highgarde roared as he fired, profanities his wife would have reprimanded him for, if he could believe that she was still alive. But she wasn't there, and he was here. Alone. A tear trailed down his cheek as thoughts of her topaz eyes overwrote the chaos before him. Praying that he'd get a chance to see their pools of beauty again before the night was over.

The ground rumbled, thunder coming from a direction that wasn't the sky. The vibrations traveled up his legs. The wendigos turned their heads, pausing their attack, giving him a chance to fire another dozen rounds before reaching for a fresh magazine.

Dorris Hackman, Denridge's eldest citizen, found herself swaddled in blankets, her misty eyes staring into nowhere as her family surrounded her and fought to keep her safe. Though their own wendigo attack had ended an hour or so ago (the Hackman's only losing three of their kin), they were reticent to lower their guard given the shrieks, screaming, and gunshots in the distance. Sally, Dorris' fifty-two-year-old granddaughter, drank from a carton of orange juice, still shivering from the memory of the attack and the cold that followed. Sally's husband, Felix Littlestowe, worked to keep the fire going, the whole room lit in the wavering orange glow of their burning books and scraps of stray timber. A leg from an old coffee table stuck out from the flames, the blackening page of a James Patterson novel curling and erupting into ash and smoke.

There were no firearms among this band of survivors. The firearms went with the hunters, and the hunters were yet to return. Machetes and carving knives were their weapons of choice, and it showed in the litter of body parts that had been brushed to the side of the room. Dark shadows of forgotten limbs that were already beginning to stink and would draw the occasional glance from each of them in turn. "Out of sight, out of mind," as Dorris would often say. Then again, Dorris was old now, and a lot of her incoherent mumbles were lost on the others.

When the third rumble came, the ground listed with it. Denridge had never known an earthquake of this magnitude and, judging by the briefness of its activity, they would never see another again. The vibrations shook the walls. Beams and doorways creaked and groaned. Bric-a-brac escaped their shelves and cupboards and shattered on the floor. Drinks spilled. Family and friends hugged each other, whispering silent prayers.

The dead rolled.

And then came the monstrous finale of this chaotic symphony. The long, howling note coming from some other world, drowning out what remained of the brief recess in the storm. Windows rattled in their frames. The remaining wendigo turned their heads, frozen where they stood. The note not unlike the rallying cry of a Viking horn put through a festival speaker until distortion broke its purity. A note of pain and wonder and fear and danger and anger and frustration and...

...and then it was gone.

For a moment, the world was silent. The world was still. The fighting stopped. Both human and wendigo ceased. For a blissful moment, there was something alike to peace.

The wendigo turned to the forest. They reared their heads to the sky and belted their shrill cries. A dozen more shots fired from the survivors, then the wendigos ran, arms pumping, leaving barely an imprint in the snow as they sped off in one direction.

Something was calling them back.

Something was calling them home.

59

CODY TREBECK

The floor shifted beneath Cody. Something wet and cold licked his face. He reached out blindly, attempting to stifle the eager white dog that demanded his attention. Kazu... That was his name. Kazu the husky. The husky that belonged to...

Cody sat up sharply, memories flooding back in a single, surging wave. His back was wet. It hurt to move. What little skin remained exposed on his face stung, and as he glanced at the tip of his nose he could see blackness where the pink should have been, his skin succumbing, at last, to the frostbite he'd tried so hard to fight off.

And there was the sky, clouds rolling like angry smoke billowing in the heavens above. Snow floated lazily around him, landing on his cheeks, his eyelids, his lips. He was outside.

Outside...

Outside?

Cody found no sign of the igloo. There was nothing, no imprint in the snow, no evidence of the frozen bricks that stacked in circles until the dome had formed, no proof that a fire had once blazed and filled the igloo with heat and smoke.

There was nothing. Only white, again.

But he had seen it, hadn't he? He had been there, inside the igloo with... He put a hand to his temple. *What the hell was her name?*

He had seen shapes in the fire. She had told him the story of her people, and the dangers that he now faced. She had bestowed upon Cody the information that could unlock the end and help free the town from this chaos...

From the wendigos.

He shivered where he sat. It took him a few minutes to realize that the snow had slowed around him, and he could now see farther than the storm had allowed for some time. Not that it helped. The floor was white, the sky was white...

The world was white.

Cody tried to piece things together. He stood, finding that his body had regained some of its strength, and for that he was thankful. Though his nose was numb and he was pretty sure his cheeks were turning black, too, there was some lightness in his mind. His arms and legs didn't hurt so much, and as he started walking, he found that he could likely carry on for some time without having to crumble again.

Confusion cuddled him like a familiar friend. He walked on, the taste of jerky on his tongue. He could swear there was white fur stuck to his clothing, but whenever he tried to look again the wind whipped and stole the evidence. He had no idea where he was heading, and the more that he walked the more he convinced himself it must have all been a dream. Why else would he be out here alone again? What had happened was clear: he had passed out in the snow, and his exhausted mind had created the illusions of company and story. There was no woman. There was no dog.

But there *had* been a dog.

Black eyes in the snow had found him. The dog had set him free from the rope.

Cody trudged ahead, whispering silent thanks that the snow had relinquished some of its ferocity. He wondered how long he had been asleep for. If, perhaps, the worst was over, and he would soon find the houses of Denridge Hills again. Maybe he'd soon be back with Alex, and all of this would be behind them. They could hop on a plane back to England and leave this nightmare behind.

And leave Sophie behind?

Cody's lip quivered at the thought of her, his lips retracing the feeling of hers as they kissed, a thousand years ago in a darkened tunnel. He stumbled. Tripped. Fell. Glanced back. Couldn't work out what his foot had caught on until he spotted the stump half-buried in the snow.

He picked himself up and brushed the snow away. He glanced at the blackened tip of his nose and tapped a gloved hand against it, feeling nothing where he should have felt something. When he lowered his hands, he saw it. The first something to have met his vision since departing from the strange house on a piece of ancient cord.

Trunks stood like earthy jail cell bars, breaking the white. A canopy of green pines filled the horizon. Cody moved closer, waiting for the image to coalesce into greater clarity before allowing himself the chance to believe in what he was seeing.

The Drumtrie Forest. He was certain that this was it. All his studies of Denridge maps had shown the town bordered by the forest. He had flown over it, had heard rumors and myths and stories from the kids and school, and now it was here. The snow ended where the forest began, and inside the trees all was darkness. Another few steps and Cody could smell the heart of it all, the musty scent of the earthen pines. The shadows whispered to him, and something flashed in the dark. An animal? More snow? It was impossible to tell.

Cody looked over his shoulder, white behind, green ahead. There was no alternative. It was as if the world had driven him here, and now all that was left to do was to follow the yellow brick road and see where it led.

Twin lumps of coal caught his eye. Kazu strode out of the white, appearing as a fluffy mass of snow by his side. Cody couldn't explain it, but something felt right about the dog's appearance. It halted beside his leg and stared ahead. Cody looked between the dog and the darkness, from canine to pine, then with a determined mask of resolve, strode on into the trees.

The ground rumbled. A monstrous sound belched from the darkness.

60

ALEX GOINS

A lex knocked three times and waited.

The children stood some distance back, warned by Alex to run away if danger were to present itself. Although the house appeared untouched by the hordes of the creatures, his mind was filled with visions of wendigo leaping from the balcony and landing on his shoulders, a crazed man or woman with a shotgun hurtling toward him, a dog, a wolf, or a bear lunging from the darkness and sinking their teeth into his flesh.

He turned to the kids, Alice cuddling up to Sophie, Damien clutching Sophie's leg. Sophie had aged, even in the short time Alex had known her. Death and worry casting shadows on her face. He hated to think how much he had changed over the last few hours.

He thought back to Tori, and their journey into the snow... the others he had lost along the way. How could someone who knew so few people in this city, lose so many so quickly?

Something moved inside the house. Alex kept a hand on the rifle behind his back. It would be a sharp maneuver to snap it out and blast his way inside, but he'd be damned if he was going to wait it out in this storm for another minute. He needed a break, and the kids did, too. If the world had become dog-eat-dog, then he was going to prove himself top of the pack and take what was his.

Anything to somehow get closer to finding Cody.

A hand on the door. It twisted. A crack opened. Inside was darkness. The cold, steel barrel of a shotgun emerged. Alex heard commotion behind him. He waved a hand to calm the kids, but he couldn't check that they were there still. Not without turning away from the barrel of the gun.

A guttural sound emitted as an eye appeared in the slit between the doors. Something that sounded oddly like a sob. Alex raised a hand in the air. "Please. I mean you no harm. I'm just looking for somewhere to get out of the storm. I've got others with me. Children. We just need somewhere to rest from..."

From what? Try explaining all of this to a recluse who lives on the outskirts of town. Someone unaffected by the wendigos' destruction. Did they even have a clue what was going on?

Whispers from the door. Hurried exclamations. A shaking hand. A young, male voice snapped. The metal latch on the door clanged. The door caught on a second latch as someone struggled to open it. The second latch came free.

Alex's face fell. What remained of his breath stolen. It couldn't be. It wasn't possible. Forget the young kid with the furrowed brow aiming a rifle at his face, the woman behind had to be a ghost. Had to be...

Tears flooded down Tori's cheeks. Her cheeks were sunken hollows, her lip bruised, her hair an untidy mess. She looked as if she was going to pass out, and as Alex stepped toward her, her body slumped. Alex batted the boy's gun away and wrapped his arms around her despite the lad's terrified shouts. Her weight fell into his arms and he fell with her, landing in a lump on the floor as her body racked with sobs and he closed his eyes to breathe her in.

The boy stood over them, grabbing Alex's shoulder, trying to tear him away. Tori shouted something incoherent and he let them be. Tori's skin was soft, her face inches from his. She held his cheeks and drew him close, their lips touching. Their kiss was desperate, feral, manic, and it was all that he could do not to cry, too. Her tongue explored his mouth, her sour breath not a strong enough deterrent to break this moment. The boy took his position by the door and stared suspiciously into the white. He shouted, but Alex wasn't paying attention, all that mattered was Tori and her cracked lips.

When they finally came up for air, they stared a while into each other's eyes. Tori's tears slowed, and the ghost of a smile flickered on her face. She ran her fingers through Alex's hair. He removed his gloves and stroked her cheek.

"Hey," he said.

Tori chuckled. "Hi."

Alex was the first to stand. He offered a hand and helped Tori to her feet. She stayed a moment in his arms before Alex turned back to the front door where the young lad watched them with a raised eyebrow. "Are you done?"

Tori laughed. Sawed her hand across her nose. "Yes."

Alex approached the kid. The kid tensed.

"Don't worry," Alex said. "I'm not going to hurt you. I've left some luggage in the cold."

"Luggage?"

Alex turned from the door and stared into the white. His smile faded as he hunted in the snow for his flock. A bolt of panic flooded through him—they were nowhere to be seen.

Slight movement drew his attention to something on the edges of his vision. He waved a hand, then cupped them to his lips and hollered. A moment later, Sophie emerged from the white with the others at her side. Damien and Alice broke free and ran ahead. Sophie was slower, more cautious. Her arms wrapped around her waist, and she gritted herself against the chill wind as she drew closer to the house.

The door closed off the storm. For a long moment they shivered in the entryway, snow melting and dripping to the floor. Damien and Alice looked from the boy to Tori, then at each other. Sophie hung her head and stared blankly at her feet.

"I suppose we should do introductions," Tori said, breaking the silence at last.

The boy glared at Tori.

Alex chuckled, though there was little humor in it. The sight of the children, thawing out from the storm, bags beneath their eyes, and the sight of Tori's bruises and cuts quickly brought the haunting reality back to him.

Tori introduced the boy as Oscar, her nephew. Alex introduced the children, taking note of how Tori's eyes widened a touch at the mention of how Sophie was one of Cody's companions. She escorted them further into the house and helped them out of their jackets. They took a seat beside the fireplace and coddled hot drinks in their hands as they allowed themselves the luxury of heat for the first time that night. The flames flickered and made the shadows dance, and the sweet smell of tea and cocoa filled the room.

Tori and Alex sat together on the couch. Oscar stroked the barrel of his rifle, occasionally glancing to the curtained window along the back wall. Alex couldn't see anything out there since, at Tori's instruction, Oscar had hurried to close the drapes before they all settled down. Oscar's face curdled, growing darker with each passing second.

"How did you escape?" Alex asked at last, the coffee so hot that it numbed his tongue. "The last I saw, you were..."

Tori nodded, neither of them needing to say what had happened in the church. Damien looked as if he was about to say something, then decided not to. Alex was thankful for that.

"Naomi found me," she said softly, a heady warmth making Alex's eyelids heavy. "They were about to take me. I don't know how much longer I could have stayed there before it was over. Karl... He loomed over me, every part of what made him human was gone and..." She hedged her words, not wanting to alarm the children any more than she had to. "Naomi rescued me. She took out two of them, I think. Maybe more. It's all a blur. Before I knew it, she was dragging me away, back here."

"Where is here?" Sophie asked, for the first time making her voice heard.

Alice rolled her eyes. "In this house, silly."

"The edge of the forest," Tori said. "Just outside the border of the Drumtrie. This is her house."

Oscar bristled. "And mine."

"And yours."

Oscar shot Tori an urgent look. She lowered her eyes, the grooves growing deep in her forehead.

"What is it?" Alex asked.

Tori took a couple of deep breaths, but it was Oscar who finally replied. "Mom's out there. In the woods. She's gone by herself." He aimed his words at Tori. "We should be out there. Getting her. Bringing her back. Those...Those things..."

"What things?" Damien asked. "That man? Is he there?"

Tori looked at him quizzically, then shook her head as she realized to whom he was referring. "No. Not him."

"Then, what?" Sophie asked, rising from her seat and heading to the curtains.

Tori jumped up, making a move to block Sophie. Oscar rose from the edge of the armchair and stepped in her way. "No. They need to see this."

"The children," Tori complained. "They can't. They're only children."

Alex stood. "What is going on out..."

Sophie tore back the curtains, flooding the room in the eerie white glow of the snow. Alice shuffled closer to Damien, taking a stand behind him. Sophie stared aghast at the world outside. Oscar returned to his seat, a grim satisfaction on his face.

Alex moved slowly to the window, the room cast in silence. There was something out there. A few somethings. And with each step closer they grew clearer.

A stretch of snow paved the way toward the ancient pines, towering taller than the house and losing their tops in the frosty clouds. In front of them, creating a barrier between the house and the forest were a dozen or so wendigos, motionless and brooding. Their dark shapes reminded him of scarecrows, stick-thin limbs a mockery of anything that could have once called itself human. Their arms were longer than they should have been, and their feet were lost in the powder. Strange-looking genitals hung like dehydrated fruit between their legs, and beyond them...

Beyond them the woods were dark.

"Shit..." Alex breathed.

"Bad word," Damien said softly.

Alice whimpered and scrunched her face into the folds of Damien's t-shirt.

"Mom's out there," Oscar announced to the room, eyes brimming with tears, though he was doing everything to hold them back. "They have her. Those things... they're guarding the forest, and we need to get past."

Alex turned to Tori. "When did this happen?"

"Not that long ago. We were gearing up, getting ourselves ready to take them on when you arrived and..." She took a few hitching breaths. "I guess that seeing you all arrive through that door was a welcome distraction, but she's by herself and, Oscar's right, we need to get to her." She shook her head. "How the hell are we going to chase them with all these kids, Alex? We can't risk their lives, too. We've already lost so much tonight."

"Don't talk as though we're not here," Sophie snapped, brow hanging low over her eyes. Her voice was flat, emotionless. "We've been through shit, too—"

"Naughty," Damien whispered.

"—and it's not over. Whatever you choose to do, I'm going with you. I've had enough of these shits taking what doesn't belong to them. Tearing through this town and taking..." Her lip trembled, words failing. She composed herself, straightening her back as she wiped a tear with the back of her hand. "Cody deserves to be avenged. The storm and those things took him, the same way they did Amy, Brandon, Travis and..." Her eyes darted to the cupboard. "There's no way I'm not seeing this through to the end."

Alex looked from Sophie to Damien to Alice. "Well, someone needs to stay here with the kids. If we're going in there, they need to be guarded. They can't be left by themselves. Not tonight. Not until this is done."

"We can't take them with us," Tori replied, casting an apologetic eye to the pair. "It's too dangerous. They wouldn't last five minutes if the wendigo came at us. They have to stay here. Someone has to stay here with them. It's the only way to keep them safe."

"Who's to say this place is safe?" Sophie asked. "Why are you so sure that they won't attack us here?"

Alex raised his eyebrows.

Tori waved a hand. "We don't have time for this. What we need to do is to decide who's staying and who's going."

Before anyone could reply, a resounding boom erupted as something crashed against the front door. Wood splintered around the hinges and a blast of chilly air invaded the room. All heads turned. Oscar raised his father's rifle...

Too slow. The figure stepped over the threshold and aimed a pistol dead ahead. The report echoed around the house. Damien and Alice screamed as they threw themselves to the ground. Tori bellowed, diving behind the protective belly of the couch. Sophie hurled herself against the wall, shrinking against the wooden boards as though they might swallow her whole and hide her from harm.

Alex grunted, bullet ripping straight through him. Blood erupted from the wound and fountained into the air as he toppled onto the rug, head hitting the floor with a sharp thud, eyes rolling into the back of his head.

Tori's screams filled the air as another two shots were fired.

The third came from Oscar's rifle.

There were no more shots after that.

61

HAYDEN LOCKLEAR

The house looked inviting. The house looked warm. Flickering light showed the tell-tale signs of the fire inside. Fire... Something that Hayden's withering body yearned for. There was a fire in his father's home, a stone chimney with a metallic grate to protect the dog from the floating embers when the fire raged and breathed its warmth into the house. His dog—a working husky that he called Dog, even after his mother and father named him Klovski —would often fall asleep in front of that fire, and Hayden would watch from the couch, waiting for the day that a stray ember, as minuscule and powerful as a toxic nymph, would float above the grate and find its way into the dog's fur. He loved Dog, but he was also fascinated by all the things he shouldn't be fascinated by. Fire, blood, death... They were all on his lifelong to-see list, and perhaps if his visions came through, he would see all three ticked off at once.

In his mind's eye, the dark fur of Dog would catch alight around his rump. The tail would be the first to ignite, embers multiplying rapidly as the dog's eyes widened and he gave a panicked yelp. Hayden would watch him, unsympathetic to his pleas, as Dog sprinted around the room. Nothing else would catch fire in these visions, only the dog, and the dog would suffer. Not because he wanted the dog to suffer, but because there was no other way to know what would happen than to witness it firsthand, was there? Would the flesh melt and the blood scrape along behind him as the dog dragged its ass on the floor in a furious attempt to extinguish its flame? Would the creature simply melt into a sack of dripping blood, the fire eventually doused by the viscous fluid? Would the fire boil the blood and cause it to evaporate? Or would it all turn into a dry, powdery residue as the dog dragged its broken body along the wood and juddered into its final resting place?

Death would soon follow, that he knew for certain. Nothing could survive the cold clutches of death in the end. Nothing could survive that amount of duress, taken by the single cruelest element to exist on this planet.

But it wasn't the cruelest, was it? Tonight had shown him that. Tonight, the world had unleashed the demons from their underworld cages and thrown them at Denridge. Hurled the snow and the ice and the winds at Hayden and his posse, and from their wombs came the monsters. While Cody and Sophie and Brandon ran ahead and left Amy to die, Hayden sneaked around in the darkness, forced to survive on his own. Travis, his so-called best friend—

'Hayden is a prick'

—refused to defend his honor. Had finally joined their side, like he knew he would in the end. Not that that helped him. Where was Travis now? Likely dead in that tunnel, devoured by bloodthirsty creatures of ice, and Hayden was alone. There they were, the remaining band of survivors, cozied up in a nice warm house, surrounded by fire, probably hugging and laughing and singing Koom-by-fucking-yah, and Hayden was alone again, left outside in the snow with nothing but a pistol for company.

His blue lips peeled back into a painful snarl. The skin cracked and bled.

Hayden's father had taken him hunting on several occasions. Together they had stalked the water's edge, lying low and hunting for seal and polar bear. Hayden was familiar with the electric thrill of a gun firing from the simple pull of the trigger, the kickback shaking bones and rattling marrow. The smell of gunpowder and iron as the dying creature bled its contents onto the ice.

Dog barking unhappily by their side.

On those trips, it could have been so easy to aim the gun a few inches to his left. Fire again. Take out the dog. His father wouldn't have forgiven him, but what did that matter? Would serve Daddy right for the belt beatings and the name calling and the late-night drinking, returning in the early hours of the morning to screaming matches with Mom and stinking of another lady's perfume, wouldn't it?

Hayden saw them in the white, visions of his parents, the pair of them screaming until their voices were hoarse. His mother slapping his father, his father belting his mother. Dog yapping at their feet. His father taking a boot to Dog's head. Dog didn't last long after that. Mom said she forgave his father eventually, but her eyes told different. Eyes can't lie like mouths can.

Hayden wasn't even aware that he was crying until the tears froze and pained his cheeks. He turned over the gun in his hand, then looked back at the house, wanting it all to be over. The barrel pressed to his temple. He applied pressure. The chamber left a dent in his skin. His finger tensed. He growled, cried, sobbed, but the wind stole it all.

To his side, his mother and father made amends, arms wrapped around each other as Daddy undressed her and pressed her to an invisible wall. The sounds of their lovemaking would follow the fight. The sound of her tears would follow his snores. The cycle would continue indefinitely, that was the way of the world.

Or had been, at least.

Hayden ripped the pistol from his head as a shadow passed across the window. He thought of Travis, of his betrayal. He thought of Cody, of the humiliation Hayden had felt at his defeat on the court. He thought of Sophie defending Amy, turning his own girlfriend against him. He thought of the girl, the tiny bitch who had sucker punched him in the dark, and how she was in there with them now, warm, cozy, loved. He thought of how unjust the world was, how all he wanted was to be understood, to have a friend who cared, to not be laughed at, to not be humiliated by his father, to see the other side of the darkness and experience a world that wasn't this one.

He was walking before he knew he was. He lumbered toward the house, the sound of their voices reaching his ear and sending pangs of jealousy through his body. What could he do now? He could hardly go in there and join the throng. Gather with the merry band of adventurers and blend seamlessly into their narrative. No, Hayden would go out with a bang. Get his vengeance on the world and leave a mark that would be remembered.

"We don't have time for this. What we need to do is to decide who's staying and who's going," a voice said. Female.

Great, they were already breaking up the pack. He had to act, and soon.

He shot at the lock without thought. In his head, the perfect movie line begged to be hollered, "Oh, I think you'll all be staying," but nothing came out. His eyes fixed on the boy's rifle, pointing directly at him. He panicked, blood turning colder than he thought possible as he aimed at the largest object in the room, the man who, in that moment, reminded him strangely of Cody. He fired. The bullet tore through the room. The man went down.

His finger tensed on the trigger, arm waving wildly about as the chaos set in. On his lips was a dark, confused grin—the mask of a lunatic—and then a muzzle flashed, something hard and heavy crashed into his stomach. Air fled his lungs, abandoning him as his friends had earlier that night.

Back when things were simple...

The world went black.

The world was dark.

Hayden closed his eyes and exhaled his final breath.

Finally, at peace.

62

TORI ASPLIN

Tori swam in an ocean of tar.

The world moved in slow motion. Each movement was a struggle, each thought rising to her memory in puzzle pieces that she had to assemble with no hands. The gunshots rang in her ears like thunderclaps, the screams of the others the painful glue that bonded the sounds. Alex lay on the rug behind her. The gunshots stalled to nothing, but the activity continued. People ran and voices called, undefined in their announcements. She pushed herself to her feet but knew she couldn't move fast enough to make a damned bit of difference. Blood pulsed around the cuts of her nose. Her head pounded.

And still this night was far from over.

Alice's cries were what finally aroused Tori, bringing clarity to their situation with stark command. Tori stood sharply, blood rushing to her head. Bile fizzed her throat. She spotted the dead boy by the front door, then staggered toward Alice who had fallen danger- ously close to the fire, the embers licking at the back of her coat.

"Come here." She pulled Alice to her chest and buried her face in her shoulder. "Oscar, check that he's down, then close the door. Damien? Damien, where are you?"

Damien's face appeared beneath the coffee table. There were cracks in the walls from the other bullets the gunman had fired. They were lucky he hadn't broken the glass.

"He's dead!" Sophie declared, dust and dirt stuck to her face. "He's dead!"

The words bounced off Tori as she turned and saw the large lump on the floor. She wouldn't believe it. Couldn't believe it. Not Alex. Not the man that had dragged her through the storm and rescued these children. Alex, the savior, the one beacon of decency which had shone brightly during the darkest night of her life. An overwhelming rush of conflicting emotions swallowed her, threatened to drown her, keep her buried under their throbbing tides. It couldn't be him. Please, no...

She passed Alice to Sophie and fell to her knees beside the still figure. Blood pooled around Alex's head, soaking into the fibers of the carpet. The stink of piss and shit came from his trousers, and in rolling him a little she could make out dark stains around his crotch.

"No. No, no, no, no..."

His head rolled back. His lips were parted. She drew closer, knees soaking up blood, hands growing slick with the stuff. She held his cheeks and pressed her ear to his lips, pressed her lips to his, tried to see through the fuzzy haze of tears curtaining her eyes.

"He's dead," Oscar said flatly, voice trailing through the house. How much death must a kid have seen to become so emotionless in the process of its declaration? The door slammed shut and the wind's cry cut off.

Though Oscar was talking about the dead body in the hall, the words resonated with Tori. In her arms was a dead man. Another. Two in one night. Stanley. Alex. Interchangeable sacks of flesh that had met the same end via different means. Her hands scrambled across his body, bloodstained palms painting his clothes, searching for the bullet wound like a dog seeking a rabbit which had just fled down its burrow. Her mouth was a rainbow of upset, the tears flowing freely. She was aware of the others moving behind her, of Alice's racking sobs, Damien's flat, innocent lines of questioning, Oscar striding over as they gathered around Alex and Tori.

Yet, she still couldn't find it. She examined his chest for the bullet wound, searched his neck, checked the back of his head. Where was the blood fountaining from? It was still flowing freely, the puddle growing, a metallic scent lingering in the air.

Sophie took the other side of Alex, kneeling in the growing lake of blood. "Tori..."

Tori ignored her, not understanding what had happened. Something was wrong. She had looked death in the eye that night, studied her enemy and grown familiar. She attacked his body with her frantic hands, rolling Alex back and forth, the blood covering so much of him that the only part of his flesh left on display was the pale skin of his face. Flecks of blood marked his white cheeks. His nose was flushed with blooming roses.

Did his eyelids just flicker?

Sophie put her hands on Tori's shoulder, trying to rouse her from her frenzy. Oscar stood behind her, rifle in his hands, shadow stretching atop the three on the floor.

"Tori...?"

"No." There was no argument to be had. Tori rolled Alex to his side, and a small pulse of blood leaked from Alex's shoulder, looking more like the ripples left in the wake of a crimson fish leaving the pond than the sprays that came before. The blood was slowing.

But there was the wound.

In his shoulder.

His shoulder?

"Oscar, go to the utility closet and get me some towels."

Oscar turned to the window, impatience in his eyes.

"Now!" Tori screamed. Oscar jumped. He ran up the stairs and appeared a moment later with an armful of pristine white towels.

"Tori, what are you doing?" Sophie asked.

Tori patted the towels against Alex's shoulder, the white turning instantly red. The site of the wound soon cleared and in the dark pit of where the pistol had caught Alex, she finally saw a glint of gold.

Acting before she could think, Tori dug her fingers into Alex's shoulder. The bullet had caught in the bone, and as Tori pinched her fingers around the metal head, fighting for purchase against the fresh swell of blood, Alex's eyes fluttered. His lips curled into a snarl and he gave a weak cry that soon grew as his eyes snapped open and pain erupted in one clean note from his lips.

"Hold him still!" Tori cried.

Oscar and Sophie obeyed, holding Alex's other arm and pressing him down while Tori fought for the bullet. Her fingers closed around the curved head, one finger scooping it toward her. Although she could feel the bullet in her hand, she couldn't see it for the blood, but now that she was satisfied that the wound was clear, she set about cleaning up the mess.

Alex writhed in pain as his consciousness pulsed back. Oscar and Sophie struggled to pin him, growing sweaty and tired as Tori took her belt and created a makeshift tourniquet, applying pressure in order to stem the bleeding. She wrapped his shoulder with the last of the cotton towels, and then sat back, hands sliding in the blood beneath her.

She nodded to Oscar and Sophie. They let go of Alex and gave him some space. Alex lay on the ground, eyes closed, nose wrinkled, gasping and panting as the pain began to subside. Tori instructed Oscar to find some aspirin, and with a little assistance, Alex took three. After a few moments, he tried to sit up, looking around the room as if he'd just woken from a nightmare, arm bent across his body in the makeshift sling Tori had fashioned.

"What the fuck just happened?"

Tori laughed. She clamped her hands to her mouth, realizing just how strange a reaction it was, but she didn't care. Relief lightened the weight that had appeared on her shoulders, and she fought the urge to throw her arms around Alex and hug him. "Welcome back to the land of the living."

"I saw a light."

"That'll be the muzzle flash," Oscar said.

Alex's brow narrowed. "The gunman... Is he...?"

"Dead." Oscar glanced over at the corpse growing cold by the door. "Yes."

"Who was that?" Alex asked. He straightened his back and grimaced as a flood of pain passed through him.

Oscar shrugged. Alice and Damien sat together in the corner of the room, arms around each other. Sophie crossed over to the body, letting out a strangled gasp when she saw the face staring blankly at the ceiling.

"You know him?" Tori asked.

Sophie nodded, unable to verbalize the answer. She struggled for breath and took a step back before tearing her eyes away from the gunman's body.

Tori turned to Alex and whispered, "Are you going to be okay if I..."

Alex waved his spare hand. "Go on."

She could tell he was lying, but she had no choice. Alex wasn't the only mess that needed clearing up.

Alice stopped crying. Damien stayed by her side, watching over her like a loyal retriever, playing the protective older brother as Tori tried to clean up the worst of the mess and remove the dead boy. Oscar helped her, the pair of them working to cover the boy in a rug so that he was at least out of sight and, hopefully, out of mind. There were some stains that would never come out of the wood and the cloth, but those could be dealt with later.

Alex shifted to the couch, lying down across its length as he spoke through gritted teeth to Sophie who had since gone silent. "One of yours?"

She hardly blinked, eyes drifting occasionally to the wendigo sentinels outside.

When, at last, the worst of the mess was cleared, Tori returned to the living room and took a seat by Alex's feet. She scanned the sea of expectant faces, aware of the subtle shift in the atmosphere. The patriarch had been compromised. There was a new leader in town.

"I think we know who's going to be staying here," she announced, the burden of her words weighing on her as she spoke.

Alex protested.

"No." She placed a hand on his chest and held him firmly down. It was easier than it should have been. "You're staying. No argument. You can't go in there like that. You can't."

"I'll be fine. It's too dangerous—"

"No!" This time it was Sophie's turn to interject. Her face wore the mask of someone much older than she, eyelids heavy, bags like wet hammocks beneath her eyes. "No more arguing. No more time wasting. We need the healthy and the able to go out there and end this fucking nightmare."

Damien flinched. Alice drew closer to him.

"I'll go." She turned to Tori, determination in her eyes. "I'll join you. Oscar will go, too."

"I want to come," Damien said weakly.

"No," Tori said.

"But I want to help," Damien replied. "I want to help you, too. I can. I promise. I've helped Alex all night."

Alex gave a reassuring grin as he shook his head. "Step down, soldier. Your part is done."

Damien's brow furrowed. He looked as if he was going to protest, then huffed and fell quiet.

Oscar stared out of the window. "We *have* to get going, Aunt Tori. Mom is out there, and she can't do this alone. Please. Let's go."

"Have you got your father's..."

Oscar motioned to the far wall where a collection of pistols and rifles were gathered, the firearms that they had originally come back to the house to collect before distraction came.

Tori looked into Alex's eyes, worry traced in every line. "Will you be okay?"

"Doesn't look like I have much of a choice, does it?"

She smirked, a hollow gesture. "We'll be back."

"I know."

He's lying.

Oscar helped Sophie pick out a double-barreled shotgun from the pile, and soon they were standing by the back door again. Tori's mind flashed with images of the previous attack, the way the wendigos worked as one to block them from the forest. When Alex had arrived at the house, she had hoped to be able to grow their numbers and increase their chances, but what hope was there now when he was in such a state?

Her hand lingered on the door. She looked back at the room, eyes glittering, taking in each face staring up at her. "You be good for Alex, okay?" she told Damien and Alice. "Do what he says and make sure he gets better. If we don't come back..." She took a long breath. "If we don't come back, seek help. Wait for the storm to pass. Try the telephone lines. Look after each other."

Alice looked at the floor. Damien nodded. Alex smiled.

And wasn't that smile the most painful part of all of this?

She opened the door and a blast of cold air met her skin. The wendigos remained silent, stoic in their positions. A slight tremor ran through her toes, or was that simply her nerves racking through her body? The answer came when a haunting sound launched from the forest, erupting from the gaps in the pines, and the wendigos all bowed to one knee.

Tori stared wide-eyed at the wendigo. When the full tremor came, she fell to her knees, too. They all did. All except Alex. The lights swung from their fixtures, trophies and photo frames crashed to the floor. Glasses shattered as they shook free from their shelves, and as the monstrous expulsion of sound grew in force, they all clamped their hands to their ears. All except Alex who turned into his pillows and did what he could to shut out the sound without triggering further pain in his arm.

Something shook in the trees. The sound faded to silence. Tori stood frozen by the door. The wendigos silently turned as one and ran back into the forest. Before Tori could ask Alex what was happening, the rushing sound of dozens more creatures came from around the sides of the house. Dark figures, blurred as they sprinted, stalked back into the darkness of the trees, the shadows hungrily claiming them. Dozens upon dozens of wendigos of all shapes and sizes, drawn back to the place from whence they came.

After a beat, there were no more.

Tori swallowed dryly. Oscar shuffled beside her, a single word melting off his tongue. "Mom..."

63

CODY TREBECK

The belching bellow stopped Cody in his tracks. He was surrounded by darkness, coddled by the trees, yet still, impossibly, he knew the way ahead.

The way to what? He couldn't answer that question, all that he knew was that the trees parted for him, moving as if by their own volition, and the path ahead was as clear as day. The thorns and leaves and detritus that powdered the forest floor was cleared from the single-track path that led ahead, winding through the boughs of the ancient pines. He could smell the passage of time, his nostrils saturated with the scent of dusty attics and molding floorboards. There was a dryness to the air as it held its breath in anticipation of his passage. A warmth, minimal, but in stark contrast to the chill from the outside world, thawed his bones and he soon found his forehead peppered in a thin film of sweat.

Things moved in the darkness. The farther in he trod, the more he was aware of them, dark figures running through the shadows. He could guess what they were, but couldn't know for sure. All he knew was that their passage was impossibly silent, and it wasn't long before the flock had passed and they were gone again. Occasionally the canopy of pines would break and grant him a reprieve from the cloying shadows, and in those brief breaks in time and space he saw the stars wheeling above him, bending and dancing along with the Aurora Borealis, the crimson phenomenon forcing Cody to think of the trails of blood left on a neck in the wake of a butcher's knife. Once more he found his thoughts filled with that strange transition of color, blues to greens to red, until the trees snatched his glimpses and the world faded to black once more.

He was barely aware of the dog walking by his side, yet to have a companion was a gift beyond his wildest dreams. For a short while he had feared that he would be alone forever, facing whatever may come his way with no one left to tell his story, but at least with the dog beside him he knew two things: that his encounter with the witch had been true, and that he wouldn't have to die alone.

Who said anything about dying?

The trees peeled apart as the road grew wider. After a stretch of time in the woods that could have been minutes, could have been days, his first real break in the blackness presented itself. A great, jagged shape lodged at the base of a tree. The bones gleamed white in the shadows, the ridges of a beastly ribcage like long, thin teeth chomping at the sky. Antlers stretched at least ten feet in either direction on the enormous stag's skull. The last scraps of flesh and meat clung to the bone, dried and forgotten over time.

How long had this creature been here? What monstrosities had picked it clean, licked the bones and chomped the meat? Well, he thought he knew the answer to that last one at least.

He stared a long while at the white stag, feeling as though this was all somehow strangely connected. There was a familiarity in its shape, an aura surrounding the dead beast that spoke of warning, of blood, of danger, and yet still he stared, stared until his eyes stung and he could picture the great beast standing on all fours, wandering through this mystical forest like a beast of legend and myth. What a sight it would have been to behold the regality of the creature, to see this giant specimen in its prime and to gaze from afar. They sure didn't make them like this in England.

Kazu whined by his side. Cody knelt by the dog and tussled his fur. Kazu whined once more, nose pointing into the surrounding darkness.

A darkness interjected by the twinkling studs of dozens of pairs of eyes, patiently waiting for Cody to continue.

64

SOPHIE PEARCE

S ophie breathed a conflicting sigh of relief as they left the white
and entered the forest.

When they left the house, she concocted visions of the three of
them crossing to the trees and entering a Wild West showdown with
the wendigo sentinels, bullets erupting from a gun that she barely
knew how to control as she fought alongside Tori and Oscar, battling
for their lives. She had gone so far as to smell their fetid stink, feel the
dry roughness of their limbs on her body, imagine herself screaming
and doing all that she could to narrow their number and gain entry
across the threshold.

But all of that had passed. The wendigo were gone.

And that was a much worse reality to comprehend.

It would be fine if they could see where they were going. It would
be fine if they knew where the wendigo had gone. Hell, it would be
even better if they had Alex with them, the man who had protected
her and the children and led them safely away from the isolated
house in the far reaches of who-the-fuck-knew-where.

But that wasn't the reality they were facing, and with each step
Sophie grew more reluctant to take another, as though the very forest
itself was creeping into her stores of courage and sapping all that

remained. The only things steeling her resolve were the woman and the boy beside her.

Well, that wasn't entirely true. There was also the third of their company. The ghost that wouldn't exit her sight.

He clung to the farthest reaches of the darkness, appearing as a white specter on the horizon. His smile was bright, the grin stretching ear to ear. His hair was tousled at the back, and he walked with a gay hop in his step, leaping between the boughs like a mischievous faun, fingers dancing over the pipe as he danced a jig and led them on.

Cody was dead. She was certain of that. But there he was, tempting them ahead, guiding the way and causing her eyes to prick with tears. Each fleeting appearance made her heart leap. Every time he faded to darkness, it sank. Cody was an honorable man, and the world didn't respect the honorable, it favored the unjust and the corrupt. Sophie had hardly known a boy her age with the courage that Cody had shown that night, the grace, the class, the personality. Denridge didn't breed boys in his stock, and now he was gone.

And all she could do was claim back his memory and ensure that his death wouldn't be in vain. There were others to protect.

Tori walked silently by her side. Sophie wondered if she knew she was crying, her face set in grim resolve but for the silvery trails. Oscar made her feel calm, the boy exhibiting the kind of strength she had only seen in a few. He wore the courage of an older man, of someone who understood what was coming, even though none of them really knew. If this night had shown them anything, it was that life was still a mystery, and that reality was fluid. The boy dancing in front of her proved that much at least.

"How much further?" Sophie asked, when she was certain that the forest had begun to repeat its patterns, throwing them onto an eternal treadmill of damnation

Tori's muttered response. "I don't know."

"We've been walking for hours."

Oscar examined his watch.

"What time is it?" Sophie asked.

"It's broken."

"Of course."

The sudden disappearance of the wendigos was the biggest concern of all. Cast into the darkness, there was no telling where they were or what they could be up to. Sophie imagined herself in the eye of a hurricane, the world fallen silent, staring up at a cataclysmic roiling of thunderous clouds, a smile on her face, knowing that the moment the eye shifted its gaze to another target, the end would come. What would it be like to die? Would there be relief in the end? She hoped that Amy found hers. That Travis found his. That Cody...

Cody waved her onward.

The ground rumbled again. A flurry of movement and wind, the colossal beating of bat wings powering through the forest and blasting their faces. They braced themselves, grimaced against the coming gust, then that, too, passed.

Tori shook her head, palms slipping against the barrel of her rifle.

Sophie adjusted her grip on the shotgun.

Oscar's eyes narrowed, face souring as the trees, at last, began to thin.

65

CODY TREBECK

S urrounded.

Cody paused, eyes scanning the trees. The wendigos watched, their circling stretched so wide that he could only see the onyx glitter in their eyes. Dozens upon dozens of them in rows, and all he could do was manage his breathing, try to calm his beating heart, wonder at the marvel of what stood before him.

Creatures of history, of legend, of the Earth. Chikuk had taught him the secrets of their birth. Creatures born of insatiable hunger, cursed with the parasitic force of greed. Yet, they were but mere servants to a larger master. A creature that had once been human, until famine had forced him to do the unthinkable.

These were his children. Minions of the darkness bound by a single cause. Their leashes had been severed, and their reign had been granted in the wake of Aklaq's death. The floodgates opened and the wrath of the wendigos was permitted to go unchecked for an entire evening, an entire week, a month, who knew how long it would all last, when the sun may once again rise?

Cody's breath fogged before his eyes. The world was cast in monochrome. He wondered what they were waiting for, for clearly their hunger wasn't enough to drive them to feast. If they wanted him dead, he would be dead right now, nothing more than chunks of meat sizzling in digestive fluids. Impossibly so, he felt safe in their presence, as if they were there to guard him, not to attack.

But where was Kazu?

"What do you want?" Cody breathed, wondering if the words would even reach them. A shape shifted, coalescing from the shadows, and as it arrived, Cody wondered how he could ever have not noticed that it was there. The great mask of bone—a stag's head, antlers stretching from bough to bough—floated in the darkness. An eternal emptiness in the place where innocent eyes once sat. The creature appeared to hover before Cody, its stick-thin arms and scythe-like fingers stretching toward his face. A voice appeared from a place where no mouth sat.

"You."

There was no more explanation. What explanation would make sense to Cody, anyway? He nodded in response, eyes narrowing, jaw clenched. The masked wendigo cocked its head and stared at Cody for a long time, before finally turning and sweeping into the woods.

Cody remained frozen, uncertain of what would come next until rough, cold fingers gripped his arms and led him onward. Two more wendigos of mask and bone guiding him ahead, leading the way as their crowd of followers closed in behind. There was no going back now.

The trees thinned, parting to allow the sky above to come into full view. There were no clouds above, there was no more fall of snow. The Aurora pulsed with feverish excitement, forming the shapes of skeletal animals and dripping with blood that dissolved into nothing before it could touch the ground. Cody tried to pinch himself, to wake up from this hypnotic dream, but the wendigos held him firmly in place. His head swam, reminding him of the strange trip inside the old woman's igloo. Where were they taking him? Why was he okay with this? What lay beyond the veil of trees as they homed in on the heart of the forest?

Grass grew around his feet, the distance between the trees spread ever wider. The wendigo with the stag's crown guided him into the clearing, a place where the ragged canvas of what might have once been a tent flapped in the breeze. A stone circle with the dark remnants of ash sat in the center. Around the clearing was a mass of human remains, men and women and children he recognized from the town, though some were far too desecrated to identify.

"Where am I?"

The stag turned, lips unmoving, the voice taking shape in his head. "Home."

The sound of something wet and meaty met his ears. A sack of liver dropped from a height, left to thwack against a ceramic floor. The hungry smack of lips was followed by the grunts of feast as a large figure crouched over something in the distance, its form shadowed by an even larger boulder that sat on the far side of the clearing.

Its back convulsed. Hands, slick with a slimy substance, pulled at the body on the ground. Trails of tendons and flesh and viscera hung between the darkened form and its meal.

Bile rose in Cody's throat. The wendigos moved around the clearing, forming a barrier of bodies that encircled him, closed off all escape. The masked wendigos cleared the way and allowed a direct path from Cody to this hulking beast, shoveling mouthful after mouthful, barely taking a breath. Cody took a cautious step forward. The ancient voice appeared in his head, "It is okay. It is the way of things."

Another step and the earthy scent reached his nostrils. He worked his way through the labyrinth of bodies, flinching only slightly when a jagged piece of bone prodded through the sole of his shoes and pricked his heel. He became immersed in the scent of death, his skin prickling, throat gagging, until all that he knew was this place, the taste of this air, the desperate, feverish hunger of the creature before him.

The boulder loomed over the figure. The figure cackled, groaned with ecstatic delight, picked at the bones of the figure, sucked the blood off its fingers, throbbed and writhed and lost itself in delirium...

A bone snapped under Cody's foot.

The Aurora bled on.

The creature froze, globules of blood dripping onto the soil, disappearing into the thirsty earth. Cody's heart stopped. His pulse beat violently in his ears.

The creature slowly turned, a face, thick with dark hair, matted with blood and chunks of gore, eyes as black as night. It fixed its gaze on Cody, a grin forming on its face, teeth red and yellow and black. It stood to its full height, an easy two feet taller than Cody. A naked man, his body showing the shadow of what might once have been muscles, but which had since deflated to a shrunken ribcage, and the coming signs of a famished stomach, his flesh caving toward his hips. A hideous sight to watch the transformation.

The worst of this man's appearance stood between his legs, a flag raised proudly from his crotch, a bulbous red head, flecked with the blood which had escaped his hungry lips. His chest heaved, his anvil hands packed with meat and organs and flesh. The monster of a man extended his hands to Cody, offering the meal as a child might offer a slice of birthday cake to their guests.

"It's good," the deep, croaking voice said, each syllable laced with ecstasy. "Imagine the greatest meal you've had, and times that by infinite." There was a wonder in his dark eyes, the man fallen under their spell. "They can protect you. They can make you family. Have you ever wanted to live forever? Live forever with those who love you? Live forever with... us..."

A trail of thick, pink saliva fell from his open mouth. Cody followed the trail until it sank into the mud at his feet. Something glimmered, and his eyes trailed to the metal barrel of the gun that lay by the corpse's side—a rifle, if his knowledge of guns was anything to go by. Not too far from the rifle, sitting crookedly where the desiccated corpse's head should have been, was another stag skull, this one looking more human than animal.

Cody put a hand to his mouth, fighting back the urge to vomit. It was all too much. To be in this place. To see what he was seeing. To be promised love and family and life. His juvenile brain had had enough wonder, and in that moment, all he longed for was the chilly darkness of his bedroom, to listen to the songs that crooned through the walls, to dance with the orchestra of whispers and whistles and wonder whether his uncle was still up writing, lost in the throes of his fiction until dawn crowed and the moon began its descent. He wished for his parents, for his sleep to be rudely broken by his phone's alarm, to taste Kellogg's on his tongue, smell the stench of BO in the school locker room, feel the elastic bounce of a basketball on his fingertips. What was this world that was so cast from his own reality, lost on the far side of knowledge and caught in the clutches of monsters? What was this dizzying redness that swam above him, casting its hypnotic glow and causing his mouth to salivate? How long could he stand here, resisting the temptation to surrender to the delicious scent that consumed his senses and drew him forward, his arms stretching out toward the hairy beast and his offering?

How long?

How long...?

The scent of death twisted, forming a sweet cocktail of treats. Sugar seduced his tastebuds. The meat transformed before his eyes into brightly colored doughnuts and cakes, dripping with melted sugar and honey. His eyes grew wide. His tongue traced his lips. He reached out, hands only centimeters from the meal as the man brooded over him, the dark shape of the Devil, it seemed, yet even the Devil must have an ounce of good inside him, surely? To present him with such delights...

And then it happened.

Cody looked up into the dark abyssal pits of the hairy man's face and behind him something moved. The boulder, previously nothing more than a hunk of gigantic rock, started to move. The rock unfurled, cracks fissuring and producing the form of arms, legs tucked underneath now stretching as the boulder shifted before his very eyes, growing, growing, growing, until the figure stood above the hairy man, easily double his height, perhaps triple, a great monster of surreal proportions.

Coarse fur matted its body, a great tufty collar trailing maned around its neck. Its arms were like tree branches, stretching to the ground in an apish way that arched its back and displayed the ridges of its spine like prehistoric spikes to the crimson glow. Its legs were long but bent, and Cody wondered how tall this creature would truly become if it stood at its full height. The top of its antlers competed with the height of the pines, and as Cody took a staggering step back, trying to process the full breadth of the enormity before him, he noticed the strangest part of all—while the masked wendigos wore their skulls in the same way that trick-or-treaters donned artificial masks for Halloween, the skull of this creature was a part of it, as if this was all somehow the result of monstrous cross-breeding between stag and a human. It made no sense. Thick muscles cording its body where the other wendigo had none, as if it feasted on their misery, and their pain brought it strength. Its lower jaw opened and closed. The creature bent low, bringing its face closer to Cody's, emitting the screeching roar of an ancient machine, fetid breath wafting over Cody and peeling back his eyelids, spreading his lips and filling his lungs with decrepit air. The wind cast from its bone mouth gushed through the clearing, billowing the tattered remains of the clothes that clung to the corpses before dispersing into the forest.

Cody swallowed, tasted death. Death stared at him in the face, its empty eyes burrowing into Cody's soul. And somehow he knew it, somehow he knew that Death had a name.

And that name was Tulimaq.

66

ALEX GOINS

Wind rattled the windows of the house. Alex doubled over, pulling at the carpet with his one good arm as he fought to hide the monstrosity from sight.

He had begun to stink already, and the children couldn't help but look over at the ominous lump wrapped in fabric. Alex felt bad for the kid, his golden heart empathizing with his attacker, even though the loss of function in his arm was going to be a burden he carried for the rest of his life.

What was this guy thinking? What was his story?

He supposed it didn't matter. What mattered now was that he protected the two children left in his charge, even if every fiber of his body was telling him to follow Tori and her companions into the woods, to help end this damned thing once and for all.

If ending it is even possible.

Alice and Damien chatted quietly on the couch, facing away from the front door. Alex drew the curtains the moment the others had left, thinking it would make him feel better. It didn't. All it made him feel was useless, as though he was cowering from the danger set before him, a danger that had followed him every step of the journey.

How could he stay here while the others strode boldly into the lion's den? How could he...

"I'm tired," Alice said, her tiny mouth fanning into a wide yawn. "Are you tired, Damien?"

Damien's eyelids were heavy, his lips slightly parted. The warm milk Alex had made for him edged closer to the lip of the cup as the boy's attention strayed and his hand tilted.

Alice screwed a fist into her eye and shook Damien's leg. "Are you tired?"

Damien nodded. Yawned. Closed his eyes.

Alex turned his attention to the dead boy.

He dragged the body to a cupboard under the stairs in spurts of energy and pain. At least the boy would be out of sight in there. They could deal with the smell later. For now, this would have to do. The throbbing in his shoulder provided a constant reminder that he should be careful, take it easy, but the aspirin did a great job at taking the edge off.

The fit was a squeeze, but eventually Alex rested his back against the door. He was sweating, despite being dressed in only his long-sleeved t-shirt and pants. He wiped his brow, then headed back into the living room to check on the kids.

They were fast asleep.

He sat on the edge of the coffee table and studied their innocent faces. Alice's cheeks still held the jowly wobble of infancy, pinched and kissed by a thousand fingers and lips. Damien's skin was pale, but this was the first time Alex had seen him truly at peace since they had fled his parents. Lines appeared on Alex's face as he thought back to Harvey and Sherri and their kind hospitality, a hospitality that ended in Harvey's death, and Sherri's... Well, Alex had no idea what had become of Sherri in the end.

Was there a chance she'd make it through this night?

Something told him that wouldn't be the case.

When the sun finally rose on this sleepy town and revealed its wounds and losses, he wondered what would become of the kid. He had grown fond of Damien, his constant chatter and his naïve optimism. But Alex never set out to be a caregiver. Perhaps someone in the town could adopt him—if there was anyone left. Damien was an intelligent boy. Curious. Sweet. Loyal. Anyone would be lucky to have him.

Their snoring was soft, the pair of them snoozing in a gentle embrace. Alice snuggled her head into Damien's collar, a small pool of drool darkening his shirt. Damien breathed heavily, mouth wide open, catching flies.

Alex turned to the window. Out there, somewhere, the fight would be taking place. With any luck, a fight to end this nightmare and bring peace to the town once more. What would the survival of these kids matter if everyone and everything else died? Wouldn't it be the best protection for the children if he actually went to the source of chaos and helped end this thing once and for all?

He found himself at the curtains with no memory of moving. He peeked between the cloth and looked out at the trees, the gaps between the boughs appearing to have grown, calling him inside, begging him to become a part of their narrative.

Alex glanced back at the kids. The rifle nestled perfectly in his hand. The chill air numbed his wound as he closed the door and staggered outside.

67

TORI ASPLIN

S omething crunched beneath Tori's feet. The wicked sound of the monstrous unknown belched through the forest. She squinted ahead, a number of dark shapes standing sentinel, their silhouettes cast in a strange red glow.

Another crunch. She looked down. Bones. Tiny, white bones.

She positioned the butt of her rifle into the crook of her shoulder and viewed the world through its sights. Her finger twitched on the trigger and, in that moment, memories flooded back of phone screens and scrolling images. Of pop-up hearts and bright blue thumbs. Of showers of praise and comments, royalty statements and advertiser emails. Admirations and adulations of selfies in front of the mirror, shallow comments and rhetorical questions. An audience trapped in her hands. People she would never know or truly care about. Not like the man she had left behind. The phone screen she tapped with her index finger more times than she could count...

This finger, the one that caressed the trigger, had it ever known how comfortably it would fit here?

They grew closer, Oscar and Sophie silent as they flanked her. Oscar copied Tori and readied his weapon. Sophie looked uncertain, but soon found her resolve. Three untrained soldiers, affected by the crushing storm, united in their final stand.

Why was it so quiet, now? What was this apprehensive breath in the world? Tori swayed the scope of her rifle among the wendigo heads, prepared for when they would inevitably turn around and come for them. Something shifted beyond the lines of creatures, something that was too difficult to see at first. A great boulder, heaving as if it was attempting to breathe itself to life. Tori's eyes narrowed as the red pulsing light grew brighter, and in the odd flicker of color the picture became clear.

The wendigo were guarding the center of a clearing, a balding crown in the depth of the forests. Two figures, one barely the size of a young man, and another towering above him, eyes locked together, quiet words exchanged, standing at the far reach of the clearing.

They drew closer, stopping a short distance from the wendigos, able to see through the breaks in their number. Sophie gasped, shotgun lowering as her eyes grew wide and afraid.

"It's him... Oh my God. It's him..." Her hands shook, knees trembling.

"Who?"

"Him... Cody. It's..." She fought with the shotgun for purchase, and as she lined up a shot, Tori grabbed the barrel and forced it down.

"Not yet."

Sophie shook her head, unable to form another clear word amidst the strange, desperate moans coming from her lips.

Oscar crept forward. So, too, did Tori. Eyes pinned on the hulking figure above the boy. The man who looked to have neared the end of his final metamorphosis, muscle beginning to wilt, flesh caked in dried blood, hair matted and wild. Karl looked as devilish as they came, even more fearsome than the creatures he now associated himself with, and that was saying something.

Karl presented something to Cody. Tori swallowed down bile as chunks of the offering slopped to the floor with a wet thwack. She lined up Karl in her sights, unable to believe what this night had come to, that she would be contemplating killing her former lover. The man she had envisioned her future with but hours ago. The man who had once captured her affections and stolen her heart.

Yet, somehow, here they were, and Tori knew that if she didn't act fast, there would be no hope left for the kid.

The thing moved behind him. The giant, quaking rock. The boulder sprang to life, unfurling from its cocoon, and a creature was birthed into the world that should never have existed. A thing that towered over Karl's shoulders, double his height, twice his width. Sophie sobbed through the hand covering her mouth, Oscar gave a muted squeak of fear, his courage finally fleeing.

Tori took a deep breath, conviction rising deep within her as she got the beast in her sights and readied her shot. The ripple of anticipation that ran through the ring of wendigos told her all that she needed to know—this creature was at the top of the food chain. This was the creature that had called its children home.

The creature lowered its head, drawing closer to the boy. Its mouth was large enough to take his head in a single bite. There were no eyes, only vapid pits of despair. The white crown of bone it wore was ancient, a grand display of taxidermized artwork. Broad, paddle-like antlers winging from its head. It roared in its lost language at the boy, and he dropped to his knees, trousers soaking up the life juice of the corpse at his feet. The boy bent low, hands swimming in the pools of viscera and gore, back heaving excitedly like a hyena wild with frenzied hunger.

"No!" Tori sprinted, broke into the ring of wendigo, aimed the rifle at the beast and fired.

68

CODY TREBECK

Time stretched into always. Those twin caves, buried deep into the skull's sockets, held the universe.

It was infinite, expansive, history gathered in a melting puddle and swirled in an endless abyss. In those immortal pools of black was love and anger, fear and pain, death and ecstasy, and somewhere in the midst of it all was his parent's laughter, his mother's sobs, his father's coughs and sneezes and snores. Somewhere in the chasm of no return was the creak of mountains and the roar and swell of ocean, salt spray flecked his face, heat roared from the infernal stony lips of the volcano's tip. The theme tune to Sonic the Hedgehog morphed into his grandmother's harp, the babble of the children in the schoolyard, the ringing of a bell calling them in from play. Car engines thrummed, wind whispered in trees, dogs barked and howled, and cats fucked, rutting to a chorus of angry screeches and mewling. The snow melted as it fell, storms clashed, tectonic plates generated friction as all the elements of the planet fought for their place, expanding and shrinking, breathing in and out, a set of godly lungs that spanned the Earth and exhaled into the cosmos.

Meat touched his lips. Something wet and iron-tasting and cold and...

His tongue touched the thick liquid, pupils dilating as he wobbled unsteadily on his feet. Tulimaq moved closer, the great bone mask just inches from his face, those eyes drawing him in like black holes as his fear and worry washed away, swirling down the drain until there was nothing left.

Cody smiled, his father's smile after six rounds of Kronenbourg and a dollop of AC/DC.

A tear.

That was sucked away, too.

The bearded man stroked his erection.

The wendigo were invisible.

All that you are is before you. That voice, a voice of the Earth. *To submit is to live a life eternal. To taste is to know the answers to life's questions.*

Cody's tongue traced his lips.

Taste the forces of life. Taste what the weak become.

The words caressed him, adding its orchestra to his lucid dreaming. The words made sense; how could he not have known this all along? That the whispered words in the dark recesses of the house were His, that the language of his worries and fears was merely that of this creature, this infinite god, speaking to him for always with words that didn't make sense until now. Relief would be kind, relief would be wonderful, to unload the pain and heartache and angst and woe that had befallen Cody since the day the phone had rung and delivered the news of his parents. He didn't want to be here. He hated life without them, without familial figures to guide him and show him what living was. All that he knew had been stripped bare and there was no one he could blame but himself.

Come...

Cody's head found its resting place on the cold surface of the creature's bony mask. Electricity hummed through his system, his hairs standing on end. Blood rushed to his loins and he understood the man frantically masturbating beside him, understood the unbound joy of becoming unchained. There was no greater burden than loss, and he couldn't carry it any longer. His shoulders ached.

His back hurt. He'd lost everything he'd known. His parents. His uncle. His friends. All he had in that moment was Tulimaq.

And the dog—his own voice, a foreign invader.

Where was the dog? Where was Kazu?

The blood coated Cody's swollen tongue. He swallowed, the strange flavor setting his senses alight. The liquid like warm whisky, burning as it descended. A pleasure he'd never get to truly experience. But the blood...

The blood...

The blood sprayed his face. The electricity peaked. A thunderclap sounded from the heavens, yet there were no clouds above.

Tulimaq roared, the force of it knocking Cody onto his ass. His hands slipped in blood. The bearded man yowled, his grip finally leaving his throbbing member as he turned his full attention to something that Cody couldn't see. An invader? Who was this intruder who had broken into camp and stolen him from his final destiny?

The bearded man stretched his arms wide, fingers turned black, bent into claws. A sagging six-pack catching the bloody light, penis like a wizard's staff as he roared and charged out of sight.

Cody looked over his shoulder, following his bearded brother as he leapt unnaturally high into the air, his full brunt and weight arcing toward a woman...

A woman? Cody blinked stupidly, metal coating his throat. A woman with a rifle. The sight aimed at the airborne beast.

And there, behind her, sprinting into the broken fence of the wendigo, was a girl.

A girl with a name that Cody couldn't remember.

69

TORI ASPLIN

Karl swam through the air in slow motion. Tori tracked his face as he sprang at her, a creature born from what had once been human, but which bore the marks no longer.

It no longer mattered. None of it did. As her finger tensed on the trigger, her mind followed their journey through time. An alpha male, approaching her in the pub, drink in hand, a grin on his brooding face. Exactly what she needed that night. To experience real, physical attraction, not just the empty words from internet trolls. A sweaty night, roasted in the heat of passion, taken by a man driven by his carnal urges. Hormones mixing like ingredients in a bubbling cauldron, setting her senses on fire. Attraction so strong that it panged her stomach. Smiles which told the secrets of her love when she posted them online. Sneaking around in the middle of the night. The thrill of getting caught. The ecstasy of his sex. Dark, mysterious eyes full of wonder, drawing her in from the very start.

A broken heart.

Shattered dreams.

A monster with death scrawled on his face.

This man was no longer Karl.

That man was long gone.

Gone before the storm had begun.

Nothing more than stains on her bedsheets.

This creature was a monster. A cog in the machine. A threat to her very existence. He had almost killed her twice already. Had bitten her neck. Had fed her to the bony wolves.

His body was white, his sagging skin clinging to his wasting figure like dripping honey. The only part of his body not colored in monochrome was the blazing redness of his cock, an extra appendage that would soon land on her. She didn't want to think what would happen if it did. The horrors he could unleash.

So, she didn't.

She didn't think anymore.

She fired.

The gun recoiled, a sharp pain throwing her arm back. The bullet ripped through the air, finding the center of Karl's face before he could acknowledge its existence. One minute he was there, the next he was no more as shards of bone and slithers of viscera sprayed in all directions. His body jerked, a trout caught on a fishing line pulled taught, trajectory harshly mismanaged. He turned sideways, still coming at her, chest spun to the skies. Black ichor fountained from the wound. Tori dived away as the thudding confirmed his landing. Bone snapped. Karl's body twitched, as though the ghost of his tongue was held to an electric fence.

Tori gasped, eyes pinned open. Black ooze dribbled into the ground, the reality of the scene enough to shatter what little belief she had left in the world she once knew.

There was no time to ponder her actions, as fetid air pulsed in her direction from the mammoth creature rising to its full stature. The small kid paled in comparison, his head trailing the monster's as it began its descent. A creature of biblical proportions, an intelligence lost in the dark wells of its eye sockets. It stood at least three times the height of the kid, and as it turned its gaze to Tori, she withered. A chamber of screams entered her mind and she threw herself to the ground, hands clasped to her ears, the rifle forgotten, the wendigos no more, all that she knew in this world existed in a tunnel of piercing shrieks.

The ground shook as it lumbered toward her. Someone cried a boy's name. Another gun fired.

All Tori could see was darkness as blood trickled from her eardrums.

70

SOPHIE PEARCE

The thing was monstrous, and Cody was nothing more than its toy. A plaything standing before it, tracking its movements as it grew. Sophie was only vaguely aware of Tori's fight with her own personal demon that sprang from the ground because Cody was *alive*.

He was *alive*.

And he was in trouble.

Sophie was slower to advance than Tori, the shotgun leveled at her eyes. There was something dark on Cody's lips, and his eyes were fixated on the beast. How the hell were three nobodies from the back end of nowhere meant to destroy something that shouldn't exist? A monster that had hibernated and chosen its time to claim the world around it?

The monster roared. Sophie braced herself against the sudden gust, laced with mildew and mold and flecks of saliva that stung as they hit her skin. The shotgun was heavy in her trembling hands. The creature brought a long-fingered hand to its chest, its intention to bat Cody away and discard its toy now that something new had caught its attention. A small hole oozing a dark liquid from its mask in the place where Tori had shot.

Sophie screamed as she pulled the trigger. Pellets erupted from the barrel, missing her mark, but still finding their way into the creature's body. One in the shoulder, another in the chest. The creature flinched but stood firm, arms stretching to the sky as it raised its head to the Aurora and gave a raucous howl. Unnatural. Warped and bent by the leanings of time. The sound of buildings collapsing and predators dying.

Though it was still very much alive.

"Cody!" Sophie cried, firing another round at the creature's stomach. Two more holes, asymmetrical, dribbling ichor. Out of the corner of her eye she could make out Tori bent low to the ground, hunched over and inactive.

What the fuck was going on?

"Cody!"

He turned as if summoned from a dream. Slow and sticky. His eyes, half-closed, found her, but though the lights were on, no one was home. Nothing whatsoever in those beautiful blues.

"Cody..." Quieter now. Tears salting her lips. "Cody... It's me..."

Cody vomited. Blood and chunks of nothing spewed onto the ground. He doubled over, body heaving from the force of it.

Which was when the creature kicked.

71

OSCAR OSLOW

C old, strong hands gripped Oscar's shoulder and pulled him back. Long black fingers digging into his flesh.

He shrugged them away, tried to fight them back. He had stayed back a beat, covering Tori and Sophie, rifle poised and ready. Then they had run—no warning, no signal—and as he tried to catch up, the creatures caught him in their web. For a blissful moment he had thought he was free to enter the circle, but the wendigos soon confirmed the contrary.

"Get off me!" he grunted, batting their fingers with the barrel of the gun. He pulled and pulled, but they only gripped tighter, fingers piercing his jacket and burying into his skin like fishhooks as a bearded creature attacked Auntie Tori and she blasted him away, as Sophie called out to the boy and fired his father's shotgun.

It was Oscar's turn to shine. He couldn't let this happen. But, fuck, did this hurt.

He groaned, turning his head as he chomped into a set of fingers on his shoulder. Something shrieked. They withdrew. He tasted dust on his tongue, the finger yielding into nothing beneath his bite. Deflating like a peach rotted from the inside, hissing air and yielding beneath his touch. What the hell were they made of?

He aimed the rifle blindly behind him and shot. Three, four, five. The fingers were still in him, but their strength faded as they dealt with their wounds.

Oscar dropped to his knees, hoping that gravity would aid his escape. Their fingers slicked out. He crawled, then pushed himself to his feet, ignoring the lightning bolts of pain that shot through his arms as he ran. Instinct drove him. Not toward his auntie, nor toward the girl, but toward the object that had caught his eye at the far side of the clearing.

The creature kicked out a mighty leg, sending the boy—Cody—flying like a ragdoll. He came at Oscar. Oscar dropped to the ground, grimacing as his shoulder yielded. He climbed hastily to his feet, making a swing to his right and out of the way of the enormous creature's path. The object was small, but intrigue pulled him, a disturbing tether that dragged him toward the white item discarded on the ground.

A bone mask. Antlers soaked in crimson. A hand once attached to arms that had soothed and pacified his cries as they wrapped around his body. A hand that had once stroked the tears from his cheeks. A hand that once ran its slender fingers through his hair. A hand now severed. Alone and removed from the mess of body that littered the ground. All that was left of her.

Oscar didn't cry. Didn't falter. There was no time. Stars wheeled overhead and the Aurora danced its waltz as he reached for the skull, hands as steady as a rock, and placed it on his head.

72

TORI ASPLIN

The shrieks dulled to a mild nuisance as gunshots rang around the clearing. Somewhere she could hear Oscar struggling. In another place, Sophie was calling Cody's name.

She glanced up and a boy was hurled through the air, arms and legs limp as if made of cotton and thread. His body crashed to the ground nearby, and the hungry wolves descended.

Dark hands reached for him, hunger lighting up dead eyes. Tori peeled her hands, sticky with blood, from her head and ran for the kid, snatching up the rifle as she sprinted on. She fired shots without looking, sent wendigos reeling backward. The kid lay lifeless and still, greedy wendigos pawing at his body...

A roar stilled them, another powerful gust of ancient air disrupting their frenzy and bringing them to a standstill. The cry was clear, an instruction to leave the boy for their master.

Tori made it to the kid's side and crouched beside him, hovering over his body like a protective mother. She had never had children of her own, was never sure she wanted them, but that didn't mean that this monster could steal someone else's. Sophie sent off report after report, the bullets finding their way into the creature's dark flank, nothing more than mosquito stings on the statue of a giant. The creature stalked toward them, a giant amongst men, coarse hair and throbbing muscle. The eyes fixed on Tori and the boy. Sophie screamed, fired the shotgun until it ran dry, then tossed the gun at the creature who didn't so much as bat an invisible eyelid.

Behind him stood the Masked Ones. A bear, a stag, a wolf. The vanguard of the damned, awaiting their master's call.

The creature was slow in its movements. Deliberate. How could something so monstrous exist? In which history class did they teach of this? The ground trembled, an impossible weight slamming down with each step.

Tears blurred Tori's eyes. "Stay back!"

Her words rippled around the clearing, then were absorbed by the forest. The Aurora chuckled, its pulsing lights giggling down on them.

"I mean it!" She stood, knees trembling, rifle aimed into the center of one of the creature's dark pits. "One more step and I shoot. This is your last warning."

Are you trying to reason with the Devil?

The creature cocked its head. Tori half expected shrieks to explode in her head again, but only silence remained. There was no more need for words, the message was clear: *It's over.*

Words that defined every step of her night, every last miserable experience since the coming of the storm and the sighting of the red lights.

It's over.

The creature took another step. Tori's hands shook. Her lip quivered. She fired the rifle, expecting a sudden burst of screaming, a well of chaos, a crumbling of the great being that stood before her.

Nothing. The bullet entered the socket, and disappeared, swallowed and no more. She fired again, catching the mask. A fracture appeared in the bone. It took another step, shadow looming over Tori and the boy. Sophie ran over to it, beating her fists against its legs, dissolving into pained screams the moment she made contact with its form, recoiling and lying on the ground as though she'd been electrified.

The creature stopped before them, eyes boring into Tori. Cody didn't make a sound. Didn't move. Tori held the gun steady, as if it would make a blind bit of difference. This creature, already littered with holes, and walking around as though nothing had happened. This creature with its magnificent size and impossible creation. This creature...

This creature, whose den they had entered, whose home they had invaded...

This creature...

She fired again.

Again.

Again.

This creature that grasped Tori in its powerful fists, pinning her arms to her sides.

This creature...

This creature that raised Tori off the ground, featherlight and fragile...

This creature.

This creature that belched its message of death at Tori, warm air flowing through the vents of a mausoleum...

This creature...

This creature that laughed.

This creature that stared.

This creature that squeezed...

73

OSCAR OSLOW

D*ad...?*
       Clear as day. He'd recognize him anywhere.

The ghost of Donavon Oslow smiled, a warmth that Oscar had only ever seen in pictures and dreams. A smile... *His* smile. A smile that stretched in time and brought wetness to his eyes.

Oscar's mouth wouldn't close. It made no sense. He was here. *He* was right there, standing in the middle of the clearing as the creature lumbered toward Aunt Tori and the boy. Standing feet away from Oscar were the Masked Ones, silent and reverent in the presence of their master, unblinking, unaware of Oscar's father standing there...

Standing. *There...*

Dad...?

He dare not speak the words aloud through fear of spooking this vision, frightening the tentative stag into the depths of the woods. He simply stared at his father as the creature loomed over Aunt Tori and the boy and blocked them from sight. His father walked toward him, growing larger, growing more real with every step. His brow was creased with worry lines, crow's feet at the corners of his eyes. His father had died young, back when Oscar was only a screaming babe, but age had followed him. His mother never told him all that much about what happened, only that his father went missing one night and never returned. He had always hoped that one day he might find his father appearing from the trees, impossibly, years after his disappearance, but never once had he envisioned meeting him like this.

Can you hear me?

A nod. That unfaltering smile. A smile laced with love.

Tori shot the creature.

Oscar fixed his gaze on his father, a ghostly hand rising to come to rest on his shoulder. There was a smell to the ghost, of earth and time and a distant whiff of cologne gone stale. He shouldn't have felt any physical touch from his ghost, but from where his palm sat, a warmth seeped into his body, a weight to the hand as it pressed on him, his father still smiling, inches from his boy.

What must I do?

His father's gaze moved past Oscar, looking over his shoulder. Oscar followed with a turn of the head, a strange mixture of grief and understanding pulsing through him as his mother appeared behind. How had he not heard her appear? How had he not felt her nearby? Her skin was pale, almost translucent. She wore the same smile as his father. Her hand rested on top of his, and for a single second they were happy. They were together. Oscar hadn't seen the woman before him in his lifetime. The Naomi Oslow from the pictures on the mantel showed a carefree woman, optimistic about a future she would never be able to claim. Here she was now, the light returning to her eyes as she looked at her husband and they wrapped their arms around Oscar. He could feel their hearts beating, could feel their weight and warmth. Could feel... *them*.

Another shot fired. Aunt Tori screamed.

Oscar looked over his father's shoulder to find Tori raised off the ground, the creature's monstrous hand wrapped around her waist.

Something pressed into the cup of his hand. He looked down at his mother's rifle—his *father's* rifle. His mother nudged him forward. His father stepped to the side.

They didn't speak, but he knew what to do. Tori's screams grew louder, taking over the clearing. Oscar calmly strode into the center of the clearing, lining up the rifle with the back of the creature's skull. A dark crack, a fissure where the contours of the bone failed to unite. In the middle of the fissure was a darkness, and as Oscar lined up the shot, he thought of train tunnels and underground caverns, places where the dark things hid in the hopes that light wouldn't penetrate.

His father's rifle was the breaker of darkness.

Go. His voice.

Go. Hers.

Oscar pulled the trigger.

Chaos broke out almost instantly. His aim was true, and the bullet was lost in the void. A wet, meaty expansion took place inside the helmet, and the creature screamed, buildings bending and machines chewing up the world. All that was human fell to the ground, hands clamped to their ears, all that was wendigo reared their heads back, stretched their arms and joined the chorus of hurt.

Oscar watched all of this passively, not understanding, protected in his little cocoon of bone as Sophie fell, Tori dropped from the creature's hand, and Cody twitched on the floor—his first signs of movement since the mighty kick of the father wendigo.

The creature whirled on him, ichor oozing from those dark eye sockets. It slammed its fists into the ground and the world leaned left, listing like a ship on turbulent waters. Oscar fought to balance. The creature sprinted toward him, using its fists as supports in the way he had seen apes move in nature documentaries. The creature drew a great fist to the sky, catching the darkening glint of the Aurora as it swung down at him.

Oscar closed his eyes.

Arms wrapped around his chest. His frozen body was pulled.

He opened his eyes and the creature was no longer there. He stood behind the monster in the center of the clearing, his mother and father standing either side of him, the way they should always have been, faces hardened as they glared at the creature now a short distance away.

Oscar lined up a second shot and fired, the bullet finding its mark in the creature's neck.

Not as effective. A bug on a windshield.

But now the creature was scared.

74

SOPHIE PEARCE

S ophie watched in horror as the creature bounded toward Oscar. Or, at least, what she thought was Oscar. It had to be him. He wore his clothes, stood with his posture...

But what was the skull on his head?

The whole reality was a nightmare, and Sophie felt as though she were underwater. As the wendigos screeched and the cries of the great beast faded, she crawled toward Tori's and Cody's limp bodies. She lay across Cody, head placed on his chest, doing whatever she could to ignore the restless wendigos that beat their chests and waved their arms and gnashed their teeth.

They were breaking formation.

What else was there to do but lie next to Cody and die? That's what all of this was leading to, right? Their inevitable deaths. Who did they think they were to cling onto what wasn't theirs to have? Maybe the afterlife wouldn't be so bad in the end...

Cody groaned. His eyelids fluttered. A wendigo leaped over them, coming to their master's defense.

"Cody?" Her words a whisper.

Cody's eyes opened a fraction, the pupils still dilated. A crust of blood on his lips.

Sophie couldn't hold back the overwhelm of tears that flooded her system, salt droplets falling on his face. "Cody..."

More wendigo leaped. A black rush of a gathering swarm of bats.

Another gunshot. Always gunshots. The drumbeat of their melancholy.

A teardrop, turned to blood in the reflection of the Aurora, hit his lip. She traced her finger across its length, wiping away the stubborn crusts until his lips were clean. Shallow breaths came from his mouth, chest beginning to rise and fall. She put her hands to his cheeks and kissed him, her own lips cracked and dry, softening as they touched his, his body responding as he returned the kiss then groaned when he tried to raise his arm to her face.

"What's wrong?"

"Broken..."

There were lumps where there should be none, and as she examined his arms, eyes darting quickly to the places in urgent need of medical attention, she caught Tori's fallen body out of the corner of her eye.

Before she could register what she was seeing, Oscar's cries pulled her attention.

A wave of creatures ran at the boy. Sophie spared a longing glance at Cody before grabbing the rifle that had fallen from Tori's hands. She sprinted toward the father beast, found the same entry point that Oscar had shot at, and fired.

She only pulled the trigger once, but three shots followed. The wendigos frenzied, dark blood spraying into the air as something ripped into their heads, their bodies, their legs, and their number began to thin. Sophie shot again at the great beast, this bullet missing its mark as the colossal thing screeched.

All Sophie wanted to do was escape that haunting shriek, but she soldiered on, even as warm liquid dripped from her ears, even as static filled her vision, she shot. Four more shots. The Masked Ones moved into the throng, running to the aid of their savior, their skulls shattering as more shots fired in quick succession. With each Masked One taken down, the father beast increased its ferocity, swinging wildly around, arms catching its own children and sending them traveling through the air. Were the shots blinding it? Were the Masked Ones in some way associated with its power? Sophie had no idea, all that she knew through her fuzzy haze was that something was happening. Someone was shooting, the wendigos were confused and afraid and, for the first time that night, it felt like there might be some semblance of hope.

She shot again, catching the father beast in the back of the head. A large shard of bone chipped off. Four more shots. Sophie glanced behind her, finding a familiar face that flooded her with hope.

Alex had come, after all.

75

ALEX GOINS

H is clothes clung to his body. Pain throbbed in his arm. The vibrations of the earth fizzed through his legs, a gash on his eyebrow where he had been knocked off-kilter and brushed the rough bark of a tree.

The forest shouldn't have been so dense, but in a strange way he expected it to be. The trees didn't want him. The world didn't want him.

The wendigos didn't want him.

He heard their din from a mile away and ran in their direction. When they came into sight, blood-red under the lights of the Aurora, all hope drained. He couldn't drink it in, there was too much, information sated his body and overflowed, pouring out of every crevice. He lined one of his rifles—for he had been certain to take several firearms from the sideboard in Tori's sister's house, strapping them precariously across his waist and back—and took a shot at the impossible mass of wendigo towering above the others. His grip was clumsy. Rifles were designed for two hands, not one.

Wendigos turned on him and charged. Bullets found their bodies.

Masked Ones swooped toward him. He adjusted, shouting until he was deaf, ignoring the tremendous screech that filled his ears with fluid and pulsed as though he was underwater. The madness was engulfing, and all he could do was shoot and shoot and shoot until the weapon was drained of ammunition, and then switch to another, and then shoot, and shoot, and shoot, adrenaline numbing the pain, coating the overwhelming agony of his shattered shoulder...

Bodies smashed into him. Hands and needlelike fingers tore at his clothes. Yet still he fired, internally urging Sophie to fire faster, to find the primal animal inside her and fight harder, that was the only way to beat these creatures, to out-animal them, to find the ancient part buried deep down and kill until the ground was saturated with blood and the quiet came.

The enormous creature swung its titanic arms, only helping their case as wendigo flew through the air, spines breaking upon impact with the arctic ground. At first, they had seemed infinite in their number, but finally they were breaking down. With each toppling of a Masked One, the frenzy grew wilder, their numbers dwindled. Alex allowed himself a moment of hope, that they might beat this, *could* beat this. Find an end to it all.

And then a Masked One was on him. His clip was empty. Alex groaned as the creature grabbed him by the throat and raised him off the ground, impossible strength in long, matchstick arms. Alex kicked out, foot finding the creature's chest, bouncing back as though he'd kicked a wall. The creature grasped his windpipe and Alex fought for breath.

The creature's mask exploded. Sophie shouted something he couldn't hear. None of them could hear anything anymore.

Alex's feet found the earth. He discarded the empty weapon and found his pistol, finger aching as he pumped it against trigger, spinning in all directions until he bought himself a bit of space among the throng to move. He worked his way toward Sophie. "How you doing, kid?"

Sophie didn't answer. He didn't expect her to.

The monolithic creature cried out into the night, flailing in all directions. It turned its head toward Alex, then froze where it stood.

Alex looked behind him as the wendigo horde stilled. Cody rose shakily to his feet, supported by a woman in a thick fur hood, a snow-white dog by her side.

76

CODY TREBECK

Cody looked at the world through the soft, fuzzy lens of a dream. A tinnitus whine rang in his head. His body ached and hurt and throbbed. Bones and limbs should not have been where they were, but what could he do? He was lucky to have survived the flight. Lucky to still be alive.

Lucky...

As the wendigos reached fever pitch, something soft and warm nuzzled against him. A rough tongue traced his lips and he wondered if Sophie was back, or if her kisses had all been a dream. A bony head nestled into his shoulder as a shadow loomed over him.

Come. It is time.

Chikuk crouched beside Cody, a strange vigor in her step that hadn't been there before. He wondered where this strange woman had come from, if Chikuk was simply a guardian angel watching over him, appearing in his mind when he needed her most. He rose to his feet, struggling against the broken bones and bruised flesh. She was strong, and here she stood.

Kazu took point in front of them as Chikuk bellowed a command and drew the attention of Tulimaq.

The giant creature stilled, venom and ferocity in those cavernous eyes. The white slate of bone was now stained with black and gray, and the creature limped as it took a stride toward Chikuk.

Chikuk spoke without moving her lips, her voice filling Cody's head and the heads of all those around. *It is time...* Chikuk raised her arms to the sky.

The edges of the crimson Aurora morphed, the vividness of their red light now showing a hint of azure and emerald.

Your time has come. You have drawn your recruits to your lair, but you may only keep one. The edges of your enclosure are drawn once more, and here you shall rest until the next king dies.

Cody's brow creased. "The next king?"

A whisper of a smile met Chikuk's lips. She nodded toward Tulimaq, to where the remaining Masked Ones stood, one of their number out of place and smaller than the rest.

77

OSCAR OSLOW

O scar met the old woman's gaze, her voice appearing in the folds of his mind. His heart paced a steady rhythm, a calm washing over him in the presence of his parents, both of them, together at last.

She summoned Oscar to her, and so he walked, unafraid and unencumbered. The monstrous wendigo watched on, a snarl hiding in the dark pit of its mouth. There was something about the woman, something that made little sense, and yet it made all the sense in the world. She was familiar, appearing as though he had somehow had this dream before, but he could not recall when.

He stood before the woman, the boy, their dog. His mother and father flanking him. The old woman looked at him with dark, button eyes and reached out a hand. He didn't flinch as she removed the bone mask from his head and stared deeply into his eyes. His mother and father disappeared, though he could still feel their presence beside him.

Are you ready, child? she asked, a hand cupping his cheek.

He nodded.

You have the strength and heart of a warrior. Our people need a leader who is strong, one who is bold and fearless and can keep the monsters at bay for the longest of time. Can you achieve that goal for us? Delay the hours in which Tulimaq shall rise again?

He nodded.

Cody frowned, shaking his head. "Can't you just kill him? End it all now? You can't let him escape like this..."

Chikuk silenced him with a wave of her hand. *The world spins in cycles. Evil shall rise, and good shall conquer. The sun makes way for the moon. Life is met with death and death is met with life, and so it shall always be. So it has always been.*

Tulimaq panted, his enormous body cresting and falling with each breath, a strange patience in the place where his eyes should have been.

You will come with me, Chikuk spoke to Oscar. *My days are numbered, but I will teach you all that Aklaq had to pass on. It is time, boy. It is time...*

She eased Cody back to the ground, then turned and started back toward the trees. Kazu followed in step, walking dutifully behind.

Oscar paused, hesitation rising as he scanned the chaos he'd be leaving behind. He searched for Tori, finding her lifeless body a few meters away, limbs bent at odd angles and a puddle of blood pooling beneath her. Nothing could have survived Tulimaq's crushing fists.

There was nothing for it. There was nothing left. His mother and father were gone. His auntie was with them somewhere in the void. Cody looked up at him with imploring eyes, refusing to believe that this chaos and destruction would one day begin again, the cyclical loops of nature taking place as the world kept on spinning.

Chikuk paused. The reds of the Aurora melted.

Oscar followed, a single tear rolling down his cheek.

Behind him, Tulimaq roared, then strode toward the trees. They parted to allow for his monstrous mass, creaking as a gully appeared to allow his passing. He stopped by the clearing's edge, the remaining wendigo slipping into the unnatural darkness as Tulimaq waited patiently, eyes fixed on Cody.

78

ALEX GOINS

A lex held his breath, waiting for the "A-Ha!" moment. Waiting for the "Gotcha!" Wondering what it was he had seen. Wondering what the colossal beast was waiting for.

The world was silent. The clearing was almost vacant. Above him, the Aurora metamorphosed into the colors he had seen in the brochures and on the internet, months ahead of his departure to the frozen north. Back when he knew what warmth was, and the biggest problems he faced were meeting his agent's deadlines and grieving for his fallen sister. Another time. Another place.

Another world.

He scanned the clearing, drinking in the devastation. Bodies littered the ground, most of them pale with black fingers and toes, some with masks of bone, and two that had once been human. The strange, mangled soup of a woman that he would never get to meet, only an arm and hand with a golden ring remaining amongst the violated pieces of her corpse. The other, a deflated body of a much larger man that somehow felt familiar, though he couldn't be sure. He couldn't be sure of anything anymore. His head swam, his tired body breathing a sigh of relief, a ringing in his ears...

And a girl.

A girl screaming words that made no sound, aiming her open mouth at Alex, waving for him to come on over to where Cody had stood...

Cody.

Alex ran. Ran as though his life depended on it. Ran over to the boy struggling to sit up, one arm crossing his chest and clamping over his ribs. Alex skidded beside him and threw his arms around him, a flood of tears racking his body at the sight of his nephew. Finally. There. In his arms.

Sophie joined in the embrace, weeping until their eyes burned and there was no more crying to be done. Weeping until Cody groaned with pain and Alex eased him onto his back. He wasn't sure how he was going to get Cody home, but he would try. Dear God, he would try.

"Are you okay?" Alex asked. It was strange to hear his own voice again, sounding as if he had spoken through three panes of glass.

Sophie nodded. Wiped her tears with the back of her hand.

The ground rumbled. Alex turned to the forest, to where the creature stood. His skin bristled. For a blissful moment he had forgotten that the father wendigo was still there.

"What does it want?" Sophie asked, her voice weak. "Why is it just standing there?"

"I don't know."

The creature made a sound, then. A low braying as it nudged its head at the group.

Alex's throat went dry. Cody forced himself up, grunting as his eyes locked onto the beast. Despite his wounds, and the unnatural angle of the bones protruding from his skin like sticks beneath wet tissue paper, he rose unsteadily to his feet.

Alex's heart raced. "Cody? What's he saying to you?"

Cody staggered forward. The beast raised its chin approvingly, black ichor dripping from its mask as the Aurora shimmered above.

Another step.

"Cody, no." Alex stepped in front of the boy. He reached out to place a hand on his shoulder, until he remembered the broken bones and saw the flecks of blood blossoming through his clothes. Cody's pupils were dilated, the whites around his eyes losing the battle as the black continued to swell. "Cody..."

Cody took another step, head meeting Alex's chest. Alex fixed his position, bracing himself as Cody pushed forward. The kid was strong, and on the next step, the boy's head nudged his ruptured shoulder. Alex groaned in pain, tears hot around his eyes. "Cody, stop."

Sophie ran behind Cody, wrapping her arms around his waist, head pressed between his shoulder blades. "No. Stop. Please."

Sandwiched between the pair of them, Cody grunted, pushing forward, nudging Alex back inch by inch. The creature growled as they clung to Cody and tried to force him back, to stop him moving toward the beast.

"Cody, please," Sophie begged. "Don't... We need you... *I* need you... please."

Alex looked down at Cody, not recognizing the boy doggedly pushing forward. His nose was wrinkled, mouth turned into a pained sneer, eyes dark. With each step his strength only grew as they made it to the center of the clearing. Far away, somewhere in the forest, a flock of birds took flight, signaling the receding path of the wendigo as they disturbed any creature brave enough to have borne witness to the night's showdown.

"Cody!" Sophie screamed, now. Hands slipping as Cody wriggled free from her grip, growing ever more frenzied with each step, as if proximity to the creature gave him power. Alex's jaw clenched, brow set, moving behind Cody as he wrapped his arm around the boy's throat.

Cody gasped. Growled. Grunted. Protested. Flecks of spit flew from his lips, and still they moved forward. Still Sophie's feet skidded, and Alex gritted against the pain as he forced both arms into play, ignoring the hot-white lightning bolts that shot through his shoulder. The creature smiled—if, indeed, you could call it that. It waited with an impossible patience, as if it could stand there for eons and still be satisfied.

Alex met the great beast's eyes, Cody only fifteen feet away, losing himself in the monster's shadow. He dug his feet into the dirt, pulled hard enough to knock Cody onto his ass, then laughed. "You can't have him. No matter how hard you try, he stays with us. He stays with me." The world blurred. Cody fell still in his arms, cradled in Alex's straddle as he stared up at the creature. "Go. Be gone. He's ours... Ours..."

Cody's chest rose and fell with heavy breaths, his eyes lowered to the floor. Sophie whimpered behind them, her fight given up as she sobbed and quivered and quaked in the great beast's presence. The creature's nostrils flared, great gusts of warm, stale air wafting toward them.

And then it was gone.

They could hear the creature lumbering for some distance, the ground trembling with each step. Alex clung to Cody, arms pinned around his chest as he buried his face into his neck, dried his tears on the boy's coat. Cody was silent, and so too was Alex. There was nothing left to be said. It was over.

It was all over.

Until it wasn't.

"Cody!" Sophie screamed, her voice slicing through this strange new silence as Cody ripped away from Alex's clutches, stumbling and using his arms and legs to run toward the pines, crouched on all fours as he slipped into the darkness. Alex reached forward, collapsing onto one arm. The world turned sideways as Cody was claimed by the forest. He shouted until he couldn't, his agony joined by Sophie's as they lay by the forest's edge, knowing already that to chase Cody would be pointless. They were in there, all of them, and this was the way of things. This was the way of the wendigo.

...you may only keep one...

Alex wasn't sure how long he and Sophie lay there in the blood-soaked dirt, surrounded by the dismembered limbs of wendigo and human alike, but soon the sky began to break. Above them, the Aurora was fading. In the distance, the ever-pervading whites and grays of the storm subsided and the first rays of dawn pinked the horizon, melting peaches back across the skyscape.

Alex shuffled closer to Sophie and wrapped his arms around her, struggling to comprehend the weight that compressed his heart. They listened for footsteps, as though Cody was playing an inappropriate prank and may soon be back with them.

Silence screamed its passing of time.

"Let's go," Alex said at last, Sophie shivering violently in his arms. For the first time that night, he knew it wasn't because of the cold. They rose, Alex grimacing as he supported Sophie and walked in the heavy silence across the clearing, eyes grown numb to the dead littered around him.

As they made it to the other side of the clearing, Alex stopped, noticing the crumpled shape lying a short distance away.

His heart broke, then. What little glue that bound the fractured remains of his beating organ dissipated. Light danced off the wet marbles of her lifeless eyes. Blue had already begun to claim the soft, warm pinks of her lips. Tori's twisted body, broken and battered, looked more like a doll's, discarded and tossed from this world. Lifeless and empty.

Alex collapsed beside her. Kissed her lips. Tried to breathe life back into her lungs.

No magic remained to revive the dead.

ALICE BOWMAN

S he pressed her face against the glass, breath fogging her view, masking the woman from sight.

It was her. She could have recognized that woman anywhere. As Damien snored soundly behind her, she fixed her gaze on the old lady, rubbing her hand across the glass to gain a moment of clarity before her breath misted the glass again. It was her. The lady from her dreams.

Alice's dreams had been her usual concoction of play, color, and sweet treats as she shifted beneath her duvet. In this particular rendition, her mother had gifted her a brand-new toy, a spinning top, and it spun neatly before her, the vibrant images of stars and moons and swirls turned blurry and into snow. Alice had been laughing, clapping her hands, begging the top to spin faster, when the woman had appeared on the cusp of her vision.

Her mother melted from sight, replaced only with the kind and wrinkled face of the old woman, kneeling beside her, smile touching her ears. *You must go, my little sweetheart.*

Alice raised an eyebrow. The top kept spinning.

Soon the monsters will come, the woman explained, lips unmoving, a dog appearing at her side and licking Alice's face eagerly. Alice giggled. *You must leave now, little girl. Happiness lives on the other side of what you don't know. Go, before it is too late.*

Alice pushed the dog away, her own smile beaming. "Is Mommy coming, too? And Daddy?"

The woman's smile didn't falter. Nor did she offer a reply. She reached for Alice's hand. Her touch was warm, yet commanding. Alice laughed as the dog took step beside her, tongue hanging out his mouth as he panted. The world was colorful, the world was bright. Stars shone brightly above. Somewhere in the distance the front door closed and she heard her father's heavy boots trailing upstairs. The woman paused, smiling down on her, a face as bright as the sun. A moment later and someone screamed, the dream turning the sound into strange music as Alice descended stairs made of snow and found her boots and coat. There were other figures around, but they kept their distance, withered trees standing in the far reaches of her mind.

The way ahead will be cold and dark, but Kazu will guide you.

Alice stepped out of her house, eyes opening fully into a world of white. The dog led the way, a step in front of her as the woman remained where she was.

"You're not coming with me?" Alice asked, spitting snow from her infant lips.

You will find the way, the woman replied. *You will find the way, and I will find my way back to you. There is nothing more for you here. Life takes many paths. This is now yours. Follow the man, and he will lead you to me. I will come for you soon.*

Alice had thought often about the old lady, even as the dog guided her to the abandoned house and found her a place to hide. Even as the older boy invaded her private hideout and held the darkened glare in his eye. Even as Alex led Alice and the others out into the snow and found the kind lady's house. At every turn she thought about her.

And there she was. Alice waved a hand on the glass to clear the fog. The woman waved a hand back, that same knowing smile still on her face, an older boy, one she recognized, standing beside her. Kazu by her feet.

Come. It is time.

Alice slid the door open and met the cold. She cast a glance back at Damien, glad to find him still asleep. She grinned, her heart lightening for the first time that night, though she didn't understand why. All that she knew was that things were going to be okay.

In the end, everything would be okay.

EPILOGUE

Rain hurled itself against the floor-to-ceiling windows. The sky outside was gray, the buttery glow of streetlights melting into dreary orbs as dark shapes flitted past the glass.

The smell of dust and paper filled the air. Warmth pulsed from a roaring fire built into the grand stone facade. A table, piled high with books, framed the man, hunched over, scribbling a signature with black pen onto the virgin pages of each copy.

The storm didn't assuage the line. Men, women, and children flocked from all over the country to catch a glimpse and claim their two minutes of contact time. Toddlers grew bored, wriggled in their parents' arms. A solitary security guard stood nearby, coiled wires looping into his ears as he monitored the queues and ensured that people didn't outstay their time at the table.

"Can you make it out to Christine, please?" The woman's cheeks were plump and rosy. A suede, crimson coat and complementary lipstick. "She's my mother. Ill, you see. She couldn't make it today, but I promised I'd get you to sign for her. She's a big fan of the fantastical. Loves your work."

Alex nodded, already scratching the pen on the page. His wrist hurt from signing, and a dull throb ached his shoulder, yet he looked as fresh as ever, offering a curt smile to the lady as he passed the book back and wished her a great day.

The queue filed down, but Alex never saw its end. He never really expected to, given that his latest book had turned into a global best-seller. The book idea that he had taken to Denridge Hills had morphed into something else entirely, fueled by a research project he never dreamed he'd survive, and would never hope to attempt again. For the last twelve months, London had reclaimed its place as his home, a strange concrete jungle of thousands of impatient creatures, barging their shoulders to claim their place on the tube, sour expressions on their faces as they speed-walked with unjust urgency through the gray-stained landscape.

A city that was infinitely better than the alternatives Alex had experienced.

For as long as Alex could remember, his feet had been itchy for travel. His entire being longed to see the world, yearned to soak up the many cultures of the globe and to lose himself in every aspect of what it meant to be human. That urgency had faded. The anchor he refused to toss from the ship had been secured the moment the wheels of the plane touched British soil. He was home. This was home. London was...

"I don't suppose you write In Memoriams?"

Alex was shaken from his reverie, a familiar voice that he couldn't quite place cooing him from his thoughts. A woman with salt-and-pepper hair, dark eyes, and a thick, gray coat. She stood out from the other preened and fashioned women in the queue, her own attire more basic and suited to the functions of a much colder climate. All that said, Sherri Dutton looked well. Surprisingly so, although age had finally caught up with her.

Alex smiled and rose from the table, offering Sherri a hug. Sherri accepted, the guard watching with a scrutinous eye and those patiently waiting in the queue prickling with jealousy.

"A lot has changed for you," she said.

"I hope that's true for you, too."

Alex offered to meet Sherri after his business at the bookstore for a drink and found the woman waiting patiently in the rain outside an independent cafe, the windows steamed with condensation and the smell of freshly ground brew in the air.

They took a table in the back corner, a young waitress trying her best not to let the tray slip from trembling hands as her eyes flickered between Alex and the drinks.

He thanked her with a twenty-pound note.

"How are you finding London?" Alex asked.

"Different. I always imagined what somewhere like this would be like; a big city, bustling traffic, grand buildings. I never really understood just how alone you could feel surrounded by so many people."

"Ain't that the truth?" He sipped his drink. Burned his tongue. "I'll be honest, I never dreamed you'd take the plunge. I figured you townsfolk would remain where you were forever. Too scared to travel."

Sherri furrowed her brow. "A lot can change. We've learned that the hard way."

Alex nodded solemnly. He hadn't waited around in the town all that long following the clear-up. The numbers of the townsfolk had been slashed by more than half, and there was a great deal of repair to complete. Alex's chief concern had been returning to the house with Sophie, ensuring that Damien and Alice were okay.

He hadn't factored in losing more of their number before the dawn broke. For the first time in some months, his thoughts strayed to the boy they had left behind, confirmed dead come morning. He thought of Alice and her unexplained disappearance...

"It's a heavy business," Sherri said solemnly, shaking Alex from his thoughts.

Alex nodded, composing himself. "That's all over, now." A group of teens turned away as Alex caught their eye. "I'm glad you managed to fight it all off. How's the healing?"

Sherri's hand moved absently to her chest. Over a year later and Alex still remembered the blank animal fury in her eyes as she had reared back to attack her own son. Even now, he looked into those dark eyes, the rings where color had once been now shaded permanently in black, and he wondered if any of those touched by the wendigo could ever heal.

"It comes and goes." Sherri sighed. "Less so these days. The... I guess you could call them 'waves' of darkness peter out in the end. They're easier to control when you feel them coming. Time heals all wounds. At least, that's what they say."

Alex cast his eyes down at the table.

Sherri reached for his hand. "It's not your fault..."

But it was, wasn't it? Alex had given up. Sherri proved that the affected could still live normal lives, so why had he given up on Cody? Was he still out there, somewhere? Lost in the woods with that beast and his minions? Could Alex have saved him? Dragged him back from the precipice and made everything okay?

"I know... It's just..."

They fell into silence.

Sherri cast her eyes to the teens, now standing at a strange angle as they tried to get a selfie with Alex from a distance. "I see the book is selling well."

Alex took a deep breath. "You could say that. I was light on certain details. Twisted the narrative a bit. But even if I didn't, there would be few who would believe that any of that was real."

Sherri nodded, her turn to fall quiet.

The coffee machines spewed out their heat, the warmth of the animated bodies inside the café only driving up the temperature. Sherri removed her coat, and through the thin white cotton of her undershirt, Alex's eyes were drawn to the dark mark on her chest, nestled in her solar plexus. He hated to remember, wondered why he'd written a book about it all in the first place, but his fingers wouldn't let him forget. For nights on end he typed until the sun rose, the book forming itself without much conscious thought. Before he knew it, he was done. His agent was ecstatic, the publishers entered the most ferocious bidding war Alex had seen. His final contract put his old agreements to shame.

A story that demanded to be written.

A story that demanded to be remembered.

"Can I see him?" Sherri asked the question Alex knew was coming but wasn't sure how to approach.

His indecision was clear enough on his face that Sherri added, "You promised. I'm okay. Honestly."

Alex nodded, thoughts straying to the kids back home. Sophie stepping into her own as chief guardian to Damien. Adopting the role of big sister to the bright, talkative boy. Alex's new apartment was large enough for each of them to have their own bedroom, and slowly they were finding their own sense of normal. Slowly they were letting the memories melt and fade into the past. Occasionally Damien's memories would trigger, and his questions would catch Sophie by surprise, but eventually they would pass. All things do.

Alex checked his watch. "Sure. I think it's time."

It's time... Words that'll echo in his head forever. Words that he'll never fully understand. Words spoken as Tori lay lifeless on the ground and an ancient woman claimed a new protector for her realm. Words spoken moments before Cody was taken by the darkness and entered the Drumtrie Forest forever...

A line from an old novel formed in Alex's mind, words uttered from the hands of a greater writer than he'd ever dream to become. Words he had since stuck on the wall above his desk to serve as a reminder that it wasn't his fault. He couldn't change what had happened. Life had its way.

There are other worlds than these.

After draining the final dregs of his coffee, Alex shrugged on his jacket, offered an arm to Sherri, and headed into the storm.

If you could call it that.

AUTHOR'S NOTES

First of all, a huge thank you for not only reading When Winter comes but sticking around for the post-credits scene—the Marvel bonus action, if you will.

When Winter Comes has been on one hell of rollercoaster ride to get to this final version that you hold in your hands. When I first started, I had no idea of the beast I was unleashing, from its first initial seed on a scrap of paper in a dingy room above an antiquated Lincolnshire pub, to the hefty tome that has been reworked, revised, and polished more times than I care to count.

I wrote my first novella back in 2015, a scrappy horror novella by the title of "Sins of Smoke." Back then I was a member of the Lincoln Creative Writers group—a collection of unique and talented individuals who gathered around the table once a month to stimulate the creative gears and place words on the paper. Every month we would probe each other with stimuli that would inform small pieces of writing, and then share our work. There would be no criticism, no critique, it was a safe zone to harbor creativity and sacrifice our digits in the name of the muses.

It was in 2016 that the idea for When Winter Comes first sprang to mind. I can't quite recall what the original stimulus was, but I sketched down a scenario on a piece of paper about a young boy cast adrift in the far reaches of an isolated Alaskan town. Cody, Kyle, Brandon, and Travis were born into an apocalyptic landscape of snow and destruction. A band of four friends, fighting to survive some kind of cataclysmic event that had struck their town.

That was it.

That was all I had to go on.

The sessions in those workshops were short, each stimulus allowed to prod the brain for a maximum of fifteen minutes. At the end of the session, I deposited my notes into my bag, and in there they would stay for another year at least.

But I couldn't get that scenario out of my head.

I've always been fascinated by destruction, and the extremes that people will go to when survival is the only option. The majority of my days are spent musing on the comforts of modern living—almost universal access to the internet, entertainment on demand, machines and robots and technologies that allow us to sit comfortably inside our homes, barely having to raise a finger (hell, in the last few years, even that strain has been removed with the birth of Alexa and other voice-activated devices)—and I will often find myself drifting into imaginings of scenarios in which the world shuts down. What would we do if the power grid suddenly sparked and failed? How would I gather (edible) food once the shops had been looted, and people had holed themselves inside their houses? I've even experienced a glimpse of that world first-hand during a terrifying drive home from work when a city-wide power cut struck and lasted for two hours. Traffic lights stalled, drivers went rogue, and a ten-minute journey home took nearly an hour of adrenaline fueled, white-knuckled driving.

I guess, then, it makes sense that I like writing horror and the apocalyptic.

So into the drawer it went, the seedling of an idea, and I moved on. In 2016 I collaborated on my first novels with Luke Kondor, writing a series about zombies birthed from fungal spores in a world where 90% of the population had been wiped out. Colin Bolton (the protagonist) set forth into a chaotic post-Rot UK, and my mind was distracted with Rotters, and Scavvies, and Millers, and...

...huskies.

Yeah, I have a soft spot for huskies.

Time span by, as it so often does, and it wouldn't then be until 2017 that When Winter Comes would rise to the surface of my consciousness again. I was looking for my next project, exploring the mechanics of writing an episodic, serialized story, when I stumbled across my original notes.

Four boys. A blizzard.

That was still all I had.

So I span some wheels.

Over the next few weeks I would create an entire cast of characters (many of whom wouldn't make their way into the final cut of the book). The town of Denridge Hills was birthed. Alex Goins appeared on the scene. Chikuk and Aklaq showed themselves in full multi-color. I created a cover for the first book and laid down the first forty pages of the story.

And then I was waylaid.

Don't get me wrong, I'm not complaining about what happened next. An Amazon heavy-hitter by the name of Michael Anderle reached out to me with an opportunity to write a number of books in his multi-million selling universe, The Kurtherian Gambit. I jumped at the chance, eager to learn, and ready to contribute. Great things were coming out of the Kurtherian Universe and I was honored to be asked to contribute. Over the next two years I worked with Michael and his team to create "The Caitlin Chronicles," a five-book series coloring in the legend of a nobody woman raised in a fortress in the middle of a forest, believing the world had fallen to shit and nothing lay beyond the zombie-infested trees that surrounded her. The process was intense, it was liberating, it was educational, and in October 2019, the final instalment (from me, at least) was published. I sat back and celebrated with a whisky, and then allowed myself the chance to look at what to work on next.

There was no competition

Denridge wouldn't let me go.

For those of you familiar with the film "30 Days of Night," I'm sure you can see its influence on this book. I still can't explain it to this day, but there's a real deep-seated obsession that I can't shake with Alaskan towns and the fact that they must survive in blocks of darkness that can span weeks. What better breeding ground for a horror story? What better setting to play with character and scenario and create something magical? Couple that with the Aurora Borealis, and the legends of the Inuit people, and you have the formula for something truly magical.

At the beginning of 2020, I committed to bringing this tale to life. Inspired by David Slade's vampire movie, as well as Richard Laymon's "One Rainy Night," and Stephen King's "The Stand," I challenged myself to create my own epic horror story. All I had to do was research and fill in a little bit of that frozen magic to get it all started.

When Winter Comes will forever be my pandemic novel. My "COVID creation." As a writer of apocalyptic events, all the stories I had spun of cataclysmic events paid off and helped me remain calm in the face of an unprecedented situation. The pandemic allowed me the time to focus, to create, to craft, and to bring this story to life, five years later. As some of you will know, this book was released episodically in 2020. I released an episode every month, using the time in lockdown to fuel my passion and unleash four young boys who had been trapped in a writer's head for half a decade. Characters like Tori Asplin and Sophie Pearce appeared along the way, shouting for their own stories to be told.

And the wendigos...

Boy, are they fascinating. The wendigos were the final piece of the puzzle. The monstrous adhesive that tied the story together. Underexplored in modern writing, the mythos of the wendigo in Inuit culture is fascinating, and although I took some liberties in the writing of this book, I have done my best to remain true and represent them as authentically as possible. If you ever get a chance to look up wendigo art and wendigo myth, I would highly recommend it. You could lose yourself in the internet for days.

Unless the power dies, of course.

And so that brings us to today. Right here. Right now. Your eyeballs on these words. I never expected this story to grow to the size it became. I never expected so many readers to dive into those first six episodes and leave such positive feedback. I never expected to have to change Kyle's name in this final version of the book (let's be honest, Karl and Kyle were far too similar, Hayden was better, and I'm not about to become another George R.R. Martin). But here we are. A revised, edited, and re-covered collection that may just be one of my proudest works to date. I'd once heard that when a story takes a bite of your heart, it won't let go. This is evidence that that may just be true.

I want to say a personal thank you to you, the reader, for not only reading this story, but making your way through these author notes as well. The journey of a novel is never a solitary endeavor, and I also want to take the time to thank a few people along the way who were pivotal to its creation and its success.

First, as always, I thank my Hawk & Cleaver brothers for all their inspiration and support early on in my writing journey. A special bonus thanks to Luke Kondor for agreeing to put up with me and my antics as we collaborated on the first full-length works that would be published with my name on them, and for being a constant reminder of the power that comes from sticking close to your truth, to your art, and "questioning the premise."

A massive thank you to the writers who have uplifted and inspired me along the way. Without the wisdom, encouragement, and support from Michael Anderle, CM Raymond, LE Barbant, Natale Roberts, Martha Carr, J. Thorn, Zach Bohannon, Sacha Black, Jonathan Yanez, Katlyn Duncan, Crys Cain, Jenna Moreci, and Helen Scheuerer (to name a few), I believe that stories like this would have at least sat dormant for another decade. I've said it before, and I'll say it a thousand times again, "Being a writer can be lonely work, but does it really have to be?"

No. No, it doesn't.

More thank yous go to my cover designers, J Caleb Clark (who created the original covers for the episodic serial), and Christian Bentulan from Covers by Christian (the artist behind the glorious blood-red Aurora), as well as Lori Parks for proofreading the work. I most certainly shouldn't (and won't) forget the endless contributions to the polishing of this work at every level from the wonderfully talented Julie Hiner. I can't express how much I appreciate the endless reads and re-reads at every level of this book's journey. A special thank you to my ARC readers, my beta readers, and everyone who has read the story so far.

And, finally, the biggest of thanks to my Activated Authors writing group. Your constant inspiration, excitement, and passion for your own creations not only fuels my own but amplifies it to extraordinary levels. You're the coal to my steam engine, and I'm forever thankful and honored to be a part of your journeys.

So, there it is. The end of the end, my friends. Who'd have thought that a paragraph of text written on a scrap of paper in a dust-filled attic room of an old Lincolnshire pub would turn into a 500+ page tome of love, horror, excitement, and misery? Who would have thought that four children from Denridge hills would fight (and prevail) in their plight to be birthed into this strange, strange world?

Who would have thought that a twenty-four-year-old wannabe writer would be sitting before you now, six years and forty-eight books later, typing the final words of an epic that has plagued his mind for years?

Life's a funny thing, don't you think?

Daniel Willcocks
Sept 4th 2021

CLAIM YOUR FREE STORY

Death Hunt: The When Winter Comes Prequel

Discover the full, untold story of Donavon Oslow in this official prequel to the When Winter Comes epic.

A white stag of myth. A mind corrupted from Abraham's Nectar. The looming shadow of the Drumtrie Forest.

Yours to claim now, for FREE.

https://bookhip.com/RMBZZL

ABOUT THE AUTHOR

Daniel Willcocks is an international bestselling author and award-winning podcaster of dark fiction. He is an author coach; one fifth of digital story studio, Hawk & Cleaver; co-founder of iTunes-busting horror fiction podcast, 'The Other Stories';' CEO of horror imprint, Devil's Rock Publishing; and the co-host of the 'Next Level Authors' podcast.

Residing in the UK, Dan's work explores the catastrophic and the strange. His stories span the genres of horror, post-apocalyptic, and sci-fi, and his work has seen him collaborating with some of the biggest names in the independent publishing community.

Find out more at www.danielwillcocks.com

facebook.com/willcocksauthor

twitter.com/willcocksauthor

instagram.com/willcocksauthor

OTHER TITLES BY DANIEL WILLCOCKS

The Rot Series (with Luke Kondor)

They Rot (Book 1)

They Remain (Book 2)

They Ruin (coming soon)

Keep My Bones

The Caitlin Chronicles (with Michael Anderle)

(1) Dawn of Chaos

(2) Into the Fire

(3) Hunting the Broken

(4) The City Revolts

(5) Chasing the Cure

Other Works

Twisted: A Collection of Dark Tales

Lazarus: Enter the Deadspace

The Mark of the Damned

Sins of Smoke

Keep up-to-date at

www.danielwillcocks.com

Lightning Source UK Ltd.
Milton Keynes UK
UKHW010448070223
416581UK00015B/699/J